THE
ARCHIVIST

THE ARCHIVIST

V S NELSON

Matador
Unit E2 Airfield Business Park,
Harrison Road, Market Harborough,
Leicestershire. LE16 7UL
Tel: 0116 2792299
Email: books@troubador.co.uk
Web: www.troubador.co.uk/matador
Twitter: @matadorbooks

ISBN 978 1803131 573

British Library Cataloguing in Publication Data.
A catalogue record for this book is available from the British Library.

Printed and bound in the UK by TJ Books LTD, Padstow, Cornwall
Typeset in 10pt Utopia Std by Troubador Publishing Ltd, Leicester, UK

Matador is an imprint of Troubador Publishing Ltd

In memory of Fay Martin,
who slipped into the Aether far too soon.

There is no God. There is no heaven and there is no hell. There is only the Aether. It follows your every moment, ponders every impulse. It is a carrion bird that has circled you from birth. It bides its time. It is patient. It does not matter how strongly you deny it or how hard you fight; the Aether will possess you.

So do not expect Death's gentle embrace. It arrives ravenous, eviscerating, devouring, desperate to consume all that you ever were, every thought, every feeling, every memory, no matter how fractured or flawed. The Aether cares not for the life you led or the beliefs you held. The Aether accepts all.

It is no secret that the Aether and I share a fractious relationship. I am its antithesis, breaking the barbs from its claws and prising its grip from the depths of your essence. I take what it covets, keeping you for myself. An opportunist, a johnny-come-lately, I am the one satiated while the Aether starves. And so, I become your afterlife, linking your essence with the living while your body rots. I am your only chance of salvation, the single raft on the Aether's infinite sea.

I also charge. A lot.

I drink my coffee. Undissolved granules float to the surface and stick in my throat. I feel indentations in the Styrofoam that don't align with my teeth. I put the cup down, pushing it to the edge of the table to avoid absentmindedly reaching for it again. I still feel new to this and nerves have distracted me; I've not bought coffee today.

No one sits next to me. The seats opposite, behind and diagonally across are empty too. Everyone knows I am something to be avoided. It is not conscious knowledge, but a deep-seated fear that lurks in the unexplored recesses of the mind. Without knowing why they are doing it, people find themselves taken to a seat elsewhere. I am abandoned on an island, beyond rescue. This does not concern me: it is all I have known.

A woman runs past the rows of waiting room chairs, wailing incomprehensibly. She kicks a bottle of water, which spills over the shoes of an old woman dressed for an evening out, and elbows her way through a glut of teenagers. The child in her arms is grey, her limbs flaccid. A nurse takes one look at the little girl and opens the door to the emergency ward. Woman and child disappear. A man two rows away rants about how long he has waited, every word punctuated with an expletive. He notices me looking and glares. Too caught up in himself to see the obvious, he soon loses interest, eyes searching for anyone else who dares look his way. There are screams from inside the emergency ward. Everyone falls silent except for the irate man, who continues to grumble about the sanctity of queueing.

An old couple in the corner ignore the commotion. They huddle together next to a wooden table cluttered with toys. The children keep their distance, too fearful to approach. They can sense what I can see; the old woman is dying. For the last two hours I have been locked in an internal debate over whether I should introduce myself. Their clothes suggest they cannot afford the service I offer. Though desperation is often good at finding cash.

The rest of the waiting room holds only the mildly injured. Even the man who periodically treats us to his rants only has a twisted ankle. He moves with an exaggerated limp to sit next to a black woman with an untamed afro. She types furiously into her phone between stolen glances at me. Our eyes meet several times and I watch surety change to confusion and doubt each time eye contact breaks. She smiles to herself as the ferocity of her typing intensifies, a chance encounter in a waiting room no doubt becoming a blog post.

I am not here for her. Or for the man with the twisted ankle or for the teenagers who huddle around their phones, two broken arms between the five of them. I need the nearly dead. Those who balance on the precipice, teetering between two worlds as they await the faintest gust to push them across the divide. Only the old woman in the corner flickers between life and death. She has folded herself into the old man, her head hiding in the crook of his armpit, his emaciated arm wrapped across her back. Like me, they know that she will die regardless of any intervention from a doctor. Unlike the man with the twisted ankle, who now raises his hand as if ready to slap away the young woman's phone, they do not demand attention from anyone else.

If they reject me, then what I am will be known to the room. I do not want that. My face is hidden as much as it can be without appearing overtly suspicious. Occasionally I read a magazine, flicking the pages at regular intervals while I study the people around me. There is something about the couple that suggests they accept the finality of death. I oppose that finality, prolonging what nature would rather destroy. I convince myself that they would reject me and, as they were my only option, decide to leave.

As I stand, the man with the twisted ankle grabs the coat of the young woman and pulls her towards him, launching into a tirade about treating people with respect. The nurses are quick to call for security, but there is no need because seconds later the young woman has him on the floor, his arm bent behind his back and a knee pressed into his neck.

Security lead the man away. The young woman speaks to a nurse. She appears keen to leave and, after a few clipped words, takes her bag and marches to the door. The nurse looks for someone to share in her incredulity and as the only other person standing, her eyes fall to mine. She looks away. Frowns.

I sit down unnaturally fast, throwing a magazine open onto my lap despite knowing that feigning interest in *Country Living* won't deter her.

She approaches, stares at the magazine with a puzzled expression. A wave of panic hits me, and I'm convinced the magazine is upside down. I check. Fortunately, it is not. Less fortunately, I appear to be engrossed in an advert for feminine hygiene products.

She notices my realisation and smirks. Then it's back to business. 'You've been here for three hours,' she says, 'and you've not signed in at the desk.'

I close the magazine and smooth the cover with my gloved hands. 'I know.'

'If you don't sign in, then we can't triage your condition and you won't be seen.'

'I am not ill.'

'This isn't the visitors' waiting room.'

'I am not here to visit anyone.'

She appears uncomfortable. Having dealt with one unreasonable man in the last five minutes, it's clear she has no desire to tackle a second. She is young, but the circles under her eyes are strikingly dark against such pale skin and every movement she makes feels delayed. Her hand is in the air, ready to call someone over. I look up at her moments before she turns away. Her finger hovers, retracts. She lowers her arm.

The nurse rubs her eyes with her palms. She likely believes this to be a hallucination brought on by exhaustion. She turns to me again, her knees bending so that her face is level with mine. Those patients who aren't too absorbed in their own self-pity are paying attention and utter the gasps that have stalked me since birth.

The nurse has yet to react. She continues to stare until, finally satisfied, she closes her eyes. It is her turn to gasp. She staggers backwards, falling over a man in a suit who tuts loudly.

'Oh my God! You're one of them!' she cries.

I did not want a scene. Checking my escape, I am on my feet before the nurse shouts.

'Wait!' She looks across the room. 'Nurse Crawley! Nurse… Jane! Jane, where did they take Mr Braithwaite?'

The other nurse looks up from dealing with an irate, red-faced man. 'Fallon, but they may have moved him again. You saw him, Jenny, he should have gone to the palliative ward.'

'This is why you're here, isn't it? For the dying.'

'It is.'

'Then why did you wait in A&E for three hours?' She's admonishing me, but struggles with the words, fighting their desire to leap from her mouth in a chaotic flurry. She shakes her head, trying to regain some composure. 'It doesn't matter,' she says. 'A man was brought in two days ago with severe pneumonia. He was transferred to another ward and his family are with him. He's eighty-four. A history of heavy smoking as a young man and a long-term bronchitis sufferer. There was nothing we could do for him.'

The nurse goes to take my arm. I snatch it away.

'You shouldn't touch me.'

She nods to herself. 'Oh. Right. Well, please come with me.'

I follow and people stand to get out of my way, some with reverence and others with fear, violently recoiling as I approach.

I watch the old lady in the corner of the room die. Peacefully, she leaves her body, her essence floating through her flesh, her clothes and her husband's arm, which is draped around her with such love and sorrow. She scatters into writhing facets of pure silver. They bury themselves into the walls and ceiling of the waiting room until the last one vanishes.

I am the only witness to her death.

The husband continues to cradle the empty shell of his wife. Soon he will realise that she has died, someone will be alerted, and people will panic.

The nurse runs, periodically stopping to wait for me as I follow on behind at barely a brisk walk. She looks irritated. If I wasn't what I am, she would have spoken up, grabbed my hand and dragged me to this Mr Braithwaite. Eventually she gives up and walks beside me.

'Does everyone forget what you look like?'

'Yes.'

'Even you?'

'Even me.'

We stand aside as an old woman is wheeled past on a bed. Half of her essence hangs from her, fluttering like a wind-tossed scarf as porters rush her to another ward. It reaches for me, desperate for a home, knowing that its current one will soon die. I reject her facets, leaving them to cling to the woman's dwindling life until it ends and they scatter into the Aether to be combined with others and formed into someone new.

The nurse looks at me again and I watch as her eyes flick over my features, moving from one to the next and then back again, as if to be certain.

As soon as she turns away, she shakes her head.

'How do you do that?'

'It is not something I control.'

'You could cause a lot of trouble with that.'

'I'm in the business of death,' I say. 'Trouble comes with the job.'

Silence stalks us through the corridors for the next three turns.

'My grandmother believed in people like you,' the nurse says as I'm led through a set of double doors. She applies antiseptic foam to her hands from a wall-mounted dispenser and rubs it in while staring at my gloves. 'Her brother, William, died of tuberculosis when he was seven. She said there were more of you around back then, but you were still expensive. Her parents weren't rich, so they could only keep William for four months. She said it helped at first, but after a while it made things difficult. William couldn't understand he was dead, and his parents cried every time they saw him. Even so, she always wanted to have her soul preserved when she died. She made us promise we'd find someone like you, but of course we couldn't, because to us you were just characters from old stories. She died two years ago.'

She's doubting herself. Doubting me. It creeps into her voice. She's telling herself that she hasn't even asked me if I am what she thinks I am. She's just assumed based on stories, but she hasn't had it confirmed. Already her walking has slowed. She thinks I'm a fraud. False hope for the family of the soon-to-be deceased.

'I know what you are thinking.'

The nurse bites her lip and checks a board that lists the patients' room numbers. 'There's an old man in there who will die tonight. His family are with him. If you're a fake, if what you do with your face is some trick, then walk away now, because if you go in there you'll break them, and no one deserves that.'

'I am exactly what you think I am.'

She nods once and motions for me to wait outside the room as she enters. After a while she opens the door and beckons me inside.

The room is full. Adults and children have arranged themselves awkwardly against the walls, balancing on windowsills or half-leaning on a table. No one speaks. Everyone watches the old man lying on the single bed. His body is thin, barely creasing the sheet. He has thicker hair than most men in their thirties. Another man leans over the bed, pressing his ear to Mr Braithwaite's mouth. Mr Braithwaite's lips move, but the other man just shakes his head. He places a comforting hand on the old man's chest before pulling it back and walking over.

He looks at me, closes his eyes and opens them again. Then he repeats, this time looking away and pausing for longer before he looks once more. He smiles as much as he can, given the atmosphere in the room.

'She told me what you were, but I couldn't bring myself to believe it.' He takes a tissue from his pocket and wipes his eyes. 'My dad can't speak. He's trying, but nothing comes out. He just doesn't have the strength. It's strange because he always spoke so much. He was one of those people who knew something about everything. It didn't matter the subject; he'd always have a few facts on it stashed away. You'd never see him without a book. Even when he was driving, there would be one on his lap. He used to love traffic jams. "Any excuse to read," he would say.

Sorry, you don't need to know this, I just... don't know what I'm supposed to do.'

'I cannot make the decision for you. But you should know, what I do will kill your father.'

'He led a good life. It should end with the dignity he deserves.'

A woman walks over. She was standing by the other side of the bed, holding Mr Braithwaite's hand. As she steps away, someone else takes her place as another family member peels herself from the wall to place her ear over the old man's silent lips.

'You can't just make that decision, David. He's my dad too.'

'If we don't, then this is it, and he dies desperately trying to speak to us while we strain to make out the words. He doesn't want to go like this, Sally. You know that as well as I do.'

'But he might—'

'He won't. You heard what the doctors told us. It's going to be tonight. That's why our family has driven hundreds of miles to say goodbye. Let us at least do it properly.'

'But what if he's a fraud?' Sally says.

'Look at him!'

The siblings stare each other down and, with the slightest lowering of her eyes, the sister acquiesces.

'My service is not free,' I say.

'Of course,' the son says. 'We'll pay anything.'

I hand him a card from inside my jacket pocket and his eyebrows raise as he reads the price, but soon he's nodding to himself and handing the card back while he ushers me towards his dad.

'If you want to say anything to him, hold his hand, or hug him, then you need to do so now.'

'You really will kill him, won't you?' the daughter asks.

'I have to.'

The family approaches the bed, each saying goodbye to their father, grandfather, uncle, cousin, with a sense of unreality, as if nothing will happen.

'Please step away,' I say, and they do.

I remove my gloves and lay them on the bed next to the old man. The family don't turn away, like I would expect. Instead, their phones are out, recording what will take place. It won't work. What a brain interprets and what a camera records are different things, but I see no need to correct them on this.

I stand at the side of Mr Braithwaite's bed and close my eyes. Everything is black at first, but soon his essence appears, a mass of writhing facets of silver threads knotted into the shape of a human. Every aspect of his personality, every memory that has clung on through the years, his loves, his hates, his shames, his fears; each one is represented in a single facet, wound into the essence that is him. I bend forward.

'Release the life you hold so tight; welcome me and leave the light.'

My forehead touches his and instantly facets flow into me, fighting each other in their desperate bid for salvation. Uncorked, they burst into the room, foolishly escaping. I reach out, pulling them in with my hands while the facets inside my arms grow longer, forming emaciated, ethereal counterparts that push through my palms and sweep the room. They race through my head and charge down my arms, right into my centre, where they collect and shrink – retaining everything that they are while fitting themselves into the space I can offer.

The family will have seen nothing of what I experienced. To them, I am a willow-bodied eighteen-year-old, barely a man, who has a face they cannot remember. I have bent over the body of their beloved relative, muttered something unintelligible, and waved my arms trying to catch things they cannot see.

A few of the older children fail to stifle their laughter while their parents slap their legs with the back of their hands, their faces sour and pinched. Annoyance seeps into the room and accusatory stares are aimed at me and the son. The sister is opening her mouth when someone screams.

'He's dead!'

The family run to him, surrounding the bed, prodding and poking, shaking and trying to wake the man I have just killed. All except for the son. He stands in front of me, waiting, hoping desperately that I am real, that a character from his childhood history books stands before him.

I could say something, but I am busy. I have a new essence inside me and if I do not bind him to me, then he will escape into the Aether.

The family turns away from the bed one by one, wanting to know what I have done. They call for the doctors. The nurse waits by the door. To her credit, she doesn't back away, but she doesn't enter the room either.

Finally, Mr Braithwaite is secured. I watch the son as the face of his father appears over my own. His mouth lifts at the corners, smiling, beaming. His eyes crinkle, then run with tears. Everyone around the bed, and those who hang out of the door calling for help, rush over, gasping and laughing and crying as they see the face of Mr Braithwaite, who lies dead only metres from them, where my own should be.

'Well, this is a surprise,' says an intelligent voice emanating from my mouth, though not at all of my doing. 'Where on earth did you find an archivist?'

2

'I'm sure it told me to dice the onions but now it says add the *sliced* onions. I must have printed this wrong or mixed up the recipes.' Richard flips the pages, stained around the edges with olive oil and dusted with ground pepper. 'Well, the onions are diced now, so there's no going back. Or do you think I should slice some more?'

'It doesn't matter,' I say. The boiling water for the pasta has made the room a sauna and the only thing the extractor fan is good for is making noise. I turn a page of my library book and it feels moist. The paper's starting to curl too, so I guess that's a fine.

'If it didn't tell me I needed sliced onions, then it wouldn't be important. Perhaps it improves the texture. What do you think, Sun?'

'I already said. I think it doesn't matter.'

'I suppose you're right.' Richard dumps the onions into the pan. They're clearly sliced. I wonder if I'm supposed to find this fake ineptitude endearing.

The scent of fried onions and burning spices fill the air. I hold back my cough, but after a while I can't stop it and it erupts in a splutter. It's so hot I'm sweating. If I lived anywhere else I'd open the windows, but not here. They're either painted shut or nailed shut, or they open a portal to hell – at least that's what I think; I can't reach that one. That means the only way fresh air can get in is through the letter box, but you're an idiot if you think propping open that piss flap is a good idea.

'So, Laure's out again. That's the fifth weekend in a row. For such a quiet girl she sure has an active social life. I can't figure her out.'

'She's a twelve-year-old girl,' I say. 'You're not supposed to figure her out.'

'Still, how does she make so many friends?'

'She's pretty, that's all anyone needs. That and a phone.'

'You're right. She is stunning, our Laure.'

'I called her pretty.'

Richard opens a tin of tomatoes and drops them into the pan. 'Same thing.'

I close my book and try to brush clear the dust jacket with the back of my hand. It comes away sticky; the flat has claimed it. I guess that means it's mine for keeps.

I get up and grab my jacket. Even for faux leather, it's unconvincingly shit.

'Where are you going?' Richard calls as he measures rock salt into the sauce, crystal by crystal.

'Out.'

'But I've cooked.'

I grab my library book. 'I'll heat it up when I get back.'

'You're only seventeen, Sun. It's not safe for you to be out so late.'

'After consulting my balance, it seems I'm completely out of fucks.' I dig into my pocket for some keys, only to find they've escaped into the lining of the jacket. I fish them out – small hands have their uses – and unlock the door. I look back and there is Richard, standing by the table, wearing an apron Laure bought him for Christmas, his pathetic eyes fixed on the seat meant for me.

'You don't care about me at all, do you?'

'Nothing gets past you.' I take my bag and leave the door to slam itself shut.

The hospital's hydrotherapy pool isn't large enough to swim in, but then it wasn't really built for that. It's warm, not far off bath temperature, and I am a slowly spinning star, watching the reflected light from the water dance across the ceiling. I've wedged some floats under the small of my back. Without them I'd sink like a rock. They say women are supposed to float better than men because of our body shape, but all those extra bits women have I'm in short supply of.

I remove the floats and let the water take me. I keep my eyes open. Water floods my ears and soon I'm cocooned by the warmth of the pool. I lie on the bottom for as long as I can hold my breath before pushing up and climbing out.

It's late. The last class to use the pool finished at six. There used to be cameras in here, but after an operator was caught selling footage of the toddler swim classes the hospital removed them – the cameras, not the operator; he killed himself when his wife and children found out. I grab the towel I left draped on a chair and dry myself as little as possible. I don't bother with a shower; I like the smell of chlorine on my skin. I imagine the chemicals cleansing me, killing all traces of the flat and the filth it flings. I climb into my clothes, my wet swimsuit beneath them, and run my fingers through my hair. The door was locked when I came here, but it's on a latch so I don't need my picks to lock it again. There's no one in the corridors and all the lights are on.

There'll be people in the hospital somewhere, there always are, but not around here. Once I ran into a cleaner and blurted out some stupid excuse, but she didn't care who I was and just went back to mopping the floor.

There's someone else in the waiting room I like, the one with the broken vending machine. The only other time I've seen people here was after a riot at the football stadium that left the hospital crammed with drunken fuckwits, all with missing teeth and ears hanging round their chins. I spent that night pushing myself around on a trolley in a twenty-four-hour supermarket. It took the lone security guard two hours to catch me. He was old and fat. I think I gave him a heart attack.

I make my way to the vending machine. It's snagged a packet of salt-and-vinegar crisps on the busted spiral. Someone has tried to drop a couple of chocolate bars, hoping to dislodge it, but they're caught too. There are fresh kick marks on the machine and someone has written a complaint and stuck it on the glass. I rip it off and reach under the flap, my hand small enough to fit through the gap, and grab the crisps. The chocolate follows soon after. I hope they never fix this machine.

I sit down and open the crisps. I almost forgot how starving I am. The smell of Richard's food haunts me, but I'll only dump it in the bin as soon as I get home, no matter how delicious it is.

I glance at the intruder, aware that the sound of crisps in my mouth is impossibly loud. Black shoes, black trousers, a white shirt under a dark green jacket, and bright purple leather gloves. They're not dressed for a late-night trip to the hospital. I get up, move one seat closer. I can't see their face, but I'm sure it's a him. It should be obvious, but there's doubt. The intruder is clearly tall, much taller than me, and there's no sign of any chest. Still, it's not obvious. I move another seat closer, then climb over a row as I eat the freakishly loud crisps. They know

15

I'm here. I can almost hear them wishing me away. It's not like I want to talk to them. I just want to see them. Something isn't right and I need to know what. After that I'll hide away, maybe take a nap in a ward or steal a wheelchair and learn to spin on one wheel. Just one look, then I'll go.

The intruder is sat right in front of me. Actually, I suppose I'm sat right in front of them. Head down and hands clasped in their lap. It almost looks like they're praying – probably praying for me to fuck off.

I eat a crisp. The intruder watches me.

'Want one?'

The intruder doesn't respond.

'It's OK, I didn't pay for them.'

Their head goes down.

'Suit yourself,' I say, and I pour the rest of the packet into my mouth.

I shift forward, ready to stand, but something's missing. I looked at that face, right into the eyes, but my memory of it has gone. Maybe I just wasn't paying attention, like when someone tells you their name and you immediately forget it. But it's worse than that. I don't even know if it was the face of a man or a woman, let alone what colour the eyes were. Surely I'm not that vacant?

My cough is so loud it's blatantly fake.

The intruder looks up and I'm doing it, I'm definitely looking at their face, thinking about their face, doing nothing but concentrating on their face.

'Crisp shards in my throat,' I say, and cough again. 'Sorry.'

They look down.

Every feature of the face vanishes. Poof! Like some creepy magic trick where the guy reaches into your brain and steals memories using persuasion. Only no one did that to me because I haven't moved and the person sitting opposite me hasn't moved and the time is still the same. Sure, if I'd lost an hour of my life, I'd be suspicious, but this is creepier than that and I'm ready to get the hell out of here when I remember something I learnt about in History.

'Are you one of them?'

'One of what?' The voice is definitely male. A soft, confident baritone that draws me in, not a brash bass that brags about conquests and sits with his legs too wide apart on the bus.

'A face stealer.'

He laughs, but I can't see a smile. He says nothing more.

'You are, aren't you?'

'If that is what you want to call me.'

'Do you care that people can't remember what you look like?'

'No.'

'I think I'd care,' I say.

'Then it is fortunate you are not me.'

He continues to stare into his clasped hands. I do the same, staring at his bright purple gloves, so out of place with everything else he wears.

'Can I take a picture of you?'

'If you wish.'

As he looks up at me, the memories flood back and I doubt that I ever forgot. Of course this is what he looks like. Of course his eyes are that colour and his hair is that length. How could I possibly have forgotten?

I slide my phone out of my jacket pocket. His face fills the screen, not blurred or pixelated, just there like anyone else's would be. I take the picture and turn myself away so all I can see is the phone and not him. His face is frozen on the screen, half smile and half look of concern. I press the lock screen button and my phone goes black. So too does my memory.

'How did you do that?'

'I did nothing; you're the one who forgot.'

'You made me forget!'

'If that is what you want to believe,' he says.

'What else can you make me do?'

'Clearly not leave.'

'Rude.' I slide my phone back into my pocket and start on one of the chocolate bars. 'Why are you here?' I ask.

'I'm ordering.'

'Ordering what? Chinese? Because if you're up for sharing...'

'People,' he says.

'Chinese brides?'

'No.'

'Oh, you mean the souls you ate?'

'They're called essences.'

'Semantics,' I say as I finish the last of the chocolate and contemplate the fate of the second bar.

'No, not semantics,' he says, irritated. 'A soul implies something that is indivisible, a single entity that represents every part of a person. What we have inside us are essences composed of facets. Each facet is a unique aspect of the person: a memory, a feeling, a response, a trait. Facets appear when a person experiences something new and leave when a person grows, either as they forget the memories or as their character changes with age. You are not one thing, you are many; constantly evolving and growing and dying. The essence you have now is not the essence you were born with and it will not be the essence you die with.'

'Well, look at you forming complete sentences.'

He looks away and there goes the memory of the left side of his face. A part of my mind tells me it's identical to the right side, but for some reason I can't bring myself to believe that.

'Sorry,' I say, 'that was mean. It was interesting, what you said. I didn't know that.'

'Most people don't.'

'And now you've ruined it by sounding arrogant.'

He's silent for a while.

'Don't you want to know why I'm here?' I ask.

'No.'

'Oh.'

'It's late. You should get home.'

I check the clock. He's right. At least Richard will be asleep.

'What's your name?'

'I don't have a name,' he says.

'Of course you have a name. Everyone has a name.'

'Just like everyone has a face that can be remembered?'

'OK. Sure. But still, people have to call you something, kind of inconvenient otherwise.'

'They call me the Archivist.'

'Well, that's a little impersonal.'

'It suits me.'

'You got me there. I'm Sun-young, but most people call me Sun.'

'Why are you telling me this?'

'So you know what to call me next time we meet.'

'I have no intention of seeing you again.'

'*You* might not, but I have other ideas.' I get off the chair and head for the door. 'So you'll be here tomorrow, right?'

He stares at me. Not saying anything. Not smiling. Just looking. I give him a wave and he turns away to focus on the floor.

I'll take that as a yes.

'I can't believe you're arguing with me at a time like this!'

'I'm not arguing with you, I'm trying to have a reasoned discussion.'

'My mother is lying there dying!'

The husband sits down and glares at me. His wife goes to her mother's bedside and strokes her hand. Two teenagers, a girl and a boy, sit with the husband, trying not to make eye contact with anyone.

Eventually, the husband stands and goes to his wife, gently placing a hand on her shoulder. 'I know how hard this must be for you. When I lost my mum, I would have given anything to keep her around... but the prices he's charging are ludicrous.'

'She's my mother and it's my inheritance, Daniel.'

'I'm not saying it's not, I just think we should sit down and discuss this properly before we make any decisions we later regret.'

'Regret?' the wife cries. 'And why exactly would I regret keeping my mother around?'

'There are other things the money could go on. Sarah will need a car to learn in next year and Mike's been after an electric guitar for months. Why don't we use your mother's money for the kids? It's what she would have wanted.'

'Oh, don't give me that "it's what she would have wanted" crap. You never spent any time with her; you have no idea what she wants.'

'Of course I know what she wants,' the husband says. 'She's an old woman who has reached the end of her very long and happy life, and now she wants to gently drift away surrounded by the people she loves.'

The wife's shoulders drop and she leans into her husband. 'Maybe you're right. Keeping her around would be selfish.' She strokes the back of her mother's frail hand. 'But then maybe this is fate,' she says as she looks at me, a hint of shock registering in the slight raising of her eyebrows. 'Finding an archivist the same day we're told to come and say goodbye. That has to mean something.'

The husband rolls his eyes and exhales deeply. I do not believe I am his favourite person.

'And I suppose this costs, or do you just charge by the dead?'

'I only charge for services rendered.'

'Well at least *that's* something.'

'Daniel,' the wife says, 'this isn't about money, it's about my mother.'

'I know,' the husband says as he rubs his wife's back. 'It's just when I think about all the money we spent on her while she was in that care home... We've not taken a holiday in two years. Losing that kind of money was bad enough when she was alive, but when she's dead...'

The door flies open and a woman rushes in. She's breathing heavily, blonde hair stuck to her face with sweat. She holds onto the doorframe for support. 'You have to come with me,' she cries, reaching for me before snatching her hand back. It's covered with blood. So is her arm.

The woman is Jenny, the nurse I met when I took the face of Mr Braithwaite. I walk to the door.

'But what about my mother?' the wife cries.

'She died three minutes ago.'

The wife collapses on the floor and a look of triumph is passed between her husband and his teenage children.

'But... but...' the wife stammers.

'I don't know if it helps,' I say, 'but she didn't look pleased.'

'Why didn't you tell me?'

'I wanted Mike to have an electric guitar,' I say as I stand. 'Children need hobbies.'

The woman glares at me. 'Daniel. Do something!'

The husband appears unable to do anything but grin.

I'm practically thrown into a car, which mounts the pavement twice before I have time to put on my seatbelt. There is a queue by the exit barrier that we veer away from at the last minute, driving through a bush and immediately finding ourselves on a road. A lorry swerves out of the way to avoid us, blaring its horn and flashing its lights, but the response of the nurse next to me is only to drive faster. She leans forward in her seat, both hands gripping the wheel so tightly that veins appear beneath the skin of her arms. She weaves between the traffic, jumps red lights and drives well in excess of any speed limit, legal or self-preservative. She does not wear her uniform and there are no hospitals or care homes where we are heading. Whatever has happened, I can only assume it's personal.

An ambulance hangs off the kerb outside a large red-brick house, a police car parked behind it. The officer inside it is on her phone. She takes one look at me and starts the engine.

I'm led up the path, past the white columns of a portico, and through the open door. A woman in her late fifties runs

22

downstairs. She has blood over her arms and dress. The nurse runs upstairs and I follow.

'Have they managed to…?'

'No,' the older woman says.

'But is she still…?'

'Yes. Just.'

I climb the curved stairs onto a landing. The thick pile carpet grows sodden beneath my feet and soon I stand in the doorway of a bathroom. Jenny has rushed inside and leans over the bath, hugging someone I cannot see.

Two paramedics work frantically at the bathroom's far end, neither registering me. The scene before them has their full attention. A broken water pipe gushes over linoleum. One of the paramedics fumbles a bandage. It falls to the bathroom floor and quickly absorbs water to join the other bloated medical equipment that floats serenely around everyone's feet.

'Please,' Jenny calls. 'They can't save her.'

The paramedics step back, awkward and silent. They look at me again and finally understand.

I approach the bath, the cold water seeping between the stitching of my leather shoes. Lying inside is a young girl, no more than fourteen. She wears a blood-stained lace dress that looks to have once been cream. Her auburn hair clings to the sides of the empty bath and the pallor of her skin accentuates her freckles and the blue of her lips.

'She's only thirteen,' Jenny says. 'You have to help her.'

The girl looks to have handcuffed herself to the taps after cutting both radial arteries with a razor blade that sits innocuously on the bottom of the bath. The skin around her wrists bleeds from deep gouges that go down to the bone. The cuts are neat, the handcuffs – and the apparent lack of key – decisive; so why has she fought so hard against something of her own doing? Everything leading up to the suicide appears planned, and then at the moment it is executed, fearfully regretted.

I move closer. An earlier attempt to free her broke the water pipe and the cuts in the handcuffs from a hacksaw are superficial. The same with the taps, which are solid and Victorian like the rest of the house.

The woman, who I presume is the mother to both Jenny and the girl in the bath, based on the collective flatness of their earlobes, strokes the hair of her young daughter. At the same time, Jenny tries to work her fingers through the handcuffs and apply pressure to the cuts. She struggles; the handcuffs are too tight to move them far enough up the arm, resulting in a length of cut that remains exposed.

A man appears in the doorway. White trousers and a salmon-coloured shirt that barely contains his gut. His face isn't as fat as it ought to be and he wears his grey hair swept back into a quiff. Unlike everyone else, there doesn't appear to be a drop of blood on him.

'And just who the fuck is this?' he cries, not even bothering to point at me.

'The Archivist,' Jenny says, 'the one I told you about.'

'Well then, what the fuck is he doing here?'

'Dad, Claire won't—'

'Don't you start that again. We'll get your sister out of this. You two,' it seems the paramedics are worth at least a cursory wave, 'don't just stand there thumbing your arseholes, get my daughter out of there. I've already called for another ambulance; it'll be here in ten minutes. Let's hope that one hasn't been packed with fuckwits.'

The paramedics lurch forward as Jenny and her mother step aside, but their attempts to free the girl are in vain. They are trained in saving lives, not plumbing, and their ineffectual use of a clearly blunt saw will do nothing but waste the final minutes of this girl's life.

Jenny stands and I can tell she wants to grab my jacket and throw me into the fray, but she knows that she shouldn't touch me and, despite the situation, shows restraint.

'Please,' she says.

'I cannot save lives; I only take them.'

'I know,' she sniffs and wipes her eyes with the back of her hand, staining her face with blood. 'She screamed. After she... She doesn't want to die. This was a mistake, but they can't get her out. At least if you're here, we'll still have a part of her.'

The girl's essence grips the body with futility. The Aether has already drawn it out and facets desperately hold on to what little life remains. They have left her extremities to gather around her slowly beating heart in a panicked cluster. And while they remain together as a single essence for now, it will not be long before they are taken and scattered to form anew.

I nod and approach the girl. The paramedics stand back as Jenny and her mother kneel on the flooded floor and lean over the rim of the bath.

'Can we hold her while you...?' the mother asks, unsure what it is I'm going to do.

'You can.'

The mother reaches into the bath and pulls her daughter into a sitting position as Jenny places a hand on one of her sister's ice-blue feet.

'Be careful not to touch me,' I say as I lean forward and slip my gloves into the pocket of my jacket.

'Just what the fuck is going on?'

'Jeremy, please,' the mother manages with shaking lips. 'You need to come here and say goodbye to our baby.'

25

'I'll be doing no such thing. Now I don't know what you think you're about to do—'

The father grabs the back of my collar and his knuckles brush my neck. I inhale sharply as I feel his facets surge into me. He lets go and staggers backwards, ripping his facets out of me as he goes. They hang from his hand like long silver hairs. They know I am there and probe the air trying to find me, twitching and flicking their way forwards, desperate for what I am. He collapses, the side of his head cracking against the sink as he falls. His vomit skits across the waterlogged floor and he slips into unconsciousness.

The paramedics are slow to react, but after a moment of confusion they take him out of the room and out of my sight. Jenny looks at me with concern.

'He won't die,' I say, and turn my attention back to the thirteen-year-old girl in the arms of her mother.

'It'll be all right, Mum,' Jenny says. 'He's real. I promise you.'

The mother looks at me with such intensity that I have no reply. I lean into the girl and press my forehead to hers.

'Release the life you hold so tight; welcome me and leave the light.'

I place my hands on the side of the bath as I stand, pulling out the brilliant facets of the girl's life through her forehead. My own facets push out from the palms of my hands to wrap around the girl. I take her into me and she leaves her body quickly.

The girl rages inside me and I struggle to hold her. Her face appears over mine. The mother screams and drops her daughter, leaving her head to crash against the side of the bath before it slides, undignified, towards the bottom.

Claire's face screams over my own. She doesn't stop. A single note of panic. I clamp my hands over her mouth. The screaming continues and I can see in the mirror that her mouth

26

has travelled through my fingers to materialise on the back of my hands.

The mother is calling Claire's name while Jenny watches, horrified.

A searing pain attacks my skin and I fall to my knees. The essence of the girl is shifting. It pulls itself from where I have stored it, an extraction that should be impossible. I feel her face lift. I try to catch it, but something pulls her with a strength greater than my own.

Her face explodes from mine. I reach out, facets streaming from my fingers, desperately trying to regain the girl, but she won't return. A swirling brilliance of gold appears above my head. It rises, whipping around the light and pulling itself together tighter and tighter until it is a ball. The mother jumps to grab it, but before her fingers brush the surface it has disappeared through the ceiling and left the room.

The mother collapses. Jenny's legs give way slowly, her eyes still on the ceiling. She holds the rim of the bath for support.

No one looks at me.

I don't understand what has just happened. I secured her essence inside of me. She should not have been able to leave. It was as if someone reached in and ripped her out. Everything inside is in turmoil and I can feel the essences of others spasming as my own recoils from the shock.

Soon, everything settles and I notice that something is not where it is supposed to be. Not all of Claire was taken. A collection of her facets remain, buried deep in my essence. I can feel them, coiled tightly into a knot. I cannot tell which aspect of Claire those facets represent; a memory, an anxiety, a fear, it does not matter. All I know is that they are immovable, wound into the very facets that define me, the facets that make me an archivist.

4

Why are the lights in this room brighter than the Sun? I shield my eyes as I slide my legs off the armrest. My mouth tastes like I've gargled bin water. I guess I should have chewed gum before I fell asleep. A crunch breaks the silence. I move my hand away from my eyes and fight the light. He's sat across from me, one glove off, eating a packet of crisps.

'Souls of the dead not enough?'

'Apparently not.'

He finishes, not offering me any, and produces a tissue from inside his jacket pocket to wipe his fingers clean. The crisp packet is laid on his lap, where he smooths it flat and meticulously folds it before tying it into a neat knot. He drops both it and the tissue into the bin next to him.

'Why didn't you wake me?'

'I didn't realise I was supposed to.'

'You're a big boy,' I say, 'you should've figured it out.'

He wasn't there the day after we first met. I waited all evening, but the only person who appeared was an old man. He saw me, smiled, then vomited over himself and passed out. I had to call someone from the reception phone to come and get him.

The only reason I kept going back to that waiting room was because I had nowhere else to be. I always made sure Laure was safe before I left, each night spent with a different friend. It's become normal. With both of her parents missing, possibly dead, there's no end of families willing to take her in.

And what was it all for? So I could hang around in an empty hospital like some obsessed stalker? I'm sure the only reason he's here is to hand over a restraining order.

I pull my pathetic self up and steal my own bag of crisps. I bet he paid for his.

'What's with the fancy gloves?'

Today's gloves are dark green. Leather. He slides the second one on and places his hands neatly on his lap.

'I am a fancy person.'

I snort. He smiles.

'You don't like gloves?' he asks.

I eat my crisps. 'Thick fluffy ones in the winter. Yours are serial killer gloves.'

'Then they are perfect.'

'I thought you saved people's souls.'

'Only if that is what you believe,' he says. 'Archivists are not unique in their claims of divinity.'

'So you're a fraud?'

'I wouldn't say that.'

He studies the clock on the wall and my eyes follow. It's nearly one.

'Somewhere to be?' I ask.

He shakes his head and removes his gloves. Apart from his face, his hands are the only glimpse I get of his skin. He studies them like he's stoned, marvelling at the way his fingers bend.

'Facets are drawn to me. I can see yours twitching inside you. They are excited that I am so near. The ones by your left shoulder poke through your skin, trying to rip themselves from your essence and dive into mine. You have an injury there. It has healed, but not perfectly.'

I rub my shoulder. That one was a door handle.

He leans forward, reaching for me. 'The closer I get, the more your facets want me. They work themselves into a frenzy, eager to flee your body. You feel a deep sense of dread. Just by sitting close to me, you are aware that something is not as it should be. You are thinking about death. You feel it approaching. An inexplicable sense that soon something terrible will befall you. That feeling is because of me, and the closer I move, the stronger that feeling becomes.'

A gasp rushes into my mouth. The walls of the waiting room close in and the light that was so oppressive when I woke up is now dim. I try to move, but it takes all my energy to push myself away from the Archivist and back into my chair. I'm heavy, a girl of lead, and I will grow heavier the closer he comes until the chair collapses and I fall through the floor.

He's still talking, but his words have slipped away. All I hear is buzzing. Flies, desperate to feast on my rotting body.

It's so cold I can barely think, but I can't see my breath. Am I still breathing? I can't feel myself breathing. I try to drag my arms across my chest but they won't move and I'm crying, and his face is right in front of mine as tears freeze, crystalising against my cheeks. I want to vanish. I curl over and scream. I make no sound.

My hands are on my face and I'm warm again. The room is light, and so am I. My cheeks are wet and I frantically wipe them dry with the sleeve of my jacket.

'Fucking hell.'

'I took that too far. I apologise.'

'Fucking hell,' I say again, angry and happy and confused

all at once. I'm breathing heavily, but that's a relief considering what I just went through. I can't help myself from smiling, so relieved to be back in this shitty waiting room. 'Does that always happen?' I ask.

'When I project the face of a person, family members want to touch it and hold me like I'm their father, or sister, or wife, so I have to repress the effect, but it is difficult and I cannot do it for long.'

'Could you have killed me?'

'It is possible.'

He slips the gloves back on.

'What do the gloves do?'

'Your facets wanted me because I was close. But you are healthy, so they would not have left your body. It is different if I touch you. If my skin contacts yours then our facets will connect, and when I pull away yours will be removed and a part of who you are will be ripped from your body.'

'So what you're saying is that you can only touch dead people?'

'And people who are going to die.'

'Not much of a dating life.'

He looks away and moves his feet like he's ready to leave.

'Sorry, that wasn't fair,' I say hurriedly.

He relaxes into his seat and looks at me square on. His face is a wonderful surprise every time I see it.

'When I take possession of a person's essence, that person dies. This is because their body is weak and the essence is ready to leave. If the person is healthy, and I touch them, then I only pull some of their facets from their essence, with the rest remaining safely inside the body. If I keep those facets, then a link is formed between me and the essence.'

'Don't they snap?'

31

'The facets I see are long silver threads coiled inside you. They are ethereal, not physical, so while I perceive them to have length, that is only the image that my mind creates. Other archivists visualise them differently, as jewels, whorls of golden dust or brilliant flashes of light. What I see is only a representation of something my brain struggles to understand.'

'So you could take some of these facets from a person and then, when they die, their essence would come to you, no matter where they were?'

'For a time, but facets are thoughts and ideas and feelings. They are changeable. If the facets that connected me to a person were a memory, and that memory was forgotten, then the link would be lost. Some connections could last hours; others, years. There is no guarantee that when a person dies, the link will remain.'

The smile is still on my face. Those few moments when I felt so close to dying are now a lifetime ago and the difference between then and now has elevated me to a sensation that's bordering euphoric. I feel lucky to be alive, as if after a near-death experience. Every day from this moment will be a precious gift. And yet already I feel the effect he had on me fading, my mood floating down like a leaf in autumn.

'Can you show me one?'

He leans forward and a sudden wave of despair grips me before he realises and settles back. The immediate rise in my spirits is like a drug hit.

'One of what?'

'The face of a dead person.'

He doesn't respond and, for the second time that night, I'm convinced he's grown tired of me. I should know better. What he does isn't a party trick. I turn around and grab my jacket as I mumble an apology.

When I look back there is someone else sitting across from me.

The face is frozen and, despite my sense of self-preservation, I lean closer. I don't feel the dread I expected and know he's holding it back like a pack of rabid dogs on fraying leads. The woman has hair that frames her face, though it's only there from the front as further round the back of his head it blends seamlessly into his. Her hair is soft and feels as real as any hair I have ever felt. I cup a thick blonde lock in my hand and lift it up, testing its weight. It's there, even though I know it can't be because it would be impossible for anyone to grow so much hair in less than a second.

'Enjoying yourself?'

I scream and rip my hand away.

The woman smiles. It's kind.

'I only ever see my husband or children, so I thought he must have made a mistake, but you didn't complain so I decided to leave you to it. I hope I'm not here as some party piece to impress a date.'

'It's not a date.'

'I see.' She nods as she speaks, her hair gently bouncing against her face and his shoulders.

'What's it like?'

'Being dead?' she asks. 'Not what I'd been led to believe, but then isn't that always the case? It's not that I was religious and felt let down by death, I was just expecting something more final. You see, there's nothing in-between. No one tells you that, though who these days expects to run into an archivist? I had dismissed them as frauds, but it turns out my husband believed and so here I am, proven wrong. Again.'

'Don't you want to be there?'

She frowns, fine wrinkles gathering at the corners of her eyes. 'I wouldn't say that. It makes it easier on my boys. They're only ten and eight and even though they knew I was dying, we didn't have enough time together before the cancer chained me to a bed. Because there's no in-between, I notice the changes more. It's only been a month and Ryan has a new haircut and Jason's wearing clothes I didn't buy him. As the gaps between visits get longer, I'll slowly become a chore and then a burden.'

'I'm sorry.' I feel stupid for saying it, but she's looking at me like she expects a response and it's all I have.

'I'm sure David will remarry,' she says. 'Not straight away, but eventually. He's only forty-three, I can't expect him to be alone forever. I wonder if he'll introduce me to his new wife – the new mother of my children. Perhaps I'll even see my boys get married. The Archivist could wear a dress and fascinator and sit next to David and his new wife in the front row. Ryan might have children; I'm not sure Jason will. Maybe I'll get to meet them.'

She sighs. It's strange how impassive his body is. People touch their face when they speak, especially during awkward conversations like this. I imagine her running her fingers through her hair or cupping her cheek with her hand while she thinks. Instead, her face is stranded, left to deal with this pause alone.

'I know that won't happen,' the woman continues. 'The time between visits will grow and so will my boys. They'll get used to me being dead and seeing me like this will just make it worse. One day it will be the last visit. They won't tell me. Afterwards, they'll stop paying the Archivist, he'll release me and that'll be it.'

'I could talk to you.'

'That's sweet, but it's my burden, not yours.'

'Can I take your picture?'

'Of course.'

I pull out my phone and take her picture. The face on the screen is hers.

'I can feel him pulling me back. I think it's time we said goodbye.'

'What's your name?' I ask.

'Karen.'

Her face is sucked into his. He moves again, looking at me from eyes I had forgotten until moments ago. I glance at my phone. The face of the woman has gone. It's now his face in the picture.

'Where did she go?' I ask, holding up my phone.

'She was never there.'

'But I spoke to her.'

'You thought you spoke to her, but it was always my face.'

'I don't understand.'

'Your senses were being manipulated. It is like pain. You feel it because your brain is told you are injured, but if that signal is blocked, the pain disappears. What I do is the same. I reach into your brain and tell it you see the face of Karen Moore, who died aged forty-two from ovarian cancer. I tell it that you hear her voice. I tell it that you touch her hair. But none of that happens and you sit there in conversation with no one but me.'

'Does that mean you couldn't hear her?'

'I could. It manipulates my senses too.'

'I don't understand. Is it real or not?'

'It is as real as you want it to be.'

I know what I saw when Karen's face appeared over his. My imagination is not creative enough to produce something with such detail. Even when I try to conjure up a face in my mind so I can dream about that person, it's always hazy. That was the face of someone who lived and died. It was real. The same is true of

35

the feeling that came over me as he moved closer. That was real too. Far more real than I wanted it to be.

'I believe you.'

He says nothing, knows there's more to come.

'And I want you to do it to me,' I say. 'I want you to take my face.'

'I can't interview a dead woman.' Detective Inspector Monique Jones uncrosses her legs and leans forward. She rests her chin on a clenched fist and studies the woman in the hospital bed. 'Can't interview a woman in a coma either.'

'You heard the doctor, ma'am. With the level of injury she sustained, we'll be lucky if she can nod, let alone speak.'

'You're right, Constable. I did hear the doctor.' The detective inspector walks over. Tall for a woman, her powder blue Merino wool suit is tight around an athletic physique. I'm convinced this isn't the first time we've met but struggle to place her.

'What if I told you I can remember your face?'

'Then I would be impressed.'

She walks away. 'I can't, of course. But that doesn't mean I believe you can reach in and pull out that woman's soul.'

'You heard what the nurses said.' Constable Wilson says. 'Even the doctors agree, he's the real thing.'

'Again, Isabella. Yes, I heard. And it's called confirmation bias. They were in emotional situations and saw what they wanted to see. There's something wrong with his face, even I believe that. But just because there is some aspect to him I can't explain, doesn't mean he can raise the dead.'

'They all saw it.'

'They all *thought* they saw it. Pick up a book. Browse the internet. These cases have a history of reappearing, especially with charlatans who have mastered the skill of appearing unsettling.'

'If you don't need me,' I say, 'there are other people who require my services.'

'Ma'am, at least let him try,' Constable Wilson says.

'Why?' Detective Inspector Jones asks. 'Because some grieving wife believes she can talk to her husband of fifty-seven years despite him being stone dead? Every video recorded by a family member on their phone, every CCTV clip, they all show nothing but him. No ghostly faces. No voices from beyond the grave. Just him.'

'That's because what he does can't be recorded,' Constable Wilson says.

Detective Inspector Jones shoots me a look. 'Convenient, that.'

The detective inspector sits on the edge of the bed and takes the hand of Melody Cross, the silence punctuated by the steady beep from the cardiac monitor. 'Who did this to you?' she asks.

I was informed by a police liaison officer that Melody was found at five in the morning by a dog walker. Victims of violence in public places are always discovered the next morning by dog walkers. Perhaps that's one of the allures of pet ownership.

The police believe she was attacked on her way home after a night out. Her friends hadn't seen her leave, though apparently that wasn't unusual as her boyfriend worked late and most nights were cut short so the two of them could walk home through the park. Only he wasn't working that evening. The dog walker who found her, a woman in her sixties with two German Shepherds and a Labrador to control, was amazed Melody was still alive. They induced a coma as soon as she was brought in and performed a decompressive craniotomy to reduce the oedema. The family have been kept out. Melody is now stable, and the police want to know who did this before they let anyone see her. Unfortunately, there's no line of questioning that'll work on the comatose.

'You might as well just leave,' the detective inspector tells me. I know the constable wants to speak up, but she'll only be put in her place for it.

If I assist the police, then I'll be expected to do so again, and any form of remuneration will be considerably smaller than what I charge for private clients. But I don't do this for the money; the cost is high to reduce the demand, especially when there's an uncertainty around my abilities. I've never been an altruist because, until now, the right opportunity has not presented itself. I will try it on and see if I like the fit. If not, I can always move to another city. I certainly have the means.

I approach the bed, careful to keep my distance. Melody, a woman only a few years older than me, lies beneath the sheets. Detective Inspector Jones stays on the edge of the bed, regarding me with quizzical irritation.

The sheets, the bed, the room, everything but Melody falls away. I can see her essence, relatively well contained in her torso but with signs of significant distress. Further towards her head, it struggles to take hold. Several facets remain in place, anchored around the areas that avoided any damage, though most have escaped and are orbiting Melody's head like the spiral arms of a galaxy. They reach into her skull, maintaining fragile contact with her brain tissue. Over time they extract themselves and join the slowly rotating mass. It will not be many days before the number of facets that have left her brain has grown too numerous for them to ever return, and while they may remain as a cranial cloud, forever just out of reach, most will detach and drift into the Aether. If Melody ever wakes, she will never be the woman who existed before the attack.

Melody's body constructs itself around her facets, as does the bed, Detective Inspector Jones perched on its edge, the room and Constable Wilson.

'The femoral shaft of her right leg has been fractured and there's considerable bruising around the area,' I explain. 'The proximal phalanxes of the third and fourth finger of her left hand have been fractured and the metacarpal bones have suffered a compound fracture, consistent with someone repeatedly stamping on her hand. Four of the ribs on her right side are fractured, as are two on her left side. Her right ankle has been dislocated, most probably as she tried to run away; the ligament has been torn and will require surgery.'

Detective Inspector Jones does not look impressed.

'Wilson?'

The constable takes the patient's notes from the end of the bed and gives them a quick scan before nodding.

The detective inspector sighs. She was the first of us in the room. Constable Wilson and I were the late additions, the former pulling me from a grieving family whose relative had died only moments before I arrived. At the time, I was grateful for the extraction.

'Just from looking at her?' the detective inspector asks.

'The parts that are hidden from view.'

'Not something I find overly reassuring.' She jumps off the bed. 'But barring some miracle, which I doubt will be you, we've no chance of identifying who did this. So what's going to happen is this. You do your thing, Constable Wilson here will tell no one that I was curious enough to agree to something so ludicrous, and once you've proven yourself a fraud, we'll go out there and let the family in.'

'That is not how this will play out. What I do to a person doesn't save them. It kills them.'

'And how exactly do you kill them?'

'I gather their essence and pull it into mine. Once an essence has been taken, the body cannot survive.'

'I think we've firmly established that I believe precisely none of that, Mr Archivist. So why don't you tell me what you do from my perspective?'

'I will touch my forehead to hers and, after a moment, I will stand up.'

'And when you say touch, is force involved? Do you plan to headbutt poor Melody?'

'No. I barely make contact.'

'I think that will be an acceptable risk,' the detective inspector says.

'I know you do not believe me, but I will kill her. You should allow the family time with her before that happens.'

'No, I don't think so. When you're in the police you can't always deal with certainties, so what you're left with is good enoughs. The problem is, what you've told me so far is not good enough to convince me that I need to go out there and disturb this young woman's family.'

'But good enough that you still want me to try?'

'I'd hate not to know I was right.'

I consider this. If I do nothing, then Melody Cross will spend the rest of her life in a coma or wake suffering severe brain damage. Her life will never return to how it was. I can give her the opportunity to speak again, to see her family. She may take the time to say goodbye and choose to leave, or she may opt to stay with me for years. I will give her that choice. Without me, she will have nothing.

Once more the room fades and Melody's facets appear. Their silver glow is the only thing I can see as the blackness of the Aether stretches to infinity. They know I am near and twitch in anticipation. The galactic arms grow, sweeping themselves across the space that divides us until the orbit collapses and they reach for me like the tail of a comet.

They are agitated. They both want and fear me. I reach out my hand to take some but they pull away like startled minnows. I stand by Melody's body and lean over. My head passes through the cloud of facets that surround her and I stop when I feel my forehead touch hers.

'Release the life you hold so tight; welcome me and leave the light.'

I stand, drawing facets from her extremities and pulling them through her head. They leave her body but are uncertain as to what is happening. Those last horrific moments of Melody's life will have been heavily imprinted throughout her essence. The damage to her brain affects the parts of her that dwelt there. Memories have been lost, cast off along with everything that believed in the inherent goodness of others. The purge that occurred in her final moments of consciousness left her with an essence consumed by hatred and distrust. It both wants me and fears me, eager to leave her failing body but unwilling to trust another.

It scatters, the facets freed from that which confined them but refusing to surrender. I grab them. I can see them writhing, caught among a knot of my own, but they soon pull free. Each time I catch a cluster it quickly disentangles, leaving me the vestiges that soon fight their way from my grip.

I watch everything that was once Melody Cross leave her body and escape into the Aether. The constant note of the cardiac monitor brings me back to the room. Constable Isabella Wilson runs to the door and calls for a doctor while Detective Inspector Monique Jones stares at me, horrified.

'What the fuck did you just do?'

I am in the corridor, leaning against a bin and waiting for the pain to stop. No one offers to help, either assuming I'm being seen to or too scared to get close. Or neither; not everyone was born with a desire to help others. I wasn't. I should go home and deal with this myself. I've been thinking that for at least the last hour, yet I don't appear to have moved.

The half-Korean girl runs over, her arrestingly blue eyes wide and expressive.

'What the shit happened to your face?'

I tilt my head back and stare at the ceiling tiles. 'Not everyone gets saved.'

'But someone's hit you. I thought—'

'He was smart enough not to use his hands.'

'A baseball bat?' she asks.

'Fire extinguisher.'

'He fucked you up good.'

'I killed his girlfriend. I had it coming.'

'You do kill people for a living.'

'I also make a point to keep their essence. This time I was less than successful.'

'You'd think in a hospital someone would have taken care of you.'

'I kept a low profile.'

'Have you been waiting for me?' she asks.

'I don't know.'

I pick something off my cheek and feel a fresh trickle of blood drip off the end of my chin.

'You should get cleaned up. If you leave looking like that, the hospital will get a bad rep.'

Without thinking, I follow her into the women's toilets. I recoil at the sight of my face in the mirror. Normally I'm pleased to see it, like the reassurance you feel after you've checked your wallet is still in your pocket.

I prod my lip. 'It looks worse than it feels.'

'That's something, because it looks fucking awful.'

'I can see,' I say.

'But you'll forget, right?'

I nod.

'Don't worry, I'll be here to remind you,' Sun says.

Blood has run down my face and soaked into my white shirt. It's not quite reached my trousers, though there are a few spots on my shoes. Sun grabs paper towels and soaks them in a sink before wringing them out. 'You should take your shirt off,' she says.

'Should I?'

'Just because you killed someone today doesn't mean you need to dress like it.'

I slip my jacket off, folding it and placing it on the side of the sink. I'm slow to unbutton my shirt. Sun watches with an unhealthy intensity.

I drop the shirt on the floor. I won't be wearing it again.

She approaches with the wet paper towels. 'Why don't I feel it?'

'I'm holding it back.'

'Is it hard?'

'It's manageable.'

'What if I accidentally touch you?'

I slip off a glove, which she puts on. It's too big, but it will do.

44

'What happened to the woman's essence?'

'She'd been attacked. It feared me.'

Sun throws a bloodied wad of paper towels into a sink.

'Is this the first time you've been in shock?'

'Shock?'

'You could have done this yourself, but instead you hid in a deserted waiting room until I showed up. If I hadn't come along, you'd have been there all night. Let me guess, this is the first time someone's hit you.'

'Yes.'

'Must be nice.'

Sun tosses another bloodied wad into the sink.

'Has someone hit you?' I ask.

She shrugs.

I can see it. The area on her shoulder where a cluster of her facets push through. It's the result of an injury, but I never asked what caused it. There are more further down her body. In some places several facets poke through, waving lazily in time with Sun's movements, but in others there is just a single thread that stands apart from the tight clusters around her bones, muscles and organs. They must have been there when we met, but I never had the inclination to look.

'I live with a bad man,' Sun says as she pads the paper towels around my eyes, the water icy cold. 'He met my mum in the park one night when she'd drunk too much and lost herself in that wooded area by the stream. She thought he was her saviour, but I could tell there was something wrong with him. My mum left after a while, didn't bother taking my sister and me, so we ended up staying with him. I think he planned it, suckered her in then drove her away. We needed someone to love us, but that wasn't going to work for him. We tried to run away, but the police always found us and brought us back to the flat. Back to him.'

'Does he hurt you?'

Sun shrugs and looks away. 'He doesn't hit my sister.'

'You should go to the police.'

'That won't work.'

Another wad in the sink. This one is slightly less bloodied than the last and I hope she has almost finished because I'm struggling to hold back the influence of my essence.

'Dying isn't the solution.'

She stops.

'You asked me to take your face,' I say.

'I thought you'd forgotten.'

'I don't forget.'

'I know what you're thinking; that I'm some overemotional teenager who can't deal with life and sees suicide as the only option. Maybe people will miss me when I'm gone? Maybe they'll cry? What, because they don't give a shit about me now, I need to teach them a lesson by slashing my fucking wrists to pieces? If you think that, you're wrong. I have a twelve-year-old sister I'd do anything to protect. This isn't a pathetic cry for help. This is a battle cry!'

She leaps at me, clasping my face in her hands and rubbing the skin of her bare arms over my neck and across my naked chest. I stagger back as she falls to the floor. I don't even think to catch her and she collapses in an unconscious heap. Facets stream out of her, brilliant strands of silver that burst through her skin and into mine. I feel them pushing into my essence, desperate for a home.

There is also the aftermath of her touch. Her hands on my face were cold from the water, but her arms were warm and the sensation was glorious. My parents never hugged me. Family friends never shook my hand or patted me on the back. The most human contact I have felt in my entire life was over in a second and now its provocateur lies at my feet.

I could reject Sun's essence and the facets that were so eager to leave would be stranded in an environment they can't survive and left to seek the Aether. But I don't do that. I gather them together and push what I can back into her body. Then, using the ethereal counterparts to my own hands, I twist what remains into a single cord that ties me to Sun. Among that cord are facets that represent parts of Sun I cannot see. Her memories, loves, hates are all hidden. This cord could sever in a day as Sun's opinions change or short-term memories of her most recent meal or the colour of the T-shirt she wore two days ago fade into nothingness. If Sun dies and the cord remains, then her facets will stream through it and come to me. The millions of individual parts that comprise Sun will remain as a collective within me until the time I release her. That is, should she come. Should she die.

Sun empties her stomach over the floor and across my shoes and the hems of my trousers. She pushes herself up but vomits again and slips, her face landing in her last two meals. For a moment she looks at me, angry that I haven't bent down to help her stand. Then she realises why.

She picks a piece of half-digested pasta from her hair.

'I was expecting my battle cry to be more dignified.'

She vomits again.

'Sorry about your shoes.'

6

It's not even late, yet I can barely stay awake. The food-stained blanket is too thick, its warmth and comforting smell of Laure pulls me under. Richard is next to me, sat perfectly upright, drinking a cup of tea. He uses a saucer despite how disgusting the flat is. Meanwhile I'm curled into a tiny ball against the arm rest, hard with age, and cocooned by my blanket. Richard would never dream of putting his feet on the sofa like I am. I think it's because he always wears shoes in the house. I've never seen him with his socks off.

He watches the TV while picking his teeth with his little finger, making insidious sucking noises that grow louder when he realises I'm staring.

'The beef was too stringy. I think the butcher ripped us off.'

'Just ignore it,' I say.

He's quiet for a bit, but then the sucking starts again. I can't hear the movie I'm barely watching.

'I need some dental floss.'

'She'll be out soon.'

Quiet again. Then the sucking. He has his phone out, shining the light into his mouth and taking a picture.

'It's between my molars. My tongue is useless.'

'She's having a bath.'

'I can barely concentrate on the movie.' He continues sucking and poking and photographing. 'She's a child, kids don't mind these things.'

'She's twelve,' I say. 'She'll mind.'

More sucking.

'Sun, this is ridiculous. If I don't get it out now, I may need to go to the dentist.'

He goes to stand but I'm up before him, the blanket thrown to the floor.

I knock on the bathroom door.

'It's me.'

Laure doesn't respond. Richard watches from the sofa. I know the layout of the bathroom and shuffle half a step to the right.

I go in anyway. Laure's head is out of the bath and her earbuds are in. She silently sings along to her music, lying in the perfectly clear water with not a single cluster of bubbles to cover her. She's too pretty. When she was younger, it was great because shop owners would give us free stuff like ice cream and sweets, but now her beauty worries me. I don't think she's noticed it, or if she has, she's keeping quiet.

I remove an earbud.

'You doing OK in there?'

'Fine,' she says.

I dip my fingers in the water and flick it in her face. 'It's getting cold, you should come out.'

'I've a solution for that,' Laure says and twists the hot tap.

'Don't stay in there all night. Our only toilet's in here.'

I try to shove her earbud back in and fail. Laure flicks her hand dry and takes it from me.

'You know, it's physically impossible to put someone else's earbuds in comfortably. It's like licking your elbow or tickling yourself.'

Laure slides it in and goes back to miming along with her songs.

I take a packet of dental floss from the cupboard above the sink. Closing the bathroom door behind me, I toss the floss to Richard, who catches it and immediately slams it on the table.

'I managed to get it out,' he says.

I'm nearly asleep when Richard's movements on the other side of the sofa jolt me into full wakefulness. I poke my head out from under the blanket to see him standing up.

'I need the toilet.'

I check my watch. It's been fifteen minutes since I got the floss. I sit up. Laure's bedroom door's still open and the bathroom door's still shut.

'Just tell her to get out, she's been in there long enough.'

'I don't want to disturb her,' Richard says as he smooths his jumper.

'Sit down, Richard.'

'Stop being so silly, Sun. I need to go to the toilet, or do you do that for me too?'

'Laure,' I shout. 'Time to get out.'

'It doesn't look like she can hear you. Oh well, I'll only be a few seconds, then I'll leave her to it.'

'Richard, you're not going in there.'

'So what do you propose? Ask the neighbours? Go in the kitchen sink?'

He hovers near the door, no longer able to disguise his excitement. He catches me looking at his erection and smiles.

'You're a grown man, you can hold it.'

'Sun, I've been holding this for a very long time. Everyone has their limits.'

He touches the handle. I'm surprised by my calm as I get off the sofa. I walk to Richard and place my hand over his.

'Don't turn that handle.'

He's still smiling, revealing teeth he cleans so meticulously that the gums are worn away, leaving them long and fang-like. A quick look at the door, a shrug and a sigh, and his attention's back on me.

'I'd hate for you to think you were in control,' Richard says as he prises my hand from his. He strokes my arm, his fingertips soft. I shiver in revulsion. Smart enough not to pull away, I stare at a stain on the wall as his hand moves over my chest before his fingers wrap around my throat.

'I thought about having you arrested,' Richard says. 'You're an embuggerance. Just think what my life would be like if you weren't in it. The things I could do! Just me and Laure.'

He throws me onto the sofa and jumps on top, pinning me. Slowly he lifts my T-shirt to expose my midriff and draws an invisible circle around my belly button before placing his sweaty palm flat against my stomach.

I screamed and kicked when this started, but all that got me was more violence. Now I accept it, thankful that Laure refuses to get out of the bath and has her music turned up so high. My heart doesn't even race like it used to. It might not be a steady beat, but I've endured this so many times it has dulled the panic.

'Richard, please,' I croak, 'she's still awake.'

Richard stops moving. His hand remains where it was, hot and clammy against my skin. I can feel his pulse through his fingers. Frozen, he stares at me, his eyes unblinking. Something in his composure cracks. He slowly lowers himself so all his weight is on me. I see the lightning-strike blood vessels in the

51

whites of his eyes, the stray flicks of hair between his eyebrows, and all the ugliness of a face so close to mine.

'You think I'm a villain, don't you, Sun?'

I don't move. Just keep watching, trying to figure him out. This happens sometimes. It's like there's another Richard in there. A decent one, or as close to decent as a Richard can be. It needs to justify itself to me. Doesn't change anything though, just says its piece and leaves.

'Nod, Sun. Come on, nod that little head of yours because I know you think it.' I nod and Richard responds with a smile. 'See, that wasn't so hard,' he says. 'Don't I provide somewhere for you to live? Cook for you? Wash your clothes? Take you places? And yet your eyes when they look at me see only a monster. But I'm not, Sun. I know me. I know better than you what's inside me. I've always known. That's why I kept away. I was good at hiding it. Pass me in the street, work with me, know me for years; you'd have had no clue what went on inside my head. But then I met you and your mother and Laure. Little Laure... You have no idea, Sun. To want someone like that but know you can't have them. It kills me. Surely choosing you is the lesser evil. Can't you see how that makes me a good man?'

'You don't get my pity.'

'I know,' Richard says. 'And I don't want it. In truth, I want nothing from you. It's always been about Laure. You know that, don't you?'

'Touch her and I kill you.'

Richard smiles and the cracks heal. His face grows hard. 'Something's changed,' he says. 'Any other day and you'd already have my cock in your mouth, anything to break that spell Laure has me under. But not today. What's happened to you, Sun? Don't tell me you've met someone. Surely there's no one alive who would care about you.'

Richard's hand slides into my underwear. I reach down and pull it out.

'You're right,' Richard says, 'we should go to your room. Wouldn't want Laure to see this.'

I bring my head up fast. Catching Richard in the mouth, I feel his monstrous teeth smash into my forehead. Moments later my knee crashes into his testicles, crushing their excitement. I throw him from the sofa before jumping off and straddling him.

My hands are wrapped around his neck and I'm squeezing so fucking hard that veins pop out of my arms. My mouth hangs open, tongue dangling by my chin. A string of saliva falls and lands on his forehead. His eyes are wide, bulging like they're going to pop and I just keep squeezing harder and harder like I'm strong enough to snap his neck and pull his head off his body, trailing arteries and veins and the inside of his throat behind it. Once I've ripped his head off, I'll stamp it into mush. It doesn't matter that I'm not wearing shoes, I want to feel his nose and cheeks under my feet, destroy his jaw and pull his shattered teeth from between my toes. I want to leave it not just unrecognisable; I want to pour what's left of his head into a cup then fucking drink it and shit him out down his throat.

He chokes out a sound and I freeze. Frantically, I pull my hands away. I can't kill him, that's not the plan. I take a step back. He's still breathing, maybe unconscious. I'm too scared to check.

I run to the bathroom and throw open the door. Laure screams, thrashing the water over the side and dropping her phone in the bath.

'Get dressed. We're leaving.'

She stands up and grabs a towel. She's not stupid, that girl. Knows now isn't the time to ask questions.

Pain engulfs the back of my head and I stagger forward. Laure catches me. I feel something hot running down my hair and when I pull my hand away, it's covered in blood. I turn and there's Richard in the doorway, saucepan in hand. I pull off the cistern cover and hurl it at him. It catches him in the shoulder and he falls backwards, dropping the saucepan.

I pull the key out and use it to lock Laure in the bathroom. She's banging on the door and screaming my name, but it's the safest place for her right now.

Richard's standing. Not bothering with the frying pan anymore, he kicks it over to the TV. My head's throbbing and I need to hold on to something or I'll collapse. Laure's still banging on the door, crying for help. The neighbours won't come; they're smarter than that.

Richard moves in streaks like torches in the night and I feel his punches before I see them. I'm thrown against the wall, slide down it and spit blood. It's never been this bad before. I hurt in ways I never thought possible.

Laure's stopped shouting and all I hear through the dull ringing in my ears is her panicked sobs.

I make it to my bedroom. Richard follows calmly behind. As soon as I'm inside, he takes my hair in his hand and yanks it backwards. I cry out, but the contorted angle of my neck twists it into a panicked choke.

'I appreciate the offer, Sun. But I think we're past that. Don't you?'

I find strength from some hidden place inside me. I stamp on Richard's foot, not enough to hurt him, but enough to produce a knee-jerk reaction. He falls forwards and I drive my elbow into his chin. He lets go of my hair. I swing around and jab my fingers into his left eye.

I run for the window, bathroom key in hand, and smash it

54

with a clenched fist. I throw the key between the iron bars and it falls through the dark, down five floors to the ground.

Richard's behind me, swearing so much the words blur into one. There's a long shard of glass left in the window. It's calling me. Wants me to take it, spin around and drive it fully into his neck. I push it out and, like the key, it falls to the ground where it shatters. I can't kill Richard. I keep telling myself this, but dear God, do I want to.

Richard throws me to the floor. I try to stand but he sits down so heavily on my stomach that I vomit.

'Sun, we both know a locked door won't stop me. I'm the one who taught you to pick locks, remember?'

He runs a hand down my cheek and his fingers play with my lips. I try to bite them, but he knows it's coming and pulls away.

'It didn't have to be tonight. You forced my hand. In a way, I'm thankful. Surely this is your blessing. I hope you know that I'll take care of little Laure. We won't be here in the morning. But for now...' he turns to the door, 'I think we can all agree I've waited long enough.'

He holds my shoulders down and kisses me on the forehead.

'Bye, Sun.'

He gets off, but I still feel his weight. The door locks and I know he'll have left the key in at a quarter turn.

I hear him cursing. He can't find his lock picks or anything that'll make a good substitute. They're all in here with me.

I manage to stand but quickly fall over. The bathroom door may be solid, fireproof like all of the doors up here, but it'll only delay Richard, not stop him, so I don't have time for this shit and my body should know it. On my second attempt, I stay upright long enough to collapse against my wardrobe.

I pull out the bag I'd hidden in the bottom and meticulously, but quickly, lay everything on the floor. There are four vials, 20 ml each containing ten percent by volume. I've looked this up. I'm just under seven stone so what I have should be more than enough.

I slide the syringe into the top of the first vial and draw out the full amount. I don't have the time to be squeamish and jab the needle into the skin behind my elbow, before pressing down on the plunger with my thumb. As soon as it's done, I pull the needle out and empty the second vial before that too enters my arm.

I've spent enough time in the hospital to know what I'm doing. An overdose of potassium chloride will cause a cardiac arrest with an asystole rhythm.

It will stop my heart.

I taste the tears on my lips before my face feels them. I'm doing this for Laure. To save her. To save us both. I repeat this like a mantra. I'm doing this for Laure. I'm doing this for Laure.

Third vial. This feels so right. So perfect. Fourth vial. For the first time I feel like I'm in control. I can't help but smile as I wait to die.

7

'He must know it's wrong,' Gary says.

'He doesn't care,' Geraldine replies.

'Then make him care.'

'I've tried, but...' Geraldine looks out the window.

'What's that supposed to mean?'

'It means I need to pick my battles, Gary. This isn't one of them.'

'He'll only do it again. How many children are you going to let him hurt before you do something?'

'Please don't be like that.'

'I'm not being like anything,' Gary says. 'It's a genuine question. How many times will he get away with acting out before it's not OK anymore? I understand that he needs time to deal with his frustration, but it can't go on forever.'

'You don't get it!' Geraldine cries. 'Luke is five years old and his dad is dead. He doesn't know how to process that. So yes, he's going to lash out and he'll probably hit a few more kids. If that means I get dragged into school to deal with the head teacher, then that's absolutely fine. But what's not OK is for you to sit there and criticise my parenting when you're the one who's not there!'

'Can you please move closer to her?'

I've tried to extricate myself from the conversation as much as possible, so it takes a moment before I realise he's addressing me. I slide towards Geraldine, sat at the other end of my sofa. She looks up at me and sees her husband, maybe even smells him. Tentatively, she leans her head against my shoulder, leaving it there for as long as she can stand. She cries a little as she straightens up and I move away as Gary whispers a thank you.

'I'm sorry, Dee,' Gary says. 'I can't imagine what it's like.'

'I've been close to telling them so many times. Two nights ago, Katie was inconsolable. I so wanted her to know you're still here, but I held back. If I told her she'd expect you to come home. She'd never understand this ghost timeshare.'

And like that, everything I am is reduced to something akin to a holiday scam. I try not to dwell on it.

'We paid for a long time. One day the children will be old enough to see me.'

'After they're over you. Once their lives are back to normal.'

'And after you've found a new man?'

Geraldine shakes her head. 'No. It was you when I was thirteen and it's still you now, even if you are corporeally challenged.'

'It means a lot to hear you say that, but you're a yo—'

His face vanishes, taking the voice with it. Something else is coming, sidling its way into me. Facets fight over themselves as they surge along the thread that extends from my chest. The one that connects me to Sun.

They push into me, storming through my body towards my head. Parts of her face grip mine like desperate fingers reaching from my neck. It is not a fully formed thing and, in the reflection from a window, I can see Sun's face conquer mine in tiger stripes.

58

As soon as she's in, Sun's body pulls her back and I manage to stand. Geraldine has thrown herself against the far side of the sofa and clutches a cushion to her chest.

'Gary? Where's Gary?'

I'm off the sofa and out of my flat, the thread in front of me glowing against the darkness of the night. It is made from the facets of Sun that I took when the connection was formed. I run past an old couple struggling with their shopping and across a road, following Sun's memories, knowing they will lead me to her.

Another surge. An influx of Sun's facets suddenly inside me. She is dying.

A car has stopped at traffic lights. It's blue, low profile. Looks fast. I get in.

'Drive!' I shout as I force my face to cycle through those I have within me, each one bursting from the mouth of the one who came before.

The driver, young and stupid-looking, hesitates at the red light before the car lurches forward with such ferocity I'm thrown back into the seat. I quickly slam the door shut and take the wheel. He lets go instinctively and it suddenly becomes more of a struggle to hold back the effect I have on him, but the last thing I need is an unconscious driver.

Sun's face is back, slowly claiming mine. The driver keeps glancing at me and whimpering, but to his credit, he doesn't slow. I've never driven a car before and after we mount our seventh curb, I get the sense he can tell.

I feel another surge; this one is weaker. There isn't much of Sun left. I pull down the visor and look in the mirror. Her face creeps over mine from the edges. She has no nose or philtrum, and her eyes are partially blended into mine.

The thread shoots through the roof of the car. I tell the driver to stop and he does, slamming on the brakes and skidding to an awkward stop. His eagerness wasn't necessary as we're still a few streets away, but I thank him for the ride and get out. The thread extends into the sky, leading to a tower block. The driver is out of the car too, shaken, and looks at me as if he should follow. As if this will be the start of a thing.

It's not.

I leave him by the car. Sun's facets continue to trickle into me as the thread that connects us flickers.

I run for the lift to find it out of order. The stairs are my only option and I push my way up, fighting the urine-thick miasma with every step. The thread vanishes as I run through its frayed end, the last of Sun's facets fleeing her body.

Ahead of me, a group of boys or men, I'm unsure what to call them, hang over the side of the railing. One of them reaches for something hidden from sight in the waist of his trousers. Another stops him.

'That's Richard's girl,' he says as I run past their music and smoke.

I jump over a pile of bin bags, most of them torn and spilling their contents, past flat after flat with no clear idea of where I need to be.

'Please stop him.'

Sun's voice. I have all of her. Can feel her essence inside me, lost and confused. I try to order it, slotting it neatly among the others.

'You're on the wrong floor. You need to go up,' Sun says. 'There are more stairs at the end. Two more floors.'

The stairs are a struggle. I'm thin, but it's not through exercise. Sun talks to me as I climb. She explains where she lives, about a man named Richard, her sister, Laure, and what she needs me to do. She planned this after the first night we met. The only thing she couldn't be certain of was whether I would help, or if I would remain at home, sat on my sofa as I gradually took possession of her essence and left her body to die.

The proof that her gamble paid off is my hand as it takes the handle to her flat and opens it.

'Save Laure first. Keep his essence. If there's time after that, try to save me. I left you instructions.'

I run to the locked door on the right, the one Sun told me opened to her room. She screams at me to save Laure and I pull her back as I unlock the door to find her body on the floor. There's blood around the back of her head and over her face, but that isn't what killed her. A note written in neat handwriting lies face up next to her left hand, and around that are four empty vials of potassium chloride and a used syringe. Next to the empty syringe are a further five vials. These are full.

It's been three minutes since I took possession of Sun's complete essence. The moment her heart stopped, the final surge of facets were flung off and her body was left an empty shell. I can return her essence, but if the body is not alive, then it cannot attach. The presence of Sun's essence alone will not bring her back to life.

The instructions are precise. I inject the epinephrine first, then the four vials of sodium bicarbonate solution. I perform ten quick chest compressions, hoping that will be enough to pump the medication into her heart.

I press my forehead against Sun's.

I have only ever taken life, never returned it. Sun is inside me, wound up tightly like bands of elastic. I push every thought Sun has ever retained, every feeling that made her cry or shriek with joy, every aspect of her personality back into her body.

The ball of potential held within the essence explodes inside her, firing the facets to wrap around her muscles and bones and veins and brain. Not everything is in the right place, but I can change that. Sun bequeathed her essence to me; that gives me control.

I close my eyes to witness the confusion in body-form that lies below me. My ethereal arms extend and manipulate, bringing order to the chaos. I move quickly, doing as much as I need to but not as much as I should. The rest will sort itself out, that or my efforts to restart the heart will fail and she will grow cold as the final flicker of light departs.

I leave Sun. There are four more doors. Three are open: a kitchen, a bathroom and an empty bedroom. A bloodied saucepan lies on the floor. I pick it up and move to the closed door, listening for hints of what I may find inside. A subdued cry. Heavy breathing. I open the door.

A young girl, Sun's sister Laure. Only twelve, she lies on a bed wrapped in a towel. She is on her front, her long hair is wet and clumps together in lazy curls. She stares at me, scared, trying not to look hopeful. Sitting on the other end of the bed must be Richard. He massages Laure's calf. Rubs his fingers down her naked leg. He is not how I imagined; young and well turned out. Most people would consider him handsome. They wouldn't expect that someone who looks like him would massage the leg of a partially naked child. In their minds, that pursuit is reserved only for the ugly, old or tragically unloved.

'You're a new face,' he says. 'You'll have to forgive me for not greeting you properly, but this poor girl was in the bath when her leg cramped.' He focuses on Laure again, running his fingers along her calf and the back of her thigh. 'Now that's interesting,' he says. 'I've completely forgotten what you look like.'

'I suggest you stop touching her.'

'I don't want to offend you, but I can manage this myself. If you'll just wait outside, Mr...?'

'Archivist,' I say.

'Of course you are! Well, Mr Archivist, how about you have a seat in the living room, and I'll be with you shortly.'

His lack of concern is unsettling. He should shout and rage, or ply me with self-pitying excuses, not surround himself with this wall of unflinching confidence.

I raise the saucepan, ready to strike, but halfway into my swing Richard leaps from the bed. I have no time to react before his foot sweeps my legs and I crash onto my back, expelling every breath inside me in a violent burst.

'At least that clears up what you're here for.' Richard's voice is calm. 'Let me guess, you made friends with the little Korean whore. I'll give you some advice: she's not worth it. If you leave now, we can forget this ever happened and I won't have to kill you in front of my daughter.'

I struggle to my feet, gasping for breath. Richard has the saucepan now. He's more practised with it than me and I feel it strike my arm only moments after I see it move. He may appear small, but he knows how to use what little weight he has. I stagger backwards, the arm he hit useless and on fire. I consider running, but what would that achieve? Despite his composure, I saw something I wasn't supposed to, and I expect there is little chance I will be allowed to leave with that knowledge.

Richard drops the saucepan. He's smiling, like he's enjoying this. There's a small bookcase by the bed on which sits a lamp designed for a child of four and a grubby coaster. He picks the bookcase up and hurls it at me. I turn as it catches me in the back, the corner digging into my hip. Books scatter across the floor and I slip on them as I struggle to escape, falling across a desk covered with neat piles of paper and rows of pens.

Richard's keeping his distance; he knows what I am.

'Sun isn't my prisoner. Take her and leave. You would be doing me a favour.'

I've allowed myself to be pulled too far into someone else's problem and can't climb out without some form of resolution. I remove my gloves and lurch forward, aiming for his neck. Richard reaches into his pocket and withdraws a flick knife. One second I see it, the next, its cool blade slides into my stomach. He quickly lets go of the handle and stands back. Blood swells around the wound and soaks my shirt.

I stagger forward, trying to fall on Richard, but he's too fast and I collapse on the floor. Hot blood runs into my trousers and the pain finally announces its presence. I hold back a moan through gritted teeth.

'Something like you is too good to die for her.'

I lie on the floor, bleeding. Richard moves closer, ready to gloat or finish me. Laure is still on the bed. We block her escape and there are bars over the window. She's watching me, frightened, but not looking away or covering her eyes, even though she must know what is about to happen.

A flash of flesh between Richard's sock and the hem of his trousers; my arm shoots out and takes it. His facets brush against mine and he stops moving. I take his hand as I pull myself up, blood running around the handle of the knife buried in my stomach.

He can feel death. Can smell it, taste it, hear it, see it. Every sense screams at him that finality is approaching and all he can do is stand rigidly as colour deserts his face and his heartbeat quickens in fear before it beats slower and slower, as if aware that soon it will be time to stop forever.

My forehead is against Richard's as I extract the facets tightly bound to his brain. They pass through his skull but do not bring the rest with them, unspooling themselves and surrendering to me in isolation. I lean forward to remove more, but they too leave the collective instead of carrying it away from the body.

Richard moans and one side of his face falls. He is a healthy man and, despite what I've convinced his mind, he is not near death. His essence and body are entangled and all I manage is to tear off fragments while the whole remains secure.

My own essence shudders, reorganising itself as facets push through my hands, my shoulders, my back, many pairs of arms nothing more than glowing filaments of silver that are seen only by me. They dive into Richard's body, attacking his chest and legs and arms and head. They scour his internals, dredging the facets that stubbornly cling to him with barbed hooks that rip and wrench. I remove him piecemeal, my facets firing into him and grabbing what they can before darting out to present their prey. He twitches, then convulses violently before collapsing.

I have killed many times. It is not just my livelihood; I was born for it. We are all approaching death, each moment that passes bringing us fractionally closer to that instant when we will cease to exist. Every time I take a person's essence, I do so before that moment. I terminate them prior to their designated end, and yet until now I have never truly felt like I have comitted murder.

Richard's body at my feet changes that. The body of a man who, despite his outward appearance, had what most people would consider evil inside him.

There is more blood around Richard than I expected. His body suffered no wounds and an autopsy would reveal that his heart stopped with no obvious cause, and certainly nothing that could be attributed to me. The blood is mine. I lost more than I expected, and my hands are ineffectual at stopping the flow as it continues to seep from around the blade of the knife.

I look to Laure for help, expecting her to be twelve and useless, but she has already shredded a pillowcase and wrapped it into a doughnut. I slide it over the handle of the knife and press down. The pain is beyond any physical sensation I have ever felt and my teeth grind against each other as sounds I have never made before escape my mouth.

I know of this neighbourhood. No ambulance will come here so I don't waste time calling one. My only option is Sun and the link we shared before her essence came to me. I could reopen that connection and use it to save myself, though to do so I would have to sacrifice Sun.

Sun, a girl I barely know who tricked me into murder.

8

There was no body in the flat. No missed calls from the police. No visits from social services. The fridge, freezer and cupboards were full, and someone had scrubbed the blood from the carpets.

There was also no Richard, and never would be again.

Laure didn't understand how he died. She was there when it happened, but according to her he just collapsed in the Archivist's arms. I tried to explain, but she refused to believe me and said it was probably a heart attack.

We've not spoken about Richard since. We will... later. Right now, his memories are raw and need time to heal before we start poking them. We've also not spoken about what else happened that night, about what he was going to do to Laure. I'm too scared to ask. Some days I convince myself that she's forgotten, the shock of Richard's death overshadowing all other memories. Then there are days when fear invades, and I'm convinced she knows exactly the kind of man Richard was. Two nights ago, she crept into my bed and cried herself to sleep with her arms around my neck. The next day she got up and made us breakfast like it never happened. Laure's carrying something, I know that much, I'm just not brave enough to find out what.

The bus takes a sharp corner and throws Laure against me. The wound in my stomach has mostly healed, but occasionally I will feel a wince of pain. Richard didn't hold back that night and I still find new traces of his anger when I force myself to look. One thing I know with certainty is that he didn't stab me, but when I woke the next morning in a hospital bed, there were painful stitches running across my stomach. I asked the doctors what happened but they had no idea, so I suspect it had something to do with *him*.

There's only Laure, me and the driver left on the bus. The last town was fifteen minutes ago and, one by one, the women with children and old ladies with shopping carts got off. Even the man with the dog who was desperate for someone to talk to eventually reached his stop, waving at us as we drove into the night.

I've no idea where I am, it's so dark outside. Even when I press myself against the window, all I see is blackness. I leave a greasy nose and forehead on the glass. It makes me smile but Laure shakes her head and looks away even though I know she's giggling.

Suddenly, what I'm following flicks to the side and I hit the bell.

'There's not another stop for a mile,' the bus driver calls.

'That's fine. Anywhere here will do.'

I get up and walk to the front of the bus. Laure follows.

The driver stops and looks at us, knowing he has to say something.

'There's nothing here but countryside.'

'We know.' I give him back our tickets. 'If someone murders us, the police will think we took a taxi.'

The driver presses the button to open the door and says nothing as we leave.

'How do you know where to go?' Laure asks me.

'I just do.' I take her hand and push through an awkward bush, dragging her in behind me.

The silver thread that extends from my chest was with me that first moment I woke up in hospital, along with the scar from a stab wound I never received. I asked the doctors what it was, expecting it to link to a heart monitor, but I was only told to rest and not worry about how I looked.

It didn't take me long to realise I was the only one who could see it. At first I thought I was hallucinating because of all the pain drugs they'd given me. I expected it to fade until one day it finally vanished, yet it remained as clear as on that first day.

I can move it with my hands. Wrap it around my fingers. I've tried to pull it out but it doesn't move, and no matter how hard I yank, there is never any pain or feeling of any kind.

When I undress and look in the mirror, it's still there, extending from the middle of my sternum, right between my breasts. There are others too, not threads that lead somewhere, but frayed ends that hang from my skin. Some by my left shoulder, where Richard threw me against a door handle. There are others too, on my legs and arms and across my back. Around my stomach, where the stitches are still raw, there's a cluster of them, waving in the air like the tentacles of a jellyfish.

They don't go away. Clothes won't hide them and I can't push them back in. They can't be cut either; the scissors just go straight through like they're threads from a ghost.

At first I thought the thread led to my death, that I could follow it my whole life and when I reached the end that would be it and I'd die, but then I watched it flicking around the room, as if what was on the other end could move.

I know it leads to the Archivist. But I can't tell Laure this; she wouldn't understand. I tried to explain what he can do but she just shook her head and said that archivists are from stories and I need to grow up if I'm going to be in charge of our lives.

So I tell her it's women's intuition that shows me where to go. One day she'll get it too.

Laure walks behind me. She holds my hand because it's too dark not to and I didn't bring a torch. The thread I follow glows, though the light doesn't touch the ground. And instead of leading us around trees it cuts straight through them, and a few times we need to back up to find a clear path through.

Eventually the trees thin, then abruptly stop. We walk across grass to the tall silhouette in the middle of the field. The person at the other end of the thread.

I haven't seen him for three weeks. Once I left hospital we returned to the flat, and even though Laure still went to school, I wasn't up to it. I felt guilty over what I'd made the Archivist do. I never expected to escape the trap I'd wandered into and once free of it, I had no idea what came next. Still don't. But then he sent me a message telling me it was time and we arranged to meet.

'Richard was seen two hundred miles away on Tuesday. CCTV caught him at the train station. After that he bought camping equipment and took a bus to the mountains,' he says.

'You went to his work and bank?' I ask.

'I did.'

'You spoke to people?'

'I did everything you wanted.'

There were two letters waiting for the Archivist in my room the night I died. One I didn't need to seal; the instructions to restart my heart. The other one was for what to do after, once he had Richard's essence.

I wanted Richard dead, but that would only make problems for us. Even if an autopsy revealed he'd died of natural causes, the police would still be left with two minors and nowhere to place them. Eventually, they will learn that Richard is dead, or missing presumed dead, and at that point I'm sure they'll come looking for me and Laure, but at least now we have time.

'You didn't tell me he was police.'

'Would it have made a difference?' I ask.

'No.'

'They protect their own. That was why I couldn't tell anyone. I tried, when it first started, but no one listened. Some of them knew, though, that I was telling the truth. I could tell from the way they looked at me, but they wouldn't help.'

Laure takes my hand. 'Richard was always nice to me,' she says, 'but it felt wrong. He was interested in who my friends were and what they were doing. At first it was nice to talk about them with him, but then he'd ask every day and want to see their pictures and read all my messages. Sometimes he took my phone and would spend hours chatting to my friends pretending to be me. He said it was OK because he was with the police. I read some of those messages afterwards. I lost friends because of him.'

'I didn't have to come for you,' the Archivist says.

I move Laure in front of me and wrap my arms around her. She's nearly as tall as I am. Sometimes I don't feel like the big sister at all.

'I am paid for the service I provide. A service that does not involve running, threatening people in cars, or murder. You took advantage of what I am and manipulated the situation so that I was placed in a position where I had to kill someone who was not ready to die.'

There's an edge to his voice. I want to believe it's put on to scold me.

71

'I could have ignored you,' he says. 'You could have died. That man could have...' He looks at Laure and doesn't say anything else.

'But you did come,' I say, only just managing to get it out.

'You were lucky.'

I close my eyes and steel myself. 'No. I wasn't lucky. You needed to do this. The mother, the one who spoke to me. She was miserable. Her children's lives will flash in front of her eyes and then one day they'll get rid of her and she'll have no idea it's coming. All you do is bring misery to people. You might pretend you can't see it, but you don't fool me. You needed someone to save. I gave you that.'

He thinks this over and as he does, his shoulders relax and he looks at Laure and me, not like we're objects, but like we're people.

'What will you do now?' he asks.

'We'll stay in the flat for a while. Laure still needs to go to school and I suppose I should too. We'll be left alone until someone realises Richard won't be coming back. He had money stashed somewhere, I just need to find it. When I do, we'll move to another town and start again.'

'Will you still come to the hospital?'

'Richard's gone. I don't need to hide from him anymore,' I say.

He nods. I can't tell if he's hiding his disappointment well or if there is no disappointment to hide.

'But if I ever need you, I can always find you.'

I twang the silver thread that extends from the middle of my chest and straight into his.

'What else can you see?'

Only the outline of his face is visible in the near darkness. The light of the moon picks out the slope of his nose and the soft swelling of his cheeks. Each time a cloud obscures the light, his face gently drifts into the black that surrounds us. His features may be hidden, but my memory of them is not. Every contour, ridge, curve and line was seared into my mind from that first moment I woke in the hospital. That he looked that way came as a shock. I may not have been able to remember the details, but surely I would recall at least the impression of a face that beautiful. I continued to doubt myself until the moment I saw him standing in the middle of the field, the collar of his peacoat pulled up against the cold and his hands thrust deeply into its pockets. On those hands would be the leather gloves he always wears, bright purple or possibly a dark green.

His face, when I saw it, was the one that I had spoken to on those nights in the hospital when it had just been the two of us in a deserted waiting room. I want to keep seeing him, just to be in the presence of someone so perfect, but us meeting is a risk that will only bring the police to my door that much sooner.

'Is he still inside you?' I ask, avoiding his question.

'He is.'

'This is where we last saw our mum,' Laure says. 'Richard was with us and we were having a picnic. She went into the woods to look for blackberries.'

'The police thought she'd run away and would come back in a few days. It's been six months.'

'Do you miss her?' he asks.

'She protected us from the worst of Richard, but then she left. She was a shitty mum and Richard was a shitty man. Their memories belong together.'

'Are you ready?' he asks.

'Don't let him speak,' I say. 'I just want to see him, to know he's really gone.'

Richard's face appears over the Archivist's. I squeeze Laure too hard and she fights her way from my grip. 'What are you doing?' she asks. I ignore her and take a step closer. The face is impassive. It stares straight ahead, not even blinking. I run a finger along Richard's cheek. His rough stubble scratches my fingertip. I pull up his top lip to reveal his teeth. The crack in his front left tooth is fixed and his gold molar is missing. When I let go the lip snaps lazily back into place.

It's a perfect likeness, both to sight and touch. I should want to hit it, tear at it with my nails and bite off its ears, but those feelings aren't there. This isn't him. It's just a veneer plastered over the face of another man who's standing in the middle of a field I was last in six months ago for a picnic with my mum. Richard's body, which lies rotting somewhere or has already been cremated under a different name in a different place, is also not him. Richard is not something you can see; he is thoughts, memories, anger, lust. All of those things are inside the Archivist. He has Richard stored like so many others, but not for long. We're going to return him to the place where those things come from. From the remains of him, others will be born.

I hope I never meet those twisted little fuckers.

'Are you ready?' I ask Laure as I take her hand.

'Ready for what?'

I can't help but smile. 'Do it.'

Richard's face lifts from the Archivist's like a sheet of paper floating in the thermals. Cracks appear at the edges before spreading to form clusters of islands. The higher they climb into the black sky, the more the islands drift from each other. Soon, they crumble. Everything shatters in an instant and Richard's face is transformed into a mass of golden particles that illuminate the space around us.

A gust of wind appears and all that is left of Richard is captured and dances around the field. A murmuration of golden swallows. Soon he is scattered so far that all I can see is black and I know that Richard has gone forever.

I squeeze Laure's hand tighter. 'That was too beautiful for him,' I say.

I am not a people person. I make them feel uneasy: either through not remembering my face, or the effect of my presence if they venture too near. Any friends I acquire are fleeting, their interest only thinly veiled displays of bravery. I exist to scare them and on the few occasions during my childhood when others my age came to my house, they would dare themselves to see who would come closest to me. It always ended the same, with children leaving in tears to suffer months of nightmares. Parents soon complained, word spread, and those visits stopped.

There was one person I connected with. Someone I considered a friend. They were cursed the moment they met me and, despite the promise genuine friendship held, it was stolen by the very thing that makes me what I am. After that, I knew companionship would forever be denied and I became as I am now.

Since then, the only people I knew were those in books, half-formed or exaggerated in ways no real person is to make them appear more likeable. It is only since gaining the ability to take the essence of a person – something I discovered by mistake when an old lady fell asleep next to me on a train – that I finally understood what people are. They are slow to comprehend, and believe they can change what has already happened by strongly disagreeing. Worst of all, they expect the laws of physics to respect their feelings.

The man who sits across from me exemplifies these traits. His daughter lies in a coma on the bed while her mother strokes her hand and talks to her in a soft voice. Anyone else would find the situation distressing: the girl will either die or never wake. I am frustrated. Emotions are a personal commodity and, like toothbrushes, I have no desire to share anyone else's. The last three hours have been a mixture of crying and shouting, with the occasional intervention of doctors who arrive by conveyor belt, make non-committal remarks and leave, never to be seen again. The parents don't know what they want and have demanded I stay until they decide. I am not beholden to them and even if they were to become physical, it is unlikely they could stop me from leaving. Frustrated as I am, I am here by enforced choice. The mother has connections with the police, who informed me of the impending death of the girl, needlessly conveyed to me with more delicate language. My presence is supposed to be a favour, though after the incident with Melody Cross, I believe I'm expected to make amends.

'Please, Darren,' the mother says. She ties a thin plait in her daughter's hair and starts on another.

'She might—'

'She won't.'

'Doctors get it wrong sometimes.'

'She's been seen by five doctors and two specialist consultants. They all agree.'

'What are you saying?'

The mother exhales, shivering slightly. 'I don't want to go over it again.'

'But she…' The father stops himself. He's a big man. Strong. Wears an expensive suit. His facial features belong to someone born to be aggressive. 'She has to come back.' He can't look at his wife or his daughter and I'm an unsettling presence in the room he'd rather forget. He speaks only to his shoes.

'She can't, Darren. You heard what the doctors said: when someone takes that much insulin, the damage can't be repaired. Not after it's got to her brain.'

'But she didn't want this,' the father says. 'She cried for me. Begged me to save her life. We have to try. *I* have to try.'

Chrissy had locked herself in the family safe room. She hid the master key, changed the unlock codes, and injected more than two thousand units of insulin into her thighs. Then she screamed and cried and begged for help while her parents, trapped on the other side of the door, did much the same. It took the fire brigade more than six hours to break into the room.

The father approaches the bed. He stands opposite his wife and cautiously places a hand on his daughter. He strokes her cheek and squeezes one of her plaits before twisting it around his finger. This is the first time I've seen him look at his daughter.

'I was the first person to hold her,' he says. 'The nurse kept explaining that she wouldn't look like a baby on TV, but I insisted that the first hands that held her were going to be mine. She was so slippery I nearly dropped her. But there she was, the world's newest person in the hands of her daddy. For the first year you refused to cut her fingernails because you were scared you'd take her fingers off, so I was there every week trimming her tiny nails with those little white scissors. I'd play with her in the evenings when I could get off work early and made sure that, no matter what, I read a story to her every single day. But it didn't matter what I did. You were always the favourite. I kept telling myself my time would come. She'd become a teenager and you and her would fall out while I waited in the wings, but it didn't happen like that.'

'She loved you, Darren. So much.'

'But never enough for me.' He sits on his daughter's bed and strokes her hair. 'The next part was going to be mine. She'd start dating boys and come to me for advice. I'd tell her what they're really like and then when she found her first proper boyfriend, I'd pretend to hate him but secretly I'd be happy that Chrissy had someone who loved her. Not everyone gets that.

'She was going to be mine. "Dad, can you come and pick me up?" "Dad, there's something wrong with my sink, can you come over?" "Dad, the kids want a climbing frame in the garden, bring your tools." I had it all planned, Kath. And now...'

'...that will never happen,' his wife finishes. 'But if you let the Archivist take her face, then we'll at least have something. We'll still get to see her. She won't grow up and she won't need you to plaster a wall, but at least she'll still be here. Our beautiful girl will get to be fifteen forever.'

He finally looks at me, registering not only my presence but also what I am to him and, more importantly, to his daughter. 'This is the only way I'll get to talk to her again?'

'It is,' I say.

'I need to tell her that I'm sorry,' he says. 'That Daddy tried, but he couldn't save his beautiful baby girl. I need to tell her that I'm not going anywhere. And I'll be here for her, even if she can't be here for me.'

He leans over to kiss Chrissy's cheek. Suddenly overflowing with emotion, he holds her tightly and weeps so much that I fear he will never let go, but then he's standing and walking away, taking his wife with him.

The room vanishes and all I see is Chrissy. She floats in the blackness. Her facets have tied themselves into a mirror of her brain. It hovers above her face, joining with the body at the neck. She is brain dead, her thoughts no longer connected to living tissue. Her essence remains whole, but these parts outside the body are lost to a place medicine cannot reach. Her kidneys, liver and lungs have also lost their facets, which, like those of the brain, have formed copies of the organs they once inhabited – spun in fine threads of silver. Machines have taken over the functions of Chrissy's failed organs, but there is no machine that will replace her brain. Starved of energy, the brain cells have died. I cannot simply push her essence back into her head because there is nothing left to act as host. This girl will never walk, never talk, never open her eyes.

I am all she has.

'Release the life you hold so tight; welcome me and leave the light.'

I bend down and touch my forehead to Chrissy's. Her essence comes to me quickly and as I straighten myself, the monitors around the bed beep incessantly before an alarm sounds. A nurse runs into the room, sees me and switches everything off.

The mother rushes to the bed, holding the body of her dead daughter while the father stands before me.

'You have her?' he asks, scared and unbelieving.

'I do.'

'Can I... can I see her?'

'You can.'

Chrissy's essence rises through me and instantly I know that something is not right. Her face flows over my own and her father covers his mouth with his hands as his eyes grow wide and wet.

'Daddy! Daddy!'

She's in turmoil. Barbed hooks scour my arms and legs, dredging up Chrissy's facets, ripping them out like matted hair. Something is taking her from me.

I fall to one knee and the father is on me.

'No, Chrissy. You stay here. You stay with me! Chrissy! Chrissy!'

His hands are on my face, trying to mash the essence of his daughter back through my skin, but it doesn't work that way and all he does is pulverise me. Her facets protect him from the pull of mine, but as she drifts away, he keeps catching my bare skin and pulling out clumps of his essence through the palms of his hands.

Chrissy's face lifts from mine. Intact and pulled by some unknown force. The father swipes for her and every time he does, her face scatters before quickly reforming. Soon the mother is by her husband's side, watching with horror as her daughter drifts away from me and into the ceiling. What they don't see is the rest of Chrissy's essence that hangs beneath her face like the tentacles of a man o' war. They emerge from my forehead, my mouth and even my chest, taking the final traces of Chrissy with them.

The moment she leaves, so too does the pain. Her face has reached the ceiling and the father has dragged the bed into the middle of the room and climbed onto it. Polystyrene ceiling tiles hit the floor and shatter as he knocks them down, desperately trying to hold his daughter one last time. As a dandelion seed in an autumn breeze, she slips through his fingers and is gone from the room.

Doctors appear and I'm led away while nurses talk to Chrissy's parents. They were here to celebrate me taking Chrissy's face, but as soon as the situation changed, their training kicked in and they responded to my failure with practised efficiency.

I'm told to sit and given a drink and even a blanket, despite the oppressive heat of the ward and the fact that I rarely remove my coat.

As I take that first sip of tepid coffee, I sense it, that tiny part of Chrissy that refused to leave. It's not an accident it is there, a careless memory or rarely called upon feeling that was otherwise occupied while the rest of the essence made its exit. This part of Chrissy was left inside me intentionally. I feel it move, seeking a part of me. It doesn't take long until it joins the remnants of Claire, wrapping itself tightly around the facets that make me an archivist.

There's a commotion in the corridor. The voices aren't raised but there's an edge to them that's just as loud. Everyone involved is desperately trying to keep their anger in check because this is a hospital and they're in full view of the public. Hands are twitching, ready to push. One of them looks at me with a flash of recognition followed by a quick turn of the head that brings that second glint of knowing. There is only one person with a face that can have that effect and it's me. Being unrememberable is my most memorable quality.

'They tell me I should go home,' Jenny says, dressed in her starched nurse's uniform. It's frayed around the sleeves and hem, her being the latest in a long line of wearers.

'You're not ready to come back,' a doctor says. He gives me a quick look and intuitively knows who I am. His expression is one of disapproval, but since I started visiting this hospital I've attained the status of a demigod and even those who don't believe are fearful to voice their opinion in my presence.

'Look at me, Sandeep. I've showered, I've dressed myself, my hair is combed and my teeth are clean. I'm not an emotional wreck. It's time I went back to work.'

'You'll still be paid.'

'It's not about the money...' Jenny stops herself with a long exhale. 'Are you free?' she asks me.

Today has not been a success and all I want is to slip away unseen. Jenny takes my silence to mean I would relish spending time with her.

'I'll buy you a coffee,' she says. 'A good one. There's a new place over the road. Sandeep, I'll see you tomorrow. I expect a full case load.'

'Jenny, I really—'

'Bye, Sandeep.'

She sits across from me on a seat that's an upturned crate, drinking something that is coffee in name only from a beer tankard. My coffee is black with no sugar. It took them five minutes to find something that resembled a cup. I already know I won't be coming here again.

She's halfway through her drink, which has a straw in it, when she laughs to herself.

'You've not asked how I'm doing.'

'I didn't realise I was supposed to.'

She scoops whipped cream with the end of the straw and eats it. 'It's not that you're supposed to, it's just what people do.'

'Every day I see people who've lost someone close to them. I don't concern myself with their feelings.'

'You'd make a poor doctor,' Jenny says.

'I'll add it to the list.'

'Have you read the story of Pinocchio?'

'No,' I say, 'but I know of it.'

'You're like Pinocchio. You're not a real boy yet. It's like there's something missing in you that everyone else has.'

'Empathy?'

'No, more than that. But don't worry, I think you'll find it.'

'I can't wait.'

She goes back to her drink, spending more time stirring than drinking.

'About Claire,' Jenny says. 'I don't blame you.'

'It's never happened before.'

'Has it happened since?' Jenny asks.

I stay quiet.

'My dad's got his lawyers involved. With him there's always someone at fault. It doesn't matter what the problem is, someone is to blame and he sees it as his duty to bring them to justice. The handcuff manufacturer, the razor blade manufacturer, the hacksaw manufacturer and, of course, the paramedics, all have some kind of legal proceedings against them.'

'What about me?'

'He doesn't know who you are. Even I don't know. Your name is basically your job title and it's not like I can draw your face – even if I could draw, which I can't.'

Jenny finishes her drink, spending too long trying to suck the dregs through her straw. The sound it makes stretches on for so long people look at us, and then at me. I hear a few gasps and some even rise from their seats with hope in their eyes.

Eventually, Jenny stops.

'They're wrong. Dr Lakhani, the senior sisters, the consultants. I'm ready to go back to work. They think I'm an emotional wreck. I'm not. I wasn't when Claire died and I'm not now. My mum? She's the one who's messed up. Keeps making cups of tea no one asks for and just leaves them around the house, then orders more teacups online because she says ours are all broken, but they're not, they're just in bathroom cupboards or tucked into the corners of unused rooms. I tried to tidy a few but she screamed at me that someone might want them, never mind that they'd been sat there for three weeks.

'Do you want to know my secret?' Jenny asks. A quick flick of her lips exposes a canine. 'Claire's not gone. I've seen you take people before and I know what the other nurses have seen too. When you let someone go, their face shatters and all the little parts shoot out in different directions. But Claire didn't go like that. She was whole. Even as she drifted through the ceiling, her face didn't change. You didn't release her like you did the others. What happened to Claire was different. Someone stole her from you.'

'It is not possible for someone to have stolen her from me.'

Jenny smiles again, this time showing all her teeth. 'And that's your problem. You're arrogant.'

'How so?' I ask.

'You think you're the only archivist.'

We talked our way past the doorman, took the stairs to avoid meeting anyone in the lift, and even waved to a confused old couple when someone in a security uniform reached for their radio. Now we're by the front door. Not just one door either, but two, like the entrance to a stately home even though it's only a flat.

'Are you going to knock?' Laure asks.

I just keep staring at the door. It's cream with gold leaf around the edges, probably worth more than our flat.

'I can knock for you. I don't mind.'

Laure reaches up to do just that. I take her hand.

'This was a terrible idea,' I say. 'He's not going to help.'

'No, I think he will.'

I miss being twelve, though I was never as beautiful as Laure. The teenage years might erode her childish optimism, but at least she'll have looks to rely on. All I've got is bitterness and breasts that didn't get past the first letter of the alphabet.

'We should leave,' I say. 'He won't want to see us.'

'You're not being like you.'

She's right. Anyone else and I'd pick the lock, throw my bags on the floor and make myself a snack. But he's not just anyone.

He's the person who saved my life. But then we were done and we said goodbye. Now here I am about to ask for more.

And what if I'm wrong and he's just another Richard? What if all men are Richards but they hide it better? He's practically a stranger. So we met in a hospital a few times? That's nothing. He's a man I barely know and here I am, stood at his door with my twelve-year-old sister, desperate for help.

'You're worried, aren't you?'

I nod and Laure takes my hand. 'I won't let anyone hurt you.'

'No, *I* won't let anyone hurt *you*,' I say, and she squeezes my hand so fucking hard that I want to know what she knows because I'm sure she doesn't know. She can't know, not all of it. Not now. Not ever.

'We can come back tomorrow,' Laure says. 'I don't mind another night sleeping under the bridge.'

The door opens and he's there, looming over us. Even in his house he's dressed impeccably.

'Sleeping under a bridge?' he says.

Laure looks up, her doe eyes pulling him in. 'It's OK. The foxes keep us warm.'

I'm too distracted by the thread that extends from my chest and dives into his to say anything. It's mesmerising, a starlight highway.

'The restaurants throw away their best food on Fridays. Some of it's not even covered in maggots!'

Too far. I flick Laure in the ear and she squeals.

'Sorry about her,' I say.

Laure sticks her tongue out at me and takes our bags. 'Mind if we come in?'

He steps aside but doesn't help.

Laure marches in and makes herself at home while I'm left stranded in the doorway.

'We didn't mean to come here.'

'Yes, you did,' he says.

'Well, I suppose we did. But this wasn't my plan.'

He looks inside. Not exactly an invitation, but it's the best I'll get. Past the entrance there's a hall with several large doors leading off it and stairs at the end. I've never been inside a two-storey flat.

Laure has vanished.

'She's in my living room,' he says.

I glance at the thread. 'Do you know what I'm thinking?' I ask, horror-stricken.

'No. That was a guess.'

He points through a doorway and there's Laure, sat on the only chair in the large room. No TV, no sofa, just a chair with a small table next to it. There's a tea coaster in the exact centre of the table and nothing else. The walls are bare and there are no curtains to cover the floor-to-ceiling windows.

'Have you just moved in?' I ask.

'No.'

'Then where's everything else?'

'This is all I need.'

At that moment I'm convinced that if I went into the kitchen and looked through the cabinets, I'd find one plate, one bowl, one cup, one fork and... well, you get what I mean.

'Yes, thank you, we would love a drink,' Laure says as she jumps off the chair and strides into the kitchen.

The downstairs of his flat is split into two halves. One half for him and the other for his clients. He explained that his business, if that's what you can call it, is mostly run from home. People book appointments to see the dead and he slots them in one after the other with an hour's break for lunch. At the end of each day, a cleaner comes to straighten everything out and he returns to his side of the flat with his single seat and bare white walls.

We're in the other half of the flat. You just turn left when you come in. This living room has furniture, paintings and freshly cut flowers. None of this was him. An early client was an interior designer and, along with her sister, they kitted out several rooms for an extra session each week for the next five years.

We're drinking expensive tea and eating macaroons left over from his last group of visitors. None of these things he buys himself; he has people for that. The only effort he exerts is opening the door. After that he just sits on the sofa and lets the dead do the talking.

'I didn't want to ask, but we had nowhere else to go.'

He puts down his cup. He is drinking water. The tea is only for the guests, which I presume means we'll be leaving soon.

'I thought you had a plan.'

'So did I. And I still do, but... we can't stay there. A police officer keeps coming round. Her name's Jones. She used to know Richard; I remember him talking about her. He said she'd slept her way to detective inspector. They weren't friends.'

'We've met.'

'The dead woman in the park?'

He nods.

'She's there every morning, waiting for us to leave. She can't come in, though, not unless we invite her. That means she hasn't got a warrant. Whatever it is, I think it's personal, otherwise she'd have someone else with her, like social services.'

'How long do you need to stay?'

'I don't know. It would be different if I was eighteen; then I could just adopt Laure and we could live together legally.'

'You want to stay for a year?'

'Eight months, at most.'

'Why should I help you?'

'We could pay you rent.'

'I don't need your money.'

'We could clean.'

'I already have someone to do that.'

Laure sits quietly in the corner, bizarrely unconcerned that we're about to get thrown out on our arses when the tea's drunk and the macaroons eaten.

'I know you don't owe us anything.'

'You're right, I don't.' He stands up and so do I. That's it, he's said no. I don't blame him, not after what he's already done for us.

'Well, thank you for the tea and the macaroons,' I mumble. 'And for, you know, everything else.' And then I'm looking at Laure as she reaches for another macaroon, and I see her smile and my mind throws together what my life would be like if Richard was still alive. Or what would have happened if I had been wrong and the Archivist hadn't come for me. If I had died, if Richard had subjected Laure to the drawn-out rape he'd fantasised every time he looked at her. Gratitude bursts from me and I don't stop to think about what I am doing as I throw myself forward and wrap my arms around the Archivist's thin torso and press my face into the recess just below his chest. His shirt is cool against my cheek and beneath that I feel something I didn't expect. Warmth. For all the death and suffering the world feeds him, his body is as human as mine. His heart beats beneath my ear, pumping hot blood and growing steadily faster.

My hands touch behind his back. That's when I freeze.

I don't feel it.

The despair he instils just with his presence is missing. My hand touches his face, making the skin-to-skin contact that saved my life. All I can feel is a cheek, warm and soft.

He looks straight ahead. Staring at the wall. His arms come down and wrap themselves around my back. He pulls me in, firmly but with a gentle restraint. When was the last time he held someone who wasn't about to die? Did anyone ever hug him? His parents? Maybe they wanted to but never could because of what it would do to them. Maybe they never wanted to. But here I am, hugging him because right now it's all I want to do. Hugging him because maybe I'm the only person in the whole world who can. And then I feel it, a shaking in his body, an uncertainty that seeps from a place inside him where his emotions are locked away. A desperate longing bleeds into our embrace. The Archivist isn't just alone, he's lonely in a way I could never understand. And so I stay there, holding him, until eventually his hands drop to his sides and I step away. We avoid eye contact as he fidgets backwards, not sure where to be. He places a hand on the back of an armchair, but clearly it feels wrong and he snatches it away before sliding it into a pocket.

'Not for eight months,' he manages.

I'm not able to process that before Laure throws herself from the chair and cries. 'First dibs on bedroom!'

The upstairs has five bedrooms; four of them are bare. He borrowed an inflatable bed from a neighbour and made a second bed from a pile of bathroom towels and his summer duvet. Laure is next to me, on the inflatable, fast asleep. We spent a long time talking but eventually I faked tiredness to give myself time to think. After that, Laure's unanswered questions became further and further apart until her breathing changed and she fell asleep.

I want to believe we're safe here, at least until I know what to do next. The Jones woman will get bored soon enough and stop coming over, but by then the estate will know Richard's left and the flat will be trashed. We already took what we could from there and everything we couldn't carry we hid. The money's not in the flat anyway. Richard was smarter than that.

I roll over, the towels moving beneath me to expose a crack of cold wooden floor that goes for my back. I rearrange everything as best I can, but I'll never be able to make this comfortable.

Bored with fighting it, I get up. There's a hoodie in my bag that I manage to find in the dark. It needs a wash but will do for now.

A noise on the other side of the door entices me. Voices from downstairs and to the right, the room where he takes his clients. There are no clocks on the wall, but it was after eleven when we came upstairs and we must have been in that room for at least two hours.

I'm about to go down when I catch myself in a bathroom mirror. Sleeping shorts that are not for public viewing and a hoodie that's unstitching itself around the cuffs. Hair and face are a complete write-off, so the less said about them the better. I'm certainly not presentable to whoever can afford the Archivist.

One of the voices cuts through the others, a shrill cry that turns to a laugh. It's a young voice. Soon I pick out more, focusing on just one while the others merge into the background. They're all young and they shout and swear and laugh.

I never questioned if the Archivist had friends, I just assumed he was alone. I'm almost certain that's what his hug told me, or was I arrogant in believing no one else considered him human?

The shorts are fine from the right angle and the hoodie really isn't that bad when you consider how late it is. As for the face and hair, well, that's what the hood's for. I go down quietly, like a child who's woken in the middle of the night and found the downstairs of their house transformed into a black world where grown-ups watch strange TV shows and every sound has an eerily seductive quality.

Sitting on the third step from the bottom, I can see through the double doors into the guest living room. I'm in darkness and if anyone were to look my way, they'd be more likely to mistake me for a ghost than a person. I want to go in, meet his friends and join the fun. I need it. But how would he explain me? And if not me, then Laure? This is our first night; I don't want us kicked out just yet.

I move closer and sit to the side of the open door. I count four girls and four boys. I can't see their faces because they've all got their backs to me, facing the guy on the sofa.

It's him. The long body and suit trousers, different to the ones he was wearing when I went to bed, with a grey shirt and burnt orange gloves. Like Richard, he wears his shoes inside the house, brown brogues against the immaculate cream carpet. Inside shoes only.

The face is not his. Same age, but that's where the similarities end. Everyone laughs at something I wasn't paying attention to. I shuffle closer, watching the Archivist work for the first time.

'There's none of that stuff in the middle,' the guy on the Archivist says. The dead one. 'You know, like sitting on a bus or trying to find something good on TV. It's just hanging out with you guys and seeing my mum. I never feel tired or hungry and there's no pain. It's pretty fucking sweet.'

They're drinking and someone takes a swig from a bottle.

'Can't drink, though,' the dead guy says. 'Or fuck. Or… well, I guess lots of stuff. But meeting up like this every Thursday is great. Maybe next time we could hit a bar.'

His friends agree and I can hear the guilt in their voices. It's Tuesday and my guess is they're not two days early.

93

'Shit! Chris, are you holding Claire's hand?'

The two sat on the floor next to the sofa jerk apart.

'When the fuck did that happen? I thought you and Amy were...' He looks down at the Archivist's hands. 'Mate, can you make your finger look like it's fucking your hand?' His hands don't move. Dear God, I would have pissed myself if he'd done that.

'It just kind of happened,' Chris says.

'Surprised you had the time with mocks coming up.'

'Mocks were over two weeks ago,' one of the guys says and quickly receives a punch in the arm.

'Really?' The dead guy says. 'Well, I guess that's fair. They're important. You won't get a decent uni offer without good mock grades. I wanted to go to Bath. Liz reckoned she'd get an unconditional offer, so it made sense.'

'You could still go,' one of them says.

'What's the point? It's not like I'll ever get a job.'

'Yeah, but for, like, the experience and everything.'

'Just drop it, Mike,' the dead guy says. 'It's not happening.'

'Liz is going to Durham now, anyway,' Mike says.

'Fuck's sake, Mike. Shut up,' Chris says as someone else punches Mike in the arm.

'Durham? Isn't that where Paul's going?'

Silence. I have no idea who Paul or Liz are, but it doesn't take a genius to work out what's happened. *Fuck's sake, Mike.*

The dead guy's face changes. He's working everything out, but in slower time than me. I guess that's fair because it's not like he has a brain anymore. As soon as he understands, his mouth shrinks and the tendons around his jaw flex.

The Archivist's body remains impassive.

'She's not visited me since it happened.'

'It's hard for Liz,' one of the girls says, a redhead. 'She needs time to adjust.'

'To Paul's massive cock!'

'Mike, what the fuck is your problem? Shut up!' Chris yells. I look up, wondering if that's woken Laure. 'Jake... look man, it's been two months. Liz's been a mess and Paul was there to—'

'What? Offer his balls for her to gobble? And two months? What the fuck? You said it'd only been three weeks. Even my mum... I've only seen her twice.'

'Jake, mate. We don't know what to say.'

'Don't you fucking *mate* me!' Jake shouts. 'You've been lying about Liz, lying about how long I've been dead. This is fucking bullshit! Argh! Move, you lanky prick! Stand up. Kick someone in the face. Throw the fucking television through the window! Do something!'

Everyone waits. The Archivist uncrosses his long legs, pauses, then recrosses them.

Jake shouts again, but it's hard to make out what he's saying because he fires the *fucks* like bullets from a machine gun. Throughout his tirade, his face growing redder and veinier by the *fuck*, the Archivist sits back impassively against the corner of his sofa, with his legs crossed at the knee and his hands resting gently on his lap.

Jake's friends are up now, arguing about what they should do. Mike tries to call Jake's mum, but the phone is slapped from his hands. Things get violent. Someone kicks over a table, toppling a flowerpot that throws moist soil over the virginal carpet. Another table goes and drinks are spilled. Someone is shoved against the wall and Jake continues his barrage, grinning maniacally as he revels in the carnage.

Then, as suddenly as it started, it stops. The Archivist is standing; Jake's face has gone, replaced by his own. The room is silent. Someone picks up shards of broken glass, but one look from the Archivist and they stop.

'Will he still be angry the next time he... you know...' Claire asks.

'He will. There is no in-between.'

'His mum said she wanted to see him next week,' Chris says.

'I know,' the Archivist says. 'I will take him outside so he has time to think. The session is now over. Leave.'

'Do you want us to...' one of the girls says, pointing to the mess.

'No. Just leave,' the Archivist says, silent rage filling those three words.

And they do. Quickly. No talk of where they should call a cab from, or if there are busses running at 2 am. They just grab their shit and get out with a silent fear I've only seen in horror movies.

'You can come in now,' he says when they've left.

Careful where I place my feet to avoid the broken glass, I make my way into the ruined living room.

'Another satisfied customer,' I say.

'It's not always like that.'

'But it is sometimes, isn't it?'

'It is.'

'Worse than that?'

'The police weren't called,' he says. 'And no one left in an ambulance.'

I bend down to pick up the flowerpot and start scooping the soil back in.

'Leave it,' he says. 'I have people for that.'

I keep scooping. His mouth moves, ready to speak, but then stops. He kneels next to me and together we scoop the soil back into the pot before we collect the broken glass. The room is far from clean by the time we go upstairs – his people will still need to be called.

At the top of the stairs, we pause.

'Goodnight,' I say.

He extends a finger and pokes me in the centre of my forehead, keeping it there for a while before pulling away. He smiles to himself and I'm so taken aback by how beautiful he looks at that moment that I don't hear him wish me goodnight or notice that he has left.

I eventually return to myself and shuffle back to the mound of towels that is my bed. Laure sleeps silently on the inflatable mattress next to me as I spend the rest of the night unable to do the same.

'We wouldn't want to keep you,' the doctor says, 'only we know you must be busy.'

She sits to my left at a sensible distance, in one of the many high-backed upholstered chairs that have been dragged into the room.

Thick columns of near-black wood support a frame, from which hang lace curtains riddled with holes. Beneath that is the bed where the patient lies. I have not seen the doctor approach the bed once, choosing instead to sit next to me and ask repeatedly when it will be time to take the essence.

'Yes, please don't let us keep you,' the soon-to-be widow who sits on my right adds. There are others in the room, perched upon woodworm-riddled furniture that's centuries old or standing against the wall, hugging themselves to keep out the chill of the large house.

I have glanced at the fireplace several times, and despite others catching my eye, no one has suggested that it should be lit. I regret accepting their offer to take my coat.

'That man is old,' I say. 'And he is ill. But he is not dying.'

'That would be your opinion, though, wouldn't it?' the doctor says.

We have been here before. She is a doctor and so only her views are valid, but at no point has she assessed the old man in the bed or made a diagnosis to inform me what exactly he is dying of.

No one else speaks or has spoken since I came here. They refuse to even look at each other, let alone the man on the bed. I have watched them for the last hour, forming connections to piece together a family tree, but I've failed to make it fit. The children have traits that don't match the dominant genes of their parents and the succession of eye colour, while not impossible, is so unlikely it's unsettling.

I could explain all of this with a few adoptions or a pair of tinted contact lenses, but I'm not hopeful for such simple solutions – nothing about this room aligns with the ordinary.

A young man in a waistcoat, thick hair swept back off his forehead, checks his watch. Others soon follow and watch-checking spreads through the room like a yawn. The young man checks his watch again and, unsatisfied by the meagre passing of time, turns his attention to what lies on the other side of the window.

'You don't need me today. If his condition worsens, you have my card.'

'Wait,' the doctor says. 'His breathing has changed. I fear it might be any moment.'

I am certain that no one else in the room heard any change in the old man's breathing. Though I detect a change in theirs, as if they have released a collective breath.

'I think that's unlikely.' I stand and take my coat from the rack.

The doctor moves while my back is turned. Someone attempts to distract me, but they are no actor and whatever it is they are trying to say comes out mumbled and confused.

The doctor is by the bed, holding the arm of the old man. She slips something into her pocket and takes his wrist like she is checking his pulse. She looks at me and shakes her head.

'His heart rate is erratic and it's getting worse. I do think you should stay.'

Unlike the man who has now retreated to the wall, the doctor can act. She continues to fuss over the patient, feeling his forehead to check his temperature and leaning over to place her ear to his lips, listening for breathing reps. I would probably have believed her if not for the outline of the hypodermic in her pocket.

I'm part way to the door when a man tries to take my arm. His fingers brush the material of my coat when the constricting fear of death ensnares him and he falls to the floor with a whimper. I don't stop and the next moment he is on his feet, smiling and uncertain.

A cough from the bed followed by the sound of distressed bedsprings stops me. The doctor stands on the other side, acting out the horror perfectly as she tries to restrain the man's violent convulsions.

I abandon my escape and return to the bed. The room falls away and the man's essence appears superimposed against his body. When I arrived it was bound securely. Areas of weakness and the natural attrition of age were present, but that is to be expected and does not mean death will occur soon.

The essence I see now is not what it was two hours ago. Whatever the doctor injected him with courses through his body, throwing out clusters of facets as it travels through his arteries and veins, forming tracks of destruction that spread through his capillaries and into every extremity. The facets collect over him in a cloud. As more leave, the anchor to the body will weaken and eventually the essence will drift away.

They shiver in my presence. I step back.

'He is dying,' I say to the doctor. She doesn't respond. There is no need. She has performed what was required of her.

The wife appears, as old as her husband. 'Please, if you can save him, do. Only, there is the small matter of payment.'

I look around the room. Grand, much like the rest of the house. I see no lack of money.

'I know what you are thinking, but Reginald and I have already signed over ownership of the house to our sons. We have nothing to our name.'

'Then your sons can pay.'

'They won't do that. But if there is something else I can offer you in exchange for money...'

I already have more money than I know what to do with, but I make it a rule not to work for free, with the known exceptions I won't repeat.

'I have some jewellery, though perhaps that is not worth enough.'

I glance at the man. His essence continues to flee his body.

'You are young. Perhaps you have a school-aged sister? I'm the governess of a very exclusive school. She could attend for free if you were to take Reginald's face. I may even have room for two.'

'Well, that's deeply unsettling,' Sun says as she sets down her fork and reaches for the water. 'So do you think they killed the old man to get us into that school or were they planning to do away with him anyway?'

'You shouldn't assume it was about you,' I say.

'"I may even have room for two." Do you hear yourself?'

'I appreciate it's suspicious.'

'Oh, we've travelled way beyond suspicious, my friend, and straight to the land of screaming fucking obvious.'

'Sun-young, do mind your language,' Laure says.

Sun looks put out. She reaches for seconds, heaping the pasta onto her plate and going for the pepper. 'They're not even pretending it isn't a trap. I almost admire them.'

'There are many ways to interpret a situation. If I had taken the jewellery, the school wouldn't have been offered.'

'She made that offer for you to reject.'

'How do you know?' I ask.

'She said it wasn't worth much; you'd have been an idiot to accept it.'

I replay the situation and Sun is right. The jewellery was a perfunctory gesture with nothing to substantiate it, whereas the school was offered with assurances.

'Will we go there?' Laure asks. She doesn't talk to me much, but I understand that. The first time we met I killed a man.

'I think you should,' I say.

'No, we shouldn't,' Sun says. 'They'll put us on their database; if the police really are looking for us then going to school will give us away.'

'You won't be officially enrolled. There'll be no record of your attendance.'

'Seriously?' Sun cries. 'So not only does this creepy lady pay you with school admission, but she's going to keep it a secret?'

'If you were officially registered, the school would know she was abusing her power and remove her. You and Laure will attend under witness protection.'

Sun's head falls into her hands. She shakes it, her sleek hair slapping her fingers.

'Will we get new names? If so, I pick Penelope Warrington-Smyth,' Laure says excitedly. This is nothing but a game for her. I may not share Sun's paranoia, but a man died to get them into this school.

'You will be provided aliases.'

'That'll be good, Sun,' Laure says. 'You've always hated your name.'

'I hate being manipulated more.'

'I know you think this has been engineered, Sun.'

'Because it has!'

'But you and Laure cannot spend every day in my flat,' I continue.

'Don't worry, we'll be out of here soon enough,' Sun says.

'That isn't what I meant,' I say. 'I have no issue with you living here.'

I look at them both, want to tell them that I enjoy their company. They've brought chaos into my routine and I'm not yet ready to return to the functional orderliness I lived before. Or the loneliness.

'So what? You think I'm paranoid?' Sun says.

'Do you really believe the police would kill a man simply to send you and Laure to school? If they know you live with me, then why not come to the door?'

There is a knock, but it doesn't happen at that moment. After everything has been cleared away and I am left alone in my living room, with Sun and her sister in their bedroom, someone announces themselves at my flat. I have no meetings scheduled for the evening and the doorman is proficient at turning people away... most of the time.

I can see through the door, see through walls and floors and ceilings, to the essence on the other side. But that is all I see. There is no body, no clothes, and aside from any distinguishing injuries, one essence looks much like the next.

I slide back the cover to the fish-eye lens. I know that the visit will be regarding a request I'm unable to refuse and I will be taken to a car and driven to a place where I will need to deal with something horrific.

'I know you can see me.'

I flip back the cover on the lens and open the door.

'Detective Inspector Jones.'

'It's Detective Sergeant Jones,' she manages with minimal venom. 'Constable Wilson's write-up of our last encounter was far from glowing.'

'It's late,' I say.

'Don't worry, I won't be driving you to see something horrific. Though I'm curious, do you always talk to yourself when you think no one is listening?'

Detective Sergeant Jones manages a smile at my lack of reply. 'Something you were unaware of?'

'Why are you here?'

'Two girls have gone missing.'

'And?'

'I want you to tell me where they are.'

'Why do you think I would know?'

'Sun-young Kang and Laure Baptiste.'

'I don't know those names.'

There's a noise behind me and I quickly turn around. Sun might be awake and wondering who is at the door. I scan the hall, but no one appears.

'There was no noise, Mr Archivist,' Detective Sergeant Jones says. 'The moment you turned your face from mine I forgot what it looked like, which meant I also forgot whether I could tell if you were lying.'

'Do you have any more questions, or are we finished?'

'You don't enjoy being on the back foot, do you?'

'There are many things I don't enjoy, Detective *Sergeant*.'

'Let me explain it like this. There is CCTV footage of Sun-young Kang at the Friedmarsh General Hospital with an unidentified person. Everyone who has reviewed the footage of this unidentified person is convinced that they have a face, but when asked to recall that face they can't. The face does not match anyone on our criminal database and it appears that not only is it unidentified, it's unidentifiable.'

'It appears your investigation has stalled.'

'It would have, that is, if there wasn't already someone in the local area who was known to have a face that's impossible to remember.'

'You cannot present two unknowable quantities and claim they are the same,' I say.

'I'm not suggesting it would be successful in a court of law. That's not what I'm here for. The only person I need to convince is myself and I've done that.'

'You have,' I confirm. 'Right here, while you stand looking at me, you have convinced yourself that I am the person in the CCTV footage. But as soon as you leave, that conviction will vanish and you will be in exactly the same position as when you arrived.'

The tendons around her neck flex before sinking back into the dark brown of her skin. She reaches for her phone, flips open the case and takes a picture of me.

'You cannot look at my picture forever.'

Detective Sergeant Jones moves so she can no longer see me and checks her phone. A tap of her fingers and the screen goes blank. Frown lines run across her forehead and around her eyes. She pockets the phone.

'I would hate to return with a warrant, Mr Archivist.'

'You don't need a warrant,' I say. 'You're free to enter.'

She can't hide her surprise. After a curt nod she takes a step forward and abruptly stops.

I am standing in the doorway. It is wide and there is sufficient space for Detective Sergeant Jones to enter. I could move to appear more accommodating, though I won't. Instead, I watch the police officer, frozen at my door.

Her pupils have shrunk and the lustre from her skin has faded to reveal a dulled plastic complexion. Her breaths are quick, occurring intermittently like she has forgotten how to take in air. Her mouth hangs open, her tongue is dry-looking and useless in her mouth of perfectly white teeth. She hunches over and reaches for the doorframe to catch herself but misses and falls awkwardly against it.

My essence, which I had extended to brush against her extremities, retreats to coil around my bones. I take a step back and slowly Detective Sergeant Jones picks herself from the floor.

'What you are doesn't impress me,' she says as she straightens her suit. 'Just because you're useful to us, don't assume you're above the law.'

I smile, not that she'll remember it. 'It's regrettable that I can't help you, Detective Sergeant Jones.'

'Sun-young and Laure lived with a man called Richard Hargrave, a constable I once worked with. Richard... concerned me. I suspect his interest in the two girls was not healthy and I can make a guess as to what happened to him. I can even create a plausible scenario that involves you.'

She takes a step away from me, the linger of despair still too strong despite my attempt to reel it in.

'Richard Hargrave was not a good man and if I am right and he is dead, then the world is a better place. But he was a police officer and we look after our own. I think you'll understand when I tell you that I need a win about now.'

'Then I wish you the best of luck.'

'I highly doubt that.'

She turns to leave. I call for her to wait. She stops, standing awkwardly after an aborted half step. She knows I will not tell her where Sun and Laure are. If she knows they are with me, then she also knows that I have no reason to supply that information. And a cowardly insult as she retreats? It's patently clear that's not who I am.

'You should have someone look at your breast.'

Her hands go up instinctively before she stops them. She's about to accuse me of something. The words she's expecting don't come out.

'Which one?'

'The left.'

'Kimberly... Kimberly... Kim!'

'Laure, there's no one here. Call me Sun.'

The way she's looking at me, I know it doesn't matter how many times I say it, she's not going to respond until I call her by her new name.

'Please don't make me say it.'

She raises an eyebrow and looks away, scanning the empty corridor before gracefully recrossing her legs. The uniform looks good on her; it's prim and crisp, and with her high ponytail she was born to attend The Greenfield. Already I picture her running across a field, slender legs caked in mud and lacrosse stick raised, ready to beat over the head of an unsuspecting midfielder.

'Fine, Florence.'

'It's important to practise,' Laure says. 'Even if I can't be Penelope.'

I know I should think of her as Florence Hastings and not Laure Baptiste, but my mind can't just reassign her like that.

'We should use our new names at home too,' Laure says.

'At least call me Kim,' I say. 'Kimberly's too long.'

'Don't call me Flo,' Laure says. 'It makes me think of the toilet.'

I squeeze her hand. Tell myself we'll be OK here. That whatever trap lies in wait is imagined. We'll be here for a few weeks, maybe a month, and then we'll be gone. Back to our old names and our old lives, just without Richard.

A pack of girls walks past. Those at the front don't stop to look at us, so wrapped up in their lives as they clamour over each other to be the next to speak. They flock around the queen, buried in the centre of the group and hidden from view, feeding off her conversation. The stragglers follow a few steps behind, still part of the group, but only in their minds. *They* see us. Appraising eyes wash over Laure, assessing her future potential as queen. The looks I get confirm I'm one of them, competition for a sliver of recognition.

And then they're gone, swept along another thread of this sprawling, escherian school.

I'm bent forward, admiring how well I shaved my knees, when I realise there's someone standing over me, so silent I can't hear a single breath. She folds herself neatly in half until her nose practically touches mine. She smells exquisite.

'Kimberly Hastings, my name is Katie Merriweather. I'm here to show you around The Greenfield.'

She straightens, pulling her delicious scent back with her.

'It's a school, I'm sure I'll work it out.'

'I doubt that. Now come on, stand up.'

'What about my sister?' I say as I motion to Laure.

'One of the lower years will come for Florence.'

Katie flashes a smile, which Laure grotesquely mimics. I want to believe it was a Florence smile, not a Laure smile, but I know my sister well enough to see when she has found one of her people. I squeeze Laure's hand, possibly tighter than I need to, and follow Katie.

Katie slows and walks beside me. Dear God, I have never

felt so tiny in my life. No woman has the right to be this tall and walk with such grace. Her limbs are long and sway elegantly with each step. It's an impractical way to move. There's really no need for her to be so sickeningly perfect.

My steps grow louder as I plod my way along the corridor. I can't weigh more than two-thirds of her, but it doesn't seem to make a difference. She must operate on special physics, the type they don't teach to people like me.

'Built in 1643 by the local friars, The Greenfield was a boys' school for most of its life until, in 1876, the school was closed due to a falling birth rate in the local population and a severe lack of funds. For thirty-five years the school was deserted, home to wandering vagabonds and—'

'Please stop.'

'Pardon?'

'That museum tour narration. Just don't.'

'You don't want to learn about the history of The Greenfield?'

'Evidently not.'

Katie stops walking. She taps a finger against her chin, right where it finishes in a neat point. She's all angles; shoulders, knees, hips and elbows, covered with perfectly white skin. She'll look frightening as an old woman, after age has atrophied her muscles and curved her spine, but right now she's beautiful.

Katie brushes a lock of wheat-blonde hair behind her ear and holds it there as she looks down the length of the corridor. 'No commentary then...' she says and walks on.

'If it's OK with you, I'd rather just look around myself.'

I leave Katie and go a different way, though every door looks the same, all dark wood with no windows into the classrooms. My old school had display boards running the length of the corridors filled with science posters and awards photographs and propaganda on why students shouldn't smoke or experiment with drugs and casual sex. There's none of that here, just dark walls on a dark floor topped with a dark ceiling.

Katie is on me like an assassin. There's a menace in her presence and my heart launches itself into my mouth. I do my best to quickly choke it down. A gentle hand on my shoulder suggests I've failed.

'You would learn more if we stayed together.'

I consider running, but one look at those legs and I know I'd be wasting my time.

'I work better alone.'

'Working alone isn't The Greenfield way.'

'Does that mean I'm stuck with you?'

'Don't make it sound so negative. I'm here to help you, Kimberly.'

She squeezes my shoulder. Her fingers are so long and thin that it feels like a spider has settled there, ready to fly at my face. I count to twenty-three before she pulls her hand away.

'Well, I'm glad at least school isn't going to be super fucking creepy.'

I'm standing in the middle of the school hall, I don't know why, as Katie briefs me on its history, I also don't know why. It's been two hours and, despite my clear disinterest, Katie appears stuck on a narration loop. I have long stopped asking if there are lessons I need to be in, or better, lessons she needs to be in. I expect to spend the rest of the month on this tour. There'll probably be a fucking quiz too.

Katie leads me out of the hall and into an enclosed courtyard. There's a break between lessons; a bell sounded five minutes ago, and the courtyard is full of girls talking and looking at their phones. Take away the grandeur of the buildings and right now this would be any other school.

'What's with the armbands?' I ask. I saw them on every girl we passed, two black ribbons tied around their upper arms. Katie pulls at one of her own.

'These are for the ones we've lost.'

'Lost? You mean they died?'

Katie nods. 'It happens. Life can become ever so difficult. It takes a strong person to know when it is time to quit. For the rest of us, the pain can sometimes be too much and so we wear these bands as a sign of solace.' Katie runs her fingers along the smooth silk of the ribbon. 'I find them rather fetching, don't you, Kimberley?'

'I don't think they're for me.'

'Shame. You would look awfully out of place if you didn't wear them.'

'I'm sure I'll manage.'

Katie sighs and looks to an archway that leads out of the courtyard. There's movement as girls stream into what lies beyond the wall. They run through the archway, bursting from the doors that lead into the courtyard and clearing it in seconds. In my old school this meant only one thing: a fight. For some reason I doubt that's the case at The Greenfield. From the corner of my eye, I watch Katie rub her arm where the ribbons are tied. She smiles to herself.

'Well, I suppose we'd better see what all the commotion is about. Come along, *Kimberley*.'

The ways she says my name like that, it's almost like she knows. I push that thought aside. I'm being paranoid, of course I am. First day in a fucked-up suicide school using a different name. If I wasn't paranoid, there'd be something wrong with me.

The wall of girls in front of us parts for Katie like she's a shark among fish. Next moment, we're standing at the front while girls fight for space either side.

A black SUV moves ponderously forward then brakes sharply. The girl who moments ago fell off the side throws herself across the bonnet. She bangs it with her fists. Grabs one of the windscreen wipers and tries to pull it off but only bends it. The driver turns on the windscreen washers and she gets it in the face. Swears like I never imagined a girl at this school could. It's music; each four-letter word delights my ears and I finally feel the magic of the school has shattered and I'm back in the real world.

She slams her palms against the glass. The driver reverses and the girl slides off, cradling her head with an arm before hitting the ground.

The euphoria of expletives fading, I see the girl for who she is. Small, with hair that is nearly black and falls around her head in half-frizzed ringlets. Large, pleading eyes and teeth that are just a little too large, leaving her mouth permanently half-open. She picks herself up, wipes the gravel from her bare arm and runs at the car. This time she grabs a wing mirror and pulls it off.

The man in the car doesn't get angry. He throws it into first and lurches forward, only to drive into a dead end. I've seen this before. Young teacher, handsome and knows it. My guess: he couldn't distance himself quickly enough from a schoolgirl crush. Now she's pregnant and he's denying all involvement. It's easy for him. He'll have covered his tracks. This won't be the first time and it won't be the last.

It happened at my old school. Two girls were pregnant when I left, though one of them must have had the baby by now. The father of one was a teacher and we all knew it, but he didn't lose his job because he taught science and they were running low on science teachers already. The other one, no one was sure. I heard some stuff about a brother.

I stick my head out to look for Laure, but she isn't here. Either that or her minder doesn't command as much fear as mine.

'Shouldn't we do something?' I ask.

'We are doing something, Kimberly,' Katie says. 'We're watching.'

'I was thinking of something a little more proactive. Like stopping her.'

'And spoil the show?' Katie pouts and turns away. The girl climbs onto the roof of the car.

'Who are they?'

'Sophia Ray. I think you have some classes with her. He's Mr Cavendish. Only been here a month, but seems to have made an impression, don't you think?'

Sophia opens the passenger-side door and jumps in. Then she's slapping Mr Cavendish and grabbing fistfuls of his hair. His efforts to stop her are pretty feeble, though I guess he doesn't want to risk harming the baby I imagined into existence.

Katie watches the scene with a malicious grin on her angular face. She strokes the black bands on her arm and looks at me. 'Kimberly, you must understand that this is a very elite school. Not everyone survives,' she says as her grin widens.

This bitch is crazy.

Without Katie's statuesque form stalking me through the corridors, I become invisible. No one questioned where I was going and, as I needed somewhere to be for a few hours, the library seemed like the only sensible choice.

Laure, being as she is, has already found a group of friends and is right now trying out for the netball team, despite having never once played. True, it's not lacrosse, but I'm sure it's only a matter of time before she's presented with a crosse and the school absorbs her as one of its own.

I like school libraries because no one uses them. In my old school it was because half of the pupils couldn't read. Here it's because although they can read, like everything else, they'd rather pay someone else to do it for them.

As expected, the library is grand, well stocked and just the right side of eerie. I find the sections on faith, religion and science and pull down books on archivism. *The Unabridged History of Archivism*, *Charlatans: A sceptic's treatise on Archivists*, *Archivism and the Power of Persuasion*, *The Truth about Archivists and Death*. The books look and smell old. A quick flick to the first page confirms it: some of these books were published more than one hundred and fifty years ago. I carry them to my table. This should kill a couple of hours nicely.

A compulsion makes me look down at the thread. It punches through the fabric of my bra, shirt and tie, then stretches across the room and out through a wall. I don't understand the layout of the school well enough to know where I am in relation to anything outside, but the Archivist told us he would be seeing a man in the park whose husband had recently died, so I suppose the park must be somewhere over there.

The thread twitches. It's gentle, as if a mouse were attempting to tightrope walk from the Archivist to me. I've not seen it do that before, not when he's taken an essence or when he's projected a face. I reach out and touch it with my fingertip when I hear the door open and jerk my head towards the noise.

I can't see the door from where I sit, but I can tell that someone is struggling to open it. Eventually the whir of an electric motor replaces the cries of old hinges and a girl in a wheelchair appears from behind a bookcase.

I half watch her as I struggle to read the same sentence six times. As soon as I'm near the end, I feel the compulsion to glance up and find the girl, only to return to the page and start over again.

She has a small pile of books on the blanket that covers her lap and hides her legs. It's hot in here; my blazer's on the back of my chair and I've undone the top two buttons of my shirt. I don't know how she can cope. Perhaps what's under the blanket is worse than the heat.

She's coming over. I stop myself from looking. Still no closer to finishing that bloody sentence, though. I've got an "elbow on the table and hand against the side of my face" pose going on just to be sure I convey the image of someone who's hard at work but it clearly doesn't register with her because the next thing I know, the bitch's wheelchair is right fucking next to me.

'People's eyes move when they read,' she says.

'Pardon?'

'Across the paper.'

'I was stuck on a word.'

'Show me, I'll help you with it.'

I shut the book and slide it away from her.

'Interested in archivists?' she asks.

I try not to look at the stack of books next to me, but my goddamn deceitful eyes can't help themselves and now I'm practically gawping at them like their subject has come as a complete shock.

'The Greenfield has an archivist.'

I can literally see my surprise reflected in her eyes. 'There's another one?'

Half of her mouth smiles and she reaches up to tuck a lock of auburn hair behind her ear to distract herself.

'So you've met one?'

'Well... you know, I've heard rumours.'

'The thing with rumours,' the girl says, 'is that you really need to see them to be sure.'

'So what do you want?' I ask.

'You're the new girl and, you know, I'd heard rumours.'

'About me? How old are you? Thirteen? Fuck off.'

'We don't talk to people like that at The Greenfield.'

I'm about to bite back, but it never comes. There's something about this girl, an unsettling intensity. Something deep in my brain tells me not to push her; it won't go my way.

'What rumours?' I fumble. I lift my palm off the table to see a perfect imprint in sweat, which I hurriedly wipe clear with my elbow.

'That you're a sweaty girl,' she says, leaning forward and staring deeply into my eyes. 'So please be careful with the books. Some of these are rather old and the school would struggle to replace them.'

'I'm not sweaty,' I say, frantically wiping my hands dry on my skirt. 'It's just this room is so bloody hot.'

The girl's laugh is bitter, like she's heard it all before and there's nothing new she could ever find truly funny. She wheels herself closer.

'That's beautiful,' she says. 'Where did you get it?'

I look down and pick up the single pearl that hangs from a golden chain around my neck. 'It was my mum's.'

'I have never seen anything like it before.'

'Really? I think she stole it from a market stall.'

'You must be very special.'

'Because my mum stole cheap jewellery?' I snort, swinging the pearl around my finger. I let it fall and it lands against my chest, just above where the thread punches through my shirt.

'It's there when you close your eyes, isn't it?'

My hand snaps up, covering the pearl, but also covering the end of the thread. She's right, I see it when I close my eyes. It shines through my hands, through books, through metal. At first I struggled to sleep with its unflinching brightness. Then, gradually, it became a part of me, like teeth – painful at first and then just there.

'Who are you?' I ask.

'Just a curious student who wanted to check out the new girl.'

She backs off, turns around and is gone.

Whoever that kid is, she knew about the thread that connects me to the Archivist and wanted to see for herself. Because she *could* see, as clearly as I can, as clearly as he can.

Just who the hell is she?

Someone drops a glass that promptly shatters. It happens behind me, so I don't see the micro-chaos that unfolds. It must have been full because I hear complaints of water-sodden shoes and the next sound is of someone falling. There's a sarcastic comment or two and then everyone forgets it ever happened.

Maeve didn't look up. She picks up her tea, steadying it with both hands. Septic arthritis has left her with gnarled fingers and fissures in her scarlet skin. She's unable to properly hold the cup, her hands nothing more than immobile claws.

Carefully she cradles the cup to her lip, manages a sip and sets it back down.

'I must've spent my whole life thinking we had more money than we really did. David took care of everything, you see. He was the one who earned it; all I ever managed to contribute was enough for the weekly shop with a little left over to put on the dogs. Never won much, mind.'

There's a slice of lemon drizzle cake in front of her. She lowers the cup and tries to take the fork, but her fingers won't close around the handle. Eventually she gives up.

'I was going to sell off equity to pay for you, but he beat me to it. The bank owns the lot. I've not the heart to tell the kids, they all think they're getting a share. My youngest, Sharon, she's just got divorced and can't find anywhere with rent cheap enough. I've already told her I'll cash in the house and give her half. The other two don't need it. They won't help their sister either. Selfish boys, I raised. Not like their dad. He was kind, was David. Bad with money, but kind.'

She attempts the fork again. This time she holds one hand in the other to help close her fingers. She nearly manages, holding the fork just off the table, but then it slips from her grip and falls to the floor. The old fork is quickly removed and a new one wordlessly appears, the handle just as thin as the last.

'I'm old.' She smiles and the wrinkles spread across her crêpe-paper skin multiply and conquer her face. 'I don't throw things away. I've got newspapers from the day of my wedding and the birth of every child, ticket stubs from movies I saw fifty years ago, even clothes I wore as a girl that my mother made for me. I've so many things, I was sure there'd be something of value. An old broach, an antique clock, perhaps even a first-edition book.'

She looks down at the fork and doesn't even try. 'You're not eating anything. Would you like the cake?'

I nod, take the cake and the fork, and eat. There's something in her eyes, a look of disappointment, as if learning that I need food has shattered my image as something otherworldly. I finish it and she sighs, staring forlornly at the plate and the few remaining bright yellow crumbs.

'All worthless,' she says. 'Junk to anyone but me. Not even the kids want it. As good as told me it's going to the tip when I die.'

'Do you want to see him again? We can go someplace else.'

She shakes her head. 'He was so happy that time we were feeding the ducks. I don't think we moved from that bench for three hours. We just talked, not about anything that mattered, just how the kids were getting on and where the neighbours had gone on holiday. It was like he never died. It was only when I looked at him, sitting so tall on your body, that I realised he was gone. But the longer we were there, it seemed the more he shrunk and the more your body became his until I swear his eyes were level with mine.'

She picks up her tea. It sloshes in the cup, never quite breaching the sides. She stares, watching it churn. Giving up, she places it on the saucer with a clatter.

'If he saw me like this, he'd know. About the house, about the money, about... him. I want his last memories to be happy ones. I can do that for him. Please, let him go.'

'Here?'

'This is where we met. Back then it was a school and this was our classroom. He was a funny-looking boy. His mother would cover his hair with brilliantine and comb the straightest parting you ever saw into the side of his head, like he was a movie star from the twenties, only his ears were too large and the birthmark on his cheek too bright – until he was old enough to grow a beard, and after that day, I never saw it again.'

'You can watch him go.'

'No thank you. I think... I think I'll just keep looking at my tea.'

The face of an old man appears over mine. It cannot see or think or talk or hear; it is just a shell. Someone's conversation stops mid-flow. Someone else swears and I can hear phones being hastily removed from pockets as people gather. This was why I chose a table that allowed me to face the corner. I had hoped not to release him here and had even agreed with the owner that we could leave via the back door through the kitchen to stop people gawping as we fought through pushchairs and squeezed behind seats occupied by the large and stubborn.

His face lifts from mine, breaking apart as it rises, trailing silver tendrils of facets among cries of, 'Ian, can you fucking see this?' and 'I'm fucking freaking out, Susan. *I'm fucking freaking out.*'

He shatters in a cloud of dust and all that David ever was passes through the polystyrene ceiling tiles of *Great Eggspectations* to a delighted crowd of gormless simpletons and his widowed wife, who watches her slowly cooling cup of tea.

'I was eight years old when I first saw him, sat at the back of the class trying to carve his name into the desk with a compass. When he looked up at me, I knew I wanted to spend the rest of my life with that boy.'

She gets up, picks her bag off the table and shuffles to the exit. People part for her. Someone even drags a table across the floor, spilling a young couple's drinks. The bell over the door chimes as she leaves.

Jenny throws herself into the recently vacated chair opposite me and calls to the waiter for a slice of carrot cake.

'Anyone ever tell you you're heartless?'

'Are you following me?'

'No, just in the area. You know you could have kept that old man inside you, that's clearly what she wanted. Or is there a limit?'

'An essence has no physical size.'

'So you'll never be full?'

'I can appear full, but I am like a hotel with an infinite number of rooms filled by an infinite number of guests.'

'Everyone just moves to an even-numbered room?' Jenny says.

'Exactly.'

'So is it money? You're already richer than Croesus.'

'The fee I charge relates to the uniqueness of the opportunity. If I helped people for free, then word would travel and I would wake to find crowds outside my home.'

Jenny's cake arrives and she starts on it before calling over the same waiter again for a coffee to wash it down. 'You're not the messiah,' she manages between mouthfuls.

'Jesus performed party tricks. He sought fame. I don't.'

'I've been reading up about you. There're a lot of books on archivists. I didn't realise how late you were to the game. Somewhere between Buddhism and Christianity is where you slot in. There were no archivists, then suddenly there were. Then, over two thousand years later, you've nearly died out.'

Jenny's coffee arrives and so too does one for me, even though I didn't order it. I come here a lot and the staff are good. Everyone who only ten minutes ago had their phones out has already been asked to leave and their empty tables.

'Islam, Christianity, Confucianism all started with a single prophet, a person who can be attributed to a specific place and time in history,' I say. 'Archivists do not have that lineage. We are like pyramids or fire, a clever idea that appeared in multiple locations at different times with no connection. However, there was one person who became the first archivist, in the sense that there always will be a first. Each country claims that their own story tells the tale of that first archivist, but there is no way to prove it.'

'Who do you believe came first?' Jenny asks.

'I can't know, but I have a favourite story.'

'Would you tell it to me?'

'Why?'

Jenny shrugs. 'Because my mum packed her bags and left home. Because my dad refuses to speak to anyone about what happened to my sister. Because even though I go to the hospital every day they still won't let me work because some bitch in occupational health labelled me mentally unstable. Because I think that what I need right at this moment is to eat cake and listen to a story.'

I drink my coffee and glance at my watch. I'm free for another hour. I was expecting Maeve to take longer, a walk in the park, an emotional farewell, possibly even a plea to extend her contract free of charge. There are other people I could see. With a single call I could have any number of families racing to meet me, desperate for the opportunity to spend more time with their deceased. But I don't reach for my phone. I was the one who killed Jenny's sister, and though her light was fading long before I arrived, it was me who ripped her from the world. I owe Jenny more than a story, but right now, it is all I can give.

'In the Yan province, before the Qin wars unified China, there were tales of a woman who travelled from village to village performing ceremonies for the dying. When someone had reached a certain age, or the illness they were suffering from had developed to where death was imminent, she would perform her ritual. Running her hands over the body, she would pull out thick threads of silver silk and throw them into the air, where they dissolved and danced in the night sky. Her ritual killed every time, though no one could explain why. Gifts and money she refused, accepting only food and shelter as payment. Once she had left, the villagers struggled to describe how she looked. Unable to agree on her appearance, there were some who questioned if she were human. Stories of her spread through China. In all of them she was described as a young woman, but more than one hundred years passed until the first stories of her death appeared. A young girl named Xiu left her home in the night and found herself by a stream. When questioned afterwards, she couldn't explain what had compelled her to leave, only that she knew she must wake. What she saw was a woman kneeling by the water's edge, dressed only in white and watching Xiu. Xiu described the woman as not having one face, but of being old and young at the same time. She said the woman waded into the stream. It was late November and the water, which reached her waist, would have been close to freezing. The woman smiled at Xiu and then her face floated upwards, only to be replaced by another face that also smiled and floated away. Face after face appeared on the woman, only to climb into the air where they shattered, filling the sky above the stream with millions of new stars. When the glow of the final face faded and only the light of the moon remained, the woman who stood in the water was gone.'

'Did she have a name?' Jenny asks.

'She may have, but she never spoke it and no one ever asked. She was unique; she didn't need a name.'

'Is that why you don't have a name?'

'It is one of the stories that led to archivists not being given names, but not the only one.'

'Don't you believe it?' Jenny asks.

'You don't have to believe a story to enjoy it.'

Jenny picks up her bag and places it on the table. She calls for the waiter as she produces her purse. The waiter looks at me, eyes widening in a flash of recognition. I shake my head and the waiter leaves us alone.

'You don't need to pay. We have a different arrangement.'

Jenny just says, 'Oh,' and returns her purse to the bag.

'You've still not told me why you're here,' I say.

'Didn't believe I was just in the area, then?'

'No.'

Jenny nods. 'Figures.'

'Go on.'

'I came to tell you a story I found online. Not one as old as yours, but old nonetheless. An archivist, young like you and in desperate need of work, stages an ambush on a dowager countess as she travels home one evening. Everything of value was stolen from her, the driver killed, and her as good as left for dead. Along comes the Archivist, travelling by foot. He sees the dowager countess, plays the part of unsuspecting bystander and does what he can to help. But she is old and her injuries too severe. He knows she won't survive and so he does what any archivist would and steals her essence. Of course, this was his plan from the start. He would present himself to the family in the morning and, along with the police, explain what happened and they would come to an arrangement. But it did not play out like that. With the hired thieves waiting by the sides of the road, the young archivist wrestled the essence from the dying woman, but could not keep it. They watched as the essence was pulled through the Archivist's mouth like a fish on a line. It came out whole, writhing and fighting, before it was whipped away and the Archivist left with nothing.

'This was when people like you were common and being an archivist wasn't special. The young archivist didn't know that the dowager countess had already made arrangements with another archivist, so that if she were to die, her essence would go to them.'

Jenny stands and slings her bag over her shoulder.

'I know my sister and she didn't want to die. You were there, you saw her wrists. She was trying to escape. Someone made her do that. Someone like you. They tricked her somehow and forced her to commit suicide. Then just like the story, they stole the essence from another archivist. I just need to find out who.'

I leave the café by the back entrance and take a side alley to the main road. No one is paying attention to me; instead they focus on a cluster of police cars and ambulances. A bus has swerved to avoid someone and mounted the kerb, crashing into a betting shop.

The police struggle to contain the gathering crowd. People have their phones out, photographing, filming, streaming. Someone tries to take a selfie with the scene of the incident behind them and gets punched in the face.

I stand at the back and watch the crowd shiver as people pull their coats tighter around themselves, look at each other like maybe they shouldn't be here and slowly move away, until the space in front of me clears and I see Maeve lying in the middle of the road. A flash of compassion catches me by surprise and I take a step forward, ready to take the essence, but I am too late. Maeve has already left her body and escaped into the Aether.

I slide my hands into my pockets and take a single step backwards before turning to leave.

If physical location and temporal proximity were of any consequence to the Aether, then I could convince myself that facets from Maeve's essence had joined with David's, and that one day a child will be born that contains a little of each of them.

But the Aether does not care for these things. Death remains indifferent beyond the end.

14

'We shouldn't eat in the library,' Laure says, 'being the new girls makes us weird enough.'

'We're not here to eat. We're here to research,' I say.

'You know that makes it worse, right?'

'Why do you care?'

Laure shrugs. 'I've made friends here. I'd like to keep them.'

'What about your old friends?'

'I can't talk to them, remember?'

'But that's not forever,' I say. 'Just until things calm down and it's the two of us again. After that, you can forget all about this place and the weird creatures that inhabit it.'

'It'll be too late by then. They already know I'm ghosting them.'

'You'll be fine,' I say. I want to tell her not to even check her old phone, but she's only twelve and has been through a lot.

I study the picture Laure has just handed me, searching for a familiar face in the mass. They're not there. I slide the picture across the table, back to Laure. 'Try Year Eight from last year,' I say. 'She might have been older than she looked.'

Laure climbs onto the table to reach the pictures mounted

high on the wall and removes the one of Year Eight. The library regulars watch. A couple mutter something. One records us with her phone.

I take the picture and scan the rows. Fourth row, a third of the way in. She wasn't looking at the camera, so I only get the side of her face. There's a list of names at the bottom and after checking a few times I have hers: Claire Montgomery. I google her on my phone and there she is. She committed suicide on the twelfth of September by slitting her wrists in the bath.

'Her,' I say to Laure. 'She spoke to me last week.'

Laure leans over my shoulder to read the article. 'She died two months ago.'

'That's my point!'

'What? That you saw a ghost?'

Someone shushes us.

'No, I saw a dead girl. Different. She said there was an archivist in the school. But it was her. *She* was the archivist, projecting the face of Claire Montgomery.'

Laure sits next to me. 'This girl?' she asks, pointing to Claire.

'Yeah. Only she was in a wheelchair. I've checked online and she didn't look disabled. In most pictures she was standing and there's even one of her on a trampoline.'

'Maybe she has a disabled twin,' Laure says.

'More likely she fell off the trampoline.'

'Are you even sure it's her? It could have just been someone who looked like her.'

'I'm certain.'

'I dunno,' Laure says. 'She's so small and grainy in that picture, she could be anyone.'

'Don't you see?' I say. 'This is why we're here. That old woman knew there was another archivist in the school and sent us in to make contact or something. Maybe they're supposed to join forces, or we've got to tie knives to their feet and force them to fight. What do you think?'

'I think you need to make some friends.'

'I don't need the distraction. This is important.'

'No, it's not,' Laure says. 'It's paranoia.'

I shake my head. 'You're so naïve.'

I expect Laure to laugh it off, but when I look over she's annoyed. It's an emotion that sits poorly on her beautiful face.

'I'm not naïve.'

'You're twelve, you don't know—'

'Anything? I don't get you, Kim. It's like you refuse to be happy. Why can't you enjoy yourself without creating conspiracy theories?'

'I'm not creating anything.'

'Oh, really? You always find something wrong with everything. I like it here. It's a good school. I have friends. Great friends. I've only just met them, but it feels like I've known them for years. Only, I'm not going to keep them with my crazy sister going around talking about ghosts.'

'She wasn't a ghost. She was an archivist.'

'So? What's the difference?'

'Archivists are real.'

Laure stands up. 'I love you, Kim.' She pauses, then whispers, 'Sun. But you kinda make my life hard sometimes.'

'I look out for you!' I'm nearly shouting. 'It's all I ever do.'

'I know. It's just...' She sits back down and takes my hand. 'Not everyone is your enemy.'

'It only takes one, Laure.'

She lets the comment slide.

'You never talk about Richard.'

'He's dead,' I say. 'There's nothing to talk about.'

'Hmm.' Her gaze holds wisdom beyond her age, but then

she's always been like that. Our mum said Laure had an old soul. I used to believe that until I met the Archivist and learnt there's no such thing as a soul. At least, not how I used to think of it.

'Laure...'

I want to tell her, but I can't. I can't even say I'll tell her another day because that's as good as telling her. I couldn't bear for her to know what Richard made me do. It would change things. She'd treat me differently because she'd be ashamed of me. And then she'd realise why I did it and feel guilty because it was all to keep her safe. It wouldn't be fair for her to know.

I pull my hand out of hers.

'Look, I'm not going to embarrass you in front of your new friends.'

Laure looks away. 'You already have.'

'What? No I fucking haven't.'

Someone clears their throat.

'You might want to get that looked at,' I shout, smiling, expecting Laure to be smiling with me, only she's not.

'What? That was funny.'

'Everyone knows what you say about the girls here.'

'And what do I say?'

'That they're stuck up,' Laure says. 'And stupid, and vapid, and that they'd never last a day in our old school.'

'Well, they wouldn't...'

'See!'

'Fine,' I say. 'I promise to be nicer from now on.'

And I mean it, I really do, it's just that at that exact moment Katie Merriweather walks into the library, clocks me, and, 'Not this cunt,' falls from my mouth.

Laure moves away from me, the legs of her chair scraping unpleasantly over the floor.

131

'So I get a message about some commotion in the library and who should I find but my newest favourite pupils.' Katie sits on the edge of the table. 'I hope you're not bothering anyone, Kim.'

'They don't appear to be struggling with their sandwiches,' I say.

Katie takes in the room and every pair of eyes looks elsewhere.

'Not eating?'

I shake my head.

'Good,' Katie says. 'You've only just arrived, so the last thing you want to do is eat in the library like these sad fucks.' She leans across the table and picks up the Year Eight picture. 'Interested in this one, I take it,' she says, tapping her nail against Claire's face. She hops off the edge of the table and hangs the picture back on the wall.

'Doesn't it bother you?' I ask.

'That Claire killed herself? No. She was suffering, so by ending her life the total amount of suffering in the world was reduced.'

'That's incredibly callous,' I say.

'I just view these things from a different perspective, Kim. Come, your presence has been requested.'

Katie takes my hand and pulls me off the chair.

'Do I have to?'

'Causing a disturbance in the library warrants a detention.'

'Of course it does. Fine, I'll come.'

I'm dragged away before I can say anything meaningful to Laure. I don't know what's worse, being hateful or Laure thinking I'm hateful. She's my sister, so I just assume she sees through all the walls I project and knows the real me. But what if there is no real me and all I am is arsehole wall inside arsehole wall? Or maybe there is a real me, but all the walls have jumbled up and she's trapped inside a maze she can never escape.

And what if she's a bitch?

I do the things I do because that's what needs doing. I never think about how I come across or if the way I act reflects who I am because I don't know who that is. I leave it for everyone else to define me.

And Laure just did. And it's not good.

This is the beginning of something. Laure, the younger sister, always so in awe of me. Is it too much to ask to keep her that way? Not in every aspect. I love her as a person as well as a sister and want to see her grow to become successful and happy and loved. But that part of her that has always looked up to me, always loved me with the desperation of a young child, can that not stay the same? Even when she's twenty or thirty, can that bit of Laure that makes her my little sister continue to flower?

Because if it doesn't then this beginning will only grow into a void neither of us can enter and she will be in her life with its popularity and socialising and I will be in mine with whatever scraps of mediocre pleasures I'm tossed.

'Another tour, is it?' I ask.

Katie shakes her head and pulls me into a corridor just off the courtyard. I'm led through doors that look as if they should be locked and rooms long abandoned. Wooden boards cover every window, and the only light comes from Katie's phone.

She still hasn't let go of my hand and I'm pulled faster than I can comfortably walk. Dust covers the floor, and we follow a track of scuff marks and footprints. It leads forwards only, not into the numerous rooms we pass, their dust pristine like a morning blanket of snow.

'Are you happy, Kim?'

The corridor turns left. More untouched rooms. Light breaks through cracks in the wooden shutters and shafts of sunlight slice the mote-saturated air.

'I've not really thought about it.'

'Happiness is a tiny bluebird nestled in your hands. You cling to it, cupping its delicate body so it has just enough room for breath. You can tell it is there because you hear it sing and feel its tiny beak peck your palms. On quiet days you are reassured by its presence, but as the world around you grows more chaotic, the song of the bluebird fails to reach you. You no longer know if it is still there. You have to see it to be sure. So you look, carefully opening your hands, nothing more than a crack, to check on your bluebird of happiness. But that crack is enough for it to escape. Gone. Fled from you through curiosity's fissure. Repulsed by your doubt, it couldn't stand to be in your presence for a moment longer. It will fly to a new home, a young child, a baby, someone who has yet to have happiness bestowed upon them. The bluebird will settle there and memories of you it will forget as it basks in the warmth and reassurance of someone who deserves it. And so you are left without the bluebird, without happiness.'

'Next time I'll just say yes.'

Katie takes me to a hall. There's a stage at the front, empty except for a chair and two Roman candles. Red curtains hang on either side, their colour dulled by age. The boards have been stripped from the windows and piled along a wall. Against the other side of the room are rolls of rugs and carpets. The stench of mould is everywhere. I hold my sleeve over my mouth.

'What is this place?' I ask, my voice muffled.

Katie taps her chin with a single, slender finger. 'If you had paid attention, you would know.'

'Fine, don't tell me.'

Katie takes my elbows in her hands. 'I will tell you again, it is no problem. You would be mistaken if you thought this was the oldest part of the school, Kim, left to fester as newer buildings sprouted around it. But no, what we're in is new. Built when the school believed it would rehome pupils from the failing Crestwald Boys, this extension was constructed quickly and at relatively little cost. It was designed to be a school within a school so that the girls and boys could not mix. Such a thing would not be becoming of a Greenfield Girl!

'As it transpired, Crestwald Boys was saved from insolvency and everything around you was surplus to requirements. Not considered good enough for us girls and because of the construction materials, too expensive to demolish, it was left to rot.'

I walk around the hall, peering through the windows, many of them missing panes where the wood has expanded and cracked the glass.

'Why can't I see it from outside?'

'Have you ever been in 23 Leinster Gardens, or 58 Joralemon Street? Perhaps you've visited 145 rue La Fayette?'

'I've heard of the first one. It's that fake address in London, the one that hides the Underground.'

'The other two are no different. What you're standing in is hidden by building facades.'

I shouldn't be surprised; the entire school seems obsessed with appearances, so why should the buildings be any different?

'Does that conclude the tour?'

Katie laughs. 'This isn't part of the tour. Any student caught here faces immediate expulsion.'

Already convinced that this is a stupid ploy to get me expelled, I ask, 'So why am I here?'

'To meet *her*.'

While I wasn't looking someone walked onto the stage and now sits front and centre between the two Roman candles, now lit. She wears a Day of the Dead sugar skull mask decorated with tiny emerald jade stones that outline her eye sockets and define intricate patterns across her forehead. Around her cheeks and down to her chin, the stones slowly change from emerald to sapphire then violet jade to form patterns of flowers and hearts. Larger stones are shaped into teeth and above the forehead are three large roses, their petals light green.

'Jesus fucking Christ, what is wrong with this school?' I mutter, though apparently not quietly enough because Katie pierces me with an icy stare.

'You must be Kimberley Hastings,' the girl wearing the mask says. 'I've heard so much about you.'

'All lies,' I say, 'except the true bits.'

The girl jumps down, her skirt billowing around slender thighs. She lands softly and tilts forward, dancing like a swan until she is in front of me.

'Do you know who I am?'

'The school's resident mentalist?'

'I am *the Archivist.*'

I feel an excited chill consume my skin. Can't stop my smile. Vindication, so rare a feeling, is mine. She stands so close I could reach out and touch her, but strangely I feel nothing of the dread a person experiences from being in their presence. I look to Katie for confirmation, but she doesn't react. Her eyes flash, telling me to pay attention.

'You see, Kim, what I do is help the Greenfield Girls.' She backs away *en pointe* before performing a twirl and dancing around the hall. 'Girls come to me, Kim. Girls who carry so much pain you can't even imagine. Girls like you, Kim. I can see it, coiled inside your essence, constricting your potential, crushing your happiness. I can free you of it, Kim. All of it. Just pull it out and offer it to the Aether. Memories, feelings, thoughts, fears, I can pluck them from inside you like a hair from your head and toss them into the Aether where they will never bother you again.'

She dances, her arms held perfectly straight as she lands a jump and transitions into a leg raise, appearing to nearly fall before catching herself at the last minute. She stops. Looks at me through the eyes in her skull mask. Blue eyes. I close my own. Her eyes are still blue.

'Take off your mask,' I say.

'If you wish.'

She unfastens the clasp at the back of her head and lowers the mask. Eyes still blue, a long face, pretty. Full lips, the odd mole, small nose. Chestnut brown hair, no piercings in her ears. Her eyebrows have a natural curve to them, no evidence of angry follicles from over-plucking.

I turn to Katie, focus solely on her, but everything is still there. The hair, the eyes, her chin, her cheeks. When I look back, her face is exactly as I remembered.

I reach out and cradle her cheek. She smiles, leans her head into it and takes my hand. She's warm from dancing, but not clammy. There's something reassuring in that touch. I pull away, not feeling the despair I experienced with *him*.

'What's going on?' I say to Katie.

'I'm introducing you to The Greenfield Archivist.'

The girl in front of me curtseys.

'No, you're not. You're introducing me to a girl who wears a mask and dances. She isn't the Archivist. Where's the real one?'

'I'm not the Archivist?' the girl asks.

'You know what you are, Victoria,' Katie says.

'Archivists don't have names,' I say. 'Or faces you can remember. And when you go near them, you feel death creeping over you like a cold mist. You have none of that. You're just some girl.'

'Oh,' Victoria says, her shoulders slumping.

'I mean, I guess you're quite good at dancing.'

She perks up. 'Thank you! Though I could have sworn I was an archivist, couldn't you, Katie?'

'We all agreed.'

'Well,' Victoria says, holding out her hands. 'These things can't be helped.'

There's a noise from the stage. Movement. Something falls from the lighting rig. A scream. It stops. Jerks. Swings.

I run to the stage but struggle to get up and eventually use the steps at the side. A pair of white legs writhe frantically. I jump in the hope I can push her up but she kicks my hand. One of my fingers bends backwards. I swear and run to get something I can drag over and climb up. I find a chair, place it under her and stand on it. I grab her feet, though it's like trying to catch fish with bare hands.

I have her, but when I push up her knees bend so the weight of her body's still on her neck, crushing it, killing her.

'Help me!' I shout to Victoria and Katie. Neither of them move, watching me with queer fascination.

'Give up, Kim. This is what she wants,' Katie says, stroking one of her black bands.

I look to Victoria. She shrugs. 'I'm not a real archivist, remember. There's nothing *I* could do.'

I'm not doing anything here and run to the side of the stage. I find some ropes and start pulling randomly because there's nothing else I can think to do. Scenery falls over and an entire lighting rig swings loose and crashes into the wall. But she's still there, legs still swinging, but getting slower.

Then I have it: the rope for the rig she's hanging from. I try to lower her gently, but she's too heavy and the rope burns through my hands. I sprint across the stage to catch her but I'm too late and she lands with a sickening crunch.

I pull the rope from around her head and massage her neck as if I can magically pop her crushed throat back into shape. If I had a pen, I could jab it in her neck, but I've only ever seen that on TV and with the amount of adrenalin surging through my body, I'd probably stab it straight through to the other side.

I check her pulse; at least that I know how to do. It's still there, but only just. I brush aside a lock of black hair from off her face. It's Sophia Ray, the girl who had it out with Mr Cavendish.

'She's still alive,' I shout.

Katie looks at Victoria, mouths 'shame' and they both turn and leave.

I check my phone. No reception. Sophia manages a breath. It sounds painful, like she might not make the same mistake again.

I struggle to pick her up. She might be light, but I'm far from strong. I could probably get her off the stage, maybe even out of the hall, but no further.

'Help!' I scream. All I hear in response is my frightened echo. Katie and Victoria have left. They set this up not to show me an archivist, but to make me witness a death.

I feel cold. Alone. Scared in a way I thought only Richard could make me feel. I look down at the silver thread that extends from my chest, wrap my hands around it and pull as hard as I can. I hope that does something.

I hope he feels it.

I hope he comes.

The porter's lodge is visible through an arch built into the limestone wall. I walk past the empty waiting area; no one appears to question who I am or why I am here.

The Greenfield opens before me. A wide gravel path that cuts through manicured lawns leads to an imposing building of white stone and large windows in thick wooden frames. I risk a look back, expecting to have been followed, but the archway reveals only the woods on the far side of the road.

The sensation comes again, pulling at my essence like the lurch from a sudden drop. I've returned the favour, but that will have told her nothing beyond my recognition. She expects me to drop everything and come to her aid. That I am doing so will appear to be luck on her part. A potential lost client, reputational damage, a taxi driver that will spend the rest of her life in a nightmare world every time her eyes close; these are the things that Sun will never know of.

Like the porter's lodge, the entrance to the white building is empty. I stop, the soles of my shoes issuing an unwarranted squeak. I can't hear any people. Even a building as old as this one, with its walls as thick as the height of a small child, should allow some sound to escape. There is nothing but the ticking of the antique clock that stands in the foyer.

I walk through empty corridors, across a deserted courtyard and past rooms with shut doors. The thread remains ahead of me, pulling me through the solitude. Another tug, this one more forceful, as if annoyed at my lack of appearance. It's the only proof I'm not alone in this school. The jarring of my essence is almost reassuring.

My way is blocked. The thread leads to a dead end. I move to the left and the angle of the thread changes. I try right and it swings back the other way. Sun is on the other side of this wall.

I hear a knock. She will have seen the thread move and know I am close. There's a muffled voice, nothing clear enough to discern.

The wall drops away. I can see essences behind it. One is Sun's, tightly bound to her, the facets that protrude from her chest joined to me. There is another person with her, but the essence is more nebulous, so it's unclear exactly where the body is. Sun appears as a jumble of iridescent threads woven into the shape of a girl. Her arms, her hands, even her fingers are perfectly clear. She looks to be stroking something. Her hand glides through the facets that billow from her lap and surround her in a cloud.

I know the signs of a body destroyed by its host. This girl has attempted suicide.

Sun and the girl vanish as the wall reappears. I see no hidden doors that will take me through the end of the corridor and double back on myself when I feel her pull the thread twice.

I stop.

She pulls it again. Only once.

Once for yes. Twice for no. I don't need to return down the corridor. If I had foreseen this situation, we would have learnt

Morse code. Everyone expects instant connection via their phones. As soon as there's no signal, we don't know what to do.

I go left. Two pulls. I stop, go right. One pull. I can't go back and I can't go through the wall. There's a door on the right side of the corridor. I presume it's a classroom. I go through it and feel a reassuring single pull. She's deducing my location based on the angle at which the thread extends from her solar plexus. I'm impressed.

The room is empty save for the usual desks and chairs. Windows are directly opposite me and I shiver at the thought of having to climb out one.

I approach. No response. I flip a catch at the top and throw open the sash window.

Then it comes. Two pulls. Not through the window.

The only other possibility appears to be a stationery cupboard at the end of the room. I walk towards it and receive a single tug in response.

Opening the door, it doesn't take me long to find a panel built into the back. I crawl into a second cupboard in an adjoining classroom, only this one is bare. Wooden boards are nailed over the windows and every surface is coated with thick drifts of dust.

'Sun?'

'Here,' she calls. I follow tracks in the dust that lead out of the classroom and take me to Sun, sat against the corridor's dead end with a dying girl in her lap.

She looks at me, her icy blue eyes rimmed red from crying. 'I didn't know what to do,' she says. 'My phone had no reception and I couldn't carry her any further.'

Back along the corridor there are tracks in the dust where a body has been dragged.

The closer Sun and I are, the stronger the link between us. Only a few metres apart, the facets wind themselves into a thread as thick as a finger. It passes through the essence of the other girl, catching the facets that have prematurely detached from her body.

I stand behind Sun, trailing the thread so it passes through her and emerges between her shoulder blades.

'Her facets were—'

'I saw,' Sun says. She sighs. 'I can't carry her and if you touch her, she's dead. We don't make a very good team.'

'She hanged herself,' I say.

Sun nods. It's clear from the bruising around the girl's neck, clearer still when you can see the damage to her essence. Considering the progression of events, it was inevitable I would deal with the aftermath of a hanging. The build, the natural curl of the hair, the large eyes beneath full eyebrows; that this girl chose a rope to end her life was not a coincidence. Someone knows my secret.

'I thought about stabbing her in the neck, to help her breathe.'

'She doesn't need a tracheostomy. The pressure from the rope has constricted her carotid artery. If the neck remains unbroken, the most common cause of death from hanging is cerebral hypoxia, a lack of oxygen to the brain.'

'Not your first?'

I don't answer.

Red tracks line the girl's face around her eyes and across her cheeks. With nowhere to go, the blood has burst the capillaries beneath her skin, giving her the weathered features of someone many times her age. I peer inside to see the regions of her brain that are already dead and those that barely hang on.

'What should we—'

'Find help. Call an ambulance. She isn't going to die.'

Sun nods and gently lays the girl down. She runs through the classroom door without a word and I watch as the thread cuts into the walls of the corridor until it aligns with the dead

143

end. Several more of the girl's facets desperately reach for it. I stand aside, pulling the thread away and leaving the facets to drown in the Aether.

It is dark. Oppressively quiet. I step away from the girl and sit on the floor with my legs crossed. The dust clings to my black trousers. I can't think when I last sat like this. Maybe when I was twelve.

I flick from looking at the girl, lying with her face turned away from me at the end of a dim hallway, to watching her essence dancing above her like a sea anemone. She remains rooted in her body. The facets around her organs and extremities are tight and there is enough of her woven through the brain to keep her alive.

The facets sway, enraptured by the turbulent currents of the Aether. The memories or feelings they contain hidden from me. With the ability to unravel them, I would discover a person I do not know. Similarities, whether arising through orchestration or happenstance, are only that. She is not her, even though every glance convinces my brain she is, and saving her life will not bring the dead back with the living. No matter how much I want it.

The Aether has never cared for these things.

I regard the girl as a stranger as best I can and think. Perhaps she was not alone in concluding death was the answer. Then a bigger question comes to mind: who interfered in her fate? Had they formed a suicide pact? And if so, what could be gained from the death of a teenage girl?

Beyond those musings, balanced atop a pyramid of uncertainty, there is only one question I desperately need the answer to: is this the work of another archivist?

Something in the girl's essence changes. Facets coiled into her fingers and toes have escaped and float outside of her body. I take a step closer and her essence dances towards me.

She is being teased apart. A thick facet, much longer than she is tall, is ripped from inside her thigh. It remains joined to her hip and shimmers in silver, the other end brushing against the ceiling. I take another step closer. It reacts, but does not seek me. The girl is unwinding.

I hear laughter.

There are footsteps from the far end of the corridor. I move away from the girl and follow the sound. The darkness increases with every step, but ahead of me there is a sense of light. Cut through it is the silhouette of a person. Still too far away to see, I focus on their essence, expecting it to leap out against the blackness.

There is nothing.

The corridor again. The silhouette moves. Raises a hand and waves. Again, the walls, floor and ceiling dissolve to reveal nothing but the Aether. There is no collection of facets woven into the shape of a person, only black. I look behind and the girl is still there, glowing in the darkness.

When I check again, there is no silhouette at the end of the corridor, only emptiness and the promise of a person caused by tricks of the light. If I focus, I can create a figure from the shadows that cling to the dimness, but it does not match my memory.

There was someone at the end of the corridor. Someone whose essence I couldn't see.

'Archivist? Where are you?'

The light from Sun's phone pulls me back and I return to her and the dying girl.

'What were you doing?' she asks.

I recheck the corridor. 'It doesn't matter.' I look beyond Sun. 'You didn't bring help.'

'There's no one. It's like the entire school's gone. Then when I found a working phone and called an ambulance, they said they wouldn't be able to get here for another hour. Something about a motorway crash. I even tried calling Laure, but it just kept ringing.'

I watch as the girl's essence unravels. The process of death, of the separation of the essence from the body, has begun and no intervention can stop it.

'No one will come.'

Sun has taken the girl's hand and moved her head to rest on her lap. 'Why?'

'This girl is for me.'

'Why would she be—'

'She is my third suicide.'

Sun looks up, holding the girl's hand and stroking her hair.

'Someone wants me to take her essence, but once I have her, she will be claimed by another.'

'Another archivist?'

'If they have already entered into an arrangement, the essence will travel to the other archivist, even if I am the one to pull it from her body.'

'You think we should leave her?' Sun says, accusing me.

'If an arrangement has been made, then her essence will travel to the other archivist just as yours did to me.'

'But you can't know that. I'm the one who called you here. Don't you trust me?'

'You never explained how you found her.'

Sun focuses on the girl, checks her pulse. She brings out her phone. Still no signal.

'I was in the library and this girl came over, started talking about the school and how it has its own archivist. Something was off about her, so I looked her up. A year nine called Claire Montgomery. She killed herself two months ago. Apparently it's a big deal and the parents are trying to sue anyone they can. So I believed her, about the school having an archivist, because that must have been her. It's not like you're that rare, right? But when I'm taken to meet her, she's not an archivist. I remembered her face, there was no aura of dread, I even touched her skin. Just a normal girl.'

'Was she there when you found her?'

'She jumped while we were talking,' Sun says as she nods towards the girl. 'Like she was waiting for us. I think someone pushed her.'

'Did you see anyone?'

'No. It's just the way she fought. I don't think she wanted to die.'

I watch as another clump of facets dislodge from the girl's forearm. Someone is raking their claws through her.

'You were right,' I say. 'There is another archivist.'

'It just wasn't her?'

I nod.

Sun looks lost, stares at the girl on her lap and pulls a face. She might not see the facets leaving her body, but she can tell something is wrong. 'So, what now?'

If she had not hanged herself, if her features were not so familiar, if refusing the bait was an option, I would leave her. Another archivist was only a suspicion until Sun met a girl whose essence I separated from its body two months ago. With that confirmed, the fate of this girl is immune to my futile ministrations.

But I will not leave her to die alone. And, of greater importance, I will not let her be taken from me again.

I step towards the girl and the facets that rise from her body wrap themselves around me. I gather them, coiling a ball in my hands as I bend down and my forehead touches hers.

'Release the life you hold so tight; welcome me and leave the light.'

Her essence slips through me as soon as I have her. She escapes in streamers through my chest and bursts into the corridor. Everything vanishes until there is only the Aether and the essence of the girl.

I run.

Sun is quick to follow. I feel her hand around my arm and desperately try to ignore the alien sensation when I lurch to the side. I look back to see there's a hole in the floor. All I can see is the essence of the girl, charging through the corridor as the other archivist reels in the remains of a life that is rightfully theirs.

'Thank you,' I say, then I am running again. Sun's hand is in mine, pulling my focus from the fleeing essence.

I free myself from Sun's grip. 'It's not that... I just, I can't focus if you...'

'Oh.' Sun takes my sleeve and once more my surroundings disappear and I chase a girl whose body grows cold in a forgotten school corridor.

My elbow catches the edge of something solid and messages of pain fire up my arm. Sun apologises but it happens again, only this time it's my shin. I feel her weight on the sleeve of my jacket. She shouts at me to stop. Her legs are not as long as mine. This is repeated with increasing volume until she resorts to her usual mode of communication and swears at me.

The essence is ahead, weaving through the school. A lure designed to lead or taunt? As the distance grows, I know it to be the latter.

I run blind, Sun reduced to cursing ballast. Only interested in the chase, the essence concludes its flirtations and leaves.

Sun shouts. Her fingers take my hand and with her fingernails she attacks my skin. I stop.

'She's gone,' Sun says.

My vision flips and we are outside, a solid wall before us. The sound of an opening door causes both Sun and I to turn. Hundreds of pupils and staff stream from the building, talking and laughing as they appear to make their way from one lesson to another. The sirens of an ambulance can be heard in the distance and inside Sun's pocket, her phone vibrates as message after message drops into her inbox.

Sun, desperate for breath, leans against me. 'Let's not read anything into this.'

16

A car drives past, shit music obnoxiously loud. The wheels catch a puddle and a wave of muddy water leaps from the road.

His movements are imperceptible. The water that should have sprayed across his trousers completely misses and instead washes over my feet.

He looks down at my soaked trainers. 'You need new shoes.'

'It's only water,' I say. 'They'll dry.'

'They're old. Your clothes too. They're full of holes.'

'Nothing's wrong with them.'

He makes a thoughtful sound, shakes his head and keeps walking. I jog to catch up. It's still raining and he's the one with the umbrella.

'Should I give you money?'

'What for?'

'Clothes. For you and Laure.'

'You don't have to buy us clothes.'

'Someone needs to.'

'I'll get a part-time job,' I say.

'Why? I have more money than I can spend.'

'Then I'll pay you back.'

He laughs to himself. 'No, you won't.'

It's past ten. Laure is alone in the flat, probably half-watching a movie while messaging her new friends. Since the library, some unspoken entity has forced its way between us. It feeds off this mutual disapproval that never used to be there and its expanding gut pushes us further apart. I still love her; it's just everything else that's changed.

I told her I was going out with the Archivist and she shrugged as if that would work just fine for her. As for *where* I'm going, I have no idea. The weather sucks and every time I complain about it he remains stoic, as if the rain wouldn't dare bother him.

Though, despite my complaints, I can appreciate the pleasure of being out in the rain. There's something special about sharing an umbrella. Not romantic, exactly. Maybe companionable; almost like we're friends, huddled together beneath a meagre shelter. The thread that ties us is the only light in the darkness aside from occasional streetlamps or car headlights. It grows thicker the closer we are, brighter too, and stretches from the middle of my chest into his. I hold my hand in front of it, but the light from the thread doesn't illuminate my palm like it's supposed to. The Archivist explained that it's because the thread doesn't exist in the physical world. It belongs to the Aether and the only reason I can see it is because of the link we share.

I shove my hand into my jacket pocket as I sidestep a puddle. A few fingers poke through the lining and into the padding and find a loose coin and a sweet wrapper that's still sticky. New clothes would be nice.

'I never said thank you for getting us into the school,' I say.

'Even though it was a trap?'

'Yeah, even though it was obviously a trap. But you knew that, right?'

151

'Someone wanted you there and I was curious as to why.'

'And I suppose us living with you rent-free meant you had no concerns about throwing us to the lions.'

'None whatsoever.'

A fight at the entrance to a kebab shop. An impossible number of people spill into the street, half of them holding food or cans of beer, the other half swinging drunken punches. It's not even ten, far too early for shit like this on a Wednesday.

Someone has a bloody nose and sits against the shop's glass front, trying to hold back the blood as it streams down his chin and soaks into his white T-shirt. Some guy's girlfriend is in the face of the shop owner. She's screaming at him, calling him a pussy, but doesn't make any moves to hit him. He's a big guy, at least three times her age and size, and has the look of a man who's seen this all before.

I take the Archivist's elbow, feel him flinch, and try to lead him to the other side of the road before we're seen.

He looks at me. Smiling, he shakes his head and walks straight for the fight. A beer bottle is thrown across the street and smashes into the side of a bus. The bus, illuminated like a new day, wastes no time driving off.

The Archivist pulls his arm in, pressing my hand against his side to feel his warmth.

We've been noticed. Heads are raised and we're being asked what the fuck we're looking at and if we fucking want some of this. Questions I've never known the right answers to.

His pace doesn't slow even though mine falters and I half trip over my feet. I've met enough drunk men in their twenties to know it's best to do everything to avoid them. Even when we lived in the flat, where Richard's name was protection enough as he was the one who kept the police away, there were always a few who'd try to start something.

Someone throws a half-full bottle of beer at the Archivist's feet and it explodes on the pavement. I feel myself pull him back, but he squeezes my hand against his side even harder as his now ruined handmade cordovan brogues trample the shattered glass. The person who threw the bottle comes forward, hand reaching behind to take something tucked into the waist of his trousers.

He stops moving and the Archivist and I walk right past him until we are in the middle of what had, until a few seconds ago, been a fight and is now a group of people staring at the floor.

The rain continues and the discarded naan breads swell and disintegrate, spilling their spiced doner meat and pickled chillies.

Someone cries. Other voices soon join. It isn't long before everyone is on the floor, either kneeling or on their side with their knees to their chest. The girlfriend who was shouting at the shop owner has her face against the pavement. Her lips are nearly fully submerged in a puddle and she's pleading to God to let her die.

I peer inside the shop. Everyone is on the floor or hunched over tables with their head in their arms.

I leave the Archivist and make for the guy who threw the bottle. The knife he had been pulling from his trousers fell from his hand as we approached and I pick it up. I check a few other people and find some more weapons. I drop the lot down the drain.

I return to the Archivist and take his arm. He's concentrating. Much of what he does, which the connection we share protects me from, occurs naturally, but to affect so many people like this, and so deeply, requires effort.

'Why?' I ask.

'I thought I would enjoy it. And I was right, I do. Very much.' He walks over to the one who threw a bottle at his now-ruined shoes and rests his foot on the man's forehead. 'He thinks he is strong because he believes the fear he instils in others is enough to protect him.' I watch as the muddied sole of the Archivist's shoe slides down the man's cheek and into his open mouth, brushing against his teeth. 'I don't like people like him.'

'Is that why we're out, to fight crime?'

'No,' he says. 'This was just an opportunity to try something.'

'And are you satisfied?'

He looks around. Those who are still conscious haven't stopped screaming and crying and begging for death. 'Yes,' he says. 'Very.'

'So why are we out?'

'We're going there.'

He points to an old building standing stubbornly between a tanning salon and a six-storey office block. I have been down this road before, it's the fastest way to get from the bus station to the middle of town, but I have never noticed this building.

Behind me a man in a bright orange puffer jacket vomits and a girl weeps hysterically as she pulls her hair. Blue lights reflect off a glass-fronted building further down the road and a siren sounds briefly, announcing the police presence as if to give everyone the chance to flee and them an easy night.

We look at each other and, without a word spoken, leave the takeaway and make for the old building.

Everyone recovers surprisingly fast, as I did myself the first time I experienced the oncoming of death in that hospital waiting room. They're soon standing, shouting about the state of their clothes and food. From the snatches of conversation that reach me, it seems the experience caused more than one of them to shit themselves.

I think it's a church. The symbol above the door isn't one I recognise though: a collection of threads in the rough shape of a person. I'm not stupid enough to not know what it means.

It's not been well looked after. The short path from the road is cracked and covered in weeds that grow as high as my knees. The building's in a bad way too; bricks are missing and more window frames hold wooden boards than glass.

'I didn't know you had your own church.'

'Most saw Archivism as a business, not a religion. There was opposition when the church formed, but that didn't slow its popularity. Then when the number of archivists declined, so did interest in the religion. There are only a few of the churches left, the rest were demolished or developed into luxury flats.'

He pulls a key from under a stone and uses it to unlock a small box on the side of the door. From there he removes another key, and he walks halfway down the path and digs up a small chest that contains another key, this one long and old-looking. I expect that to be the door key, but he removes a brick from the wall and slides the key into the hole. He turns it and I hear a click. A small door swings open and out comes another key.

'It's a good job it's not raining,' I say. I've got the umbrella now, leaving him to get wet.

'Not my arrangement,' he says, two keys in hand.

'Isn't it your church?'

'It's a church that worships me, but it isn't mine.'

'What's it liked being worshipped?'

'Tedious.' He puts the two keys into the door and turns them in different directions.

The door swings open and I collapse the umbrella and give it a good shake. There's a small porch where a pair of indoor shoes wait for him. He takes off his own and slips them on.

'What about me?'

'Are your socks wet?'

'Yes.'

'Then you should take them off too.'

I follow him, my bare feet leaving moist footprints on the freezing flagstones of the porch. There's a door ahead of us and he knocks on it lightly before opening it.

'Antoinette, it's me.'

The Archivist's voice is soft, never raised, and exudes a quiet confidence that would take any normal person a lifetime to master. It is a voice of certainty and reassurance, but one thing that it is not is a voice of warmth.

Except for those three words.

Antoinette, it's me. The depth of meaning in the way he spoke those words reveals something about him I never thought possible. His voice was lighter, almost playful, with the accompaniment of unuttered laughter. Whoever Antoinette is, she's important to him.

I dwell on our shared time beneath the umbrella and feel like an idiot.

A thin woman in her sixties wearing a bright yellow saree appears from behind a corner. Her head is shaved, leaving her with white fuzz over her scalp. She wears earrings that are too heavy and stretch her lobes, and a blue scarf that trails along the floor.

'Did something happen to your calendar?' she asks.

'I'm experimenting with spontaneity,' he says with uncharacteristic lightness.

The Archivist steps into the room and places a small box on the table. Antoinette walks up to him, puts her hand on her heart and bows. Her left arm doesn't appear to move, hanging limply by her side.

'More diamonds, I take it?' Antoinette asks, picking up the box.

'Jadeite,' the Archivist says.

'Such a waste of money,' Antoinette scolds. She opens the box and I get a peek at a ring with a large green stone in its centre. 'You know I like my jewellery tacky and cheap. I'm not Eliza Doolittle. But I thank you for the gift, even if it will spend the rest of my life in a drawer. Now, come in.'

The Archivist takes off his coat and hangs it on a peg by the door. The room is warm, a fire burns to one side and everywhere I look there are haphazard piles of books on tables, the floor and the arms of chairs.

I take my coat off and move cautiously towards the fire. The rain was cold and I need the heat, but this is not my domain and Antoinette eyes me with something that is only imitating friendship and feels far from welcoming.

'Sun-young,' he says. 'My ward.'

'Ward?' Antoinette and I say, her with a note of amusement; something I don't match.

'Her sister, Laure, too. They needed a place to stay.'

'Well,' Antoinette says. 'I'm sure that any *ward* of yours is welcome here. Please, make yourselves at home. I'll brew some tea. Oh, and try not to touch the books. It's only ever me here so I tend not to bother marking the pages. Knock one on the floor and I won't have a clue where I'm at.'

Antoinette leaves and the Archivist sits on a two-seater leather sofa in the middle of the room. I go to sit next to him, but he shakes his head.

'She won't like it.'

'I'm not that wet.'

'No. That I don't affect you. That you can... touch me.'

'Oh,' I say and perch on an armchair that has books open on the seat. I'm close to the fire here and turn myself to get more heat before giving up and sitting on the mat in front of the hearth like a cat.

'So what is she, like a priest?'

'She's a historian.'

'Then how come she lives here?'

'Because she can. The church has gone and no one else claimed the building.'

'Is all this stuff from other churches?'

'Yes, stolen mostly.'

I'm not dry, but the fire has warmed me enough for plumes of steam to billow from my wet jeans and I feel like a superhero who's about to transform into their next-level body. I get up and look around the room. Among the statues of archivists, open books and frescos complete with sections of wall, are photographs. Some are in frames, but many of them are stuck to the wall with tack.

I take a while to recognise Antoinette. Possibly ten years younger and with long hair that reaches past her shoulders, dark, not like the grey it would be now if she let it grow. Next to her is a small boy dressed in black shorts and a blue shirt that's buttoned all the way to the collar. They're sitting on a blanket having a picnic. It's a warm day and the sun is in their eyes. Antoinette has a hand up to shield herself. The boy is squinting.

He hasn't changed much. He's taller now, and his face has aged from a boy's to a man's, but it's clearly still him.

'How long have you known her?' I ask.

Completely ignoring what Antoinette said, he's picked up a book from the back of the sofa and is casually leafing through it.

'Since I was eight.'

I leave the picnic photo to look for others. Some are of him as a boy and there are some where he is older. There are photos of others too, people whose faces leave me as soon as I look away. I'd forgotten what that felt like. I look at them again and the face returns, but then as soon as my eyes leave the picture, the memory is whipped away like a tablecloth trick.

I pull a picture off the wall and hold it next to another to look at both at once to see if it's the same archivist, but my mind won't register two of them at the same time.

There's a picture of him again. This time he looks about four. He's sat on a wall with the sea behind him. There's a woman next to him in a blue dress with an uncomfortable scowl on her face. On the other side of her is a man holding a baby. No one looks happy. The baby is crying and the Archivist is looking away from everyone else so that only one side of his face shows.

I want to ask but hold back.

'Yes, that's my family,' he says from the sofa.

'How did you—'

'Antoinette doesn't move the pictures and I can see where you're standing.'

I want to ask more questions, but it doesn't feel right. Everything in this place reminds me how new I am. He had a life before me. Maybe not filled with friends, but still filled with people who know him better and deeper than I do. And what am I to him anyway? A lodger? His ward?

'They're still alive,' he says. 'I don't see them much, but I know where to find them.'

'The baby?'

'My sister, Veronica. She's a year or two younger than you. I've not seen her since we were little.'

'You don't have to talk about it, I'm just your *ward*.'

I think he's about to say something, tell me I'm more than just a teenager who needs a place to crash while she and her sister avoid the police, but of course that's when Antoinette returns carrying a cup of tea with her one working hand.

I take the cup because it seems like the polite thing to do but I've not yet made up my mind on tea. There's not much to it.

'I keep them around to stop myself forgetting,' Antoinette says, nodding towards the pictures.' It doesn't work. Still, it's nice to know I'm never too far from his face.'

I take a sip of the tea. I'm not convinced, but smile anyway. Antoinette and her hawkish eyes see straight through me, which is probably why she says, 'Worth waiting for, wasn't it?' and all I can do is take another sip, smile again and nod like the stupid gimp I am.

'I take it I'm the first girl he's brought over.'

'Not at all,' she's says as she pats me on the shoulder and returns to what I guess must be a kitchen for more tea. Jesus fuck, why must I swagger into conversations with these ridiculous proclamations of importance?

Suddenly, I appreciate the bitterness of the tea and look to him for some kind of follow-up, but he has turned away and I can't tell if he's trying to hide his smile or if it's something else altogether.

Antoinette returns with a cup for him and contemplates sitting on the sofa, but opts for the chair instead. 'So, what's brought you here? Not that I don't appreciate the visit, but you're one for routine and today's date doesn't end in a zero.'

'I want to know if there's another archivist in town.'

Antoinette laughs, her emaciated body shaking beneath her saree. 'What on earth makes you think that?'

'Things have happened. Essences were stolen from me. Only another archivist could do that.'

Antoinette gets up and takes a large leather-bound ledger from a desk. She drops it into the Archivist's lap and settles back into her chair. 'Look for yourself.'

He opens the book and flicks through the pages. I can't see it from where I'm standing, so I move behind him to read over his shoulder. Antoinette catches my eye and frowns.

I lean right over the back of the sofa, my hair brushing against his shoulder. In fine handwriting are lists of dates of birth, places of birth and dates of death. All of those with a completed date-of-death column have a neat line scored through them. As he flicks through the pages, the spaces between the dates of birth grow from days to months to years to decades.

'You're too close,' he whispers.

I back off, try to pretend I feel unwell, but I don't want to put on too much of a performance because suddenly that sense of self-importance I swept into the room with feels deserved.

'I learnt that another two have died since your last visit,' Antoinette says. 'One was over a year ago. She lived in Chile and it took a while for the news to reach me. The other one was in Italy. He made it all the way to ninety-eight. Another two years and I would have crossed him off anyway.'

'Why?' I ask.

I get a look that tells me this is not my home and I should know my place. I go back to the fire and sit on the rug. Antoinette's smile appears warm now, as if her approval of me is related only to my proximity to the Archivist.

'I can't hear of every death and so when a known Archivist reaches 100, I cross them off and assume they're dead. Some may live longer, but not by much. As I'm sure he's told you, his body is as human as mine or yours. It is only his essence that is special.'

'Only twenty-five left,' he says from the sofa.

'And most of them very near death.' She turns to me. 'The one closest to him in age was murdered last year at forty-seven.'

He shuts the book. 'So I'm still the last?'

161

'I'm afraid so. You're also the only one in the entire country. It's conceivable that one of the others may have travelled here, but they are all very wealthy people and I see no reason why they would spend their remaining years stealing essences from a newly realised Archivist. The chance of this being orchestrated by one of them is remote, verging on ridiculous.'

'Just to be clear,' I say. 'There are only twenty-five archivists in the whole world and the next oldest is in their fifties?'

'Sixties,' Antoinette says. 'A Japanese lady.'

I stare at the Archivist, aware that my mouth is hanging open. 'No wonder you're so fucking smug.'

17

Two male police officers, neither of whom reach my shoulder, escort me to the crime scene via a circuitous route to avoid a gathering crowd of forty-year-old men eager for a distraction from their park run. I use the gate to scrape mud from my shoes; another pair ruined.

A hastily erected tent in a children's play area surrounds the central section of a climbing frame. A mother approaches with three children and a baby and an argument with a policewoman quickly ensues. Audible to anyone within five hundred metres, it becomes apparent that if her kids aren't allowed on the swings, there'll be another crime scene. She is more dragged than led away, her children appearing unphased by her expletive-rich ravings and the grotesque detail she includes in her threats of violence.

My escort raps his knuckles on the fabric of the blue and white tent.

'The death bringer's here, best ship out.' The officer smiles at me. 'Everyone gets a nickname.'

'I was hoping for Mr Sunshine,' I say.

Inside the tent a girl lies slumped on the metal base of the climbing frame, her head against a yellow wall scrawled with obscenities. The blue dress she wears rides up and the awkward way her legs stick out is undignified, bordering obscene.

Blood runs from her left eye into the swath smeared across her cheek. The air pistol is on the floor next to a phone. I crouch down. Bloodied thumb prints cover the screen. She must have used it after touching her ruined eye. There's nothing to suggest she was trying to call someone, though it's likely she began to fit before she had the chance.

The tent, climbing frame and body of the girl dissolve.

The airgun propelled the pellet with insufficient force to exit her skull, burying itself through her eye before losing momentum in her brain tissue and causing a frontal lobe haematoma. There's a clear void of facets along the pellet's line of travel, leaving the girl with a slowly spinning well of bright silver threads around her left eye.

Little else appears damaged, bar the signs of old injuries naturally accrued through childhood. Even standing close to her, the facets don't seek me out with any sense of desperation. That her injury was self-inflicted doesn't appear to be in question, and if it was an attempt at suicide, then at the very least it was poorly thought out. Suicide should be decisive, with no margins for error or possibility of survival. Should this girl recover, she would only be blind in one eye with moderate brain damage.

But the circumstances are not different and once more I find myself before a teenage girl who has unsuccessfully attempted to kill herself. That I will, through some possibly convoluted means, be placed in a position to take her essence is a *fait accompli*, along with the fact that her essence will be taken from me only for a collection of facets to remain.

I go to leave but the bloodied phone demands my attention; so too does the feeling that her reaching for it after she shot herself was out of a desire to be saved. The same could be said of Claire's attempts to pull herself free from the handcuffs after slitting her wrists, or Chrissy's pleas for her father after overdosing on insulin, or even Sophia Ray's screams and desperate writhing after hanging herself. None of these suicides were decisive, nor were they attempted without immediate regret.

I leave the tent.

'Why has the girl been left like that? Where is the ambulance?'

'We were told to call only you.'

'By whom?'

My escort looks back to the group gathered by the roundabout, his face a snapshot of confusion. Slowly it dawns on him that they've made a mistake.

'She isn't dead. You need to call an ambulance,' I tell him.

'Yes... fuck! Why didn't we call an ambulance?' he shouts to the group. 'Did any of you call an ambulance?'

They shake their heads. A few point to me before realising the idiocy of their gesture. Whatever I am, supernatural entity, religious deity, fraud, confidence trickster, I should not be the first call made by the police upon discovering a teenage girl who has shot herself in the eye with a pellet gun on a Sunday morning.

They're on their radios, shouting for an ambulance, cursing their stupidity. Some approach the tent, but see me and back away.

They are not at fault. Someone wanted me here. Someone with enough power to pull the strings of the entire police force as if they were marionette puppets.

I return to the girl. There is little change; the deterioration of her essence that I expected hasn't occurred and, so long as the ambulance arrives, my services won't be required.

I handle her carefully, my gloves providing sufficient protection from the attraction of my facets, though a few times I'm forced to pull away as those that have been cut free from the dying portions of her brain seek refuge.

I lay her on her side and already she's breathing more easily now her chin isn't resting against her chest. I pull the hem of her dress down and cover her with my coat. The day's warmth hasn't fully announced itself and the metal of the climbing frame sucks away the girl's heat with voracity.

Someone enters the tent. The entrance is behind me and I wait for the doors to flutter shut in the wake of a hasty retreat. I glimpse the hazy reflection of a person standing in the dull steel of a slide. I admire their fortitude.

'It's been noted that the suicides started at the same time you came to our attention.'

Detective Sergeant Monique Jones waits at the far end of the tent, though that is not an appreciable distance given its confines. The struggle to be near to me is evident from the perspiration that's broken out on her brow and the hand gripping the tent's edge.

I pull my facets away from the extremities of my body, a swarm of wasps between two clasped hands. The relief on Detective Sergeant Jones' face is visible.

'Sadly, correlation does not equal causation,' Jones continues. 'A shame. Would make my job easier.'

Aspects of the girl swing towards me. I duck and step away, forcing Detective Sergeant Jones further into the tent. She checks the girl over and soon realises that a projectile fired into the eye is beyond her police first aid training. Not wishing to do anything to make the situation worse, she tucks my coat under the girl's legs and checks the pulse at her wrist.

'I should apologise for that lot outside,' she says. 'They're scared to believe. It's easier to laugh you off as a clairvoyant with dowsing rods.'

'What do you believe?'

For a long time there's only the sound of Detective Sergeant Jones' breathing.

'I wish I knew,' she says. 'Initially, I was certain you were a fraud. Now I'm not so sure. Just because I can't work out how the trick is performed, doesn't mean it's not a trick.'

'And the girls? Do you believe I'm the reason they're dead?'

Detective Sergeant Jones sits on the metal platform, next to the dying girl. She still struggles in my presence, despite moderate efforts on my part. Though it is true, I could do more to ease her comfort.

'That depends how you view it,' she says. 'Devout followers of religion have committed atrocities in the name of their gods for thousands of years. No one blames the gods.'

'They were still the catalyst.'

Jones presses herself further into the cold steel and, sensing no antagonistic agenda, I pull my essence through me so that it protrudes from my back. She allows herself to sit more comfortably next to the dying girl as we wait for the ambulance. 'Thank you.'

'I am not a god,' I say.

'What you do, or what you claim to do, is not explained by science. So if you're not a god, then what are you?'

'When I was young, I told my father that science couldn't explain archivists. He was quick to correct me. Science couldn't explain archivists *yet*. I made him feel uncomfortable, so he spent more time with my sister than with me. That's why I remember the few meaningful things he said. "Enjoy your mystery," he said, "because it won't last."'

'He sounds smart.'

'He is.'

'I expected you to say was,' Jones says.

'Everyone struggles to imagine me as part of a family.'

'It's like learning that celebrities shit.' Jones slides off the steel platform. 'Though I shouldn't be surprised, considering your family of strays.'

'You'll have to elaborate.'

'Sun-young Kang and Laure Baptiste. Though they go by Kimberly and Florence Hastings to their friends at The Greenfield. Officially still missing.'

'I wondered why you were enduring my presence for so long.'

I allow my essence to flow into its home. Jones scowls and uses the metal railings of the climbing frame for support.

'None of what I've told you is on record; the result of some private detective work.'

'And your demand?'

'No demand. I want you to know I know and... to be mindful of your actions.'

'Then what do you want from me?'

'Nothing.' Jones crosses her arms over her chest and thinks better of it. 'I didn't know you could detect cancer.'

'I only suspected. I can see when something is wrong; the cause of the wrongness is not always clear.'

'In that case I've spoilt the surprise. I've already begun treatment. The prognosis looks good because I caught it early. The doctor was surprised; the lump was so small she could barely feel it. I am not definitively stating that what you claim to do is real. Only a fool would ignore coincidence. But if you hadn't said anything, I wouldn't have booked a private scan.'

'Not ready to commit?'

'Not yet. Though I understand why others believe. No demands. No misogynistic dogma. No divine punishment. Just you and death.'

'I keep things simple.'

'Perhaps that's your problem. As for Richard Hargrave, he remains missing and police effort remains devoted to finding his last recorded whereabouts and unpicking the events that brought him to that location. But, off the record, if Richard is dead, then the world is a better place for it. And if, like I suspect, you're offering a place to live and education to the two young girls who were last with him, then I will do everything I can to stop the police knocking on your door.'

'Detective Sergeant Jones—'

'Monique.'

'Monique, while I clearly do not understand what it is you are insinuating... thank you. Regarding her,' I angle my chin towards the unconscious girl, 'there is no need for me to stay.'

'Remain in the park. The situation may change.'

'It invariably does.'

Winter warmth swaggers into the day with a cocksure lateness. The pond in front of me, which is used by children for paddling in the summer, adults for sailing model boats in the autumn and as a toilet for dogs year-round, reflects the growing dazzle of the Sun. The benches that surround it are empty except for me and a girl who sits on the opposite side, feeding herself and the ducks chunks of baguette.

Moments where I find myself with little to do are rare. Sun has taken on the role of organising my time in exchange for a wage that I was looking for an excuse to provide and now nearly every moment of my day is accounted for. She even took it upon herself to contact today's appointments and cancel after the police called.

I take out my phone. Once used only for calls, the screen is filled with apps and games downloaded by Laure. I try one and soon lose interest, the purpose beyond me. I look at my photo album. Bare until Sun and Laure moved in, it's now filled with photographs of the three of us, though none taken by me. I select one where we're sat on the sofa together. Sun's finger is poking my cheek and Laure is smiling. I change the phone's wallpaper to that image and lock the screen. I unlock it again, see the image and can't help myself from feeling something. I go into the settings and revert the wallpaper to the default image of ocean waves.

I glance at the girl sitting on the bench by the far side of the pond. She's looking at me. From the way she's positioned, I think she's been looking for a while. She waves and goes back to pulling chunks from her baguette and eating them, occasionally tossing some to the ducks.

I don't know where to look. Any interest in my phone was quickly exhausted and aside from closing my eyes and feigning sleep, there is nowhere for me to focus without appearing to be directly ignoring her.

My eyes catch her again. She hasn't moved and raises a hand. I'm expecting her to go for the bread, but she pinches the air level with her eye and pulls something unseen.

I look away, but can tell she's shaking her head. I turn back. She does it again, pinching the air and pulling.

I focus on the girl as the park melts into blackness.

She isn't there.

The park returns and there she is, sitting on the bench, teasing an invisible thread. I force the blackness to descend again, but her essence refuses to appear. I look to the play area, much further away than the girl, and the police appear as human-shaped knots of brightness that move with hurried panic. The park runners are there too, though their numbers have waned with many of them realising there is an entire day ahead of them and little visible through the fabric of a tent.

I hold my hand over my face and pick out the hundreds of facets that mimic the shape of my bones and tendons in intricate near-perfection. I lower my hand to my lap and the darkness of the Aether returns.

The girl is not there.

I stand and the park surrounds me. The girl grabs the air with her fist, this time tugging it violently. I'm already walking around the edge of the pond when Monique runs over.

'Something's happened! Her pulse has dropped and there's still no ambulance.'

The girl has picked up what's left of her bread and waves at me before walking towards the woods. Monique catches my interest.

'She connected to this?'

'I think so.'

'I'll get someone to follow her. You're with me.'

The girl's facets are flung from the skull and spin around her ruined eye socket. They twitch as I approach, desperate and craving. I instinctively take a step back and catch Monique's foot. She collapses, holding her head and crying out. Someone comes to help her stand, but takes one look at me and thinks better of it. I move away and Monique quickly recovers.

'The girl's essence has changed.'

After several breaths Monique stands and brushes the wooden chips from her coat.

'Perhaps a warning next time.'

'Of course. I'm sorry.'

'Good job it's a quick recovery. However, we have an issue. Fights have broken out at the football stadium and all available ambulances, including ours, have been routed there to deal with it. We've already lost one of our cars and another's about to leave.'

'So what of the girl?'

'Look me in the eye and tell me she isn't dying.'

She is dying. I can see it more clearly than Monique ever could, just like I could see her own marker of death wedged deeply into her breast tissue. The girl's essence is being shaken free of the body and it will only be tens of minutes before the two part ways forever.

'The girl,' I say. 'The one by the lake. You need to find out who she is. That's your priority.'

'No, my priority is not being left with another dead body at the hands of an archivist.'

'That girl is involved.'

Monique looks to the dying girl. 'She did this to her?'

'I believe so.'

'And is she like you? I thought there weren't many of you left. It would be strange to find two in this park.'

'I don't know what she is,' I confess. 'She isn't what I am. She could be something different.'

'And what about the one who attempted suicide?'

'Put her in a car and drive her to a hospital.'

'If I move her and she dies, then it's on me. My career won't take another death.'

'Then leave her here to die. At least by putting her in the car you will have done something.'

'You should do what you're here to do,' Monique says. 'Take her soul or her essence or whatever you call it.'

'She is only dying, she's not dead yet.' A sigh escapes me. 'These girls place themselves in this state because of me. I don't understand why they are doing it or what they hope to achieve, but I am the reason this girl shot herself in the eye. If I take her essence now, then whoever coerced her will have won. If she is taken to the hospital and recovers, then I win.' I look through the tent and watch as more facets desert her brain to join the growing whorl that has all but encompassed her head. 'I need a win.'

Monique's eyes meet mine. 'We both do.' She picks out the remaining police officers trying to work the crowd and a pair that wait by one of the cars, ready for the call that'll take them away. 'But if I move her and she dies on the way to the hospital, then that'll be on me.'

'What do you propose?'

She motions with her chin towards the crowd. 'Cause a scene.'

'I don't perform.'

Monique laughs. 'Performing's all you do.'

I fight through the crowd, the once-hot bodies of the runners now cold, clammy and pathetically middle-aged. I avoid their moist limbs more for the sake of my shirt than their wellbeing.

A few feel the effect and stagger away from me into others, who are too preoccupied with what's happening inside the tent to catch them.

A face comes over my own. Her name is Beryl and she died two months ago at ninety-seven. No one sees the face appear, but it isn't long before they hear her. Beryl likes to talk and when I watch her family during our scheduled meetings, I get the sense that they've made a grave mistake.

A few people look as Beryl describes the scene, commenting on the unsightliness of the crowd and bemoaning the cold, which, incidentally, she cannot feel.

Then Beryl's face shifts, pulling to the right as a second face appears, this time a man named Jason. He died at twenty-six in a motorbike accident and will be with me for another two months to attend the wedding of his little brother, where he is to be best man.

The right side of my face is Beryl. The left side of my face is Jason.

People look now, attracting the attention of others. They start screaming. Jason is quick to understand what's going on and taunts the crowd while Beryl continues her stream-of-consciousness report, oblivious to what's happening in front of her.

A third face appears: Jasmin, forty-five and a long-distance goods driver who had a stroke at a motorway service station at three in the morning. It was her idea to attempt projecting more than one face at a time during a conversation with Sun one evening last week when she needed female advice and I did my best to ignore everything they said.

I see what I've created as a brief flash in the glasses of a balding forty-year-old man misguided enough to run towards me before realising his mistake. Jasmin's face has pushed Beryl's and Jason's further round the sides of my head so they appear over my ears. It is a step too far for the crowd and people try to escape in a clumsy surge, appearing to actively hurt themselves in their attempts to flee the horror before them.

I cannot blame them. The composite of faces was not as neat as I had expected; the features are warped and bloated and the eyes are either small like pinpricks or horrifyingly large and detailed.

I need more practice.

With the crowd dispersed, I vanish the faces and walk briskly to where Monique is sitting in an unmarked police car. She's on the phone, but when she catches my eye the call is swiftly ended.

'I want you in the back,' she says as I open the passenger door. 'I can't imagine good things will happen if you make me faint at the wheel.'

I close the door and move in next to the girl, who sits propped up against the other side. I've not even been told her name.

Her facets are onto me, seeking me out with gleeful curiosity, and I do all I can to push myself into the door.

Monique drives exactly as I would expect her to. Half of the football pitch is ruined as her tyres churn the grass before the car finds road and the concealed blue lights flash on. The road is hers, at least in her eyes, and the other cars become nothing more than an inconvenience as she pulls around them with seemingly no awareness of the lives inside.

I was focused on the girl the moment it happened, drawn to the wound in her eye and noticing that her eyelid appears undamaged. She was staring down the barrel of the pistol when she shot herself.

Noise. Then a feeling of weightlessness. More noise. Shattered glass. And, finally, weight and a lot of pain.

I know I lost consciousness only because I regain it to find Monique pulling me from the car by my shoe. There are cuts to her face and the arm of her coat has been ripped. She stops to retch. I try to stand but only manage to roll onto my side.

I see the police car. It's on its roof, the lights still on. There's a substantial dent in the passenger side and, on the other side of the road, a black car has ploughed through a shop front. It reverses out, removing the entire window, and takes off down the street.

'Where's the girl?' Monique cries.

I see her, folded in half against an industrial bin at the side of the road. I don't need to check to see if the girl's body is a shell; I know her essence has already left.

After the impact from the side, the car rolled and the girl, with her facets desperate to connect, was thrown across the back seat. Her face connected directly with mine and in that instant I had her.

And then someone took her from me.

18

He was slipping in and out of consciousness when they brought him in. The Jones woman called his flat and I hung up three times before answering in a Welsh accent to be told he'd been taken to hospital.

At first I thought it was a trap because there's been a spate of those lately. This might have been a lure to get me to the hospital only to arrest me as soon as I walked through the door. But that didn't make sense. The Jones woman rang the Archivist's house expecting to find me. She knew where I was, probably also knew which school I went to and the names Laure and I were using. More than that, she knew about the connection I had with the Archivist, which means she's not just been watching us, she's been listening too. I bet they have his entire flat bugged. I know some of his essences have committed crimes because I overhear them talk when he thinks I'm asleep. I bet the police overhear too.

So either I'm not a suspect in Richard's disappearance or the police value the Archivist's life more. I value his life too, certainly more than mine, because after a paranoia-filled minute of indecision my shoes were on and I was running to the hospital. I later learnt there was a car waiting for me.

When I got there, no one knew what they were supposed to do. The Jones woman was there, ordering people not to touch him – not that anyone looked too keen to get stuck in as every time they got close, they either fainted or vomited.

Was I emotional when I saw him on the stretcher, not even lying on it properly because the fucking paramedics couldn't even manage that? Yeah, I guess I was, but he was unconscious so at least he didn't see. A nurse tried to pull me away when I ran over and took the Archivist's hand, but he got too close and stumbled, screaming manically until someone dragged him away. I guess the Archivist's essence was a hot mess because the effect was worse than normal. Half of the corridor looked to be suffering and there I was, holding his hand and stroking his hair. I knew what would happen as soon as she said he'd been hurt and at that moment everyone else understood it too. I became Dr Kang. Or Dr Hastings. Honestly, I don't know who I'm supposed to be anymore.

That was three weeks ago. He's out tonight with Laure, some secretive event he thinks I don't know about. It involves one of his clients. He's been cagey about it, but that's understandable considering his attire for the evening.

The Archivist and Laure bonded while he was recovering at home. It was strange to see them together, but what was really strange was that I never stopped to worry about it. I don't trust men, not after Richard. When we're out I glare at everyone we pass to make sure they're not checking Laure out. The Archivist isn't like that. He's never looked at Laure the way Richard did. At first they ignored each other, then after the accident she decided he was the big brother she'd secretly always wanted. Not only is he OK with this, it seems he actually likes spending time with her. I wonder what people would think if they knew Death's gentle side.

It suited me for a while. Things with Laure have been difficult. She still thinks I'm out to get rid of her friends and I still won't tell her everything about Richard. Then when I talk about archivists, she looks at me like I'm insane, even though she lives with one, and goes off to read to him. Sure, he can read himself, but it's become a thing they do. Only thing is, now it's no longer the Archivist and me, it's the Archivist and Laure. I tell myself it's just a phase because I'm the only person who's not dying who can touch him. That must mean something.

I find the first key. Where I'm supposed to put it, though, I have no idea. I'm sure there was something up the path, but when I dig it out, it's clear that it's for a much larger key that I've no hope of finding.

'Fuck it.'

I pull the lock pick tools out of my back pocket, undo the bow and unroll the brown leather pouch onto the front step. It takes me about five minutes before the door swings open. It's an old mechanism with two locks that need to be activated at the same time in different directions; the usual tricks for the tumble locks don't apply here.

I slip off my shoes and take the indoor shoes left out for him even though they're far too big. I bang my elbow on a door and it swings against the wall with a bang, announcing my intrusion. Antoinette's shaved head appears from the other side of the sofa. Startled for a moment, she picks herself up and closes the books that lie open around her before walking over.

'Sun. How did you...'

I hold up the lock pick set then slide it back into my pocket. 'I used to live with a police officer; he taught me a few things.'

'I didn't think lock picking was part of their training.'

'It's not, but he wasn't exactly a stand-up guy.'

'As you've made it inside, I suppose I should offer you a drink,' Antoinette says.

'That's OK,' I say as I walk into what passes for a sitting room. 'I basically broke in.'

'You can drop the basically,' Antoinette says as she moves some books off the sofa to make space. 'I take it he doesn't know you're here.'

'I said I had somewhere to go. He's not really the type to pry.' My eyes scan the books and piles of notes. There's an open laptop on the floor that Antoinette quickly closes with an outstretched foot. 'What is all of this?'

'Research.'

'On archivists?'

Antoinette looks at me like I'm a complete idiot and I say, 'OK, yes, obviously it's going to be on archivists,' to which she smiles, and I almost get the sense that she wants to talk to me about it even though I've just broken into her home.

'You could call it my life's work, but I think that diminishes what I've managed to assemble. There are a lot of half-theories I've borrowed from other historians, many now long-dead, and amalgamated into a single defining theory on archivists. I've even thrown in some original ideas of my own, when I've had them.'

Antoinette picks up her laptop and places it beside her. 'There's nothing secret in here, it's just unfinished and I reserve the right to change my mind. Unlike any other world religion, what archivists do is real. It has been documented for more than two thousand years, but never understood. This is my attempt to explain exactly what an archivist is before they die out completely.'

'Do you know why they're dying out?' I ask.

Antoinette shakes her head. 'No one does.' She gets up, the many necklaces she wears chiming against each other. 'You know what? This conversation deserves tea, even if you don't.'

180

She's been researching archivists since she was twenty and, by our third cup, she's admitted to being sixty-seven. The death of archivists isn't the only clock she's fighting.

By cup number five, and increasingly frequent breaks for the toilet, Antoinette has tidied up her books and put away her laptop. Taking this as my cue to leave, I stand.

'Sit.' She walks over to a part of the room hidden by an alcove and returns with a photograph. 'You didn't come here to listen to me talk about my research, but I thank you for the opportunity – sometimes hearing it out loud helps. Here.'

I take the photograph she offers me and recognise him instantly. He's younger, maybe twelve, sitting with someone on the sofa I'm sat on right now. Several pillows form a wall between them, but despite the physical separation there's a sense of closeness about the pair that secretly wills for that wall to be torn down.

She looks to be the same age as him, has dark hair that falls over her shoulders in those big curls only European girls get. Big eyes too, round with a border of white that surrounds her iris; not like mine, which are partly lost to my eyelids even when I look surprised.

'Martina De Luca,' Antoinette says. 'The only true friend I've ever known him have. Her father was interested in the church. He used to have a great uncle who was an archivist and he would drag Martina along when he wanted to spend time in the library or just sit and swap theories. One day, the Archivist was here too, helping to organise my research. I watched Martina as she came in, curious as to what she'd make of him. It was the only time I've seen the exact moment a person falls in love.'

'He had a girlfriend?' I blurt, more to myself than Antoinette.

'I doubt he saw it that way. Despite how he may appear to you, he was still a young boy and careless with feelings, as young boys often are. But they were close in a way I struggled not to envy. She would sit with him and sometimes they would talk and sometimes they would read and sometimes all they wanted to do was sit in silence.'

'Martina, she's...'

'Yes. She's dead. I suspect he's not mentioned her.'

'Never.'

'There are few moments that truly define a person. Moments that change someone so profoundly that that change can never be reversed. For the Archivist, the death of Martina De Luca was that moment. Though he never spoke it, not even to me, he loved her. Profoundly. I doubt he will make that mistake a second time.'

Antoinette sighs, looks at our empty cups and decides against number six. I don't think she considers it to be late. I search the wall for more pictures of the Archivist and Martina, struggling to believe that he could have ever been in love and feeling guilty for even knowing. If he wanted to tell me he would have, or perhaps he introduced me to Antoinette knowing I would come here and she would be the one to reveal a past he was too embarrassed to share. Knowing that he has come from a place of pain, just like I have, bonds us in a way I didn't expect.

'He's visited me several times since you and your sister, Laure, moved in. I didn't approve. Not that I was against him helping two young girls, but I saw it for what it was. He couldn't save Martina, so instead he will save you.'

I'm about to say something, but Antoinette holds up her hand.

'Martina was fourteen when she killed herself. We should have seen it coming, but none of us realised how deeply in love she was. She wanted him to have her essence. And she wanted to be his first. But he wasn't fully realised and there was nothing he could do to stop her from being pulled into the Aether.'

'She should have known he wasn't ready,' I say. 'Surely he would have told her if he was.'

Antoinette freezes. When she moves again, it's to pick up her empty cup of tea and stare at the pattern of leaves in the bottom.

'Perhaps Martina thought she would be different; the spell to wake the sleeping prince.'

'Perhaps someone told her he was ready?' I say.

Antoinette's gaze is cold and our eyes lock. She's the first to blink. 'You think that forgetting his face is the only effect he has. There's more to him than that.' Antoinette stands and glances towards the door. 'I think it's time you left.'

I didn't mean to accuse her like that. The words were out before I had the chance to stop them. I feel bad, but I also feel I was right. There's something about Antoinette that wants to possess the Archivist. She's not just studying him, she's worshipping him.

'Before you leave,' Antoinette says as she sweeps her way around the sofa. She stands in front of me, tall and angular. I try to imagine how she must have looked when she was twenty and about to begin a lifetime of fruitless research, but the image doesn't come. She looks like she's always been in her sixties, like it's the only age she could ever be. 'Don't fall in love with him,' she says. At first I hear it as a threat, as if what happened to Martina will happen to me, but there's genuine concern in her voice.

I remove the shoes and put on the most expensive trainers I've ever owned.

'I'm not the type to fall in love.'

She smiles. 'No one sets out to fall in love, it's something beyond our control. It can't be reasoned with.'

'He really doesn't strike me as boyfriend material.'

'He is the closest thing to a god that walks among us, the link between the living and the dead, a presence that even science cannot explain. He will pull you in whether you want him to or not. If you were smart, you would take your sister and get as far away from him as possible, but already I can tell that you think you're somehow immune. But you're not. No one is.'

'You?'

'Are old. And foolish. And... going to sleep for a few hours.'

'Can I come back?' I don't know why I asked that. After breaking in and accusing her of being responsible for the death of a fourteen-year-old girl, I can't imagine she'd ever want to see my face again. But, to my surprise, Antoinette smiles and tells me she would like that.

She's harder to read than he is.

The playground in Watervale Park wasn't where Tegan Caldwell died – that happened in a totalled police car – but it was where she decided to end her life. Where she pointed an air pistol at her left eye and fired a 5.5 mm lead pellet halfway through her brain. It is her symbolic place of death. And though there's the odd bouquet of flowers tied to a lamppost at the site of the crash, the playground is the home of Tegan's shrine.

The letter sent by the school claimed it was an accident. Death by misadventure. Tegan had found an air pistol in the park and was looking at it when it accidentally went off and killed her. They were very clear: this wasn't suicide, just like Chrissy and Sophia's deaths weren't suicides either. Chrissy died due to a mix-up with her medication and Sophia was killed in a car crash – no mention of hanging. Katie Merriweather, Head Girl and also one of the three witnesses to Sophia's death, addressed the entire school between sobs, explaining how Sophia had been run down when a drunk driver mounted the kerb.

The Archivist told me the truth. Tegan makes four.

The gate to the playground creaks behind me and Lara Chin, a girl I've noticed but never spoken to, strides in wearing a purple evening dress and carrying a bouquet of flowers. She keeps to the path as best she can to avoid the rotting wood chips and stands beside me.

After a silence, in which we stare motionless at the shrine, I ask, 'Was she your friend?'

'We spoke sometimes,' Lara says, 'but I don't think we were friends.'

'She was in my French class,' I say. 'I didn't sit near her.'

'Did you bring something?'

'A bear,' I say. 'The one holding a little balloon that says sorry. Been there two weeks. It's looking grubby.'

'They'll clear it away soon. Kids will want to come and play. The shrine's too morbid for a park.'

'What will they do with it?'

'Throw it in a skip,' Lara says. 'It's all meaningless anyway.'

'So why bring flowers?'

'Because they're going to rot somewhere. Why not here?'

Lara pokes the flowers through a hole in the fence next to an almost identical bouquet that's starting to weep.

'How often do you come here?' I ask.

'Every night. I live close and my mum likes fresh flowers.'

'Do you care?' I ask, immediately feeling like an insensitive shit. 'That she's dead, I mean. Like, does it actually bother you?'

Lara shrugs. 'A bit. Maybe.' She looks around. 'I guess not. I thought coming here might help me feel something, but it's been two weeks. So I leave some more flowers, wait for about ten minutes, then go home feeling exactly the same as when I came.'

I sit on a swing. Lara comes over, looks like she's going to do the same then decides against it. I take off my jacket and toss it over the shoe-scuffed plastic.

'Sit,' I say, and Lara does. She's a delicate-looking girl. The cut of her dress accentuates a slender waist that's normally hidden among the puff and fuss of a school uniform.

'There aren't many Asian girls at school. I bet people think we're friends.'

Lara laughs. 'Kimberly, you're as Asian as fish and chips.'

'Yeah, I suppose you're right. Is Lara your real name?'

'Xiaozhi. We moved here when I was eleven. Before then I'd never spoken a word of English.'

'You sound like you've lived here all your life.'

Lara shrugs. 'Spend enough money and you can teach a monkey to write its name.'

'What's with the dress?'

Lara looks down and fingers the purple fabric. 'No idea. I don't remember putting it on. Have you ever had that? You find yourself doing something you don't remember starting, or standing in a room you don't remember entering?'

'Yeah,' I say, 'but I usually stop short of evening wear.'

Lara shrugs. She does that a lot. 'Maybe I'm going somewhere later.' She looks up, studying the rusted chains of the swing.

I lean back and kick my legs up to get the swing moving. A sharp tightness attacks the scar from a knife wound I never received. Most of the time I don't even realise it's there, but then suddenly I'll get this wave of pain. Once that happens, I remember; like when kids cut themselves but only cry when they see the blood. Everything inside me feels tangled, like my skin and muscles are tied together all wrong.

I bend over and swear. C'mon, obviously I swear!

'What's wrong?' Lara asks.

'Just a scar.'

'What happened?'

'Nothing really,' I say. 'It's not mine.'

'Not yours?'

I catch myself, realising what I just said and how stupid it sounds. I'm ready to shut it down, make up some crap about mixing up my words or not listening properly. But I don't. Maybe it's because I can't forget what Laure said about me. If I am going to give one of these girls a chance, why not Lara? How long has it been since I've had a friend? A year? Maybe I also see something of an outsider in Lara. After all, she's the only other Asian girl in a school whiter than an Aryan Brotherhood convention. It might be clichéd for us to be friends, but I don't think I care. Baby steps.

And so I tell her. Not everything, but enough. It feels good to talk about him. I don't tell Lara that we live together, only that an Archivist saved my life before someone stabbed him. The connection he made with me saved his life and left me with a scar that was meant for him.

Lara's leaning in, both hands gripping one of the swing's chains, her face pressed against the metal links.

'I don't understand, why did you get the scar?'

'He said it's because facets hold memories, only they don't just hold the memories of what we think, they also have the memories of what happens to our bodies. When he put some of his facets in me, they remembered being stabbed, and that changed my body so it was like *I* had been stabbed. Then when he took some of mine, they were facets that hadn't been stabbed and so had no memory of it. They changed his body, healing a wound they couldn't remember. He didn't take everything though, only enough so it wasn't fatal. We shared the wound and now we share a scar.'

'That's fascinating,' Lara says. She's really staring at me now. It's intense. I don't think she's blinked for at least a minute. 'Are you still connected to him?'

I nod and start to swing, slowly this time so I don't upset the scar.

'I think I'll always be connected to him. It's like we swapped kidneys, but the veins and arteries are still there, stretched between us. Only it doesn't look that gross. It's actually quite beautiful.'

Lara slides off the swing and walks over to Tegan's shrine.

'So does that make you an archivist too?'

'No,' I say as I jump off the swing and grab my jacket. 'I still remember my face.'

'Oh.' Lara rearranges some sodden plushies. 'I was hoping you'd know if Tegan's death was an accident.'

'No accident,' I say. 'She killed herself, just like Claire, Chrissy and Sophia. The school's just covering it up to save their reputation.'

'I think so too,' Lara says. 'Do you know, these suicides only started when Mr Cavendish arrived.'

'Except Claire,' I say. 'She died about a month before. I thought he might be the cause. It's neat. Mysterious male teacher comes to the school then suddenly girls start killing themselves. I doubt it's that simple, though.'

'It might be. They all visited his hotel room.'

'What?' Something inside me changes. Excitement boils. How am I only learning this now?

'I take it he's not invited you,' Lara says with an impish grin.

'No!'

'Room 1214 at the Grand Plaza Gardens.'

'Why is he inviting schoolgirls to his hotel room? Or don't I want to know?'

'He calls them extracurricular activities. I guess that's accurate.'

'Have you been?' I ask.

'That would be telling.'

I need to go there. Tonight. Now. It doesn't matter how late it is. I have too many questions and, like rabbits, they just keep breeding more. If I don't get answers soon, my head will explode. A few questions leak out to ease the pressure.

'Does the school know?'

Lara laughs and shakes her head. 'Really?'

'You're right, stupid question. OK, how about this? Why do the girls who visit Mr Cavendish kill themselves?'

'I don't know. I think you'll have to find out for yourself.'

'Room 1214, right?'

'That's the one.'

I'm nearly out of the park when I hear Lara call my name. I turn around. She looks scared.

'Why am I over here?' she asks.

'What?'

'The swing,' Lara says. 'I was on the swing.'

I go to her, put my hand on her shoulder. I'm not great at reassurance unless it's Laure. Everyone else feels alien.

'You got off the swing,' I say. 'We went to Tegan's shrine and talked about Mr Cavendish.'

'Did we?' Lara says. She looks scared, takes in her surroundings then finally shrugs. 'You told me you had a scar and then...' she holds up her hands, confused. 'This happens sometimes. I feel like a puppet and someone new has taken the strings.'

'Like the dress?'

'Yeah,' she says and smooths the fabric. She looks fearful, as if wearing the dress means something bad's coming her way. 'I need to go.'

'Wait,' I shout as she's by the gate. 'Can I get your phone number?'

'Monday,' she says. 'Let's have lunch together.'

'I'd like that.'

And then she's gone, lost to the dark. And here I am, sat on a swing doing nothing when I know I should not be on the swing and should be doing something. The hint was there, a cry for help. Eventually I move, jumping off the swing and running out of the park. Only I can't find Lara anywhere. I tell myself she doesn't really need me, that my five foot one would be no use against whatever's troubling her, and anyway, I'll see Lara on Monday for lunch. I tell myself it will happen, that we'll have a good time and slowly become friends.

I don't believe a word of my lies.

Silver trays with elaborate arrangements of champagne flutes and canapés float on the fingertips of waiters who move unseen by the crowd. Women in expensive dresses talk with careful control over their volume, allowing the music from the string quartet to explore the full vastness of the hall as the clink of glasses surrounds them like gentle rain. These women, goddesses of social interaction, move from person to person with an almost impolite efficacy, clocking their next target only moments after engaging in pleasantries with their current. When the transition is made it is slick, all parties wordlessly agreeing to break contact before gliding to their next in a string of interactions.

My own attempts to master this dance are hampered by an inability to coordinate my limbs with any sense of grace. I'm told to relax, but not too much. To keep my head up, but avoid making my presence too obvious. To keep my arms by my sides, but not let them hang. And always to remember *heel toe, heel toe* and let my feet do the thinking.

I catch the eyes of the wrong people, hear an irritated *tisk* after each one, but in every case the damage is done and conspiratorial whispers ensue or, even worse, I am approached with bright smiles and outstretched arms.

A woman in a deep green ball gown drifts my way, mouthing a name to herself, the raised intonation of a question audible only through the lines of confusion that ripple her forehead.

'Genevieve, my dear!' she calls, ready to greet me with exaggerated air kisses, which I deftly avoid with a backwards step only to be met by a clicking of the tongue. 'The rumour mill has been busy publishing stories of some horrific accident.'

'I stubbed my toe on the way over,' Genevieve laughs. 'Hardly horrific.'

Her voice emanates from my mouth, not that anyone around me can tell. To them I am respected architect Genevieve DuPont, wearing her face to an award ceremony. Sadly, it is not the only thing of hers I am wearing tonight.

'The strangest thing,' the woman says. 'I hope this is not another ploy to promote some garish new concept; remember how badly it went last time?'

'It's hard to forget, Tiffany, as you seem to mention it every time we meet.'

'Oh, you're exaggerating,' she says in mock horror, knowing perfectly well that she is anything but. She flags a waiter and plucks two champagne flutes from his tray.

'None for me,' Genevieve says. 'Doesn't agree with my medication.'

'I don't believe I offered,' Tiffany says as she folds herself into the crowd and vanishes.

'Please try not to flinch so much,' Genevieve snaps. 'These people are supposed to fear me.'

'Genevieve!' someone else calls out, appearing from the crowd with the same mysticism Tiffany used to vanish. 'Oh, my dear! Candice told me you'd met an accident while overseeing construction of that monstrous library.'

'Verity, I can assure you I would never design something that justifies the term *monstrous*. And as for an accident...' I hold my hands to the side, palms up. This is one of several cues.

Verity releases a long 'hmm' and looks me up and down. I avoid doing the same, not wanting to remind myself of the hip and bust padding that had been purchased from a website marketed to drag queens.

'If there was no accident, then how do you explain your absence in Dubai? You never pass up an opportunity to flog those ostentatious skyscrapers to the Sheikh.'

'An illness. Nothing overly concerning but enough to take me out of the game for a few weeks. I'm still technically recovering. My doctor was horrified when I said I was planning to attend tonight, but this was hardly something I could miss, don't you agree?'

'And who is this with you?' Verity asks with a nod towards Laure.

'Daughter of a friend. Whip-smart and all-round good egg. I offered to bring her along, show her that women can succeed without picking pubes out of our teeth.'

'What's her name?'

'Unimportant,' Genevieve fires back, clearly having forgotten. 'This is a business where one makes their name.'

'Very true. Still,' Verity muses, 'it is strange to see you with a child.'

'The day may come when I have one of my own. I am only forty-two and have more than enough eggs in storage.'

'Wouldn't consider getting pregnant?'

'Oh no! Far too busy for that. If I ever have a child, it would be a surrogate all the way.'

This complication had not been one I had anticipated. It was only after we entered into a contract that I was made aware that Genevieve had her eggs frozen at twenty-six in preparation for a career that would extend through her fertile period and firmly into the menopause. In discussions with her parents, she has raised the possibility of having a child to a mixture of delight and horror. Her mother's enthusiastic response was that you can buy false breasts that lactate. I need to find myself a better lawyer.

I touch my chin, a cue that I need the toilet. Genevieve excuses herself and I weave my way through the crowd with Laure by my side. Several people appear, ready to intercept, but likely the look of reproach on Genevieve's face is enough to put them off. Tonight is supposed to be about her and any distractions as a result of my bodily functions are entirely unwelcome.

'Wrong door,' she mutters under her breath and quickly laughs off her mistake to the elderly woman watching from the door to the women's toilets.

Laure looks concerned but follows anyway. For most of the evening she has been quiet, watching intently as Genevieve has conversed with an endless convoy of fans and critics. Her attendance is a result of my inability to open packages in private and, instead of claiming the silicone hips that I lifted from the too-discrete packaging were a mistaken order, I proceeded to explain what they would be used for. I bought her silence in exchange for an invite and a new dress.

I choose a cubicle with the most open doors either side and banish Genevieve's face. There's a mutter of protest as she realises what's happening, but it's soon cut off. My essence bursts from the knot in the centre of my chest, flowing into my arms and legs, filling fingers and toes with warm relief. The toilet seat is, of course, down, and I sit as a sense of completeness overtakes my body. I am satiated, overfull and a little giddy at being myself in myself. Everything is where it should be. I exhale a bliss-tinted moan, not even caring who hears.

Genevieve was convinced that people would know the truth if they felt even the slightest tinge of unease. I saw no need in pointing out the substantial news coverage of her death from a collapsed wall and agreed to her terms as best I could for no reason other than the practice would do me good. Archivists are akin to virtuosi in that they are born with something special that sets them apart from mediocrity, but like a piano or violin, the techniques required to harness that inbuilt talent need time to be mastered. I know from what Antoinette has taught me that I am far from the archivist I could one day become, that there are elements of archivism, like the suppression of my essence, that can be controlled, and that such control will only be obtained through practice.

I pull my facets away from their homes, binding them deep within me to restrict my aura of dread, as Sun refers to it, and allow myself to pass as human for at least another forty minutes. It takes longer this time around, like I'm forcing my begrudging feet back into high heels knowing full well they've swollen in protest. After five minutes, I have everything where it is supposed to be, though perhaps not as neatly as before I stepped into the venue; stuffed and crammed as opposed to folded and ordered.

I leave the cubicle, the face above my shoulders still mine, and approach the mirror. Often when I see my face, it's a pleasant surprise, the same as knowing your wallet is exactly where you left it. Even with its thicker shoulders and, as Genevieve put it, forgiving bodice, the dress detracts from the usual relief. It mocks my face, the satin and chiffon reminding

195

me that I am nothing more than a puppet made to dance for the entertainment of others. What I think and what I feel are unimportant so long as everyone leaves satisfied by the experience. Antoinette tells me I walk only a step behind God while the rest of the world struggles to keep pace miles behind. I readjust a bra strap, bringing my left silicone breast back in line with the right. When I catch up with God, we'll be having words.

A cubicle door opens behind me and a new face appears in the mirror.

'Red is not your colour.'

'It was not my choice.'

'Genevieve DuPont?'

'Is alive and well,' I say.

'You can't possibly expect me to believe that.'

'There is a contract in place that forbids me from implying otherwise.'

Monique Jones leans forward to check her make-up. She takes a small bottle of perfume from her bag and sprays it under her neck. Cinnamon and vanilla. Almost unrecognisable, I would have thought Monique someone else had she not spoken first, her natural afro released from its regulation suppression. She catches me looking.

'It's a liability when I'm on duty. Too much to grab.' She reapplies a deep red lipstick, lustrous against her dark skin. 'My girlfriend once worked with DuPont. A visionary and cunt in equal measure, according to her.'

'You're not here because of me?'

Monique's laugh is more snort than titter. 'You were the last person I expected to find in the women's toilets.' She wipes an eyelash from her cheek. 'Dress aside though, you look well. How do you feel?'

'Fine. I have more control over my body than most. I heal fast.'

'And has this been scientifically documented?'

'Not yet,' I say. 'The girl by the pond, did you find out who she was?'

Monique shakes her head. 'Not her and not the driver of the car.'

'Don't you find that suspicious?'

Monique tugs the hem of her dress. 'Yes,' she says. 'Yes, I do.'

The only other occupied cubicle opens and Laure steps out. Immediately, she spots Monique and her eyes grow wide. She fumbles for the door as if retreat is an option, though soon gives up and strides towards the sinks, mustering as much nonchalance as can be bestowed upon a twelve-year-old.

'That's a lovely dress,' Monique says. 'Expensive.'

Laure washes her hands. Stoic. I pass her a rolled towel.

'Not many girls your age here tonight. You're lucky.'

Laure drops the towel in the bin. Facing me, she silently pleads for us to leave.

'Laure...'

Her eyes go wide and she shakes her head. 'Florence' desperately squeaks past her lips.

'Detective Sergeant Jones is not our enemy. She knows exactly who you are, where you live and which school you attend.'

Monique smiles. 'It's Detective Inspector Jones again. Do the right thing and sometimes the right people notice.' She extends a hand for Laure, who ignores it and gets her shoulder squeezed instead. 'Those times I came to your flat weren't meant to intimidate you.'

Laure looks away.

'Does it scare you, that place?'

'No,' Laure says. 'It's just a flat.'

'Even after everything that happened?'

Laure shrugs. 'The flat didn't do anything to us. It was all Richard and he's—'

'Missing,' Monique catches her. 'We don't expect him to return. For now, the flat is under our possession. There are still clothes and books in your bedrooms. If you want them back, that can be arranged.'

'You've been to our old flat?'

'It's my job,' Monique says. 'Someone has to water the flowers and I'm the one with the key.'

Laure says nothing. An awkward pause rapidly unfolds.

'I think it's time I left you ladies to the rest of your evening,' Monique says and, with one final check of her hair, she is out through the door and Laure and I are alone.

'Sun won't like you making friends with attractive police officers at fancy parties.'

'Then it's a good job that Sun isn't going to find out.'

There's a moment of mutual understanding. A scent of kinship. During the first few weeks she lived with me, Laure was more pet than person, appearing to exist only in the places I did not. Something changed after the car accident, and during my recovery I spent more time with her than Sun.

'Why…' She falters. She looks down, then back to me. 'Why *are* you wearing a dress?'

'As opposed to?'

'What you normally wear.'

Laure had not been present during the conversations between Genevieve and her parents when a plan for the evening had been formulated. She did not hear Genevieve proclaim that if the masquerade were unsuccessful then her company, which was paying for a substantial share of an archivist's time, would lose millions. Laure and her sister have only known me to project someone for the benefit of others, never to embody the deceased for financial and reputational gain.

'Genevieve chose the dress. It was part of our contract.'

'Ah.' Laure looks at herself in the mirror. 'Who's Genevieve?'

'Pardon?'

The sense of disbelief in my voice is enough to stop Laure. 'Who's Genevieve?' she repeats.

'She's my client for tonight.'

'Oh. I guess that's why everyone's talking about her.'

Laure spins on the ball of her foot. The fuchsia dress dances around her calves and in a moment she will be back through that door and consumed by the bodies and noise of the LET Architect of the Year Ceremony, and I will lose the chance to confront the feeling of unease I have felt ever since Laure first looked at me.

I allow Genevieve DuPont's face to materialise over mine.

'We're still in the toilet? Oh for fuck's sake, you're being paid to mingle not piss and shit. Get out there.'

Laure is by the door. She holds the handle, ready to turn it.

'Come on,' Genevieve says, 'the girl's ready.'

I don't move. Neither does Laure.

'There are already more rumours about me than birds in the sky, so if we could not spend the next twenty minutes locked in a toilet that would be really fucking smashing.'

'Why are you saying those things to me?' A source of light in any room she enters, Laure's brilliance dims.

'I'm not talking to you! I'm talking to that bloody archivist who's charging me ten thousand pounds for every hour of this fucking charade.'

I vanish Genevieve's face.

'Why are you swearing at me?' Laure is on the verge of tears.

'It wasn't me, it was Genevieve.'

199

'Who's Genevieve?' Laure cries.

'The lady on my face.' And as soon as I say it I know, like I have always known, that Laure cannot see her. That she can only see me as I always am. 'I'm sorry,' I say. 'It wasn't me saying those things.'

'Yes it was,' Laure says. 'It was you. It's always just you.'

I look at myself in the mirror and there is my face, every detail exactly as it was the last time I was allowed to remember. I look at Laure again, her green eyes bloodshot with tears, her blonde hair tied into a skilful chignon that she mastered after a five-minute internet video, and the memory of my face vanishes. Like the fading remnants of a dream in those first moments of wakefulness, everything I piece together is wrong and no matter how hard I focus, I cannot find what for certain I once knew.

'Can you remember what I look like?'

Laure nods.

'All the time?'

Another nod.

'When you're near me. Do you ever feel unwell?'

Laure shakes her head and slowly leaves the door. As she walks over to me her body and the walls drop away and a tightly coiled mass of facets in the shape of a girl approaches. They do not flinch. It is like I am not there. And then Laure is directly beneath me and her arm is rising into the air, throwing off its ethereal glow.

Her fingers touch my chin, yet my essence does not tempt her. When she moves away, there is no connection between us, and she is her and I am me.

'I know what an archivist is,' she says and I go back to seeing her as her. 'But I also know who Jesus is, and Mohammad and Moses, and I don't believe in any of them either.'

'You think I'm a fraud?'

'Just because a lot of people believe something doesn't mean it's real.'

'Sun believes,' I say, as if that's justification.

'Sun needs someone to believe in.'

'So why me?'

'Why not?'

Laure walks away and I reach out to take her hand. It's small and cold but also somehow warm. 'You know you're different, don't you?'

Laure shrugs. 'Maybe. Or maybe you're not wearing anything at all.'

'Pardon?'

'The Emperor's New Clothes.'

'Do you think I'm crazy?'

'Yes,' Laure replies without pause, 'but you make Sun happy. Me too.'

'So...'

'So I guess you'll go out there and pretend to be a dead woman called Genevieve and everyone will believe you because that's what everyone else is doing.' Laure smiles. 'Don't worry, I'll take care of myself.'

'I hope you act surprised when they call my name,' Genevieve whispers.

I bring my hands to my face and wiggle my fingers.

'Fuck's sake, I'm not seven,' she chides. 'Bring your left hand to your mouth and look around until you make eye contact with someone. I'll mouth "oh my God" and then you walk up the steps and onto the stage.'

A woman in her fifties, whose head is so bald it reflects the spotlights like a second moon, opens an envelope. Her eyebrows, which more than make up for her sparse scalp, are raised and she whispers in the ear of the woman to her right.

'And the winner for best hotel is the Budapest Belle designed by Genevieve DuPont, who, despite what I've been led to believe, is in the building with us tonight. Genevieve, dear, why don't you give us a wave and dispel those ghastly rumours.'

Hot white lights swing towards me, so bright I'm worried they'll bore through the dress, padding and even Genevieve's face to reveal me, naked, confused and wearing high heels. Instead, I'm greeted by applause interspersed with gasps of surprise. Women with long gloves clasp their hands beneath their chins.

'You of all people shouldn't conspire with the rumour mill, Maude,' Genevieve says as I fight my way through waves of air kisses.

My foot is on the second step when I hear a scream. Followed by a second. Followed by a third. I turn as the scream count rises and catch the last moments of a person's fall from a balcony before the ground abruptly stops proceedings.

People gather, obscuring any chance of a view, before recoiling at the horror by their feet. Through the cracks I see an overextended elbow joint and a leg with an open fracture at the calf; no face yet, but the skin is young and already a feeling of dread awakens inside me.

There are calls for an ambulance, but they soon fade as the futility of the situation becomes apparent. The ambulance will arrive, but it will leave with a body.

What repels everyone else draws me in and I feel the grip on my essence slip and intuitively the women around me step back. Genevieve is quietly asking me to stop, telling me that it is her night. That she worked so hard. That she deserves this. And with each step these pleas fade. Fear wraps itself around her words and she begs me not to look at the girl's body, so broken and contorted, so much like her own when the partially constructed wall fell and crushed her four weeks ago.

And there I am, stood before a teenage girl in a purple dress. Not dead. Never dead. But not long left. Broken arms and legs, a face that half compacted the moment it struck the marble floor tiles. Facets fly off her like the seeds from a field of dandelions, whirling around and working the crowd with far greater success than I could ever manage.

'Shouldn't we do something?' Genevieve finally stammers.

'Genevieve, look at her,' Maude, the bald woman, says.

'But there must be something… at least until the ambulance arrives,' Genevieve says. 'Or we could put her in a car. Tiffany, you've still got that sporty number, haven't you? That'd get her to the hospital in a jiff.'

'The seats are white!' Tiffany cries. 'And besides, if we move her…'

'Well, I don't hear your ideas!'

Everyone is looking at Genevieve, the screams and cries long-silenced. There are no clinking glasses or muted conversations, only the rasping breaths of a dying girl and the tinnitus hum of collective expectation.

An old woman fights her way to the front and stands beside me, looking down at the broken girl.

'I remember a thirteen-year-old girl bursting into my office long after everyone else had left for the day,' the old woman says. 'I was pulling an all-nighter, but even by eight I knew I was wasting my time. Inspiration's like that; some days it's with you and others, it's flown off to accompany another. So there she was, wearing clothes that must have been made by her mother and holding a cardboard model of a church. No appointment. No reference. Certainly no manners!' The old woman leans

203

down to check the pulse of the girl and moves some of her hair to hide her ruined face. 'I told her to get lost and without a word she did. She came back the next night though. And the next. And the next. I remember saying some unpleasant things to that little girl. Words one fires at adults, not children.

'How was I supposed to work with this girl showing up every night? So sick of seeing her, I let her enter. In she traipsed, put down the model and launched into one of the best honed pitches I'd ever heard. As for the model, a church that she'd converted into apartments, well... it wasn't brilliant. But it was good. Better than I'd expect from a child, and straight away I knew who'd been squandering my inspiration.'

'Meredith, I... this is all very flattering, but that girl will die if we don't do something.'

'I've not finished, Genevieve. What I want to say is that I didn't truly appreciate your talent back then. By the time you were eighteen, though, I knew. You were gifted, Genevieve, truly gifted.'

I feel Genevieve's face freeze.

'You have always been thin. That thirteen-year-old girl in her crooked gingham dress was more in need of a meal than architectural guidance. Thin, but never like this. When I look at you head on, I'm convinced that it is you I'm seeing, even though I know for a fact that this is not you, Genevieve. It's when I'm not looking that something relaxes and what I thought I saw becomes something a little different. Taller, I think. More awkward. You've always been water, flowing into a room and filling it to the ceiling with your presence. Tonight, you are a brick.'

'Meredith, I—'

'You being here has been wonderful, and while there are those who might claim it to be in ill taste, arriving to an award ceremony only weeks after her death is exactly what I expect from Genevieve DuPont. But don't you think it's gone far enough?'

'I, no,' Genevieve stammers. 'This is my night! I worked so hard for this. You can't just...' She bites her lip. I feel a sharp pain and realise I am doing the same.

'Don't be perverse,' Meredith says. 'You have had your life. It was truly a tragedy how soon it ended and for that I am so sorry. And this girl here, she is going to die too. But if you let the person beneath you take her soul, then at least she'll get to say goodbye to those she loves.'

Meredith steps away and Genevieve is silent. People wait, some appearing to discuss plans for if Genevieve doesn't leave willingly. While the power to remove her is mine alone, I am bound to her wishes by a contract I have no intention of breaking.

'Save the girl,' Genevieve whispers.

I tilt my head back and open my mouth. Genevieve dissolves and flows across my face and into my mouth like collapsing dunes of sand, and then I am me in a red dress. There is the usual assortment of gasps, though more laughter than I'm used to.

I'm on my knees, my forehead touching the girl's.

'Release the life you hold so tight; welcome me and leave the light.'

She streams into me, feigning relief. I release every essence I have. They burst from my centre, concealing me in a silken web. The girl is there too, her facets confused by the introduction of others. I work fast, weaving my chrysalis, watching as it grows hard and people are disorganised, merged and folded into each other. I feel the pull on the girl and reel in the essences. They grow opaque as the shell around me shrinks until all I can see is solid silver. Another pull. I feel exactly where it is coming from. Know how far away they are. North and no further than four miles. I pull back, my library of essences pulling with me. A fight against another archivist. But I am many and they are one. I give no ground, determined to claim the essence as my own. It takes time, but I will not taste defeat again. I am violent, vicious, a salivating Rottweiler with an arm in my jaw, tugging with feral ferocity.

And then it snaps. Whatever memory or feeling that was being used to link the girl to the other archivist is broken and vanishes into a state of nothingness.

I break from my cocoon as facets group themselves back into their essence and the dead are once more themselves, individual, unique. Her too, safe and no one else's but mine.

There is applause when I open my eyes and while I cannot be certain exactly what they saw, from the expressions on their faces, I can imagine it was unlike anything their architect brains could create.

Cutting through the clamour and satisfaction of taking the essence of the dead girl by my feet is the knowledge that something is not where it is supposed to be.

I look to my side. Laure is not there. Through the crowd, dissolved into the forms that only I can see, still no Laure. Not hiding among them, not hidden in a different part of the building.

Gone.

No... taken.

20

Obnoxious lights from the Grand Plaza Gardens burn the night, announcing the hotel to anyone foolish enough to look. I did; my eyes still fucking sting. It's no better when you're inside. Everything's wrapped in those long fluorescent bulbs and anything not draped with lights reflects it like a hall of mirrors.

I stand to the side as a couple enters, loud and laughing. They wait by the lifts and he attacks her with a hungry kiss. She catches my eyes and rolls hers. I bet he paid for her, not that I judge. A gentle chime, a swish of doors and they're gone.

I catch myself in the mirrored ceiling, so small on the polished lobby tiles. Someone behind the reception desk notices me, appraises my puffer jacket and instantly decides I'm not a guest. They march over, sharp heels clicking double-quick. Mouth open, ready to ask what I'm doing while I blink away the balls of light orbiting my vision.

They don't manage that first word because someone else appears, walking even faster and looking even more ridiculous. He takes the receptionist's elbow and leads her away, furiously whispering into her ear.

Interesting.

I try to catch someone else's eye. Manage a few guests, but they're not important. A couple smile, a few sneer and one pulls out his wallet, waving me over. I look away and head for the bar. I'm too young to drink and certainly look it. The bartender checks me over, but a quick glance at the man from before and he looks the other way. Taking this as an invitation, I sit on a stool, helping myself to handfuls of peanuts and other snack-type things I can't name. They taste good.

'Can I get something to drink?' I ask.

The bartender can hardly ignore me; I'm the only one here and he's not even distracting himself by polishing glasses like in the movies.

'You get one drink. No alcohol.'

'White peach nectar.'

He takes a can from the fridge, not bothering with a glass and ice. I'm halfway through it when someone taps me on the shoulder.

'The lifts to the upper floors are over there,' he says, pointing to the line of gold-fronted doors.

I'm about to ask why I care when he says, 'Room 1214. Best not dawdle.'

I choke on the drink and manage a hurried 'OK' before sliding off the stool and scuttling to the lifts. As soon as that man pulled the receptionist aside, I knew something was off, and I guess I was right. I was expected. Though I wonder if it's because I am me, or because I'm a teenage girl and they assume I'm here to see Mr Cavendish. Surely he can't afford to bribe the hotel staff to safely deliver him young girls? He's only on teacher money.

The corridors either side of the door to room 1214 stretch into nothingness. They have that look about them, like if I try to run down one, I'll only end up here again, back at the door to 1214.

No escape. This is where I'm supposed to be. I tell myself that's true. I'm meant to be here because inside room 1214 is where I learn what's happening with the girls and what it's got to do with the Archivist. Because it's him they're dying in front of and him they're giving a part of themselves to. What Mr Cavendish has got to do with this, I've no idea, but once I'm on the other side of that door, I'll know.

The man in the suit slipped me a key card as I left the bar. Makes sense; it's probably not a good look for the hotel to have teenage girls waiting around to be let into the rooms of older men. Much easier if we can slip in and out like we belong, especially with the number of girls Mr Cavendish has apparently entertained.

I wonder if that's what he's expecting from me, if he's expecting me at all. Part of me feels like I've been led here, tricked into believing I came of my own free will. I will open the door and Mr Cavendish will be on the other side, waiting, ready to do to me what he does to every other girl who visits. And what is that, exactly? Not even I'm convinced it's sex; not with all of them. It's too scandalous to be true. But it's something bad.

My hands shake as I insert the key card into the lock. It takes a few goes to get it in. I can't believe I'm here, willing to enter the hotel room of a man I know to be bad. How have I not learnt my lesson? But one look down this Möbius corridor and I know I've nowhere to go but through this door.

Do I sneak in or throw the door open wide? Before I realise what's happening, I smash the door against the wall. Loud purposeful steps, head high and eyes searching. This is the Sun-young I know, not that scared girl in the corridor. More importantly, it's the me I want Mr Cavendish to know. I didn't arrive a victim and I don't plan to leave as one.

Only, it's not just Mr Cavendish. He's with a girl, has his arm around her, whispers into her ear. On the other side of the girl is Victoria, watching me with a hawkish smile.

'I almost convinced myself they were rumours,' I say, 'but it's late, you're with two schoolgirls in a hotel room and *what the fuck*?'

'You can't just barge in here!' Mr Cavendish shouts.

'Oh? Are you the fucking can't-police now?'

'This is my room and that language is inappropriate.'

'My *fucks* are inappropriate, are they? Because I think on a scale of one to whatever the fuck's going on here, my language is about a three.'

'It's a pleasure to see you again, Kim. Wonderful night, isn't it?' Victoria rubs the girl's back while I breathe and glare and clench my fists and slowly realise I need some kind of follow-up.

I grab the girl a little too roughly, pulling her from Mr Cavendish's embrace and back to the door. 'Stay there.' It's ruder than I intended, but right now I own the room and I want to keep it that way.

'Sir, please...' the girl cries and I move to block her.

'I know exactly what you and everyone else thinks of me,' Mr Cavendish says, 'but that's not why she's here.'

There's something on the floor. I bend down and snatch it. 'Another step and Mr Pen'll take a cruise down Urethra Boulevard.'

He winces. Stops. Takes a step backwards.

Victoria pulls herself from the sofa like she's gracefully falling in reverse. 'I like you, Kim. Always so quick to fight. You make things interesting.' She comes closer, past Mr Cavendish and to the other girl's side. 'But not everyone is your enemy and not every teenage girl needs saving.'

210

The girl throws her arms around Victoria and the pair gently lower themselves to the ground.

'Poor thing,' Victoria says. 'She was a daddy's girl. Loved him more than the night has stars. He left, though. Told Nicola she'd ruined his life, that she was an accident he'd begged her mother to abort.' Nicola muffles her cries into Victoria's shoulder. 'The Greenfield doesn't care that she's broken. They expect perfection, not silly teenage emotions.'

Mr Cavendish has snuck up beside me and I look stupidly to the pen in my hand and drop it on the floor.

'The visits?' I ask.

'Counselling,' Mr Cavendish says. 'I was the pastor in my old school. When I asked why The Greenfield didn't have one, I was told a counsellor wasn't needed.'

I feel like I'm staring at a jigsaw puzzle with the pieces flipped over. It's complete, but not what I wanted.

'We're lucky to have Mr Cavendish,' Victoria says. 'Without him, I'm sure we'd fall apart.'

'Then why are you here?' I ask.

'Escort duties. You can't expect a teacher to entertain young girls in his hotel room alone. There are rules about such things and if Mr Cavendish broke them, I'm sure he'd receive a visit from the *can't-police*.'

I want to believe they're lying to me so badly that I stare into Victoria's eyes like I'm one of those people who can *just tell* in the hope she'll reveal the truth, but she just looks back and smiles.

'Nicola,' I start. 'Is this true? You're not here to...' I awkwardly point to Mr Cavendish with my head.

'My dad just walked out on me,' she spits. 'So no, I'm not here to fuck a teacher!'

I might not be able to detect lying, but I sure as shit know what anger looks like. I mumble an apology. Mr Cavendish looks at me like he's gloating, almost daring me to make a scene.

I take a backwards step as Victoria unwraps herself from Nicola and stands. She shuffles forward and takes my hands.

'Suspicion eats away at you like woodworm,' she says, gnashing her teeth. 'If you don't do something about it, you'll be full of holes.'

'I—'

Victoria lets go and places her finger against my lips. 'We're here to help the Greenfield girls; unload their burdens, calm their fears. This is not a space where girls come to harm. This is a space where girls are healed.'

'How can you say that?'

'Very easily,' Victoria says. 'Flappy lips and a wiggly tongue.'

I step into her and look up, my nose practically touching her chin. Ignoring her stupid comment, I ask again. The anger rises with every word.

'How can you say that? How can you stand there and tell me that anything you do is in the best interests of Greenfield girls when you and that Amazonian bunny boiler did nothing but watch when Sophia Ray hanged herself?'

A slight slip of composure, but not enough.

From the floor, Nicola says, 'Hanged herself? I thought she was hit by a car.'

'You could have cut her down. Called an ambulance. Even screaming would have fucking helped. Something! But you did nothing. You just watched. Then when you got tired of that, you left. So no, I'm not convinced that you have the best interests of the girls at heart, and no, I'm not convinced that Mr Cavendish invites them over for counselling sessions. This,' I say, 'has clearly been arranged for my benefit because we all know Nicola's going to kill herself.'

Nicola cries. Understandable.

Aside from the brief slip, Victoria's composure doesn't change. She still looks down at me, smiling like I'm insane. She surrounds me in a hug, her soft arms desperately trying to comfort me. But I'm angry and hard; it must feel like hugging a stone.

'Not for your benefit, Kim. For Nicola's benefit. Or did you think you were expected?'

'Of course I was expected! The guy in the lobby gave me the fucking key!'

'He just knows a lost soul when he sees one and wants to help. I said it before, didn't I? Not everyone is your enemy.'

'Then explain Sophia! Explain it to me like I'm a child!'

Victoria's arms go slack.

'Is this another one of your stupid tricks?' I shout. 'Like when you pretended to be an archivist? Because if you're too scared to answer, then I already know.'

Victoria staggers backwards, her hands in the air, violently tugging something I can't see. She's crying. Screaming. Fighting something in her imagination just to make a point that she's weird. She's faking it. I turn to go. I won't learn any more here.

That's when Nicola screams.

I look back to see Victoria sliding across the floor, only there's nothing pulling her. Mr Cavendish has backed off to the other side of the room and hovers by the bathroom door. Nicola too has retreated, hiding behind a table.

I run closer, trying to understand. Victoria's hands are in the air, grappling something unseen. Her legs are in front of her, feet braced against the carpet. Nothing pushing. Nothing pulling. Her cries are real. Large painful tears roll down her face. She pleads to let go.

She's whipped off the floor and crashes into the large window with a smack. Everything beyond it is black, the ground so far below. She's spread against the pane, pinned. She screams again. I run over. I can't help myself despite what I think of her. My heart hammers away, shouting for attention as my hands fumble for Victoria's leg, trying to peel her off the window. Everything inside me screams to leave her and run. This is some witchcraft shit right here and I have enough Archivist shit to deal with already.

A crack. Something shifting. Dust and dried plaster fall from above the window. Another cry from Victoria. Blood drips from her mouth. From her ears, her eyes.

'Please!' she cries, her words a sodden mess. 'I can't. I'll die.'

'Do not lose her,' comes a voice from the corner. A girl on a chair, swathed in darkness and silent until now. She must have been there the whole time. She looks my age, dressed in black with equally black hair, long and straight, and one of those severe fringes that looks scared of her eyebrows. There's something unsettling about her, almost otherworldly, as if she doesn't belong in a room with lights and people.

'I can't!' Victoria wails. I feel the pain in her voice, want to look away but can't.

'You will not let her go,' the new girl says. Firm. I was wrong. I'm not in charge of this room; I never was.

Victoria's cries stop. She falls from the window, catching herself only seconds before her face smashes into the glass-topped coffee table. She's quick to wipe the blood from her mouth, but all she manages to do is smear it.

'You have her?' the new girl asks, the one with the fringe, but Victoria's already shaking her head.

'It broke,' she splutters.

'How pathetic,' fringe girl says. She points at Mr Cavendish. 'You, take her away and find out what happened.' But Victoria's already on her feet and running out the door. Mr Cavendish shrugs.

'Just go,' fringe girl says. 'And don't expect to sleep tonight.

You too, girl. After that, I doubt you'll be needed.'

'Needed?' Nicola says. 'But I—'

'Just go.'

'Well, as everyone's going,' I say, shuffling towards the door, 'I guess that means I should probably head home. Don't want to miss that last bus, you know.'

'No, I think you'll stay here, Kimberley. Sun-young Kang.'

The door bangs. I look around. It's just me and fringe girl now.

'You know my name? That's... worrying. But seriously, I think I'd better go.'

'The boy will have locked the door,' she says, 'and that plastic card in your hand only gets you in. But I'm in no hurry, so you're free the try it.'

'Free to try it? Seriously? Well then, I'm just gonna fucking do that, aren't I?'

I really hope I don't sound as scared as I feel.

'Yep. Definitely locked,' I say, trying the handle for the eighth time.

'You're free to try the window too,' she says, 'but I wouldn't recommend it, we're awfully high up.'

'No, you're good.' I walk to the sofa in front of fringe girl and let myself fall into the cushions. I study her. She hasn't moved since I entered the room. She's just sat there, watching and controlling. She doesn't look like she'd be much use in a fight, so why am I so scared?

'What happened to Victoria?' I ask.

'Weakness. The girl has delusions of grandeur, but she's as pathetic as they come.'

'Something threw her across the fucking room!'

'We're not here to talk about that girl,' she says. 'It's you I'm interested in. You see, I've heard that you made a connection

215

with an archivist. Only it's more than just a connection. There is a part of the Archivist in you and a part of you in him. That makes you useful.'

'Concerning.'

'No need for concern, Sun-young,' fringe girl says with a smile that radiates malice. 'You might become part of something great. With a life as worthless as yours, I'd expect you to find the prospect exciting.'

It's bad enough knowing your own life is worthless; worse when someone you've never met thinks the same. If she's trying to win me over, she's not doing a great job.

'So what now?' I ask. 'You've kicked everyone else out and locked me in. What comes next?'

Fringe girl smiles. Lights fade. I search the room, watch colour bleed from the peach walls, scarlet lampshades and the blue sofa. The girl has her arms up, fingers outstretched. I get my phone out, ready to call him. I'm in way over my head here.

I gasp so violently I nearly swallow my tongue. My phone slides from my hand. I try to move, but it's happening again. I've become the girl of lead. Even turning my head is impossible; it's grown so heavy the slightest twitch will snap my neck. Cold tears roll down my face.

'Fascinating,' she says. 'He's woven so deeply inside you. You're keeping him alive, do you know that? If you die, you take him with you. The same will be true for him, I expect. Your lives are intertwined. Watch.'

Despair fades like parting clouds, revealing fear, longing and hunger. Something else is in the room with us. It wants me with a desire not even Richard's lust for Laure could match. I wish for despair to return, a duvet of protection with me, a small child, huddled beneath it, hiding from the monsters under my bed.

The room, already stripped of colour, dissolves as if it were painted with sand and attacked by wind. I look down, can't see my hands. Look at the girl in front of me, can't see her either. We've been replaced by knots of thick ribbons, each one a different colour. They become my hands, my legs, my feet. They are the girl.

I look below. Other knots of coloured ribbons lie flat, asleep in beds. Some move through the corridors, pushing something, carrying something. I see pairs of knotted ribbons walking hand in hand. I see others having sex.

I look down at myself. See the ribbons that extend from my chest, fluttering in the space before me and stretching all the way to the Archivist, far in the distance. Everywhere there are people, some so small they're nothing but a dot. The longer I look, the more I see. If I were here long enough, I'm convinced I'd see everyone in the world, looking straight through the Earth to those who live on the other side.

This is what she sees. Not the same as him, whose facets are thin threads of silver. She has gifted her sight to me, but why?

'Look down,' she says. The ribbons where her mouth are move along with her tongue, throat and lungs, everything inside that's needed to speak. Even the ribbons in her brain twitch, thinking the words moments before they're spoken.

Ribbons that extend from her fingers, shades of violet and turquoise, follow the thread from the Archivist. They sidle up to his facets, sneaking their way inside me. Following the Archivist's path, I watch as they infiltrate my essence. I see how deeply he's worked his way into me and watch as she follows, using him to weave herself in.

Victoria was never the Archivist. It was the girl in front of me whose name I don't know. This girl who is now inside me.

I wanted to know what went on in 1214, and now I do. It was never about Mr Cavendish.

217

'They'll want to talk to you.'

'Not tonight.'

'That's not how this works.'

'I'll speak to the police when Laure is found.'

'You don't know she's been taken,' Monique says. 'She just witnessed a suicide; she's probably hiding.'

'She's not answering her phone.'

Monique shivers, rubs her goosebump-riddled forearms and checks behind her.

'I can call her in, but the station'll know who she is. Richard's only been officially missing four months.'

'What if they brought her to you?'

'Again, that's not how it's done.'

'Then change it.'

'Look,' Monique says, 'when girls Laure's age go missing they're either found in a few hours hiding under a bed or they're never found. We start down this road and she's either safe or you're about to bring a lot of attention your way just for someone to piece together what happened between you and Richard.'

The ambulance leaves, taking with it the body of a girl. They don't put the lights on. She was clearly dead – even without a doctor to declare it. Women hover uncertainly around the entrance, unsure if removal of the offending item means the night's back on. A few pass me on their way to a taxi. One wolf whistles. I'm a man in a dress until they get close, then I'm Death in a dress. It would be comical if I let it, but the fear that engulfs them is my doing and they hurry past, one kicking off her high heels and leaving them behind. Another vomits as she runs, holding onto her friends for support.

Then they're gone, out of my sight and beyond my influence. They laugh like children back in the real world after leaving a haunted house, overcompensating for their recent terror.

'Girls are killing themselves because of me.'

'We *suspect*,' Monique says.

'You suspect. I know. Tonight I took an essence and because of that things will change. I was not meant to take the essence; it was a carrot dangled before me. The girls came first and now that I have one, something else wicked this way comes.'

'And you know who's doing this?'

'I don't know who and I don't know why. What I do know is they will need someone else to make their point.'

'Laure Baptiste?'

'I don't believe in coincidence.'

Monique nods and looks through her phone. 'I'll call in some favours. They'll keep it quiet until she's found.'

'Thank you.'

She breathes in, braces herself, then steps closer and extends an arm. Her hand comes down hard on my shoulder, shielded from my skin by the meagre dress material that does nothing to keep out the cold. She squeezes reassuringly for as long as she can manage, all the while making eye contact like it's a bet. Finally she's forced to let go and staggers back a few steps.

'Doesn't get any easier,' Monique says as she composes herself.

I pulled some facets from her hand where our skin made contact through the chiffon's loose weave. One hangs past her knee but the others detach and drift into the Aether. She will never know what they contained, now lost to her forever. I hope it was something that caused her pain and that through an act of solidarity, a burden on her life was removed.

'I'll be in touch,' Monique says and holds up her phone.

I raise a hand to wave, but she's already broken into a jog and I'm left alone, wearing a dress and freezing. I project Genevieve's face but keep the rest of her concealed. She acts as my shield, convincing enough in the half-light that I don't warrant a second glance, leaving me to decide what needs to be done.

I produce my phone from the small bag I've had slung over my shoulder all evening. I scroll down to Sun's number and stare at it. I won't call her until there's news, good or bad. It'll make her angry, but right now the situation is delicate and, if I'm right, and Laure will be used against me, then Sun riding in on a wrecking ball and tearing people's heads off will only make matters worse.

I kill the screen and put the phone away. The event hall is before me, a monolith rising against the purple-hued night. I strip it down. Brick by brick, segment by segment, the Aether consumes the building. A second reality. Dimensionless. Timeless. The Aether always was and always will be. No paradise. No damnation. The Aether is death and rebirth, where we came from and where we will return to.

I see it always, creeping around the periphery to remind me of what I am. I grew up believing that everyone saw this darkness encroaching their vision. When I learnt it was only me, it became another wall of isolation. As I grew, I understood how to control what I see, and while I cannot eradicate the Aether entirely, I have learnt to focus elsewhere so its presence is only hinted at.

When I wish to see the essences that shine against it, I bring it to the fore. Permeating matter like tar, it consumes the world of science to supplant its own existence. Unknown and unknowable. I am nothing more than its gatekeeper. It scares me, and I think it knows.

Everything around me, myself included, has been replaced by the Aether's perfect blackness. Inside the event hall people move around the upper levels, either unaware of the dead girl or uncaring. People in their houses, asleep or watching TV, become contorted knots of threads in human form. No faces, no skin; everyone looks the same, distinguishable only by size.

I push my sight further and hundreds of lives wink into existence, their facets indistinct until they are nothing more than points of light.

I concentrate on the area around me, inside the event hall and nearby streets, hoping her small stature will mark Laure out, but there is nothing besides scuttling and staggering adults making their way home.

'You won't find her like that.'

I jump and Genevieve's face recoils into me. There's no one there.

Reality snaps back. Dark, but blinding when compared to the Aether's void.

A girl stands before me wearing a knowing smile, her left eyebrow raised. I allow the Aether to consume the world and she is gone. I pick out the movements of others, then hold my hand to my face and study facets as thin as silk threads moving within my flexing fingers.

The Aether withdraws and she's still there. The girl. The something. Not quite like me and not quite like everyone else, yet ordinary in appearance; your average person would see nothing awry. She appears to be a schoolgirl, older than Laure but younger than Sun. One of thousands. And yet, something about her is not as it should be.

'You're easy to find.' She runs a finger along the thread that extends from my chest. 'One way leads to you and the other to Sun-young. I may not be able to do all that you can, but this I can see.'

'What are you?'

'Not a thing as grand as you. I'm a throwback. Fractured. Half-formed. A cake removed from the oven too early. A distracted idea that forgot what it was supposed to be. A dance in the dark with no one to applaud. I am a what-never-should-have-been that marches to war with a shield of dreams. I am a use. A commodity. A mistake.' She smiles again. 'Victoria to you.'

'You took the girls.'

'Took them back, you mean. They were mine first.'

'You're responsible for their suicides.'

'I'm responsible for ending their pain. They're in a better place now.'

'The Aether is not a better place.'

'Really?' Victoria says. 'Says who? You can feel its influence just as I do, but you do not know it. Its hunger, its insatiable desire to possess is not born from malice. The Aether loves us. It is desperate for our return. Every moment we live only causes it more pain, so it is no surprise that its pull is so strong, its desire for our death so fervent.'

'You do not understand the Aether.'

'I can see your anger. Your essence crashes like breaking waves hoping to dash me against the rocks, but my ship does not sail on your sea.'

'Why can't I see your facets?'

'Because you don't know how to look.'

I take her chin in my hand. No curious facets appear to burst through her skin when I pull away.

'You're warm.'

'You should fear me,' I say and, as I do, I know it to be true.

'Why? You can't hurt me with your essence so that means your only option is physical violence, which I doubt you'd resort to. Besides, I'm not here to play antagonist. I need your help.'

'Why would I help you?'

'Because you want to find Laure Baptiste.'

'Where is she?'

Victoria spins on the ball of her foot. She dances around me, takes my hand and pulls it towards her. 'I can't tell you that until you help me.' She has my hand in both of hers, holding it just under her chin. 'You think I'm the enemy, but I'm just like you, a pawn to be sacrificed.'

I wrench my hand away. 'Tell me where Laure is.'

'I know you're worried about her, but she won't come to any harm.'

'Tell me.'

'Anyone else's essence would have been flayed and scattered to the winds. Did you know your anger could kill? And without you even laying a hand on them. No evidence, just a body stripped of life with not a mark on it.'

'Tell me.'

She holds up a finger, fixes me with the stare of an interrupted teacher. 'Not me. Not yet, at least. But you will work it out with enough time and my essence will be revealed to you, offering itself for manipulation. Not Laure, though. Never Laure.' Victoria holds up her arms. 'She asked me if they hurt. She had no idea who I was and said that if I ever needed someone to talk to, I could talk to her.'

Victoria's arms are slim, hairless and, aside from a few tiny moles, unblemished.

'Laure sees what I hide.'

The skin of Victoria's arms unfolds, revealing itself marked with scars that run in parallel lines from her wrist to her elbow. Some appear fresh, the newly formed scabs stained red with blood.

She flicks her wrists and they return to how they were, delicate and unmarked.

'People see what I want them to see. My arms, my legs, everything. I wear this body like a mask. I even fool myself. When I look in a mirror, this is what I see now,' she says, pointing to her face. 'But not Laure. This doesn't work on her. Do you understand? She's immune to my arms. Immune to your essence. Immune to everyone like us.'

Immune. I never thought of it that way. That moment in the bathroom, Laure became someone else I could connect with. Someone who doesn't fear being in my presence. Someone whose essence won't be scoured from a single touch. But her immunity means more than that. She is someone I can never save. Someone whose death will unfold without my interference. She will slip through the cracks in the barrier I create between life and the Aether. She is immune and, because of that, her death will be final.

'She is a threat to you,' I say. 'That's why she was taken.'

'A threat to someone,' Victoria says. 'But she was kind to me, so she won't be harmed.'

'And if I help you, you'll tell me where she is?'

Victoria nods. My essence calms, retracting itself to nestle sedately inside my body.

'I want to know what I am,' Victoria says.

'I don't know the answer to that.'

'The old woman in the church does. I only want to talk, but she won't let me enter. I told her what I was and she called me an abomination. Said I was unholy. A walking blasphemy. She must have stories about people like me in one of her books. Tales of the half-formed, the fractured. I just want to know what becomes of us.'

I call Antoinette. It's tense. She never mentioned Victoria's visits. Never mentioned that there was someone so close to being an archivist living in our town. Her defence is much as Victoria said, that the girl is a throwback. Despite her protestations, Antoinette will see Victoria. She can't deny my requests. I am her god.

'She'll see you,' I tell Victoria. 'Tonight.'

'Thank you. Laure has been taken to the old paper mill.'

'You know I'll go straight to her.'

'I know.'

'Then why tell me?'

'Because you and I are pawns, Mr Archivist. And it's time we fought back.'

22

I try to touch my face. Slap myself instead. My stinging cheek tethers me like an anchor. Without it, I'd drift somewhere else. Where, I don't know, but somewhere I don't want to be, that's for sure.

I look around. I'm in a hotel room. I remember coming here, eager to find out what happened to the girls who visited Mr Cavendish, only the door to the room was really the entrance to a tunnel and the further I walked, the darker everything became. The stuff at the start, with Nicola and Victoria, I remember; after that there's not enough light and my memories become blotchy and imagined. Something strange happened to Victoria. Everything after's gone.

The room's still dark, but it's the kind of dark I'm used to. Only the emergency exit light's on and all I see are the dim outlines of things. I get up awkwardly, waving my arms for balance like I'm on the back of a moving truck, even though everything's perfectly still. It's just me that's all fucked up. I try to find a switch and knock some shit over. Nothing breaks. My finger feels raised plastic. I push it. A crappy bedside light turns on. It's enough to help me find the next switch, and the next.

Each one makes the room that bit brighter until every light I can find is on. I stumble between sitting area, bedroom and bathroom, look behind curtains too. I'm alone.

I find my phone halfway under the sofa and check the time. It's after two. Shit, it was before eleven when I got here. The Archivist will wonder where I am, but there are no missed calls. He'll be in bed and so will Laure, with no clue I'm still out.

I practise walking. It takes a few goes but eventually I manage to cross the room without looking like I've downed a bottle of vodka. The last thing I need is to walk home looking drunk; I'm an easy enough target as it is.

I get out of that hotel so fast that I think I'm in a dream and the scenery's been changed around me by invisible stagehands. I go to follow the thread home but can't focus on it so use my maps instead. I've not been out this late since Laure and I moved in with the Archivist. Guess I've had no need to. I miss this. Everyone's asleep and it feels like I've been gifted an empty world.

I need to go through the centre of town to get home. The illusion of solitude is quickly shattered by noise and lights as drunk students and large groups of women in their forties hail taxis raucously and invade my world. It sets me on edge and I try to avoid being seen, even if it means leaving the comforting glow of streetlamps.

I take one of the side streets, stopping when I see myself in a shop front. There are no mirrors in the flat because the Archivist says he doesn't see the point in them. Laure and I have adapted to life without a reflection and fix each other's hair every morning. Aside from a fleeting glance in the toilet mirrors at school, I don't see myself anymore. My hair's grown. I kept it short so Richard couldn't grab it if I ran, but not so short that I appeared boyish and he'd look elsewhere. Before, the bottom was level with my chin. Now it's touching my shoulders and I could probably pull off a ponytail.

A second face of tangled ribbons lies beneath my skin, lagging behind every movement by half a second. I pull at it but it doesn't move. I shake my head and it whips past like a lazy shadow desperate to escape, and then I'm still and it sinks into my skin and hides.

I close my eyes, count to three and turn away from the mirror. I get why the Archivist doesn't like them.

I'm hungry.

I am in a brightly lit takeaway, eating a kebab. I don't remember coming here. I wanted something to eat and now I'm eating. Maybe I've got superpowers, even though everything about me feels wrong. Not just my head. It's deeper than that. The me that is *me* has been disconnected from my body.

The doner meat is cold and the fat has congealed. I'm holding one of those pickled chillies I normally hate but when I look down again, I can see I've eaten it right to the stem. Even the seeds are gone.

It's just me and the table and my cold doner kebab with its slimy meat. Reality appears through origami folds to reveal other tables with other people eating other late-night delights. I have seen this place before. I walked past it with the Archivist when a fight spilled into the street. It's quiet now. There's an old woman in the corner surrounded by shopping bags, a couple in their forties who don't look like they've been out this late since they were teenagers, and a guy in a dirty tracksuit who sits at an empty table playing with a sachet of salt.

There's also someone sitting in front of me.

'How are you doing, Kim? Or should I do away with that and just call you Sun?'

I stare at her and fill my mouth with soggy pita bread. Doner meat dangles from between my lips and I suck it up like spaghetti.

'I don't remember ordering this.'

'That's because you didn't,' Katie says. 'Someone left it half-eaten on the table before you came in.'

'Oh,' I say. More of the kebab finds its way into my mouth. 'That'll be why it tastes so bad.'

'One of the reasons. How about we just...' Katie goes to move the kebab but her fingers flit around the edges as if it's a dead cat. She bats my hands away as I try to grab more of the meat and the next thing I know, she's stood up and carried the entire table away, upending it into the bin.

'My kebab...'

'Don't worry, I'm sure you'll be seeing it again soon.'

Katie takes my wrist and leads me into the street.

Then we're in the park and Katie is talking to me even though we were leaving the kebab shop just a second ago.

'What the fuck do you want?' I ask, interrupting Katie midway through something I don't remember her starting.

'I'm helping you get home, Sun.'

'I don't need help.'

'Didn't you see the man sat behind you with his hand down his tracksuit bottoms? Because he would almost certainly have carried you into his van had I not been there. He looks like the type who builds a basement to fuck his kids in. I doubt you would have enjoyed your time together.'

'You shouldn't judge people on their looks.'

'Perhaps not,' Katie says, 'though he was masturbating rather furiously.'

'Oh… So how did you know I was lost?'

'Nicola. Though finding you wasn't trivial. Fortunately, I know a lot of people and there aren't many five-foot half-Korean girls in a bright pink puffer jacket out tonight.'

'Five foot one.'

'Of course you are.'

Things feel clearer. I know who I am, where I am and where I'm going. Everything around me makes sense. It's dark. We're cutting across a field towards a path lined by streetlamps. The town is behind us and the silent world is mine again, only this time I share it with Katie.

'I think I was wrong about Mr Cavendish,' I say.

'How so?'

'I believed the rumours. Thought he was sleeping with those girls, but that's ridiculous, isn't it?'

'It does seem unlikely. This isn't a soap opera.'

We walk on, over the path and across another field. I don't know why we didn't get a taxi. I suggested it, but Katie said it'd be better to walk.

'Are you all right, Sun?'

'Yes. Why?'

'You're lying on the floor eating grass.'

As soon as she says it, I taste it in my mouth and spit it out. I could have sworn we were walking next to each other. Katie helps me stand then spends at least five minutes knocking grass and dirt from my clothes.

'I don't think you're feeling very well, Sun.'

I nod and hold on to Katie for support. There's something dishonest about this girl. It radiates from her, cultivating cancers of distrust in anyone stupid enough to get close. I think she knows it. I think she loves it.

There's a pond in front of us, the water black and menacing.

As soon as I see it, something in my stomach flips and I throw Katie off and run for it. The kebab makes an appearance, spreading over the surface instead of graciously sinking to the bottom.

A second heave and more appears, its stench somehow fouler this time round. More on the third. A few mouthfuls of bile and saliva on the fourth and then nothing.

'Children play in that pond, Sun. My cousin Quin likes to sail his boat in it, wading up to his knees and spitting water at the sail to capsize it.'

One more spit. 'And?'

'And now I will find watching him highly amusing.'

I'm on my hands and knees, ready to stand. Katie has moved back, not keen on watching pita bread and pepper skins float across the water.

My face appears in the water as the disturbance calms and the surface returns to a black mirror. There's something alive in there. Colours glowing in the darkness. It is on me. In me. Around me. My face falls, sliding off my head and creeping down my neck. I reach out to save it. My hands just keep gripping the cold concrete lip of the pond when something else appears.

Knotted and twisted and blindingly bright, they unfurl and stretch to take my fallen face and return it home. A twitch. A wave. With another blink they're gone. My face in the black water stares back at me, confused and relieved.

I walk over to Katie, sat on a bench and illuminated by her phone. She's frowning.

'Fucking girl,' Katie mutters under her breath. 'Not you,' she adds quickly.

I reach for her phone, watching as ribbons of facets trail my arm and sink into the fabric of the jacket. I pull back and shake my hand in front of my face. Everything lights up as facets burst from my skin, unable to keep up with my blurred fingers. It goes dark again when I stop.

'Did you see that?'

'You waving your hand in front of your face? Yes. And it concerns me, Sun.'

'I need to see him.'

'Who? Oh, why pretend I care? It's not like anyone would stay up this late for you. No, we've something else to do as Victoria has decided now is the appropriate hour to take an interest in the church.'

'I don't care,' I say and follow the ribbon back to the Archivist. Didn't it used to be a silver thread? No, it's always been a ribbon, I'm sure of it. I look along it, following as it stretches into the woods. That's not where home is. Where is he? And who's with Laure?

Home first to check on Laure. Small sleep. Find the Archivist. Big sleep.

Katie grabs my wrist. 'You're with me.' I try to pull away but she's freakishly strong and, despite tugging, I don't even shake her arm. 'Victoria's gone to see the hermit in the archivist church. I need you to get me there.'

Katie lets go. There are marks where her fingernails dug into my arm. One of them bleeds.

'Use your phone.'

It takes me a full second to realise that Katie's slapped my ear. Sound goes funny. It is perfect in one side and there's a shrill ringing in the other.

'I know how to use a fucking phone.'

She's looming over me, her head fully angled down. Lightning bolts of red flash in her eyes. She takes my shoulders.

'Victoria is a liability. I can't have her deciding to do things on her own. So what I need from you is to get me into that church so I can get Victoria home and away from that woman.'

'Antoinette? She's just a historian.'

'Exactly.'

'But—'

Katie throws me backwards. The grass here has been walked on so much it's nothing but dirt and I hit it hard. First my back then my head. I'm engulfed in white. More than just seeing stars. I'm knocked out of myself. A twisted mass of me, bright fidgety ribbons, float up from my body. I close my eyes against the glare, but it makes no difference. Perhaps what I'm seeing isn't really there. Or maybe this is something I don't see with my eyes. I hold my hand up to my face and while streetlamps in the distance and the half-illuminated view of Katie vanish, the facets remain.

I feel cold. Incomplete. This is pins and needles of the soul.

I watch the parts of me that escaped float down, extinguishing their light as they bury themselves into me. Something is very wrong. So wrong it could kill me. I might not trust Antoinette, but if anyone knows what's happening, it will be her.

I hold out a hand and Katie pulls me up.

'OK, I'll come with you.'

Katie smiles, radiant and perfect. 'I thought you might. And, Sun, I do apologise for the violence. But you know all friendships have their difficulties. A little bit of conflict can really bring people closer.'

'Works for me.'

I kick Katie between the legs.

'That was for Sophia.'

The taxi driver complained from the moment I entered his car until I closed the door at the old paper mill. He had children who would be up in a few hours and he needed to get home to take them to school. The dispatcher didn't tell him how far he'd have to go. He wasn't supposed to be on tonight, but Christian sprained an ankle on his niece's trampoline and so here he is in the middle of nowhere driving some cross-dressing queer – no offence or anything – to some poofter orgy and no, I won't be waiting for you here, mate.

He leaves faster than he arrives. Without the glare of headlights, I struggle to make out the row of chimneys against the moon-tinted sky. Reluctant to reveal themselves, they shuffle into my vision one at a time, bringing the building below with them. A few abandoned cars, a van that looks like someone lived in it for a considerable period, even an upturned bath and an assortment of flowerpots have made their way to the mill.

Laure has not.

I was tipped off as to our arrival when the taxi driver yelled that we were 'finally fucking here' and at that moment

I did away with the physical world only to see that Laure, or at least her essence, was elsewhere. The mill, however, is not deserted.

The screech from the door does little to mask my arrival. Fortunately for me, the element of surprise was lost the moment the taxi driver revved his engine and barrelled down the road. I flick back to the Aether. They're at the far end of the building directly in front of me, hidden behind several walls.

I use the torch on my phone. As I step between support columns and steam machines whose function I couldn't guess at, shards of metal hamper my progress, snagging my dress and gashing my skin.

Sun and Laure are the reason I am here. I have become something to them. Perhaps not family, but a facsimile of one. They are not my clients and I am not beholden to them through a contractual agreement. The reason I provide for them is because I want to. Now that someone has taken one of them from me, I cannot do something I want to do and that, above all, is what frustrates me.

Should any permanent harm come to Laure then I will have been denied the option to provide for her indefinitely. I suspect that will anger me and essences will swiftly find themselves detached from bodies.

The second set of footsteps are louder than mine. I raise the light enough to see someone step out from behind a wall.

'I'm sorry to disappoint you, but Laure Baptiste isn't here.'

'I know.'

A pause.

'An abandoned paper mill... this isn't a movie.'

'It seemed clichéd,' I say.

'You still came, though.'

'Yes.'

'And what a fetching dress you have on. I wasn't expecting you to have made such an effort for little old me.'

I passionately wish I was wearing something else.

Ignoring his comment, I step closer. A face I have seen before is revealed in stark grey shades. He was there when the school governess's husband was killed, wearing a waistcoat and periodically checking his watch. Like everyone else in the room, he radiated no emotion when the old man died. Even when I offered to project the face of the deceased, there was no inclination that he or anyone else wanted to talk with him.

I still have the old man inside me, one of several I have never projected since taking possession of them. They don't even know they're dead, or that some part of them remains tethered to the physical world.

This man is an agent of the one who orchestrated this, not the orchestrator themselves.

'You're going to tell me where Laure is.'

'No, I'm not.' A shake of the head. A casual kick sends something rolling across the floor. He folds his arms and casts me a look that's almost pity.

'You know what I am. You should be afraid,' I tell him.

'And yet here I am, not bothered in the slightest,' he says with self-assured confidence.

My essence creeps along the floor in a fog, seeking its prey. 'Your lack of concern is because you don't understand.'

'No,' he says and pulls something from behind his back, 'it's because I've got a fucking gun, you dickhead.'

The gun presents a problem.

'And now,' he says, levelling it at my head and walking closer, 'you'll be coming with me.'

I'm forced into a car.

'Put the seatbelt on,' the man says. The gun doesn't waver from my face as he starts the engine and clips himself in. 'I know exactly what you are and exactly what you can do. The second I feel ill, I pull the trigger. Understood?'

'Yes.' He won't remember the look of contempt on my face, so I ensure the feeling is carried in that single word.

He jams the gun into my crotch. 'Just because you're in a dress doesn't mean you don't have a cock. Not that I imagine it gets much use.' He stares, waiting for a response. When he realises there won't be one, he mutters to himself and laughs. 'And don't worry, I asked for an automatic car especially, so this hand can stay right here.'

He pushes the gun harder into my crotch and accelerates away from the paper mill. Reining in my essence to this degree takes considerable concentration so I search for a landmark to focus on, but there is nothing visible besides passing trees. Light from the thread is the only permanent feature in the landscape, so I use that. I follow it as it streaks across fields and cuts through rows of trees and the occasional road sign. The thread does not lead to my flat. Sun is not at home.

Hopelessness invades me. The last true archivist and I cannot keep safe the two people I have taken into my care. The girls who died by my hands only to be stolen from me, another mark of my incompetence.

And Martina.

Martina, who so desperately wanted to believe that my archivism had been realised. Her admiration so bright I couldn't bear to extinguish it. Had I understood the depth of her devotion, I would have crushed the lie. But I didn't, and she left this world to be ravaged by the Aether.

As despair joins hopelessness, the grip on my essence slips and the position of the gun is rearranged, pressing down harder.

The driver says nothing, struggling to control his car at such speeds around the winding roads of the countryside. I regain control and the force lessens.

'See, not so hard,' he says as we fly over a cattle grid.

I focus on the thread again. Not the end that leads to Sun and wherever she may be, but the bright light that dances around my silicon-enhanced cleavage.

We're approaching lights, other cars, sleeping buildings. He says nothing for a while.

Occasionally the force of the gun against me lessens when an unexpected bend appears in the road, but even these he manages with a single hand on the wheel, throwing me against the side of the car. Another bend, clearly signposted, though he doesn't brake until the last opportunity, and I'm thrown towards him. I rip my essence from my arm and shoulder, forcing it deeper inside as my extremities experience a taste of death.

I bump into him only briefly. He doesn't comment, just keeps driving, unaware that he almost had cause to pull the trigger.

Arrogance is to blame, though I challenge anyone who has grown up being treated like a demigod not to present as an adult with an over-developed ego. I expect the same is true for members of the royal family.

Antoinette was always the first to caution me; that is, in the moments between praising my divinity. Her lessons on archivism clarified that the unfavourable elements of society would desire my abilities. What would I say if approached to take the essence of the head of a drug cartel? A dictator? The linchpin of a child trafficking network? 'No' is unlikely to be an option, especially considering I am the only archivist under the age of sixty. Knowing that I am unique has fooled me into believing that, like Jesus, I am untouchable, conveniently forgetting that the Roman Empire's treatment of Jesus was not commendable towards the end.

'I'll miss that school,' the man says. 'It was an odd job, for sure. I've never been an intellectual, but a part's a part, isn't it? Didn't like the name Cavendish though, would have preferred something shorter.'

We pass a gritter that showers the windscreen with salt.

'I've never done anything like that. A few minor parts in plays, once got picked for a shampoo advert, but I celebrated too early and woke up four hours late. I turn up at the studio and there's the guy that holds the boom mic lathering up his hair with all the cameras on him. Stopped drinking after that and decided to take things seriously.'

It's so dark that I barely notice the slip into the Aether. His essence sat beside mine, facets wound between the fibres of his muscles and coiled around every bone. I watch as they ride the movements of his jaw. He takes this as a sign of interest and continues to talk. I nod intermittently, but his ego drives the conversation more than any input from me.

We stop. The engine idles. I leave the Aether to find us at traffic lights.

'No one'll admit it,' he says, drumming his fingers on the steering wheel, 'but it's not like girls magically become fuckable at sixteen. Never touched them, though. The money was too good. But there was this one girl, Sophia. They told me to break her. I asked her over one night. Couldn't believe it when she came. We'd literally just met and there she was, all eager to see me and everything. So we hung out and I got her a few drinks. It didn't take much to get her clothes off. I took some pictures because that's what they wanted. Next thing she's in my bathroom throwing up, so I took her phone

239

and sent the pictures to her mum. Man, was she pissed when she found out. Worked though, because a week later Sophia killed herself. That's what they wanted, you see. Dead girls. It's messed up, but who am I to object? If it wasn't me then it'd just be some other guy. And I needed the money. Anyway, there's far too many fucking people on the planet. A bit of a cull's probably a good thing. But, man, did those girls love me. I tell ya, some nights I nearly broke my dick off thinking about them.'

It is bizarre how the mind processes contempt. I would have assumed that after being kidnapped, and with a gun pressed against my crotch, my feelings of hatred towards that person would be saturated. However, it appears this belief was wrong as that paraphilic confession has summoned fresh disgust from somewhere deep within me that I doubt existed before I met Sun and Laure. Before, I had only myself to consider, but now I am consumed by outrage on behalf of the sisters.

'Archivists are dying out,' I say. He's driving erratically, taking corners too late and not slowing before the blind summits on this single-track road. He looks at me, mouth open, before focusing on the road again. I continue, surprised by the steadiness in my voice. 'A friend of mine, though I suppose she is more of a mother figure than a friend, has spent her life researching the cause of our demise and has yet to come up with a theory. Though she has pointed out that as the population of the planet increases, the population of archivists decreases, as if one is there to balance the other.'

'Uh-huh,' he says. Eyes on the road.

Facets push through my skin like saplings. They probe the air, pulling others with them until my face and body bristle with spectral crop. They cocoon the driver, leaving enough of a distance so as not to pull at his essence and bring about the feeling of dread that accompanies ethereal meddling. They are everywhere, streaming from me, through the material of my seat, the roof of the car, even cutting into the asphalt beneath us. Each ending centimetres from the man, surrounding him on all sides. When he moves, they move. Flowing. Dancing. Waiting.

'I think my friend is partly right,' I say as we drive over a dual carriageway. 'There are so many people on Earth that no one has time for the dead. Perhaps we should just let them die and be done with it? Though I wonder if it's not the *number* of dead that has driven archivists into extinction, but the *type* of dead. Archivists don't often provide sanctuary for altruists. Our clients are the rich, the greedy, the devious. Their existence is prolonged and denied to the Aether, the place we go when we die and the place from which we are born. The Aether created me as it did you. And because it is denied sociopaths like you, it will not create another like me.'

'What the fuck are you talking about?'

I shake my head. 'Never mind.'

The sphere of facets dive into his head like needles. They wrestle his essence away from his cranium, throwing facets out of his skull in clumps that burst in the air.

His arm goes slack as messages from the control centre fall silent. In my haste to stop him from pulling the trigger, I forget to take the wheel. I reach for it now, but my returning vision of the real world reveals I'm too late and we drive off the road. I do what I can to avoid the trees, the wheel jerking violently in my hands. I pull on the handbrake and the car skids. We hit something I can't see and I'm thrown to the other side of the car. The man next to me follows suit and his head hits my shoulder before he's tossed back to collide with the window, cracking it.

A deafening bang. My ears ring until long after the car has rolled to a stop in a field of rapidly waking cows.

I am in pain, but it is minor when compared with the last time I was in a car accident. My body is not unduly warm, which I take as a sign that the gun was not pointing at me when it discharged.

The man next to me is silent and in a brief panic I imagine him with the gun in his hand, only this time pointed at my head. My foot kicks something hard. The gun is in my footwell and I nudge it towards the door. With no weapon the man has no power over me, and my essence relaxes to fill my body and the space that surrounds me.

There's a gasp to my right. Blood is over the back of his seat and down his shirt. His eyes are wide and every movement of his mouth produces a thick gurgle. He spits blood onto his lap.

The bullet entered his throat, ripped open his trachea, and exited through his spine before travelling through the headrest and out of the car via the roof.

Facets stream from the wound in his neck, brain, organs and everything else that's shutting down. His body is a sinking ship; the facets are desperate to flee in the hope of rescue from the Aether's seas.

'Release the life you hold so tight; welcome me and leave the light.'

I touch my forehead to his and gather his essence with a single sweep of mine. The fear in his eyes leaves and he slumps forward in his seat.

I sit for a moment, regarding the dead man next to me. I wonder how tall he is. Five foot ten? Five foot eleven? Shorter than I am, broader too. Not perfect, but near enough. His clothes are not to my taste though. A little too brash, the uniform of men who drink too much and spew misogyny. Though, on balance, I prefer them to the dress.

The door opens on the third kick, cutting a furrow in the mud as I force it wide enough to get out. One headlight still works, but apart from that everything is black. I use my phone to find the road, following our tracks to the break in the fence.

At the road it becomes clear I'm near nothing of use. The town is miles away, wrapped in a hazy orange blanket and, aside from my phone, the only light comes from the moon.

No one is coming to rescue me.

This is good.

I project the man's face as I walk back to the car and instantly he talks.

'Where the hell has he gone? Shit! I can't feel my legs. Or my arms. What the fuck? Am I being carried? Hey! Put me down! Where are we going? Yeah, the car's crashed, I can fucking see that. Call an ambulance or something. Hey! HEY!'

The driver-side door opens easily. The interior light reveals someone in a dress slumped over the steering wheel.

'I've fucking killed him! SHIT! SHIT! SHIT! SHIT!'

I pull the shoulder back and the body falls into the seat. The head rolls back, its dead eyes briefly catching mine. That shuts him up.

"What a fetching dress you have on. I wasn't expecting you to have made such an effort for little old me," I type into my phone, holding it up to my face for the dead man to read.

It's not that I can't speak, it's that I can't hear it if I do, and neither can anyone else. The brain has been manipulated into believing that my face is not there; hearing my voice would reveal the deception and so the brain silences it.

He screams. I cover my mouth with my hand to muffle the sounds, but each time I pull it away the screaming restarts. I am bizarrely concerned that someone will appear from behind a hedge despite standing in an unremarkable field in the middle of the night.

I take the head of the dead man, still warm and sticky with his blood, and hurl his essence back inside.

He flails. Looks at me and tries to scream. The air has left his lungs and so the only sound left to him is a pathetic wheeze.

'Who sent you?' I ask.

With no heartbeat he quickly dies. I catch his essence before the Aether closes in. Once more his face is over mine. He's still screaming, but it's different this time. Guttural and interspersed with deep sobs that rise from my stomach.

I throw him back into his body. There's not enough time to ask the question before his essence drifts away, unable to cling to the tiny pocket of life that remains.

I catch him. Throw him back. This time he only blinks before escaping. I pull him into me and lean over to unclip his seatbelt. He falls to the floor in an undignified heap, saving me the task of manhandling his corpse.

I straighten him out, then I'm on my knees, hands together, giving him chest compressions. I breathe him back into his body. Technically brain dead, under normal circumstances he would be in a coma. Fortunately for my unnamed kidnapper, I am with him, and while I continue to artificially pump his heart, my essence is busy ensuring that his facets remain active, even as the flesh they're forced to cling to slowly dies.

I doubt that he can hear me or see me, but he is awake and he can feel.

I pull my hands away from his chest and leave him to die for the fourth time. Death is not something I have experienced, but I have heard many first-hand accounts from clients who have been asked by curious relatives. There is no definitive answer as to exactly what transpires at the moment of death. The one thing the dead do agree on is that they are thankful it only happens once.

His face creeps over mine and as soon as his mouth has formed he pleads with me to stop. He is crying. I graciously allow him time to compose himself.

'An archivist,' he says. Tears and sputum, likely mine, run down his face. I unfold his handkerchief from the pocket of the trousers I wear and dry us both. 'Thank you. Look, I just work for her, you know? It was a job and they're hard to come by. It was an audition for a play, a solo. There were five roles, some old, some young, nothing I hadn't done before. When I got the call and the part was mine, I was over the moon, but when I got back to the theatre I was bundled in a car and driven to some hotel room. I don't know where. That's when I met her and she told me what she wanted me to do and how much she was going to pay. I couldn't say no to that.'

I clap my hands in front of his face.

'Too much backstory. I get it, you're not interested. But this woman, right? Called herself the Jade Archivist. Rich too, and powerful. The police, criminal gangs, telecoms companies, she had an in with all of them. Ever find yourself without phone signal? That'll be her. Thing is, she's after you. I don't know why, but me being at the school and all those girls dying was for you.'

I walk back to the road.

'You know, I think this will be good for me,' the man says. 'Kind of like a fresh start. Here, could you put me in a new body? Someone younger, nineteen or twenty? Handsome, but with a twist that makes me kind of interesting so people can't look away? I reckon if I give it another go I could do it. Talk to the right people, get seen in the right places. First movie by the time I'm twenty-two, shouldn't be too hard.'

I pull him back. Perhaps he does deserve a second chance. His only part in this was to accept a job and, while his death was an accident, it was technically an accident I caused. For that alone, I owe him the rest of his life back.

But what he said about the girls in the school will not leave me. Did he have those thoughts when he looked at Sun? At Laure? I do not want an essence that holds such disgusting feelings inside me. Also, I cannot imagine I will soon forgive the gun against my crotch.

His essence explodes from my back, shimmering in hues of gold to be claimed by the Aether.

24

The gate closes with a gentle clang. A few steps down the path and there's Victoria, on her hands and knees in a flower bed. She brings up a clump of earth and rubs it to nothingness. Muttering, she keeps digging, losing herself in the spikey hedges that snag her clothes.

'Victoria.' Katie stands over her, arms neatly crossed.

Victoria jerks at the mention of her name. She looks up, guilty and afraid. The dynamic between the two of them is not what I experienced in school. There, Katie appeared a sidekick to Victoria's claims of archivism. In front of the Archivist church at three in the morning, Victoria is a child caught up past their bedtime.

Katie looks at me.

'There are a lot of them,' I say and knock on the door. It opens immediately. Antoinette's saree has changed from yellow to purple and she wears a scarf of the same colour over her closely cropped hair.

'You are not the visitor I'm expecting.'

I point to Victoria. She has removed herself from the garden and stands awkwardly as Katie vigorously bangs soil from her coat.

'He said I needed to find the keys.'

'He was joking,' Antoinette says tersely.

'So I can come in?'

'I cannot refuse the request of an archivist, even at this hour.'

Antoinette stands aside and we follow her into the church that doubles as her house.

'Take a seat,' she says once we're in what she uses as a living room. 'Not you, though,' she says, pointing to Victoria. 'You sit on the floor.'

Silently, Victoria obeys.

'Sun, make sure they don't touch anything.'

Antoinette leaves. She's reluctantly brought me over to her side. I suppose I should be flattered that I'm thought better of than a fake archivist and a complete stranger.

'Victoria, it is time to leave,' Katie says, having refused to sit. 'It is late and your parents will be worried.'

'I've been trying to get in here for a year, I'm not leaving.'

'You know I can make you leave.'

Victoria takes a cushion from the sofa and sits on it. 'And I can make you leave your body.'

Katie shuts up and looks at me as if there's something I can do. I part follow their conversation, but there's a mirror in front of me so the whole time they speak, I watch my face flow in and out of itself. Even when I'm perfectly still there are undercurrents that make my cheek bulge or one of my eyes swell. I look at Katie then back to the mirror, where my chin has been pulled round to my ear. Then back at Katie. Either she can't see what's happening or she's too caught up in Victoria to notice.

Antoinette returns with a tray of tea. It looks heavy, but she manages it with only one working hand. She sets it down and looks at Victoria disapprovingly as she passes her a cup.

Victoria is quick to thank her and comment on the church and how interested she would be to learn more about Antoinette's research. Her brown-nosing doesn't get a response.

'Sun, you don't look well,' Antoinette says as she sits and tucks her bare feet under her legs.

'I don't think I am.'

'You should sleep. Most of this place is filled with my books, but you should be able to find a bed in there.' Antoinette points to an archway that leads into a large hall where books have been stacked to create walls. A slight knock and the whole lot would come down, crushing whoever lay sleeping beneath it. I might have been welcomed with tea, but I'm still another woman in the Archivist's life as far as she's concerned. An unwelcome presence at best.

I decline. If I need sleep, I'll take it on the sofa and talk to Antoinette in the morning. Whatever's going on has something to do with my essence and if anyone knows how to fix that it'll be her. Katie's reaction to Victoria's threat is another reason to stay awake. There's more going on between them than I realised. Just because Victoria isn't an archivist doesn't mean she isn't dangerous.

'So,' Antoinette says, regarding us with humorous suspicion, 'it's gone three in the morning, I've invited you in and we're sat in my living room drinking tea. At what point does someone explain what's going on?'

'What's going on is that I am an archivist and you refuse to let me into a church that's supposed to worship me.' Victoria squares up to Antoinette, who casually blows on her tea.

'My dear, you are nothing more than the Joseph Smith of Archivism.'

'I am not!'

'There are very few people who know as much about

archivists as I do and I can promise you, young girl, you are most certainly not an archivist.'

Victoria stares Antoinette down, her eyes sunken beneath angry brows and her mouth pulled in tight. I think she's holding her breath, reduced to a child used to getting her own way.

With a gasp she relaxes and sinks to the floor by Antoinette's feet.

'If I'm not an archivist, then what am I?'

Antoinette puts her cup on the floor and takes Victoria's hand. She runs her thumb around Victoria's palm then gently cradles her face.

'Sit on a chair.'

Victoria nods and sits, defeated.

'You're not unique,' Antoinette says. 'There have been others like you, but not many. Rare when compared to an archivist, but rarity doesn't make something special. I will admit, albeit reluctantly, that you possess elements of archivism. Let me guess, you can take a person's essence, but not without considerable effort, and when you do there is always something lost?'

Victoria nods. 'I can't keep them.'

'The Aether is taking its rightful possession.'

'I don't even know it's happening, but then I look inside myself and it's gone.'

'So why take them if they'll only be lost?'

Victoria looks at Katie, who's shooting her daggers, and I take this pause in the conversation to indicate that everyone in the room would like to hear something from me. I shift on the sofa, drunk through lack of sleep and also probably because there is something profoundly wrong with my essence, and kick over my empty teacup.

'Sun, you really should get some sleep.'

I hold my hand up and waggle a finger at Antoinette before pointing it at Victoria. 'She's not an archivist *anything*.'

'Sun-young.' Victoria shuffles to the edge of her seat and removes her thin jumper. Holding out her hands, she says, 'Take them.'

I give an involuntary glance towards Antoinette for assurance. She nods and I slide off the sofa and take Victoria's hands.

'Watch carefully, Sun-young. All is not as it seems.'

I look down at her hands. Smooth, flawless. She has the skin of a model. A flurry of moles appear, settling where perfect unblemished skin had been moments before. Not just moles but pores and hairs, marks and scars. The skin of her hands flips like tiles, cascading up her arms. Her entire body changes and my perception of her blurs and refocuses as my brain struggles to understand what it's seeing. Shorter with a bit of heft to her figure. Not fat, but not delicate like she was before. Her face has changed too and while her hair is still brown, the lustre's been stripped away.

Victoria smiles. She's shed her beauty, not to reveal ugly, just average. I let go of her hands and take a step back so I can see her better. There are scars up her arms, deep ones that required stitches, which run from her wrist up past her elbow. There is another scar on her face and, when I look again, her jaw doesn't sit right.

'Thith ith how I really look.' Not just how she looks, how she sounds too.

'You're not a fake?' I manage.

'No, I am. Look at me! Everything ith fake.'

'I was so certain you weren't an archivist.'

'And you were right. I'm not. I'm a thomething elth.'

'You are an archivist,' Katie shouts. 'Don't let them tell you you're not. And put that body away, it's disgusting.'

'Thith ith me!'

'No, Abigail is you.'

Victoria sits, her body folding itself to become thinner, longer and prettier, so that the moment her bum reaches the seat cushion she looks how she's always looked to me. Like a dead girl called Abigail. Her smile is weak and again I struggle to understand the hierarchy between her and Katie.

'Abigail was my friend. We were out hacking when something spooked the horses. I was thrown onto a barbed-wire fence and that's where,' her arms flash back to her own for a moment, revealing the scars, 'and,' her perfect jaw is wiped from her face and I can see where it must have broken, only to be reattached after hours of surgery, 'came from. Abigail mithed the fenth, tho I thought she wath fine. But she'd landed on her neck. After I had freed mythelf, I tried to help her thtand. Doing that mutht have killed a nerve becauth next thing, she wath dying and I wath holding her and bleeding and when she left her body, I caught her. I felt her inthide me and I knew I wath different.' Victoria's face is her own again, or at least the one I know as hers. Abigail's, I suppose. She crosses her legs and falls back into the seat. 'Abigail was three years older than me. I always wanted to be her. So graceful. So elegant. Always talking in riddles I'd pretend to understand. It seemed obvious that I'd become her. Her essence left slowly. A few facets here. A few facets there. Then, after a month, there was nothing left but this shell.'

'Can the Archivist do that too, make himself into another person?'

Antoinette can't hide her smile. 'If that girl can do it then of course he can. He hasn't even begun to approach the limits of his abilities. He's too busy making money and saving girls in distress.'

'That last comment felt a little pointed.'

'You're one of many, Sun, no need to feel special.'

That's the Antoinette I expected.

Katie stands. 'Victoria, you know what you are and have been welcomed into the church. It's time we left. I will call for a car.'

'But I don't know what I am,' Victoria says.

'And she has not been welcomed,' Antoinette finishes.

'I'm with Katie,' I say, forcing the shudder that follows just to piss her off. 'It's so very late and I need to get home. Katie, please call a car or, better yet, a fleet of beds on wheels, and I promise to be grateful until the next time I see you.'

Katie gets out her phone and types a message to someone. 'I don't know why you continue to fight our friendship, Sun.'

'It's largely because you're a cunt. Antoinette, I'm sorry for, you know, being here so late and bringing these two into your home.'

'He told me to expect an unusual visitor,' Antoinette says as she gathers the cups. 'Victoria, I think I owe you an apology. I *don't* but I still think it. You might not be an archivist and I expect that as you age, the abilities you possess will fade like a child's imagination. But if you were to come here again you would... be allowed to enter. There has been little study on those like you and I'm sure if we spent some time together, I could learn something.'

Victoria throws herself from her seat. 'Can I hug you?'

'Absolutely not,' Antoinette says and she leaves for the kitchen.

If Victoria is dejected, she doesn't let it show. She flicks through Antoinette's piles of books and the carefully written notes that cover every flat surface while Katie stares at her phone, anxiously tapping the screen.

'Do you know of many archivists?' Victoria asks.

Antoinette comes back into the room, finally looking ready for sleep. 'They are what I spend my life researching, so yes, I've come across a few.'

'Have you heard of the Jade Archivist?'

Katie drops her phone.

'Every researcher knows the Jade Archivist,' Antoinette says. 'Why do you ask?'

'I want to know if she had a granddaughter. Someone like me.'

'I can't imagine there were many people like you, and certainly not in any book I've read. I think I had something on the Jade in the nave.' Antoinette leaves and returns with the book. She rests it on the arm of the sofa and talks while flicking through the pages.

'She was born in 1524 to a family of some wealth. There would have been no expectation that she would become an archivist by trade and she was married at nineteen to a man who took little interest in her, or supposedly, anyone else of her sex. Despite the negative effect that many archivists have on people, the Jade was known to charm anyone she met. You must remember, this was when archivists were not rare or revered and, much like a weaver or apothecarist, were unwelcome in high society.'

'What happened to her?' Victoria asks.

'I believe she grew bored,' Antoinette says, looking up. 'Imagine having god-like powers and never using them. She ran away from her husband and the comforts of minor aristocracy to become a practising archivist, culminating in her appointment as the first mistress of the Guild of Archivists and being given the name Jade. Only the guild members ever received a name, either a precious stone or mineral. It makes her easier to research.'

'And a granddaughter?'

Antoinette runs her finger along a page until she finds what she wants.

'She had a number, it seems. There isn't much on them I'm afraid. Accept that...' Antoinette pauses, focusing on the book. 'One moment.' She picks up another book, heavily annotated in pencil, confirms something and returns to the first. 'She had a granddaughter named Victoria, the oldest daughter of her oldest daughter. It says here she—'

Katie leaps from the sofa with a gazelle's grace. She lands, one hand on the floor to steady herself, and takes something long and shiny from a table piled with letters. Antoinette doesn't even scream as Katie pounces. The golden blade of the letter opener catches the light for a second before Katie slides it into Antoinette's left ear.

Antoinette's emaciated body floats to the floor, meeting it with a dull thud. Blood oozes from her ear and fills the scratches and grooves in the wood.

I run to her, instinctively pulling her head onto my lap. The letter opener has been forced in as far as the handle. Whether I leave it or remove it, her brain has been sliced and the meagre experience I gained as a pretend doctor will do nothing for her.

Katie pokes me with her foot. 'Come on, Sun, the car will be here soon.' Utterly unconcerned over the murder she's just committed, Katie picks her phone from the floor. 'You too, Victoria. Beds await.'

'Victoria, you can—' but the shock is fading and she already knows what I'm going to say. She just needs to hold on to Antoinette until we find the Archivist.

Katie stares up at the ceiling and groans as Victoria fights through the tables and books to reach me. 'For fuck's sake, can we please just go home?' Then she's in the air, flying over the back of a sofa, and catches Victoria in the side. Victoria struggles to fight back, but the body beneath the dancer's shell isn't used to exercise, whereas Katie's muscles look honed from years of lacrosse.

'She's leaving!' Victoria screams just before Katie flips her onto her back and straddles her, pinning her arms. I see no essence, but there is a subtle change between holding a live body and a dead one and, as Victoria screams again, I feel that change and look around as if I might glimpse Antoinette escaping into the Aether.

Victoria grows slack and Katie lets go of her arms but remains on top.

'I killed her to protect you, you know that. Don't you, Victoria? Just like how you killed those girls to save *her.*'

'I didn't kill them,' Victoria's voice is only a whimper.

'You know what you did to them; what you put inside them.'

'I was saving them.'

Katie shakes her head and bends over so her nose hovers over the tip of Victoria's. 'You manipulated them, getting under their skin because that's what *she* wanted from you.'

'I freed them from the pain of the physical world.'

'The pain of the physical world is all there is. You sold them lies, Victoria. Fed them bullshit and called it honey. If you want to pretend they're in a better place, then you do that. Doesn't change the truth, though. At least *I* knew it was wrong. But after Daddy jumped off a bridge I've been living in a fucking semi. I'm doing this for money. You just want to please your dear old granny.'

'Shut up, you fucking psychopath.' Katie looks up and I drop a vase the weight of a small child onto her head. It catches the back of her skull, hits the floor and rolls towards the sofa.

'I was expecting it to smash,' I say to Victoria, who lies pinned under Katie's unconscious body.

I retrieve the vase and throw it at the corner of a stone wall where it rapidly disassembles in a highly satisfying manner.

'Much better.'

I go to pull Victoria up but she's already free, standing over Katie and violently kicking the unconscious girl in the stomach and head and legs. Flakes of her shell crumble and drift away with each onslaught, revealing the true Victoria beneath.

'Victoria, stop!'

I run at her. Victoria straddles Katie now, hands around her throat. She bashes her head against the ground again and again. Then she's on top of her, their faces touching as she probes Katie's cheeks with her fingers. She breathes heavily, lips against Katie's ear.

'I lick your wounds and cleanse your face, I erase the signs of your disgrace. I remove you from the taunts of all as I steal your mind and rip your soul.'

I have my hands on Victoria, desperately trying to wrench her off Katie. Victoria doesn't budge. She is stronger than me. I go for her face, working my fingers around her eyes and mouth. I feel something pulsing through her. Something of Victoria. Something of Katie. And also something of me. My essence, unsecured, flaunts its disobedience. It interferes with the flow between the other two. Caught in the stream, it tugs at me.

I'm turned inside out. A pained scream escapes, followed by a louder scream from Victoria. I lose sensation in my arms and legs. My hearing cuts off abruptly. Then my sight.

After that I don't know where I am.

Or what I am.

Or if I *am.*

New clusters of stars appear the longer I stare. They combine to form unnamed constellations, creating images that will be forgotten the moment I look away. I focus on a pinprick of light that has pierced the firmament directly above my head. Has anyone else spent so long watching this single star, an uninspiring choice in a sky of thousands?

Hours lost in the depths of space were highlights of my childhood and the telescope from my father one of few meaningful gifts. The nights when I struggled to accept what I was drove me into the garden, where I would set up my telescope and scour the sky, marvelling at how insignificant I was.

After the vastness of the universe had doused my anxiety, I would be left to contemplate the interplay between matter and what I knew of the Aether. One, governed by the immutable laws of physics and the other, dimensionless, timeless. If life existed among the stars, would I grow to become its only method of communication: messages sent through the Aether from an alien's essence? These thoughts would fuel greater flames of unease as my role as an archivist on Earth transcended to an emissary of the stars.

A face hovers over mine and, for a moment, it blocks the sky. The face is concerned, and the lips move though make no sound. The stars return, not just around the head, but through it. The face in front of mine is translucent and emits a gentle glow that overpowers many of the dimmer celestial bodies while allowing the brightest to shine through.

I know that face.

His name is Joe Daulton, crushed by a collapsing wall on a construction site during the renovation of a listed manor house. It was well known that the building presented problems for a redevelopment project. That Joe's death resulted from intentional weakening to the manor house's structure became a widely held belief. The case is going through court and, despite being deceased, Joe has appeared as a witness – the retention of his essence paid for by the prosecution. He has not been allowed to speak to his family.

I notice my clothes are damp. I place a hand on the ground and feel grass slick with morning dew. Carefully, I sit up. My eyes fall from the stars to the field of people that surround me. Joe Daulton offers a hand to help me stand. I try to take it, but our skin refuses to connect, his hand sailing straight through mine. Unaided, I stand. Joe smiles. I can't hear his laughter. He goes to clap me on the back but once again his hand meets no resistance and comes out through my chest.

Joe gestures to the people around us and, inaudibly, though clear enough from the movements of his lips, questions what transpired to create this situation, though more succinctly and with unnecessary expletives.

I'm unable to stop my eyes from looking down. Joe is naked. So too is everyone else. Naked and dead.

I leave Joe behind and walk through the crowd. Some shy away from me, covering themselves. Others shout and gesticulate wildly. The lack of noise and ferocity of their speech make understanding them impossible, though considering the situation the gist of their meaning is easy to infer.

While some are focused on me, others appear to have engaged in awkward conversations. I watch a small group introduce themselves, laughing at their shared nakedness. They shake hands, quickly realising they can touch each other. Then they hug and silently cry. All around me people are hugging anyone they can see, running around the field as if suddenly awake. They jump and race and laugh and embrace.

For a second I close my eyes and the silence descends. It is cold and the need to make my way back to Sun so we can find Laure intensifies.

I approach a man who stands alone, naked and self-consciously cupping his genitals with both hands. He is David Bellfield, a long-distance lorry driver who died of a heart attack at sixty-two. Unmarried and with no children, David contacted me prior to his death after his doctor warned him that a sedentary lifestyle and severe obesity were accelerating him towards his final moment on Earth. He told me he feared being forgotten and had inadvertently saved a small fortune over his lifetime, not uncommon with single men who want for little. He paid for twenty years of my time. Only a brother in Sydney ever talks to him. Their weekly call rarely extends beyond seven minutes and in that time, they talk of the same friends they've not seen since they were children. After each call, the brother asks me to release David's essence and send him the money his brother had set aside.

David smiles uncertainly as I approach. Standing before him, I lean forward, and my head passes through his protruding stomach. Despite being able to partially see through him, light from the stars cannot break through his shell. I am surrounded by space, the inside hollow, its walls a golden mosaic reflecting a light with no source. I angle my head to look up his arm. The tiles continue down his forearm and to his wrist, where they branch into curling fingers.

I step inside him, bending down to keep my head from poking through the top of his. Inside his skull I can see the protrusion of his nose and eyes and when he opens his mouth, the back of his throat forms from nothing and suddenly there are teeth and a tongue, which disappear the moment his mouth closes again.

I step backwards and exit David to find that a small group has gathered around him. Someone is talking to David, resting a hand on his shoulder. This soon turns into an uncomfortable hug between two naked men in their sixties. That hug is followed by another and another. After each hug, a reprimanding glare is cast at me and I wonder if it is considered impolite to stand inside the spectral shell of the dead.

Threads that run along the ground tie me to the gathered ensemble. I pull the one attached to David and watch as he disappears, only to feel him moments later take root inside me. The last two men to hug him follow after. The group are quick to understand what is happening and silently plead to stay. They hold onto each other in the vain belief that collectively they have become stronger than me. I steal one held in a tight embrace, causing the person left to desperately hug the air before I take them too. I am all that keeps their essence from being devoured by the Aether and yet they're indignant over their treatment.

I pull them in faster, avoiding eye contact before they're ripped from the field. A feasible explanation for their expulsion formulates that involves Sun and somebody interfering with her essence. Whatever happened to her was transmitted to me through the link we share and spread to the remnants of the eighty-six lives I have inside me.

Eighty-seven.

I absorb the remaining ghosts with little fanfare, pulling in many at a time, and marvel at their ability to communicate. Inside me they are separate, tightly packed into an infinite honeycomb with no ability to break from their cells. To watch them as they are now is to have characters from two different books in a library enter into conversation. There is no mechanism for it to be possible. The shock transmitted through my link to Sun has introduced an element of chaos into my essence. How this will affect me, I do not know, but the change appears permanent.

Only a handful of essences remain. I don't even cast them a cursory glance as they struggle to communicate before I pull them in. I have eyes on only one. Standing calmly with arms by her sides, jutting hips and protruding ribs the sign of a body failing before its time, and of a curator too occupied with their work to care. There is a sense of sorrow about her smile, but it is only a sense because she is where she always wanted to be. This is the fulfilment of a promise made by a boy of eight.

'Antoinette.'

She nods and stands to the side. Behind her is the other essence I took possession of tonight. She's bent over trying to cover herself. Quickly she gives up and throws her hands down. Straightening up, her stare dares me to look anywhere but her eyes.

She points to her mouth, then to me.

'You want to speak to me?' I ask.

A quick nod.

Only Antoinette and the teenager remain on the field; the other essences are back where they belong. Antoinette points to her face, then to mine.

'I will.' I turn to the girl. 'Her first, then I'll let you speak.'

She smiles her understanding and disassembles like a collapsing tower of wooden bricks. Her facets race across the floor and I have her again. Now it is only me and Antoinette.

I gently wrap my arms around her, careful not to breach the membrane of her image. She returns the hug as ghostly hands reach across my back. I close my eyes and imagine I can feel them. We made an agreement that I would take her essence in exchange for the church the first day we met. I remember her explaining to me what it meant to be an archivist, something that was regarded as an inconvenience by my parents, who spent the first seven years of my life searching for a cure. It was Antoinette who proclaimed that I was born an archivist and I would die an archivist, despite their futile machinations. She taught me that I was something to be revered and worshipped but also something that would evoke a primal fear in whoever I met, and that any friends I hoped to make would eventually be driven away. The only reason I survived is because Antoinette prepared me for the life I would be forced to lead.

I withdraw Antoinette.

The light from my link to Sun stretches across the field. Should Sun die, then, like Antoinette, she would travel that link to me. But my link to Sun is not like what I shared with Antoinette. Antoinette's link was only temporary, formed from facets that could die and vanish into the Aether as memories were forgotten or impulses rewritten. To maintain the link with Antoinette, I reformed it every time we met to be confident that something would remain should she die.

The link I have with Sun is greater, formed of shared facets, which creates a permanent connection. Part of what I am is inside Sun and part of Sun is inside me. Desperate to save both of our lives after the death of Richard, I gave too much of myself and took more of Sun than I had the right to take. Beyond the link visible to both of us, Sun is unaware of the depth of connection we share. She deserves to know, but not until I understand it myself.

I set off across the field as Antoinette's facial features trickle over mine.

'You can spend a lifetime studying something and yet still be completely unprepared when it happens to you.' Antoinette pauses. 'Of course, you can't respond. We must work on that. What I wanted to say was that I'm sorry. I didn't wake up this morning expecting to die, but an opportunity presented itself and I let nature run its course. Don't be too hard on the girl. Not that I'm above revenge, I just think she's mixed up in something bigger than her. They all are. Even you.'

The thread leads through a small wood and I'm forced to climb over a barbed-wire fence. The dew-clad grass is replaced by cold mud and the light from the moon is obscured by trees. I continue into the darkness, forced to diverge from my intended path as the thread cuts through tree trunks and thickets of brambles and holly.

I had believed that I was too special and too wealthy to ever feel cold and wet. Tonight has proved an interminable lesson to the contrary.

'What I want to tell you is that I may have made a mistake,' Antoinette says. 'That young girl you sent to my church... your church, I suppose... is something I hadn't encountered before and I hope that, despite being in this state, I will have the opportunity to continue my research in some form. Not a topic for now, but something about you has changed. The death experienced by those inside you is not what it was before the events of tonight. Oh, watch out for that—'

A branch catches my face and I feel a cluster of Antoinette's face tear off mine. I look back, expecting a wedge of flesh to hang from a thorn. Nothing is there and when I hold my hand up to my face, I feel her dry skin and delicate wrinkles.

'I expected that to hurt. Clearly death holds some advantages.'

I try to say sorry but my brain refuses to process the sound.

'Someone is very interested in you,' Antoinette says abruptly. 'I'm sure you've realised that the recent spate of suicides was an attempt to grab your attention. Victoria was a part of that, she admitted it herself. There is more to this than Victoria and tragic girls. Somewhere I have made a mistake and there is another archivist in this town. I don't know who they are, but they want you. Anyone willing to sacrifice the lives of children to get your attention doesn't have your best interests in mind. You should leave town as soon as you can. Leave the country, you have the means. If they can be used against you, then take Sun-young and Laure, otherwise leave them. *Your* life is what needs preserving, not theirs.'

I emerge from the wood onto a road. The thread cuts through another field thick with mud. I take the road instead, keeping the thread to my right.

'I wish you could reply.'

Antoinette's face folds away. I cough, just to make sure I'm in possession of my voice. I believe what she told me. Even in her descriptions of archivism and the power I wield, she was never one to overstate. If Antoinette tells me that my life is in danger, then it is. If I had not known Martina, not met Sun and Laure, then I would follow her advice. To leave this country under a false identity on a chartered plane to a foreign land would be the most sensible course of action to prolong my existence. But experience has made me into something greater than life support for the dead. Even if I could convince Sun and Laure to come with me – assuming I

265

can find Laure – that wouldn't stop whoever is after me from further killing.

If my life is in danger, then what of Sun and Laure? Laure has been kidnapped and someone has interfered with Sun's essence. Was that the other archivist, torturing Sun, aware of our link in order to send a message? With so many girls dead to suicide, what difference would two more make?

My essence flicks the air, scouring the trees. I allow the anger to course through me, excited by it. If I run, then they won't stop killing until they find me. I also won't get to punish them for the death of Antoinette.

That would be a great shame.

26

Everything falls back where it belongs. Fingernails on fingers. Hands on arms. These things were there before, but misaligned. Now they fit perfectly.

I stand. Toes, feet, shins, knees and thighs all neatly aligned. My insides have been removed, washed and neatly repacked. I'm made anew. Sun-young Kang, steaming hot from the oven. Or possibly cloning vat. If I find my old body shoved in a bin, I'll look the other way.

A valve turns and memories from old Sun-young flood my new brain. I run to Antoinette and roll her over, hold my ear just above her mouth and try to detect the rise and fall of her chest while ignoring the blood that has trickled through the perforation in her eardrum and pooled on the floorboards. I count to ten, then twenty, sixty, two hundred and fifty. No movement. So obviously dead.

I sit back and stare at her open eyes. On TV someone always closes them, but I don't feel up to that. The best I can do is get her off the floor and onto the sofa. I slide my hands under her body. She's wet. If she'd known she was going to die I guess she wouldn't have drunk so much tea, but she didn't know and so here I am with her piss-soaked corpse. I lift her up, the body under all that silk unsettlingly light. There's a blanket on the back of a chair which I lay over her. I contemplate whether to cover her head and decide that would be cruel.

I take a step back.

The longer I'm with her, the creepier this gets. She's going to look at me, I just know it. Then her mouth will open too wide and darkness will come flooding out to consume me.

That's a point, why is it so dark in here? Was it always this dark? The lights are on but they're useless. I'm sure it's intentional. Or has Antoinette's death affected them? I want him here. When faced with a dead body, it's always better to stand with Death by your side.

I wait for the light to return. When it doesn't, I convince myself that it's always been this dark and walk back to Antoinette. She'd look asleep if it wasn't for the eyes. My hand snatches out to close them. It's a bodge job. One is almost shut while the other is still wide open. Sadly, it's as much dignity as she'll get from me. I need to get out of here.

'I hope you're with him,' I say.

I take a recent photo of him from near the door and lay it on her chest. I take one for myself too, not that I need to remind myself what he looks like. Just because. Another catches my eye. Not so prominent, it's the one with him sat next to Martina on the sofa Antoinette now lies dead on. Neither one of them smiling, but there's something in their closeness that radiates happiness.

A knot forms in my stomach. Self-respect tells me to leave the picture here. With my head in control, I pocket the photo, knowing there should be something of Martina in his flat, even if it's only a picture.

Out the door and I'm running. I can't remember the last time I ran anywhere. Not like this, high on endorphins, thrilled by the sound of trainers smacking asphalt. The ribbon before me is the brightest it's ever been and I follow it along roads, through gardens and under bridges. It pulls me forward. Fills me with energy. Antoinette and death are behind me and he is ahead, reeling me in.

I crash into him a few miles past where the final bastion of suburbia gives way to fields. His hands clamp my arms. I look up and blurt.

'Antoinette is dead.'

He smiles. Then it's not his smile, it's Antoinette's. Pale pink lips rise almost imperceptibly at the edges and her near-white skin crinkles around her eyes.

I don't say anything and throw my arms around him.

'I didn't think you were all that fond of me,' Antoinette says.

'I'm not,' I say into his shirt, 'but you didn't deserve that.'

'I'm not so sure. Death hid a few surprises, even from me. Though I think some of those may be unique to him.'

I let him go and step back.

'What's it like?'

'Being killed was more painful than what I'd planned. The Archivist and I have had an arrangement for many years and it didn't involve stabbing.'

'They fought,' I say. 'I tried to stop them, but something weird happened that knocked me out. When I woke up, they'd gone.'

'Not the stupidest girls, then. Despite appearances. Sun, look. You don't need to feel sorry for me. We both know I'm where I've always wanted to be.'

'I know. Doesn't make it right, though.'

'Things are what they are. Archivism teaches that there is no wrong or right because there is no heaven or hell, only the Aether. Even if you're taken by an archivist, the Aether will get you eventually.'

Antoinette's features sink into his skin too fast for either of us to say a meaningful goodbye.

'Isn't that a little rude?' I ask.

'You will see her again,' he says. 'There are more pressing matters.'

Of course, Antoinette's body.

'I didn't call the police,' I say. 'Figured you wouldn't want them poking around before you got there. You didn't say your thing. That's important, isn't it?'

'It's not important right now.' He looks towards the town, eager to get moving. 'Antoinette is with me and her body can wait until morning.'

'OK. Let's get home before Laure wakes up. She'll freak out if we're not there. Well, maybe not freak out, but she'll certainly eat the last brioche.'

I'm hit with timelines and movements and questions like *why are we so far from home?* and *wasn't Laure with you at that awards evening she blackmailed you to go to? You know, the one where you had to wear a dress that you thought you could hide from me?* And eventually, 'Where the fuck is my sister?'

He's been caught. Thick clouds of fear spew from his pores, engulfing us in the stench of desperation.

'Don't you *dare* tell me you've lost her.'

He's inexperienced with this level of fear. Doesn't know how to play it. He looks everywhere but directly at me. Puts his hands in his pockets. Takes them out. Puts them back in again.

'We need to go.'

'Go where? Where is she?'

He takes a step then stops. 'Not here.'

'Do you even know?'

'The police are looking for her.'

270

'*The police!* How long has she been missing? Why the fuck didn't you call me?'

'I was going to call you when she'd been found.'

'Dead or alive?' I scream.

Throbbing orbs of blackness engulf the edges of my vision. Something's growing inside my head, pushing brain tissue aside as it swells to fill my skull. Is he doing this? Attacking me in the hope I'll calm down? I haven't felt the fear of his presence since that night in the hospital. Could this be another of his tricks?

I stumble. He catches me and I'm lowered to the damp ground. He looks scared, but a different kind of scared. Concerned.

'You know what I did to keep Laure safe.' It comes out a rage-filled sob. I take his arm and squeeze it too tight. 'And you *lost* her.'

'Laure was taken.'

'Taken?'

Anger is the perfect barrier to fear. It constructs an impenetrable wall around me, blocking all reason and logic. Anger is powerful, a comfort blanket I reach for more often than I should. It burns hot, but it burns fast and the wall that should protect me is soon a ring of cinders and I'm left alone, standing in the middle wondering if I subconsciously want this. That perhaps fate stole my sister because a month ago I said my life would be easier if she wasn't in it? I didn't mean it, even Laure knew that. She just smiled at me in that way she does and told me as much. If she knew it was a lie, then why didn't stupid fate?

'Who took her?'

'I don't know.'

'It involves the suicides, doesn't it?'

'It's probable.'

271

We're walking back towards civilisation. Not because we know where we need to be, but because Laure sure as shit isn't hiding in the trees.

'There was another suicide,' he says.

'What happened?'

'She jumped from the upper balcony ring. Fractured her skull when she landed.'

'Let me guess, she didn't die straight away; you took her essence then someone else stole it.'

'They tried to steal it.'

'You have her?'

He nods.

'Then bring her out. She might know something about Laure. Let's good cop, bad cop this shit.'

The face is not even fully formed when I shout, 'Where the fuck is my sister?'

Blurred cheeks and pixelated eyes dive beneath his skin.

'That's not how we speak to the dead,' he says.

'I'm the bad cop.'

'She can't speak to me.'

'Fuck it. So it's bad cop, bad cop.'

'Be polite,' he says.

'Naturally.'

I've never really paid attention when he projects a face. One moment he's him and the next he's someone else. But if you focus, you can see the change. His face is no longer one thing, it is millions of little things, as if his skin and features have turned to sand. An unfelt wind runs over him, pushing some areas down while pulling others up. His nose may fall while his cheeks rise, or his jaw may shrivel as thick drifts gather across his brow. If I were to touch him now, I'm sure my fingers would sink straight through his skull.

It doesn't normally take this long for a face to appear and I wonder if this is another form of manipulation. A watched face never projects, just like a watched phone never rings.

I quickly look away.

'I guess that's lunch off.'

That voice... I've heard it before. I'm ready to bad cop the hell out of this but when I turn, I see the straight black hair that hangs over his shoulders, the inquisitive eyes and delicate mouth of a girl I know. And just like that, my anger dissolves.

'Lara.'

The ways she looks at me, I'd know she'd shrug if she could.

'I... I... my sister, do you know where she is?'

'No.'

'Get rid of her,' I say.

Shame overwhelms me. I can't look at her. It was only, what? A few hours ago. We were in the park together in front of Tegan Caldwell's shrine. Even though we'd never met, I knew there was something off about Lara. I should have spent longer looking for her, made sure she got home all right. But I didn't and now she's dead.

She's still there.

'It wasn't your fault,' she says.

I need to find Laure. My legs are desperate to run to her, but there's no one telling them where to go. They're impatient, twitching, and they stamp the ground so everyone knows it.

'I need to find my sister,' I say, and instantly feel like a massive shit because Lara is dead and I'm acting like I don't care. Except I do care, only I can't care right now because I don't want my next conversation with Laure to be when her face is on the Archivist's body.

'I know, Kimberley. I just want you to tell my mum what happened to me. She won't have seen this coming.'

I sigh. 'It's Sun-young. Kimberley was just a stupid name I had to use at school.' I look at Lara, see the pain in her eyes, and know that I can't get rid of her. She deserves something from me, even if it's just a few minutes. After that, my legs can go wherever they want.

'OK,' I say.

'Thank you,' she replies.

We walk through fields, occasionally following paths until they become lost to trees and darkness. With Lara behind me I can forget that she's dead. When I hear her voice, I imagine it coming from her. Imagine her wearing the same purple dress she had on in the park, clutching the flowers she left where Tegan Caldwell shot herself. I imagine her struggling to climb fences and ruining her shoes attempting to cross fields of mud and stagnant water.

The image collapses when I turn around. Her head is too high, balanced precariously on a serpentine body. Loose black hair falls over the shoulders of a denim jacket and I know if I tried to touch it, I would feel each strand beneath my fingers despite them not being there.

A theatrical duck under a branch that didn't register with me, Lara's head in danger of rolling off, and we're walking side by side. These clothes aren't the Archivist's. The trousers hang above his ankles and the salmon shirt is spotted with blood. These are Mr Cavendish's clothes. I won't ask why he's wearing them; the answer is obvious.

'Why did you do it?' I ask.

'I didn't,' Lara says, her voice quiet.

'But...'

'I know I'm dead... but I didn't jump.'

'Someone pushed you?'

'Sort of.'

'I don't understand,' I say.

'I failed my grade eight piano last summer. It may not seem a big deal, but it was to me. My mum had already bought a Bösendorfer as a reward; I'd passed every other exam so why wouldn't I pass this one? When I failed, it wasn't like I'd just failed this one exam, it felt like I'd failed everything. Then I really was failing, maths, science, French. All my grades went down. That's when Mr Cavendish invited me to 1214 and I met Victoria.'

'And she did something to you?'

Lara nods. 'There were other girls there. Claire, Chrissy, Sophia, Tegan. And, well, you know what happened to them.'

'So that's why you took flowers to Tegan's shrine?'

'I knew it was going to happen to me too. Victoria needs certain types of girls: sad girls, unfulfilled girls, guilty girls. She wanted us damaged. Said she could fix us, that we are all made of different parts, some good, some bad. If we joined with her, she promised to take those bad parts away and make us good again. We all wanted that. We wanted to live, all of us did. But then Claire killed herself, then Chrissy, then Sophia. Tegan and I knew something was wrong, but we never spoke about it. We wanted to, but the words just didn't come, like someone was stealing them from our mouths. Then she died too.'

'Victoria did this to you?'

'She put something inside us. We would do things, only it wasn't us doing them. We were just watching.'

'Like the dress when we were in the park, and when you didn't remember getting off the swing?'

'It wasn't me talking to you then. Someone else... we were sad girls, but we didn't want to die. These weren't suicides, they were murders.'

'Lara, I...' I want to take her hand, tell her how sorry I am, only it's not her hand and no matter how sorry I feel for a girl I've just met, it's nothing compared to how scared I feel for Laure right now.

'I don't know where your sister is,' Lara says, either sensing my thoughts or understanding that the look of worry on my face isn't directed at her. 'If I did, I would tell you.'

'I know,' I say. It fits together now, the girls, the improbable number of suicides in one school. It was all for him, so that these girls could die in front of the Archivist and have him take their essence. Why? I don't know that yet. But there's something else missing, a link that should be there but isn't.

'How did you know the Archivist was going to be there?' I ask. 'He didn't even tell me where he was going.'

'Victoria had someone arrange that.'

I hold a gate open and with the next step, road replaces mud. 'Katie?'

'No. An adult. They drove me from the park. They didn't speak, but I think they were female. The car didn't smell like it belonged to a man.'

'What about the other girls?'

'The same, I think.'

'Who was she?'

'I was never told. All I had to do was get in the car.'

'You must have known something!' I cry in frustration.

'I knew I was being driven to my death, Kimberley! Sun-young. And I knew there was nothing I could do to stop it. I wanted to scream, but my mouth wouldn't open. I wanted to jump out the car, but my hands wouldn't move to open the door. If there is some grand plan, then I wasn't part of it, I was being used just like Claire and Chrissy and Sophia and Tegan, just like the Archivist and just like Laure.'

'What do you mean, *just like Laure*? You said—'

'That I don't know where she is. And I don't. But I know what Victoria wants. She wants sad girls. Girls who hide their despair with bright smiles, good grades and perfect skin. Girls who fit the Greenfield mould but are rotting inside. Your sister is missing, put the pieces together.'

'Laure's not like that, she's happy.'

'That's what Claire's mum said after Claire slit her wrists, and what Chrissy's dad said after she overdosed on insulin. Sophia's brother said that he'd never seen his sister cry. And Tegan, she spent her spare time reading stories to little kids in the library. That's the point, it's invisible.'

'Get rid of her,' I shout to the Archivist.

It's him and me again. We walk for a few minutes in silence. I'm shivering, my legs disobeying me and struggling to keep a straight line.

'Laure isn't like that,' he says.

I want to tell him I know, but would I be fooling myself? Laure doesn't know what I'm capable of, of the things I let Richard do to keep her safe. If I can hide so much from her, then what could she be hiding from me?

'I need you to speak to Lara again.'

'No.'

'Do you want to find Laure?' He knows not to wait for a response. 'Ask her what she smelled of.'

'The woman in the car?'

As he nods, Lara's face materialises from golden dust in a single wave that starts at his chin and rolls upwards to replace his features with those of a dead seventeen-year-old.

'What did it smell of?'

'Oh.' Lara seems confused. 'We're still here?'

'The car. You said it didn't smell like a man's. What did it smell of?'

'Perfume.'

'Any chance you could be more specific?'

'It's been a little while. Let me think.'

'It was literally tonight.'

Lara smirks. She knows something I don't and doesn't want to share. I tell myself that unless it's got anything to do with Laure or what that car smelled like, it's unimportant.

'Apples and something sweet. Vanilla, I think.'

Her face is gone and he's off. Walking fast, then running. I can't keep up.

'Where are you going?'

He slows enough for me to catch his expression. He's angry. Really fucking angry. We're running past houses where people sleep and I'm sure that whatever's coming off him is giving those inside nightmares.

I grab his wrist. 'Who was it?'

'Monique.'

'The Jones woman?'

He's silent. His eyes focused and mouth pinched. He pulls his wrist from my grip to take my hand. Running faster than I can match, he drags me along like a small child late for school. His speed and anger are fuelled by a sense of injustice over Laure. He would not run with such abandon if he was the only one wronged. He's acting this way because he cares.

My shrivelled heart swells.

Stupid! How did I not see what is so blinding with hindsight? Was I so wrapped in my own divinity that I could not connect the young lady in the waiting room, who frantically typed messages on her phone, with meeting the impeccable Detective Inspector Jones a little over a week later? She was there, watching as I interacted with Jenny Montgomery, the ED shift nurse, whose younger sister was the first to die. Then at the scene of Tegan Caldwell's attempted suicide, that I now know was murder, Monique had been there. I suspect that she was also responsible for the attending officers calling me to the scene before the ambulance.

When I refused to take Tegan's essence, it was a car crash that resulted in my unwitting killing of the girl, something Monique must have orchestrated in that hurried phone call. Then tonight, before the death of Lara Chin... I am disappointed in myself for not finding it suspicious. Monique approached me during my only visit to the toilet, conveniently; the only time that evening I was not projecting the face of Genevieve DuPont.

And after, with Laure missing, it was Monique who I entrusted to find her. Monique who said she would call in favours to find Laure without raising suspicion. Monique, who had been the one to take her.

'How do you know she's here?' Sun asks. The block of flats where she and Laure once lived with Richard, before us.

'Monique was at the award ceremony. She asked Laure about the flat.'

'What did she want to know?'

'If Laure was scared of it.'

A resigned laugh from Sun as we stop at the entrance. 'And here we are.'

'What do you mean by that?'

'You've been played.' Sun holds the door handle but doesn't open it. 'That woman doesn't care if Laure's scared of the flat. She was planting a seed, one that would take all night to grow in your unquestioning soil. Don't you see? Apart from Sophia Ray, who hanged herself in front of me, Monique either brought you to the girls or brought them to you. Now she's done it again.' Sun's hand is white. Tears roll down her face. She still won't open the door. 'You'll go into the flat, find that Laure has killed herself and take her essence. And then I guess I'll keep living with you and Laure's face will float around on your freakishly long body and maybe that will be OK because this is my fault, because my sister wanted this and I didn't realise.'

My arms think for me, wrapping themselves around Sun. Can she feel my heart beating? If she stood back, she would see its frantic rhythm punched into my shirt. Fear and guilt. I will not save Laure. Her essence is impervious to me and it would not matter how fervently I tried to possess her, she would never come and all I could do is watch as the Aether feeds on her like vultures on carrion until every bone is picked clean.

Sun returns the hug and for several moments we stay that way until the intimacy becomes too much and I pull back.

'I've never felt so comforted by such an awkward hug,' Sun says.

She refuses to step into the building, so I leave her waiting outside as I climb the stairs, breathing lungfuls of air thick with stale urine.

The door to the flat is unlocked. My mind jumps to the conclusion that it was left open for me and that Sun was right. Laure has been placed here to be found.

The flat has changed since my last visit. It is cleaner and the air, while not fresh, is laced with the scent of artificial fragrances that battle the odours from outside. The bedroom doors are shut. I know which room is Laure's and stand before it. A single flick of my perception and I would know if her intact essence was inside. I don't want to know, not yet. What would I tell Sun if her sister was dying? If I could not save her? Without Laure to protect, Sun's life would lose its immediate meaning and she is too impatient to search for another.

I open the door. A yellow haze suffuses the room, the meagre curtains unable to block the lights from outside. It is a small room, decorated with optimism to cover areas of damp with bright posters and neatly arranged stickers.

There is a shape on the single bed, hidden beneath the covers. I step closer, carefully avoiding empty water bottles and packets of food. There is a torch and a book, a plastic bag with a clean change of clothes. I check behind me and the fuchsia dress Laure wore earlier tonight hangs from the back of the door.

The room is not silent. Slow breath in, a slight pause, slow breath out. I pull the duvet back. Blond hair covers the pillow to the extent where I can't tell which way she's facing. Finally, I allow the room to fall away and there before me are the complex twists of an essence. It is alive, unhurt, bar the occasional stray facet. I reach out. The essence is inert in my presence. A flick and my finger fights its way through locks of hair, pushing them aside to reveal the sleeping face of Laure Baptiste.

I call Sun. Two minutes later she's beside me, watching her sister sleep.

'I think now's a good time to sit,' Sun says and sinks to the floor. She holds her head in her hands and exhales her relief in large breaths that shake her body.

'We should get her home.'

Sun nods, tries to stand but fails. She looks up and holds out a hand. After too long I realise I'm meant to take it. I pull her too sharply and she stumbles to her feet. I'm unused to being anyone's physical support.

'Those aren't her pyjamas,' Sun says. 'The clothes in the bag aren't hers either, someone bought them especially.'

The same will be true of the food and book. Laure was brought here by someone, almost certainly Monique, not to be harmed. The door was unlocked, so Laure could leave any time. Why she stayed here is unclear. Perhaps she was too tired to leave, or didn't know that she could. Maybe it was neither of these things and Laure stayed through choice.

'I don't want to wake her,' Sun declares. 'I want her to wake up in her own bed with no idea how she got there.'

Sun wraps the blanket around Laure and lifts her from the bed. Out of the bedroom and into the living room, a quick dash and Laure is nearly dropped on the sofa.

'When did she get so heavy?' Sun asks, rubbing her arms.

'She didn't. You never exercise.'

'You don't know what I get up to.'

'I can see inside you.'

'I'm gonna shut that down right now. So how do we get her home?'

Laure's face is pressed against the back of the sofa and the blanket has fallen away to reveal blue pyjamas that have ridden up her back. I take the blanket and cocoon Laure.

'Don't get too close,' Sun warns.

I could lie. Carry Laure as if to touch her would be to steal away folds of her essence. But I have already withheld information from Sun once tonight and so I reach out to press my finger against Laure's cheek.

'What are you doing?'

'Nothing.'

'You'll hurt her!' Sun runs around the back of the sofa and grabs my wrist with both hands. She's ready to pull me away and stops, unsure if she will make it worse. We stay like that, my finger a loaded gun against Laure's face.

Slowly, I pull away with Sun still attached to my wrist.

'She's immune.'

'What? To dying?'

'No. To me. She remembers my face.'

Sun laughs to herself and looks away. 'So do I.'

Stunned silent, I can only reply with a slack-mouthed stare. Not even I am allowed to remember my face.

'Ever since we got this,' Sun says and twangs the thread that stretches between us. 'I thought it made me special. But now I learn Laure's the same.'

'You should not envy your sister,' I say despite envying them both for knowing something of me that I do not. I try to catch myself in a reflective surface so I can at least know how I look at this instant, but despite recent efforts to clean, nothing is polished enough to capture my image. I reach down, scoop Laure into my arms and walk towards the door.

'I can never take her essence,' I say as we step onto the corridor, the first hints of morning sliding into the night. 'When Laure dies, her essence will belong to the Aether and the Aether alone.'

Sun strokes Laure's head. She moves her hair out of her face and rearranges the blanket so only a pair of closed eyes and nose poke through.

She whispers something in Laure's ear. I pretend not to hear and we descend the stairs and leave for home.

'My phone's not working.'

'I'll try mine.'

'Don't worry. I'll get it.' Sun reaches into the space between me and her sleeping sister. 'Dead.'

'It was on eighty percent when I last looked.'

Sun tries turning it on. Nothing happens. The same with hers.

'I guess this endless night's finally taken its toll on our batteries.'

I nod agreement, though suspect there is something else at play.

It is not far to walk and Laure is not a heavy load. The silence, however, weighs on us both. There is no easy conversation to be had after the night we've experienced and despite finally walking home to our beds, where we will probably spend the rest of this new day, we are not the night's victors.

'The lights are already turning off,' Sun says.

Morning may be soon, but it isn't here yet. Today will be a Sunday and so far there are no cars on the road. Without the occasional light from passing headlights or our phones to act as torches, we are reliant on the streetlamps to find our way.

They are all off. We are not surrounded by complete darkness, but the lack of artificial lighting feels malevolent. So too the lack of people.

'Does this feel a bit—' Sun stops. The light just before us turns on. The only artificial light in any direction. Even the traffic lights have winked out.

'I was going to say ominous,' Sun says, 'but that feels a little redundant now.'

We walk towards the light. As soon as we step into its glow, it is off and the next light comes on. The environment is being controlled, exactly as it was when Sophia Ray hanged herself.

To impress or intimidate, this display has failed at both. Exasperated, it signals that my night is not yet over. To ignore this would likely put Sun or Laure in danger.

One after another, lights turn on to form a path that winds into the distance and out of sight.

'Subtle.'

'What waits at the end of those lights is dangerous,' I say. 'They are not for you to follow.'

Sun wants to fight but knows that to take a sleeping Laure into whatever's at the end of the trail is unwise.

Laure wakes of her own volition. I put her on a bench and Sun takes shoes from the plastic bag she carries and puts them on her sister. Laure slumps forward, wrapping both arms around Sun, and smiles at me.

'You are a strange one,' she says, still half asleep.

Sun helps her stand and places one arm around her shoulder, the blanket shared between the two of them.

'Whatever's at the end of those lights, end it tonight,' Sun says.

I nod and Sun and Laure vanish as they step through the terminator created by the light above. I look down the path. It illuminates little save the occasional bin or wooden bench.

Victoria was right. I have allowed myself to become a pawn in someone else's game. That I have survived this long has been only through the careful positioning of someone unseen. I am not so deluded that I believe my survival will see me topple the opponent's king. I have been used, manipulated, hospitalised and humiliated.

My essence unfurls, cutting through the surrounding air, curling around trees, twisting through blades of grass and extending deep into the ground to explore the remains of long-forgotten dead.

This ends tonight.

The path created by the lights is long enough to make its point but not so long it loses relevance. The car parked beneath the final light is large and black, as you would expect of a car that waits at the end of a trail designed to display an intimidating level of control.

The light behind me has vanished and soon it is only me and the car. Without pause I open the passenger-side door, slip in and say, 'Good evening, Monique.'

A slight gasp of shock followed by a swallow of guilt.

'When did you realise?' she asks, not as confidently as I would have expected, seeing as I'm the one she played.

'Not soon enough.'

She starts the car and doesn't speak again until it stops twenty minutes later.

'You'll find her in there.'

I gently close the car door. The last part of our journey took us through a gatehouse and along a tree-lined driveway to the remains of a substantial house that looks to have been gutted by fire. The entrance is intact, though the wooden door has not survived. I step over the threshold. Small trees and bushes grow between cracks in the floor and there is nothing above me but stars.

A brief glance into the Aether to find who I am to meet and I turn left into the ruined house. There are rooms that escaped the brunt of the fire and others where I must question if I've left the house completely. Large sections of it exist only as a shell, the fire consuming the wooden floorboards and ceilings entirely. Holes in the brickwork show where they once were. Doors above me open into nothingness.

The house is not infinite. The route I take is not direct. I have been summoned here and have no desire to be punctual. Was this the house of an archivist? Is this the culmination of life as a god, both the display of wealth and the likely arson that destroyed it?

I finally allow myself to be led and enter one of the few rooms with furniture. Sat upon a large wingback chair is a woman of around twenty-five. She regards me warmly. A smile and coy recrossing of her legs does little to reassure me. A step closer and the woman is gone, replaced by a man in his late fifties, the skin on his face webbed by spider veins from excessive alcohol consumption. Another step and another change. A girl of only ten with clothes and a haircut from a different time.

A new person appears with every step I take. There is no visible period of transition, each body instantly usurping the place of the last.

I stop short of a pair of shoes owned by a man in a large black overcoat and bowler hat. He looks around the room and my eyes follow. Heavily damaged by the fire, one of the exterior walls has been lost and those that remain end at the tops of the door frames. The parquet floor is surprisingly intact.

The man in the bowler hat, whose heavily weathered skin

suggests he did not die prematurely, dissolves into a woman wearing a green dress that covers her legs all the way to her equally green shoes. Her pale arms are bare, one resting on the arm of the chair as the other crosses her body so that her hands touch.

Her smile is mischievous. Green eyes devour me.

'Welcome to my home,' she says, sweeping a hand around the charred remains of the house. 'I am the Jade Archivist.'

28

Lights extinguish as the Archivist recedes. He passes behind a wall and is gone. I wait for him to turn and catch me staring. It doesn't happen. I guess it's not one of those moments.

Laure floats towards the nearest bench, taking the duvet with her.

'I can call a taxi,' I say.

'It's OK. I just want to sit for a bit.'

I join her and she folds the duvet around me. 'Do you remember what happened?' I ask.

'Yeah.'

'Did anyone...'

'No one hurt me, Sun. It wasn't like that.'

'I was really scared.'

'I know.' She takes my hand. 'You took it out on him, didn't you?'

'Not exclusively.'

Laure rests her head against my shoulder. Another year and she'll be taller than me. I want to ask how she's feeling, but don't know the right words. Sat here with her warmth and sweet smell, it seems impossible that she could ever feel sad. The idea that she may one day become suicidal is laughable. And so all the doubt and fear that consumed my brain with its anarchic riot grows silent. It returns a few stolen tellies, patches up some shop windows and goes back to its life. Slowly things return to what they were.

I know I should do more. Think more. Feel more. Keep some worry behind for Laure, but everything is so calm, I'm convinced it was all for nothing. I take her hand and squeeze.

'What happened?'

Laure smiles. 'You think slowly.'

'What?'

'You were staring at me for like ten minutes.'

Was I?

'It's been a tough night,' I say. 'Sorry things have been weird between us.'

'*Things* haven't been weird,' Laure says. 'Just you.'

'Cheers.'

'You're welcome, sis.'

'Tonight. In the flat. Was it the Jones woman?'

'Yeah, but it's not what you think. She didn't kidnap me. I mean, I didn't want to go with her, but a girl had just died and he was right there with her. I wanted to go home. She said I was in danger and she'd keep me safe. She was nice.'

'Why didn't you say anything? You should've messaged me.'

'She took my phone when we got in her car. That was scary. But then she said it would be a good idea if I hid somewhere tonight. She must have planned it because she had these pyjamas and food for me.'

'But why did *you* need to hide? Why not me?'

'Because I can't see what he does,' Laure says. Then, more quietly, 'You know that, right?'

If the Archivist hadn't just told me, I don't think I'd believe her. Though I guess part of me knew something was different about Laure. She never complained of feeling unwell near him and would laugh whenever we walked past the living room when he was projecting the face of a client. I'd have to gag her and run upstairs. I never thought she couldn't see it, though. That's like someone saying the moon landing didn't happen or the Earth is flat. You know it's not true so think something's wrong with them for not understanding what's so obvious.

'She said she was going to take care of us. No police. No care homes. She has an older sister who always wanted children but never married. She wants us to go there and see if we like each other.'

'No,' I say. 'I want to stay with him.'

'She said we wouldn't be able to after tonight.'

'What do you mean? What's going to happen?'

Laure looks away. 'She didn't say.'

'Right, get up.' I pull Laure off the bench and throw the blanket in the bin. She glares at me, wrapping her arms tightly across her chest. I toss the plastic bag at her feet. 'There's a toilet behind those trees, get changed.'

'This is why I didn't want to walk all the way home,' Laure says. She picks the bag up and jogs to the toilet block. I follow. Someone's smashed the lock and I hold Laure back, checking that it's empty before we enter. It's even colder inside than out. Laure locks herself in a cubicle and I perch on a sink.

Maybe home is the safest place for Laure. The Archivist is in danger, as I'm sure he knows. If we go to him, then we'll be in danger too. But the Jones woman had been told to remove Laure and, despite how nice she may have been, I doubt it was for Laure's safety.

Laure steps out. Trainers, jeans, jumper and a coat. I take the pyjamas off her, still warm, and throw them in the bin. The lights are back on when we step outside. I check my phone; that's working too.

'How are we going to find him?' Laure asks.

'The ribbon,' I say.

I have explained it to her enough times to predict the rolling of eyes and scoff in her voice as she says, 'I thought you called it a thread.'

I ignore her and call a taxi. I've had enough with walking.

Ten minutes later and we're in the back of a car. The driver takes one look at us and says it's too late for a couple of kids to be out. I tell him it's practically morning, so it's early. He doesn't say much to that and instead complains about the night he's had and how he should have finished hours ago. Apparently, it'll be a miracle if he doesn't fall asleep at the wheel and kill us all. He doesn't offer to call out another car. I can only guess he's been waiting for someone to die with.

'You two had better be going home,' he says. 'Where's that?'

'Go straight on,' I say. The ribbon cuts into the back of his seat and out the windscreen.

He turns the car off, undoes his seatbelt and swings himself round, wedging his belly and fat head between the front seats. He doesn't have one of those plastic screens that stops you from stabbing the driver in the back or vomiting down their neck, so we get the full sensual experience. If he said he'd not left the car for a week, I'd believe him.

I breathe through my mouth and look away from the meat graveyard between his teeth.

'Look, love. That's not how it works. You give me an address, or you piss off and walk.'

I pull a fifty from my pocket. 'You'll get another when we get there.'

He snatches it and starts the car.

'He puts fifties in my purse too,' Laure says. 'The dinner ladies won't accept them.' She sits back and watches the world pass through her window. I can't do the same, so focused on the ribbon, so focused on *him*. Willing him to suddenly appear in the headlights, but after every turn it's just more fucking glowing ribbon with no end in sight. Why did I let him go alone? I'm such a coward.

I hold Laure's hand for the entire journey. The taxi driver follows my instructions and does a reasonable job of not saying *stupid fucking bitch* too loudly every time I make him go back the way we've come. Even exposed to his misogyny, Laure seems calm. My finger finds her pulse; it's slow and steady. Nothing phases this kid. She knows what I'm doing and smiles.

'It'll be OK,' she says.

Great, now *I'm* the one being reassured. 'Yeah.'

'It's nice to see you care about someone who isn't me.'

'Well, he did give us somewhere to live,' I say.

Laure tickles my palm.

'You were so jealous when I was spending time with him.'

'No, I wasn't!'

Laure smirks. 'You kept following us into rooms and then leaving again without saying anything. Other times you'd just glare at us when you were pretending to read.'

My head falls into my hands.

'Do you think he noticed?'

'Oh yes.'

'Well, that's just fucking fabulous.'

'I like him too,' Laure says. 'At first I hung out with him because it was funny to wind you up, but then I did it because I wanted to. He's so calm and confident. I feel safe when I'm with him. I don't think I realised how bad Richard was until I met him. I never knew men could be good like that.'

'He's one of very few,' I say.

'Are we really going to save his life?'

'We're going to try.'

'Wrong!' Laure says. 'The answer is *yes*.'

She's got me there.

'What the fuck are these girls talking about?' the taxi driver mutters, taking a corner a little too late and sending us to the other side of the road.

The ribbon leads us away from civilisation to an estate surrounded by a stone wall at least four metres high and probably hundreds of years old. The taxi driver won't stop complaining and the two times he swerves off the road through lack of sleep feel deliberate. I pull out another fifty and he shuts up.

We pass a gatehouse with turrets either side and continue along a drive protected by orderly rows of trees. I move to the middle seat and watch the ribbon's trail. It cuts a line through the drive and into the ruins of a house. The driver stops the car by the remains of an entrance and grabs the money from my hand.

'Go on then, out you get.'

The concern he showed when we first got in was lost during our second circuit of the ring road. I expect he'd be quite pleased to discover he'd driven us to our brutal deaths on the morning news.

'Come on, piss off.'

We jump out and he speeds off down the drive. We hear the screeching of brakes and a bang. After a few seconds the car starts again and soon it's too far away to be seen or heard.

'We'll get the bus next time,' Laure says.

I squeeze her shoulder and take in the scene before me. What is this place? I've lived in this town all my life and not only have I never seen it before, I've never even heard of it. Was all of this someone's home?

I follow the ribbon, walking next to the wall. Laure, who had climbed into a dried-out fountain, is quick to get out and follow.

'Are you impressed?' I ask.

'Obviously he's going to be here,' she says.

'What makes you say that?'

'The ambiance,' Laure says, smirking. 'It's perfect.'

'Aren't you at least a little curious how we got here?'

She stops to look in a window. 'Not really. You're probably tracking his phone. Seems like the kind of thing you'd do.'

'No, it isn't! I don't track your phone.'

'You're not in love with me.'

'Laure!'

She laughs and runs off. I catch myself reflected in a window. My face is red. *Buggerbollocksfuck.*

I find Laure hiding. 'I hear voices,' she says.

I cautiously look around the wall the ribbon cuts through. He's not on the other side so I take Laure's hand and lead her forward, holding a finger to my lips. This is dangerous, but how dangerous, I don't know. There were no other cars when we arrived and it's not like the house is guarded by a trigger-happy SWAT team. If anything happens, at least Laure and I can run away.

We move forward, careful to avoid stepping on the splintered legs of rotten furniture or scattered china cups from an overturned dresser. There's still so much of value here. And with so many walls missing we wouldn't technically be breaking in. The fire must have been years ago, looking at the state of the furniture, and yet there's no sign of any graffiti or evidence that a wing of the house has been used as a crack den. In fact, it looks like no one has been here since the day of the fire, but how can that be possible? I'd like to think I've dealt with enough shit recently to be forgiven for not knowing about this place, but the entire town?

Or maybe this really was an archivist's home and, just like their face, any memory of this estate is stolen the moment you look away.

Laure pulls me behind a wall and points to the other side. The Archivist is there, standing in front of a woman in a tall chair. They're not in the next room, but the room after that, or possibly even the one after that. With the collapsed walls, it's hard to tell where one room ends and another begins.

There's not much left of the house this far out and I take Laure's hand as we weave through the ruins of an al fresco dining room, complete with table and plates.

The woman leans forward and I finally see her face over the side of the chair. She's younger than I expected, though I know not to be fooled by that after seeing what Victoria could do.

I pull Laure behind a bureau and ask her what she sees.

'She's old,' Laure says. 'Really, really old. Why, what do you see?'

'She looks about forty. Long red hair. Stunning, but also quite severe. Her face is all angles.'

Laure smiles and shakes her head.

'Are we supposed to be scared of her?' she asks.

I tell myself yes, but the look of disbelief on Laure's face makes me doubt that this is the person responsible for murdering five teenage girls.

We position ourselves to get a better view of the Archivist and the woman in the chair. I want to get closer, but with that comes the risk of being seen. Fortunately, it's so quiet I can hear them clearly from a whole room over. He will know I'm here through the movement of the ribbon. I study his face for any hint of a scowl or flick of the eyes. His poker face is impeccable, though I wonder if that woman really is an archivist; can she not see the ribbon too? And if she can, why hasn't she said anything, or at the very least sat forward and looked our way? Perhaps we're not a threat. Or perhaps she wants us to see what will happen next.

If she wants to make us sweat, it's working. I unzip my jacket.

Victoria bumbles into the room. She looks to be herself, with scars running over her arms and across her jaw; the shell of Abigail no doubt lost to the Aether. She trips on a collapsed door frame only to be caught by Katie, who looks disgusted to be touching her. Something in the Archivist changes when he sees them. His stance before the woman on the chair was powerful and firm. The arrival of Victoria and Katie has stripped him of a level of control as power turns to anger and anger turns to hate. His muscles, tight and concealed, twitch beneath his clothes, ready to attack. I can't see them, not from so far, but something is sent through our connection that confirms his lust for revenge.

'You are late,' the woman on the chair says.

Katie fixes her hair. 'It's been a fraught night.'

'She killed Antoinette,' Victoria blurts.

'I'm sure she had good reason,' the woman says. 'Antoinette was a pathetic sycophant and an exceptionally mediocre scholar. I had no need for her.'

I would die if the look the Archivist gave the woman was ever directed at me. He walks towards Katie, the desire for vengeance surging through the ribbon with such force it's frightening.

Please don't do it. Please don't do it. Please don't do it.

To her credit, Katie has enough sense to step backwards and look scared, but it will not save her and she is falling and she is on the floor and Victoria is rushing to her and cradling the body of her friend.

'Please don't think you've inconvenienced me,' the woman says. 'Her use ended the moment Victoria arrived.'

Victoria, desperately clinging to her friend, pushes her face into Katie's and starts reciting something I can't hear. She pulls away then tries again, harder. Then again, so hard it looks like she's headbutting her. Again. Harder still. Again. Again. Then she stops and pulls Katie's body onto her lap. Rocking slightly, she sings to herself while stroking Katie's hair.

'I'm glad you understand,' the woman says. 'Some people need to die so we can get what we want. In my case, longevity, and in yours, vengeance. It normally takes years, for an archivist to take a life so easily from a healthy body, if they ever can, and here you are, only realised for a few months and that's the second time you've murdered. It feels good, doesn't it? To know you can kill with no fear of recrimination. We take life in a way that science can never explain and no court can convict.' She sits back so I can't see her face. 'You enjoyed it, didn't you? You're still smiling.'

He looks away to compose himself. She was right, from the moment Katie's essence was flung from her body, he smiled for longer than I have ever seen.

'It is a shame what is to become of you. Had you been alive in another time, I expect we would have been friends.'

I grab Laure's hand to remind myself she's here and now is not the time to do anything reckless. She feels cold and when I look at her, I can see how scared she is. What she sees is not the same as what I see, but we both know that Katie Merriweather is dead.

29

My body is no longer mine. Thin tendrils of light extend from the Jade's fingertips to pierce my chest and head. She has disconnected my internals. I have no choice where I look, when I blink. I try to talk, but that too has been taken.

Even my breathing is not under my control. My heartbeat is steady and measured, not influenced by my sudden paralysis. Is that also the Jade's to manipulate? And if so, how simple would it be for her to make it stop?

Her fingers play an etude with my essence. Buds flower inside me. The clusters of facets left by Claire, Chrissy, Sophia and Tegan unfurl, spreading through me with malign possession.

'A little of me in a little of them hidden inside a little of you.' The Jade leans forwards and thick waves of red hair cascade over her shoulders. 'But it is sad to see you so helpless. The last embodiment of a god, born to a collapsing dynasty. So much potential. Maybe you would have been allowed to achieve it had Antoinette Caton not sequestered you for herself. It took so long to find you that I nearly gave up.'

She sweeps a lock of hair behind her ear and sits back in the chair. 'But here you are with me. Where you belong.'

She looks to the girl I know to be Victoria only through her lack of essence. Her appearance has changed. This must be her as she really looks, covered in the scars she revealed to me in the alleyway after Laure went missing. Irritation flashes in the Jade's eyes. I cannot move my head to follow her gaze, but my mind, at least for now, remains my own. I allow the Aether in. The blackness where I know Victoria to be is on my right, cradling the body of Katie while desperately trying to gather her essence. She is failing. Much of Katie is already lost and Victoria is unable to take possession of more than a few facets at a time. She focuses on her brain in the hope it retains her memories, leaving other aspects to drift away before the Aether violently snatches them from existence.

'I bear you no ill will.' My vision returns to the Jade. 'Of the eight billion people who live on this planet, you are one of the most extraordinary. Do you ever think on it? So many people. So banal and undeserving of the life they've been gifted. And then there are those like us, with the power to connect the living with the dead. We are dying and very soon we will be gone forever.'

The body she wears is a mask. The figure sat on the chair has already lived and died, yet the emotions come through. If she really is the Jade Archivist, then she is impossibly old, and it does not take much in the way of deductive reasoning to conclude that she will use my life to further extend her own.

'You wonder about Victoria. My eldest daughter, Elizabeth, was incessant with claims that Victoria had the mark of an archivist. I told her that no archivist had a face that could be remembered and soon grew deaf to her appeal. It was the night I was to take the essence of a minor noble that the truth confronted me.'

The Jade turns again to Victoria and the world slides from photons to facets in time for me to see Katie's essence flying from her body. Even the snatches buried inside Victoria's void are extracted, leaving nothing but darkness. Victoria cries and the Jade continues.

'The noble, a boy of seventeen, was wounded while hunting the week prior and, after much consultation, his physicians agreed there was nothing further they could do. They brought the boy to me on a night when Victoria was staying, a concession I had made to end her mother's blasphemous claims. A horse had trampled the boy, leaving him severely disfigured. Most of the household fled when he arrived. A foolish few peered beneath the blanket that covered his face and regretted the impulse for many years.

'With such an uproar it was no surprise that the child woke. Drawn to the boy while others ran, those who saw her that night claimed she was possessed. I do not know if her actions were conscious, but when I arrived the disfigured face of the dead boy was upon the body of my granddaughter, Victoria.

'I tried to take the young noble from her only to find that she possessed but a few fragments of him. Some remained in his dying body while others had already been snatched by the Aether. All I could gather were remnants and when I projected his face he would only scream.

'Word spread that the prince had died en route to my home, and all who spoke a different story were soon silenced. After that night I refused to return Victoria to her mother. She did not protest.'

The Jade holds out her hand to Victoria and the girl appears by her side. Victoria tries to hide her tears by projecting the faces of others. Smiling, cheerful faces, but incomplete faces with missing chins and ears, or cut in half across her mouth. She settles on one that is only a pair of eyes, bright and blue with long dark lashes. Tears appear where the projection meets her skin and run down her cheeks and over her lips.

'That was over four hundred years ago,' the Jade says. 'But they are always the same. Incomplete. Fractured. After the tragedy that befell the first Victoria, I insisted that with every new life, the first daughter of my first daughter be given that name. In that way the wretched cycle of their existence continues. Not one has lived beyond fifteen.'

I feel my mouth loosen and fall open. I close it again. Work my jaw from side to side. I try to move my arms and legs, but they remain outside of my control.

'I do hate to be the only party in the conversation,' the Jade says.

'What happened to your granddaughters?'

'I'm glad to hear you were paying attention.' She reaches for Victoria with her gloved hand and pulls her close. 'Our flesh betrays us. It atrophies while our essence grows fat on experience. Nature has played a cruel hand by allowing one to outlive the other. But if there were a way to transfer that essence into a new body, then why would you not? A blood connection helps, but it is a body that has known the essence of an archivist that is crucial. The missing part is someone to transfer me. When the Guild was still in existence, I would have had no issue finding an archivist willing to sacrifice themselves. As we are now a dying breed, a little more coercion is required.'

Victoria wrenches herself from her grandmother's grip. 'No! You're lying!' she cries.

'Sweetness, I can assure you that I have no time for lies. You should feel honoured. I am the greatest archivist who has ever lived and it is thanks to you that I will continue living.'

'And what happenth to me when you've thtolen my body? Where do I go?'

'Like the girls from your school, like your friend Katie, your purpose will be over. Really, that was a very silly question.'

I hear Victoria run. The Jade looks unconcerned. She watches me, looks up and my neck loosens. I try to speak, but it appears I am to be silent.

Victoria comes back to us. Monique follows closely behind, pressing a gun between the teenager's shoulder blades.

'It pays to have a small number of people who can be relied upon in times like these. There are few who would willingly orchestrate the deaths of teenage girls for my selfish desire to live. Fortunately, I was able to procure the services of Detective Inspector Jones for a reasonable price.'

Monique is silent as she points the gun at Victoria's head. She will not meet my gaze. Her expression is not one of triumph. For her this is not a planned unveiling where she revels in the brilliance of her deception. Monique's face emanates nothing but profound shame. She has been caught and her selfish desires exposed. If I had control of my essence, I would push fear so deeply into her mind it would drive her insane. But I am not and what little control I have has been rescinded, and once more I blink only at the Jade's command.

Victoria is kneeling beside me. Crying.

'Pawnth thacrificed before the queen,' she splutters. 'And where'th my knight?'

I have nothing. There are no tricks, no clever manipulations of the Aether, no subtle twist of facets that will allow me to escape. There is no part of me that I retain control of; physical, ethereal, everything belongs to the Jade. I am, as Sun would say, completely fucked.

The Jade removes her black elbow-length gloves and drapes them over the side of the chair. Her bare arms, pale and lightly freckled, reach out. The moment her finger touches my temple, I am gone.

The whiteness is so pure it should hurt to look at. It doesn't. It is above me. Below me. Surrounding me. I'm lying on its flat surface. It is different to the sky. When I look at the space between my hands, palms pressed flat against something, it is not a surface I see but a whiteness that stretches forever. I move a hand away; it leaves no mark. I punch it and it makes no sound.

I am warmed to my core, but there is no air. I exhale onto my arm and feel nothing. I do not hurt and, despite not sleeping for almost twenty-four hours, I am not remotely tired.

However, I am a little crestfallen to discover that I'm naked.

I walk. There is nothing before me, nothing behind me, nothing anywhere. No dot or mirage on the horizon that may or may not become something of value. I walk only because it's what I feel I need to do. As for which direction I take, I doubt it matters.

I wonder if I am dead? Is this the Aether?

If so, I'm underwhelmed.

Something appears from the nothing. I didn't walk towards it. It's just there. A dog, running around my feet. It's incomplete, missing two of its legs and half its tail, but it runs like it hasn't realised. It sits on ghost limbs, expecting something of me. I ignore it and it whimpers. A cat runs over. Only the right side of it exists, yet it moves as if it were complete. The dog gives chase and soon both are lost behind the beginnings of a building that appears to unfold from the nothing. Individually laid bricks lose their distinction the higher I look, blending into an amorphous wall of orange until they lose their colour completely and pencil lines stretch into the sky to define what the building will become.

There are more of these buildings around me, half constructed and half architectural sketches drawn onto the air.

They don't appear, they are here as if they had always been here and I am here as if I had always been here. Like neither I nor the buildings had noticed the other.

'Wear this.'

A voice from behind. Soft fabric on my shoulders. I slide my arms into the sleeves, look down and see I am wearing a black kimono embroidered with gold. I tie the cord around my middle.

'It was the most appropriate thing I could find.'

I turn around and there is Antoinette, dressed in orange robes that flow across the floor. She slides her arms around my waist. I can feel them. Thin, comforting, they constrict me with a fierce strength. My own engulf her shoulders. After a time, we part, and she reaches up to touch my cheek.

'Where am I?'

'We have no name for it.'

'This isn't the Aether?'

Antoinette shakes her head. 'This is the place inside you. It didn't exist before our nudist jaunt in the field.'

'Where is—'

'Somewhere else,' Antoinette says. 'When you arrived, we decided it would be best if I met you alone.'

I run a hand along the kimono's sleeve. It feels real.

'Everything here takes time. But it's not time as you know it. Sometimes it runs a little slow and sometimes a little fast.'

'How long have you been here?'

'Long enough to learn everyone's names and life stories.'

'I didn't think you were sociable.'

'There are no doors here to shut or walls high enough to hide behind. I had little choice.'

'So why am I here?'

'How on earth would I know? You're the archivist.'

Antoinette sits on a pencil-line bench. I join her and feel solid support. The buildings retreat, and the whiteness by my feet shimmers with the hint of a lake. The sketch of a fish breaks the surface and dives under with a blue splash.

'Impressive.'

Antoinette laughs. 'You should see Genevieve DuPont's creations.'

'So is this it?' I ask, my understanding of the situation infantile. My essence has been sucked inside itself to a place where those in my possession can interact. They inhabit an afterlife of accidental creation, their essences growing from the new experiences they share with their fellow dead. They build memories, forge bonds and flex their imaginations in a world that bends to their desires.

They are alive. But if I am here, then surely I am not.

Antoinette takes my hand. 'Your skin is softer than I imagined.'

'You were the one who told me I'd never do an honest day's work in my life.'

'True. And no. This isn't the end. We're not connected to you in the way you might expect. We don't watch the world through your eyes. We're cut off from almost everything that exists outside of this place. But this place is inside your essence, which means that when something happens to it, we know.'

Antoinette points up. Cracks appear in the whiteness. Some are far off, ripping through the surface of a dome that encloses us. Others are much nearer, ripping apart the air directly in front of me. I walk towards one to peer inside. Beyond blackness. Beyond nothingness.

'Is this—'

'The Aether? Yes,' Antoinette says. 'We do what we can to hold it back.' She closes her eyes and the cracks disappear.

'Some of us were too curious and the Aether stole what it could.'

I tell Antoinette about the girls and what their essences left inside me, and of the Jade Archivist. There are moments where her immediate concern for my wellbeing is replaced by academic curiosity and her questions probe the nature of the Jade, notepad and pen appearing in her hand. I worry that I am wasting time. Antoinette assures me that is not the case, but her explanation of exactly how time behaves is conjecture and with the encroaching influence of the Aether, it will only grow in complication.

'I don't even know why I am here.'

'Because this is where you are safe and have the time, twisted as it might be, to think. What the Jade is doing to you, she is doing to your essence, and here you are inside it. The fragments of those girls are hooks, you need to work them loose.'

'How?'

'I can't help you there, I'm afraid. But I know someone who can.'

Antoinette waves a hand and we are no longer sitting on a bench. Lara, the girl who jumped from the upper balcony of the exhibition centre, stands before me, wearing the dress she died in.

'Follow me,' Lara says, and I leave Antoinette behind in the partially completed town and enter the whiteness. I look back and there are the people whose essences I have taken. They're in their houses, conjuring walls and doors into existence, sitting down with a partially formed cat on their lap or watching me leave as they clutch the beginnings of a window frame. They look concerned.

'Why are we walking?' I ask.

'Some places are difficult to find,' Lara says.

307

Whiteness pervades. The village has vanished, so too the people. We walk in silence. My heart doesn't beat. There is no air to be drawn into my lungs. When I attempt to measure the passage of time by the steps I take, I fail to count beyond seven. I don't feel hunger or thirst. We could have walked for thirty seconds or seven months, I wouldn't know.

A knot of colour in the whiteness. Lara says, 'Found them,' and then we are there, stood before Claire, Chrissy, Sophia and Tegan.

The girls appear as solid as we do, but do not seem to have noticed our approach. Each is immersed in a task, interacting with something unseen by us. As we watch, a pattern emerges. They are repeating moments of their life, the memories stored in the facets that were left inside me.

'Have you spoken to them?' I ask.

'We can't,' Lara says.

She approaches Tegan Caldwell, who sits at a desk we can't see and cries. Lara reaches out and something pushes Tegan from her. The other girls follow, skidding across the floor in their individual bubbles. We follow and are instantly by them.

'They don't respond, it doesn't matter what you do. We've even tried crashing them into each other; they just don't care. We can feel them tearing this place apart, but we've no way to stop them. It's not something we're supposed to do.'

'Antoinette said I need to unhook them. How do I do that?'

'You're thinking like an archivist,' Lara says.

'Because I am one.'

'These girls don't need an archivist.'

'Then how do I fix them?'

'You fix them by not trying to fix them.'

'I don't understand.'

'Antoinette said you wouldn't.'

Lara conjures a chair and sits. I try to do the same, but nothing happens. She creates one for me.

'I thought you'd be god here.'

'Apparently not.'

Lara leans forwards to study the girls. 'You see us as threads, that's what Antoinette told me.'

'Yes. But that is only how my brain represents the complexities of the human essence. Every archivist sees it differently.'

'Those threads mean something,' Lara says. 'They're not just thoughts and memories. They define who we are. It only takes one traumatic experience or crippling obsession to ruin someone. You can't unpick it without unravelling us completely.'

'So what am I supposed to do?'

'Leave the thread in.'

'But—'

'That was our mistake. We thought Victoria would pull the rotten threads from us, but instead she used them to murder us. Don't believe you can fix people with reason or force. When someone shares their story with you, listen, be there for them, support them. Not everyone needs a white knight to ride in and slay their demons. Our demons are *ours* and they're not going anywhere. We need to learn to live with them.'

I stand and the chair vanishes. Lara remains seated.

'I will make time for you,' I say.

'I'm not going anywhere.'

I pass through whatever membrane had blocked Lara and the whiteness transforms into a tidy bedroom with a single bed in the corner, a floor-to-ceiling bookshelf and a small desk.

Tegan Caldwell creeps in and gently closes the door behind her. She sits on the bed and takes a framed picture from the desk. It is of her, younger than she is now, and a girl of about ten who looks to be her sister.

Tegan holds the picture and does not move, does not say anything, does not cry.

She can't see me and I abuse the gift of invisibility to snoop around the room. Only it quickly becomes clear that this is not her room. The clothes in orderly piles inside drawers or hung from rails are too small for Tegan and have not been worn for some time. More pictures, these pinned to a notice board and bleached by the Sun, depict the younger of the two girls with similarly aged friends on a trip to a theme park. Then there are the indentation marks in the carpet from heavy machinery and numerous stains from vomit and other bodily fluids. A wall someone has punched through and poorly repaired. The polystyrene head for a child's wig.

Lara is right, I cannot fix this girl. The strength associated with these emotions has allowed her facets to cling to me with maddening desperation. She will not be prised off through force and neither will the others.

The memories and fears associated with a facet have always been hidden from me, and yet here I am, stood inside one. If I can change the Tegan in here, then I will redefine a part of her essence and possibly persuade it to loosen its grip.

I touch Tegan on the shoulder. She jumps.

The picture is lowered to her lap. She does not look surprised to find me in her sister's room. She is hopeful, desperate. I sit next to her on the bed and imagine what I would want to say and how I would want to make her feel if she were Sun.

'Is she your sister?' I ask.

Tegan nods.

'What was she like?'

310

30

I began to forget. The shape of his jaw. The colour of his eyes. The unhurried way he spoke. Those looks he gave me when we sat in his living room doing nothing that told me he was glad I was there.

The ribbon grew dull. I pulled it, hoping to wake him. It didn't.

Then he opened his eyes. It must have been only seconds, but they were the longest seconds in recorded history. Knowledge of him flooded me. I remembered him like I always had, since the day he saved my life. The image I have of him when I close my eyes is sharp, whereas everyone else is a hazy blur in the shape of a person. From every angle, from far away, from up close, I know him like I have never known anyone before and never will again.

The ribbon that leads from me into him dances in a thousand colours. He is no longer kneeling, subservient before a superior archivist. He is standing with his head back and arms waiting purposefully by his sides. Inhumanly beautiful, he is half god, with one foot in the world of the living and one in the world of the dead. There is something in his calmness that intimidates and, if I had the skill, I would remember this scene and paint him.

'You think you've helped them,' the Jade Archivist says. 'But I have no use for them now.'

Faces flash over hers. Claire, Chrissy, Tegan and Sophia. She wears them as one, their features rippling as they crash into each other. They lift from her and the fullness of teenage cheeks and lips and hair are revealed as nothing more than a paper-thin mask that quickly fractures and burns to dust.

The girls are snatched. Not by the Aether. By him. Shards of gold cut through his clothes and attack his face. They slice into his eyes and bury themselves deep within his skin.

He doesn't even move.

'Impressive,' the Jade says, 'but then I would expect nothing less. With so few of us left, mediocrity wouldn't do.'

'I will take that as a compliment.'

'Indeed I intended it as one, though I know flattery will not get me what I want, which is why I want to offer some constructive criticism. You see, you have it all wrong. You are not here to save anyone. You provide a service just like everyone else and for that you charge a reasonable fee. What you can do should not be given away. You are not their god, so don't let people fool you into thinking you are.'

'You're in no position to tell me what to do.'

'Oh, but I am,' the Jade says.

The Archivist walks away. Any control she had over him gone. I nearly take Laure's hand and run over when the Jade changes. Her face becomes younger with delicate features, a thin nose, eyebrows so fine they're barely there, and soft, freckled cheeks. She sweeps blonde hair from her face where it falls to the side, just short of her shoulders.

'If you try to save everyone, it only hurts more when you fail.'

Her voice has changed. He stops.

'Jenny?'

I know she's dead, but my stupid brain can't stop itself from wanting to know who the hell Jenny is.

'A little more perceptive than you. Her sister recently died and she believed another party was to blame. In fact, she was so convinced of this that she tried to enlist the help of an archivist she knew.'

'You killed her.'

The Jade meets his accusation with a placating smile. 'As you may have gathered, it's what we do. I couldn't have her telling you who I am.'

'You didn't have to kill her.'

'And you didn't have to kill Richard Hargrave or Katie Merriweather. We kill because we can and, more importantly, because we like it.'

He doesn't respond. I never thought to ask if he enjoyed it. I just assumed he did it because he had no choice.

He looks at his feet. He must know I'm here and that I'm seeing and hearing everything and that I know what it means. He doesn't just kill people because he must, he does it because he wants to.

Something in the Archivist's silent admission resonates with me. What he does is not just a job. It is so much greater than the clinical procedures of a hospital. It is raw, visceral. It is human death. Our end. That he enjoys it excites me. I know that any sane person should fear him, but how can I fear the person who took pleasure in the killing of my abuser? It is another flaw in his character, one that makes him seem less godly, more human. More like me.

'What I didn't need to do was keep her,' the Jade says. 'I have no intention of letting her family see her. Doubtless they will have realised she is missing, but a body will never be discovered and they will allow themselves to believe she ran away over the grief of losing a sister.' The Jade changes. She has the same face but different clothes, tighter fitting and more modern. 'When I am inside Victoria, I will need a new shell. I certainly won't make much of an impression looking like that.' Victoria looks away. 'I think this young woman would be perfect for my next appearance.'

'You lost your control over me.'

'Very true and a great shame. A lot of people died for that and you wasted it. Monique, get the girl.'

There's another girl? Wait, she's coming this way! It's me, I'm the other girl. Fuck!

Monique comes straight to me. I take Laure's hand, ready to run, but grab only air. She's not here. When did she leave? I'd been so mesmerised by the Archivist that I never thought to check on her. I nearly call out but Monique is now standing in front of me holding a gun. She's shaking her head, telling me not to try anything, and I keep my mouth shut. I'm marched to the Jade, though in a way it's not the Jade, it's some pretty girl the Archivist knew and never mentioned.

'You were supposed to go home,' he says, his voice terse like I'm just a kid.

I don't know what scares me more, the gun or his anger. I try and make light of the situation.

'Can I go home?' I ask the Jade. 'It's just, I don't think I want to be here anymore.'

The Jade ignores me. Not even a smile. At least, not one I remember.

'I told you it was going to be dangerous,' the Archivist says.

'I didn't think you meant *gun* dangerous!'

'Oh,' he says, 'and what kind of dangerous were you hoping for? Knives? Ninja stars?'

'I don't fucking know!' I cry. 'You said there was going to be trouble and I didn't want you facing it alone. OK? So, unless you've got any practical advice that's actually going to help, then maybe we just drop it. I'm here and Detective *Cunt*stable Jones is pointing a gun at my face. That's what we're working with now.'

The Jade's sigh draws everyone's attention back to her.

'For over a year I've been watching and in that time you've shown no emotional attachment to anyone apart from Antoinette. I thought about using her, but it would never have worked. She was devoted to you and would happily sacrifice her life before I'd extracted what I needed.

'I was beyond incredulous when Monique told me you had taken in a pair of strays. It was not an arrangement I expected to last, yet here we are, months later, and not only do they still live with you, but it seems that you've become attached to them.'

The Archivist shifts uncomfortably. 'Sun,' he says, 'stop smiling.'

'Sorry, it's just... I'll stop.'

'The connection you share poses a problem,' the Jade continues, still wearing the face and slim body of the Archivist's friend. 'If I threw her out, you would only throw her back in. Her life. Her death. They are your playthings, not mine.'

'I help you or Monique shoots her?' he says.

'Not fatally,' the Jade says. 'It wouldn't do to have Sun fall into the Aether, only to drag you in after. Let's hope the pain of a shattered shoulder blade is enough to earn your cooperation.'

Monique stands behind me and I feel the metal barrel of a gun pressed against my shoulder. I can't help but look at him. Can I really expect him to sacrifice his life for me? She's not even going to kill me. His life is worth more than my pain. If I were him and Laure were me, I'd let her do what she wanted to me, anything to keep Laure safe. But am I really worth that much to him? Sure, it'll hurt like holy fuck, but a competent surgeon will be able to fix it. So I may never manage a cartwheel; it's not like I'll die.

I feel the gun twitch. She's going to shoot me, I just know it. I prepare myself to move as if I can duck away fast enough to dodge a speeding bullet from a gun that's literally touching me. Breathing, loud and fast. I try to control it, which is nearly impossible, but eventually I do, even though I have to hold my hands over my mouth. It's still there. These aren't my breaths and they're not his either.

A bang echoes through the ruined building. The corner of the chair the Jade sits on explodes in a storm of wood dust. The Jade's image flicks chaotically from person to person, combining and contorting. Before she has settled on an appearance, Monique is in front of her, pointing the gun at her head.

No one is looking at me, so I check my jeans. I only pissed myself a little bit.

'That's not how this'll go down,' Monique says.

'Oh,' the Jade says, unconcerned, 'and why is that?'

'You never told me.'

'What, dear?' the Jade says, now wearing the skin of an old woman. 'About the cancer in your left breast?' The old woman melts and the Jade becomes a man in his forties. He is smartly dressed, wears a watch that is too large for even his meaty arm. He runs his hand through his thick hair, leans forwards and rests his chin on his fist. 'I was expecting this sooner,' he says.

'I... I didn't think anyone would die,' Monique says, the gun wavering.

'A police detective and you didn't think anyone would die?' The image of the man peels away to reveal the same glamorous

316

woman she projected when I arrived. 'I find that hard to believe,' she continues in a silky voice. 'You are not an idiot, Detective Inspector Jones. I knew you didn't believe in archivists, but when it finally dawned on you that we were real there was already blood on your hands. If anyone learnt you were culpable for the deaths of five schoolgirls it would mean the end of your career and decades in prison. Staying loyal to me was the only way you could save yourself. So you see, Detective Inspector Jones, you are not an idiot. You are a coward.'

The Jones woman opens her mouth at the same time the Jade flicks her wrist. A searing light blinds me as Monique's essence explodes through her back. Millions of tiny ribbons escape into the violet sky and the body of the Jones woman crumples to the floor.

'I expect she had more to say, but I've no interest in hearing it.' The Jade claps her hands together. 'Oh, please don't look so shocked. Monique was due her betrayal, it just came later than expected. Though you shouldn't begrudge her, what she did took courage. And, Sun-young, please stop staring so intently at the gun and let's get this over with.'

'No,' I say and back away from the Jade and the gun, which I guess I was staring at a little too much. 'You can't kill me and now that Monique's dead, neither can she.'

'The detective inspector was never going to shoot you; I'm not barbaric. She was only here for you to watch her die.'

My chest violently constricts, forcing the air from my lungs. My panicked cries become little more than a silent wheeze.

'I do not need weapons or the police to intimidate,' the Jade says, 'only my archivism. Only despair.'

A deep cold enters through my clothes and burrows into my skin. My flesh and blood freeze, muscles crystallise. The first rays of morning light are hurriedly withdrawn and darkness cloaks me.

I have not felt this since I made the connection with him. I wait for it to pass, knowing that the Jade is manipulating my essence and none of this is real. The light will return, and with it the warmth.

I wait.

The cold does not pass.

Time does.

My frozen insides grind against each other when I finally move. I am still at the house. The chair where the Jade sat is empty. The Archivist and Victoria are gone. The bodies of Katie and Monique have decomposed. I don't remember what happened. Did the Archivist sacrifice his life to keep the Jade living in the body of Victoria, or is it the Jade who is dead?

I must have been knocked unconscious. That nobody came for me leaves me hollow.

My movements are heavy. The effort to lift a leg and place one in front of the other drains me and it takes minutes to cover a distance that should take seconds. I call for Laure. My voice is weak, even I struggle to hear it.

I want to run through the ruins of the house, tear it apart and find Laure, but my movements are too slow and it's unlikely she's still here. I feel for my phone, but what I remove from my pocket is a slab of slate. It slips from my feeble grip, shattering when it hits the floor.

With nowhere else to go, I walk to the Archivist's flat, following roads in the hope I'll find a taxi. Silent street after silent street greets me and it feels like hours until I'm there, though with no phone I don't really know. I moon-watch, expecting it to shift across the sky like the sun. It doesn't move from where it hangs above my head. It's only a sliver, even the dark part you can sometimes see is missing. I reach up to touch it and could swear that it passes through my fingers. After that it moves further away and everything becomes a little darker.

It's the only light I have, I shouldn't piss it off.

No one is in the flat. I drift from room to room like a ghost. Someone lived here, but that looks to have been a long time ago. The lights don't work and when I look up there is the sliver of moon. It must have followed me in.

I'm hungry. Inside the fridge are stacks of grey cubes the size of my fist that glisten in the feeble moonlight. I pick one up. It's spongey and moist, and without thinking, I take a bite. All I taste is cold. I look through the cupboards: more grey cubes. I eat two.

I try the phone, the computer, the television. Nothing works. I drag a chair over to the large window in the living room where he meets his clients and part the heavy curtains. I sit and wait for it to be morning.

I thought I knew how loneliness felt. I was wrong.

The moon is outside now.

I wave to it.

It doesn't wave back.

There are no lights. Even other towns, that I should be able to see from up here, are dark. It could be the time, or maybe there's been a power cut. Occasionally, I see movement. On the street or on the other side of a window in a different building. People. I will try to talk to them in the morning.

It must be late. I don't want to sleep because I don't know where Laure is. I tell myself that she's with him and they are safe somewhere together, but if they are safe together then why aren't they safe with me? They're either safe and they chose to leave me behind or they're not safe at all.

I go into the other living room, the one that's meant for us, and take a picture off the wall. It's the three of us. We spent the afternoon on the common. I had this great idea to fly kites, but we sucked, even though there was so much wind the trees were bending. It was the Archivist's idea to take a picture. It was cute the way he suggested it, though he'd hate me for saying so.

I scan the wall for other pictures. They don't look how I remember them. Laure and his head are twisted so I can only see the back of their hair. I'm looking forward, but my eyes are too wide and my smile stretches the full length of my face.

I take it anyway and go upstairs to Laure's bedroom. I'd hoped the room would smell of her, but it smells of nothing at all. Even her stuff doesn't really feel like hers, they're just clothes and pens and books, not Laure's. The photos on her wall are all wrong too, the heads are twisted to face away from the camera. All except mine. I've mutated in every picture. My features are either too large or too small; in some they are in the wrong place. I'm missing an eye in one picture, in another I have three.

I climb into bed, curl into the foetal position and cocoon myself in the duvet. I wait to become warm, but it never happens. Eventually I sleep.

It's still dark when I wake up. I have no way to tell the time so don't know if I've slept for eight hours or eight minutes. I lie with my eyes closed and fail to fall back to sleep. After a while I slide out of bed. I'm still cold. I contemplate finding something to eat, but the hunger isn't there. I don't even need the toilet.

The outside is grey, and my moon still hangs over my head, stalking me. I lie on my back and watch it. After a while it creeps closer, curious. The craters in its surface become clearer. It's definitely the moon, just not how I remembered.

I leave the flat to find someone. When did I last hear a noise that wasn't the squeaking of my shoes? I sing to myself, some old songs my mum must have listened to. I don't remember learning the lyrics and wonder how long I've known them. My voice croaks the first few bars but after that it's something resembling a tune; good enough for a choir, not solo material.

My voice cracks in response to my heart rate, faltering with every corner I turn. The night doesn't belong to me. Sleeping families aren't tucked into their warm beds and late-night taxi drivers aren't speeding through the deserted streets, taking their last passengers home. This night feels empty of any life except mine. I want it to be morning so desperately that I tell the moon to fuck off and it shoots up, plunging me into darkness. I pad the ground for somewhere soft to wait it out and try to sleep. Miraculously I do and when I wake again, the moon is back. I apologise and call it beautiful. It hovers closer, though still seems wary of me. This is what I get for being such an arsehole all the time.

I find someone. They're standing at a bus stop staring at the timetable. I try to run, but my legs can't manage more than a shuffle and it takes an age to reach them. They don't look away from the timetable. I touch their shoulder to get their attention and accidently flick a shard of them onto the floor where it shatters, just like my phone did. They move and their crystal body cracks, disassembling into chunks that fall away to smash at my feet.

What was a person crumbles into a pile of black sand. I poke it with my foot and feel it crunch underneath the sole of my shoes. The noise is welcome against the silence.

I place a hand on my stomach and feel the cold suck away what little heat I have left. I'm freezing from the inside, starting with my heart. I will soon become a pile of black sand. It is my fate, as inescapable as the passing of time. I should feel scared, but what I experience is beyond that. I've already resigned myself to that fate. My survival is not hopeless, it is utterly without hope. They are different. Only people who have been here would know that.

I return to search the ruined mansion. Sometimes I need to stop for sleep and every time I wake nothing has changed, it's just me and my moon. Because I have no way of telling the time I don't know how long it takes before I'm talking to the moon regularly. It started in the house, on the second-floor parlour room that was missing three of its walls. I made some comment about the size of a bed. After that, every thought that popped into my head was voiced. At first these nuggets of insight weren't directed anywhere in particular, but soon they were asked directly of the moon. It didn't matter that it never spoke; the sound of my voice was enough.

Time is passing. I can feel it in the cooling of my body. I lost my left hand. I was in a different town and just caught it on the corner of a building, then heard it crack and fall to the floor. I didn't even try to catch it. I'm not fast enough. That was the day I saw someone moving inside a building. They looked about the same size as Laure. When I got there they'd already gone. It's happened a few times since then. I don't know why Laure would run from me, but I'm convinced it's her.

I'm getting slower. When I walk, I need to sleep a few times before getting anywhere. I've met other people too, though there's little left of them. Where I can, I avoid touching them, but sometimes I need the human contact so badly that I can't stop myself. They shatter every time.

I haven't been able to move between the last five times I've slept. I don't know where I am apart from that I'd come here to find Laure after another argument with the moon. I think it wants me to give up looking because it hides every time I mention Laure's name. It's jealous, I get that. But it needs to be reasonable. Laure is my sister and it's just my moon.

The moon left two sleeps ago. I miss it. Nothing moves anymore. Not my mouth, not my eyelids. No matter how hard I strain I can't see anything. I wonder if my moon's turned sweet on someone else.

No light. No noise. No movement. Nothing but fear. Nothing but fear for a very long time.

I gasp. So much warmth. So much light. I can move, and quickly fall over. A woman sits on the chair before me. It takes a moment to process where I am or who she is. Then it comes.

The Jade Archivist.

She smiles at me and motions to the figure on my right. He is on his hands and knees. Tears stream down his beautiful face. He looks at me.

'Martina.'

Of the many things experienced through life, I have always felt that mutual love was the most improbable. The chances of falling in love are small, especially when considering the general banality of the average person. The chance of that person you have fallen in love with also falling in love with you is even smaller. That this happens to anyone has always been one of life's greatest mysteries. And yet it happens.

It even happened to me.

I was in love with Martina De Luca. Of greater significance, Martina De Luca was in love with me. We never spoke of it. It was simply assumed that the other knew and so the subject was never broached. But each of us could tell. When a love is that strong, it is hard to miss.

Yet we could never touch. Even being too close would affect Martina and there were times when she would lose consciousness just from sitting on the sofa with me. Being young and determined to taste the tiniest slither of human contact, we found a solution in gloves. Martina would knit these, adding layer after layer of wool so there was no chance our fingers would accidentally slip through the weave and meet.

Her gloves were always the most vivid colours, burnt orange, purple, electric blue. I have them still, though they are too small for my adult hands.

Despite our unspoken love, each day that passed only brought disappointment as my archivism failed to appear and I felt Martina's affection for me wane. How long would it be until my appeal as an oddity exhausted completely? Any longer and she would have stopped accompanying her father to the church and someone or something else would have consumed her attention, leaving me with only the devotion of Antoinette and the fearful affection of my family for company.

So I told a lie. An old woman, believed to be in good spirits after leaving her local salon, had not given the road her full attention when stepping off the pavement. A passing lorry struck her, and she became wedged in the wheel arch. It was fortunate I was nearby, and that I felt the pull of death. I did not take possession of the dying woman's essence for long, as when I projected her face she begged to be released, leaving no evidence for Martina to scrutinise.

I could not predict what would follow only days later. Martina arrived with her father, as usual, but after a short time with me she left for an anteroom where Antoinette stored yet more books. She rang a handbell at the same time she kicked the chair from under her. Summoned to her suicide, there was nothing I could do. I tried, watching as Martina became increasingly desperate. In her dying state, she realised that I had lied and we would not be joined in death.

A year of searching a dead world. A year of unquenchable thirst, of interminable fatigue. A year of knowing that she was with me, wanting only to goad and punish. Finally, I have her. I pull her in. Wrap myself tightly around her. Tell her how sorry I am. How much I love her.

She struggles in my embrace and I realise my grip is too tight and she cannot breathe. My arms slacken, though not by much. Her hair is darker and straighter than I remember. Her skin tone is different too.

She is warm. I am warm. Cold for so long, the warmth is unbearable, then welcome, then necessary. Colour imbues the sky. The air tastes of decay and freshness.

My arms fall to my sides. I am not holding Martina De Luca. I am not in that dying world. A year's worth of memories spin into facets with such haste they struggle to retain their purpose and rapidly decohere, leaving nothing but an impression of despair.

The girl on my lap is Sun-young Kang. She is not a replacement for Martina. Feelings of guilt over my lie should not be funnelled into her and I will not achieve atonement through acts of kindness directed at someone else. Altruism is not in my nature; and I know that had I not met and lost Martina, I would never have helped Sun in the way I did.

The Jade Archivist regards me with cruel approval. 'Worse than death, wouldn't you agree? Not that I would expect you to capitulate over something so trivial. But the girl? I could create a personalised hell and force her to endure a thousand years of torture in minutes. Her heart would beat, her blood would flow, but her mind would be destroyed. Is that what you want for her?'

There is no response I can give. I want to relinquish responsibility by distancing myself from Sun. If our friendship was only an afterglow of my feelings for Martina, then Sun would mean nothing to me and her fate would be of no concern.

But she does mean something to me. I feel like a different person in her company and while I may have once claimed the feelings of others were not my concern, that is no longer the case for Sun and Laure.

'Why does he have to die?' Sun says. Still on my lap, she looks at me and there is an understanding that we both experienced something that no one but the other could ever comprehend. She stands and holds out a hand. I take it, even though I don't need to.

'You think I'm jealous of his youth? Perhaps... but there are things I can do that would take him lifetimes to master.' The Jade extends an arm. The last vestiges of youth that clung to forty-year-old flesh wither to reveal skin that hangs from feeble muscles and brittle bones. 'Everything dies. Even the Aether will die. Our essence may not decay with our flesh, but that does not mean it is immortal. We lose facets every day as memories are forgotten and impulses rewired. I am not the same person who assumed this body eighty years ago and when I leave Victoria's body, I will be different again. But there is one part of me that can never be allowed to die. Archivism is woven so deeply into us that without it we would unravel, and so, when an archivist assists me by placing my essence into the body of my granddaughter, I take from them what I need.'

A door swings open, redundant as little of the wall remains. Laure walks casually towards us. She waves at Sun, then at me.

'So... is it OK if we go now?' she asks.

The Jade doesn't look away from me. 'Move and it's ten years of hell for Sun.'

Laure walks over and hugs her sister, then approaches the Jade, thrusting her face obnoxiously close in a defiant show of bravery.

Facets leak from the Jade to constrict Laure's legs. They work their way up, curling into her body and infiltrating her mind.

'I heard what you said about my sister,' Laure says. 'You want her to suffer.' She sees the gun on the floor and after a few seconds, bends down to pick it up. 'It's really heavy!' she says to Sun and points it at the Jade.

Curves of light in their millions pour from the Jade, arcing through the air before turning their attention on Laure. I focus on the Aether; never has it blinded so completely. There are no eyes to shield when viewing this cut of existence, leaving me little choice but to endure its brilliance.

The Jade's presence slams into Laure. Facets devour with animalistic hunger. They wrap themselves around the unsuspecting essence, attempting to wrench it from the body. Laure's image swells, consumed by the torrent of invaders. Every aspect of her existence is claimed. The slightest impulse and the Jade could scatter Laure across these ruins like seeds tossed to the wind.

'She looks angry.'

Laure's voice.

My vision leaves the Aether and there she is, stood before the Jade, a mixture of confusion and amusement. The image disappears, to be replaced once more by the Aether and the Jade's struggle.

Laure is immune to everything the Jade attempts. So resolute against a rage grown over centuries, she has no idea of the onslaught inflicted upon her, of the alien presence that has invaded her body or its futile determination to destroy her. Her casual resistance only angers the Jade further and waves of her essence threaten to crash into Sun and me. I hold them off where I can. The Jade can never hurt Laure; the same cannot be said for the rest of us.

'I know I can't see what you see,' Laure says. 'But I think that means you can't see what I see. Right? She's really old. And terrified. She's looking right at me and she's crying because that thing she's trying to do to me isn't working.'

I take Sun's hand and lead her away. She fights me, wanting to be with her sister. Fear has silenced her, but that instinct to

328

protect will never leave. I pull her back with such force that I can see the damage it causes. The link we share will not be enough to protect Sun if she gets too close. I do not want her lost to the Jade's fury.

Now it's only Laure and the Jade.

'Monique and Katie, they're dead, aren't they?'

Laure looks to me and I nod.

'If they'd been shot, then there'd be blood. So I guess that means this old lady did it and if she could do it to them, then that means she could do it to all of you.' Her grip on the gun tightens, a resolve settling on her face. 'I don't believe in any of this. If you were me, you'd see two teenagers wetting themselves over a little old lady. But just because I can't see it, and just because it's not real to me, doesn't mean it's not real to you. I heard everything she said. She wants to kill you and torture my sister and there's no one but me who can stop her.'

'Don't!' Sun screams. 'Don't kill her. Don't let her make you a murderer.'

Laure beams at her sister. 'I don't know how to fire a gun,' she says before pistol-whipping the Jade.

The Jade's essence retreats. The body she wore vanishes and for the first time I see the real Jade Archivist. Except that it is not the real Jade Archivist; that body died centuries ago. This is the body of her granddaughter, Victoria. The last in a long line to be sacrificed.

Sun pulls herself from my grip and runs to Laure. She throws her arms around her, taking them both to the ground.

'Where were you?' Sun asks.

Laure fights her way out of her sister's embrace. 'I needed to pee and when I came back everything got really weird, so I hid.'

'OK. That was smart.'

'Obviously,' Laure snorts.

'The gun part, not so smart.' Sun takes the gun from Laure, removes the clip then throws them in opposite directions.

'We'll need to pick those up,' I say. 'This isn't America.'

Laure goes to where Victoria has slumped on the floor. 'She's not waking up.'

During those hours I was inside myself, which amounted to seconds here, the Jade had already used me to push a substantial amount of Victoria's essence from her body. It remains attached to her, a tree of light growing from her head, sprouting branches that hang to the floor. This is the first time I have seen Victoria's essence, the influence of the Jade granting me the ability. I try to coax it back into its body, but it resists my effort to tame it. To fix Victoria will require time and concentration. It is not a task for now.

'We need to take her somewhere.'

Sun approaches Monique's corpse and takes the car keys from her front pocket. 'Monique... do you—'

'The Aether,' I say.

'What about Katie?'

I look to the body of the teenage girl I allowed my rage to kill and ignore the question. Sun is aware enough to understand and approaches the Jade while I pick up Victoria. Laure looks to Monique and I shake my head.

'Are you just going to leave her here?' Laure asks.

'Someone will come looking for the Jade.'

'And then what?'

'Monique and Katie will be taken care of.'

'That doesn't sound very nice.'

'That's what happens when you get mixed up with not very nice people,' I say.

Laure dashes to the edge of the room and returns dragging two lengths of thick velvet curtain. She drapes one over Monique and one over Katie. 'Should we say something?' she asks.

'No, I don't think so.' I reaffirm my grip on Victoria. 'Sun, it's time to leave.'

Sun, sat on the arm of the chair, has the Jade's face in her hands and turns it towards me.

'I wonder if anyone will miss her.'

'She's not dead,' I say.

'So she can still sting me?'

'She may be dangerous.'

'Are we just going to leave her to die? Isn't that a bit cruel?'

'What do you recommend?'

'Break her neck? Shoot her in the head?'

'I kill people for a living and never once have I resorted to breaking a person's neck.'

'Oh yeah!' Sun says, 'The archivist thing. You should do that.'

Should I? Archivists follow no code that denounces the killing of another archivist as sin; however, we are endangered. Should this end with me killing the Jade, either directly or through inaction, or am I to show clemency?

'I don't think you should kill her,' Laure says.

'Why?'

'People who kill old ladies go to hell.'

'Then that will be something to look forward to.' Laure should not be here to see this, even if she cannot actually *see* it. 'I suggest you wait by the car,' I tell her. Laure runs off and I lay Victoria back down. 'Sun, get off her. You're right. She needs to die.'

'I don't think that's what I said.'

The Jade stirs as Sun shuffles off the seat. Her withered hand moves in an explosion of speed and takes Sun by the neck. The Jade's body shifts. The image I can no longer remember is replaced by the form of an old man in a great coat and top hat.

He expands, peeling off the Jade. His features lock in fear. He can see me, calls out for salvation before the Aether snatches him with ruthless efficiency. Another person, a young woman in a corseted dress and bustle, appears. She too sees me and cries out as cracks appear in her face and along her arms and legs. The Aether steals her too as another appears over the Jade, followed by another and another.

Thousands of essences stream from the Jade and the dead become the sky.

32

The old bitch is on me. Swollen fingers, red with blisters and cracked skin, wrap around my throat. Her grip is weak. She barely chokes me as I watch the thousands of people, knotted ghosts of brilliant white, escape her body. They make eye contact, their mouths moving silently as they come for me, sensing I'm something I'm not.

A shiver, but not in my flesh. Its a deeper sensation that occurs elsewhere, in the other part of me. The me that is truly me, not the meat sack pinned to the floor by a woman in her nineties.

Eventually, the dead realise their mistake and leave me alone, gasping for another to take them. They scatter and merge, forming a solid whiteness in every direction. The Jade evicts them; I think it's intentional, though don't know why. What little weight she's got left is on me, lying awkwardly with one gnarled hand around my throat and her shrivelled body covering mine. I'm strong enough to push her off, probably even strong enough to hold her over my head and throw her out a window. But I don't move. I'm frozen. My breaths are quick, my fingernails claw the ground. I want to flee, can't bear to be trapped under her like this, her body on me, her crotch pressed against mine.

The face hovering above me is not the Jade's. It is a man's face, so like Richard's I almost believe it's him, like she's reached into the Aether and pulled him back to taunt me. Then he's gone, his essence evicted into the growing cloud above us.

Another face appears. Another Richard. The same hazel eyes and weak chin, though his nose is stubbier and his ears smaller. He is not Richard, and neither was the man before him. But he looks enough like him that the Jade must know because Monique knew, and now what I endured in the flat has been weaponised to cripple me. And even though there's a rational part of my brain that screams Richard is dead and the weight on top of me is not the weight of a thirty-seven-year-old with an eager erection that digs into my thigh, but the weight of an old woman so close to death that the shock from clapping my hands would be enough to kill her, I still can't move because no matter how many months it has been or how safe I may feel in the presence of the Archivist, what Richard did has poisoned me to the core. He tracked his muddy boots through me and while I may be able to cover up the stain of his presence, the filth will eventually soak through.

I was an idiot to think his death would be the end of it. His presence has always been there, a face in the crowd, a scent on the bus, the unconscious touch of a stranger that fires burning needles into my skin.

I can never be rid of Richard Hargrave. He took me and changed me and now I am someone I wasn't before. This Sun-young will always be the Sun-young Richard created. His actions infected me, memories of him a cancer, malignant and inoperable. I know how I appear to others. Fierce Sun-young. Pugnacious Sun-young. What would they think if they knew how completely one man had cut me down?

But the Jade knows. Face after face of Richard clones. To think she has so many thousands of people inside her that she can create a category entirely to torment me.

She lets go of my throat, realising from the look in my eyes that her feeble grip is not what keeps me pinned.

'I had hoped to avoid this,' the Jade says. She's another Richard clone, but something about her is fading and she does not manipulate me in the way that she should. Cracks appear in her face and the rancid breath from her dying body, that I should not be able to smell if the illusion were complete, rolls into my mouth and up my nose with every word.

'You will have forgotten me,' she says. 'That was intentional. Sadly I cannot return those memories to you in a dramatic reveal. When I left the hotel room, I reached into you and stole what I wanted. The Aether was quick to feed. You see, it is interested in you and what you have shared with the Archivist. Very interested.'

She twangs the ribbon and I feel my essence resonate.

'He is changing you. I doubt he is aware of it, but when he shared himself he infected your body. I expect you have seen something of a person's essence. He is making you like him.'

I want to speak. Instead, I panic. My breaths are large and ragged, gulping down her vile stench as if greedy for it. I retch and feel her hand, cold and scaly, on my cheek. She snaps my head to the side as I cough a mouthful of vomit onto the floor.

'I wonder what you would become if I let you live,' the Jade says. 'It is a pity I shan't find out.'

The Richard she wears is so fractured the effect has gone. It's shattered glass, distorting the features beneath it, part hers and part those of a man who probably died more than a hundred years ago.

I wiggle my toes, flex my fingers. The person on me is not Richard. Not even close enough to fool my most vulnerable fears.

I push my hands against the weathered floor and slowly sit up, taking the Jade with me.

I see emotion on her face, but there's a flash of another man, even more cracked than the last, and whatever I saw in the Jade's eyes is forgotten. A shame, because I bet it was fear. Fear that she has no control over me. Fear that she's lost. Fear, because if she knows as much about me as she claims, then she knows that in about ten seconds, things are going to get unpleasant.

'You were Troy to his Trojan Horse,' she says, sliding off me, her legs useless and her arms barely strong enough to catch her. 'He opened you up, Sun-young, and hid among your darkest crevices. But the foolish boy forgot to close you, allowing all and sundry to enter.'

She's lying on her back, both hands in the air. I think she's trying to defend herself, even though I'm not convinced I'm up to punching an old lady in the face, no matter how much of a murdering cunt she is.

Her hands are around the ribbon that extends from my chest and before I realise what's happening, she's pulling it and something inside me shifts. I bring my hands up, ready to push her away, only they don't work anymore. Floppy and useless, I slap them against her face before my elbows go too and I'm a puppet and someone's cutting all the strings.

I look down to see her dredge my insides. Like an eyebrow hair with an impossibly long root, the ribbon keeps coming out of me as my extremities grow cold and alien.

The more she pulls, the less I feel. It's no longer a single ribbon, bright and thick, but a complex lattice in a thousand colours, a delicately interwoven web of my essence that the Jade is ripping from my body.

This is me. My thoughts, my memories. More real than if she'd taken a knife to my stomach and exposed my guts, the

336

Jade has reached in with her hooks and is slowly teasing my essence from the only home it has ever known.

I'm blind. Cold. No longer feel things the way I felt them before. Then I see the Aether. It's calling for me. It loves me.

But that's not where I am going. No, the Jade is sending me somewhere much worse.

I call Sun's name; she doesn't respond. Laure runs over from the car where she'd been waiting and crashes into me.

'What's wrong?'

'Sun. I can't see her.'

'What?' Laure says. 'She's right there.' She points, squinting. 'I think she's wrestling the old woman. I'll go see what's wrong.' And with that she disappears into the maelstrom. I try to follow, only for the dead to force me back. They are insane, beyond desperate. Their expulsion from the confines of the Jade is so sudden that there's no time to adjust to an outside world they haven't seen for hundreds of years, everyone who once knew them having long-since died.

The dead feel the Aether, as do I. Its presence a maleficent growth, a salivating hunger, manifesting as a pressure in my skull. For them, with their lack of physicality, something else. But I know they feel it. I can see it on their faces, features wound from knotted facets; they fear annihilation.

A scream, though I do not know from whom. I cannot see Laure or Sun. I try once more to breach the melee of dead, but unlike for Laure, they are impenetrable. Those at the edge come for me, snapping at my essence, pulling me apart. I'm quick to retrieve what they take, ethereal limbs darting out to prise the stolen facets from their frightened jaws.

Silver threads shoot across the sky. A connection between the Jade and those the Aether hasn't yet claimed. She does not bring them back, but instead wields them as weapons. Massive arms taller than buildings form around her, each one thousands of dead strong. They swing at me and I'm forced to run. Ducking an attack, I dive behind a desk for cover and instantly realise my mistake as the dead sail through all matter, their matted essences crashing into me. I'm thrown across the room and land awkwardly by a wall no higher than my knee. I use it to stand, only to jump back as another arm whips past my face. Facets reach for me, poking through the powerful knot the Jade has woven. Individually they want me and several are strong enough to pull away and dive into my skin only to be swiftly rejected.

Another swing. The movement is too fast and their grip too weak. They are flung off and any connection to the Jade severed, allowing the Aether to swoop once more. I watch as it drags its prey through the barrier and to a place beyond my sight.

The arms that protect the Jade grow bloated and warped as she releases more essences into them. Those at the very edge struggle for purchase and the Aether picks them off at such speed that the afterglow of their existence casts a halo.

Releasing those she has within her and using them as weapons demonstrates a degree of control I never imagined possible. Despite bringing me here to steal my archivism and kill me, it is difficult not to be impressed when witness to such power.

Another attack. This one catches my leg and I feel a part of my essence rip away. There is pain and a loss of something, but now that it is gone, I will never know what. I trip over a stack of ruined books as all sensation leaves my leg, my head crashing into a toppled cabinet.

I sit, dazed. The Jade's attacks are precise. She avoids my archivism while hitting me with enough strength to stop me from getting near her. I do not know what she is doing, only that she means to keep me away.

I stand. Fearing for Sun and Laure, I don't pay close enough attention to my surroundings and the dead envelop me. I drown in them. They fill my mouth, my nose, my ears, dive into the pores of my skin. Their facets weave themselves into mine. We are meshed. One. They lift me from the floor of this ruined room in the Jade's once-grand home. I try to move, to fight, but they are bound to me so tightly that I cannot even twitch.

And then I am free, moving through the air at speed until a wall appears to arrest my flight. My shoulder strikes it first and something inside the joint snaps. I cry out as I fall to the floor. In a misguided attempt to catch myself, I manage to place my hand beneath my back only for the impact to shift my weight entirely to my fingers, which soon yield in the wrong direction.

I swear like Sun on a bad day as the dead escape the Jade, fighting through the mallet fists in the hope that a speedy defection will forgive all ills.

They stream into me, beautiful and horrifying. Their eager desperation, their prayers for salvation. I cannot possibly take so many and when I refuse their adoration switches to bitter rejection. They attack as individuals, not under the control of the Jade. The Aether is quick to consume them, but many avoid it for long enough to unleash their frustration on my essence. They mean to destroy me, drag me into the Aether.

I fall to my knees, ready for them to take me. I have not often thought of my own mortality. I live to prolong others. My life is a service to those who can afford me, it is not a destiny I control.

Something pushes through my skin. An essence. A life. David Bellfield, the long-distance lorry driver who died of a heart attack. His essence swells until it forms a cage around me. He is unable to speak – I have not projected his face. More appear, other essences curled up inside me since their death; their continued life of little interest to those who remain.

I did not consciously release them, though I expect that my despair may have opened a door to those unwilling to have their home destroyed. If I die, then they die too. Again. Permanently. I should not be surprised that they would sacrifice themselves to protect what little they have left, though I find their bravery touching.

I stand as the dead renew their attack. David Bellfield is the first to be taken. I do not even attempt to save the scraps of facets that remain, the onslaught is so brutal. Others are quick to take his place. They are glowing threads, an armour woven from lives that are no more.

My own facets push through the cracks, spectral arms that elongate, growing and bifurcating like branches. At their ends, claws. They rake the air, ripping apart the arms that protect the Jade and scattering the dead. Those the Aether is too slow to claim, I pull into me, bolstering my defence.

I run for the Jade, for the knotted wall that surrounds her. I tear it open, ripping essences apart, pulling more and more into me. I am Hunger, devourer of lives. They flow through my fingers, down my arms, and into my centre where they are knotted so tightly that the ethereal light that bursts from my stomach blinds.

I fight my way forwards, carving a tunnel to the Jade while I grow fat on the dead. They stream into me, all excitement and relief. I consume them by their thousands, taking no time to assess what I have before devouring more. They do not sit well inside me. They should be ordered and stored correctly. An essence requires no physical space, the facets, though I see them as having shape, are massless, sizeless quantities of thought. I could hold every life on the planet inside me if I wished, but not all at once. To reuse the analogy, I may be a hotel with an infinite number of rooms, but if everyone arrives at once, the reception gets a little crowded.

An involuntary expulsion throws hundreds from me. No longer attached to the Jade, they once more become the prey of the Aether. I watch as they vanish from the sky. Their arms spiral as they attempt to swim back. For others the shock of such a sudden eviction takes longer to appear and the Aether claims them before awareness arrives. Their faces still smile, their eyes remain alight with joy and then they are gone, snatched from the world of the living to be dismembered and reborn.

The Aether, glutton that it is, feeds with abandon. Only a peripheral entity before, the lives on offer have brought it one step closer to the physical reality. It becomes a presence in a dark room. A person standing behind you, warm breath on the back of your neck. Lights on and they disappear, but the moment darkness arrives, they're back. Following you, never seen but always felt. The Aether may be here for the thousands that fill the air, but that does not mean I am ignored. I am its antithesis, denying it what it craves the most. And it wants me, more than the wisps and wraiths of decaying lives it delicately plucks from existence. More than even the Jade, who has kept it waiting for so long. To the Aether, I am the ultimate prize. The last in a long line of delicacies. And it wants me now, while I'm still fresh.

I push forwards, the Jade, Sun and Laure obscured by the dead. I'm disorientated. Every direction I look, all I can see are the frightened masses of dead. Above me, they blot the sky, and below, where they swim around my feet, even the floor is obscured.

Another release. Jenny, whose essence I had for less than an hour, flies from my back amidst a hundred others. I'm quick to turn and throw out my arms to catch her. Hers is one life that deserves to remain tethered to me, if only so she can live in the place inside me with the essence of her sister, Claire.

But I am not fast enough, or the empathy I claim to have is not great enough to drive my conviction, and the Aether has her and she is gone from existence.

Another essence, a brilliant diamond among the dross I have gathered. I feel it leave, violently thrown out as I struggle to process those I now possess. This time the conviction is there and I have her, my ethereal arms long and sinewy, my hands holding all that remains of Antoinette Caton. But I am not the only one who has her. The Aether pulls, expecting me to yield. I do not, and sense its satisfaction as it drags Antoinette into itself, bringing me with it. Into death. Into darkness.

Only it is not dark. The curtain has been lifted to reveal brilliant fractals of every colour. They merge into each other, seeming to grow larger until instantly appearing small again. The heart of the Aether, beating in time with the flow of the colours, overpowers me with its love. I relax; waves of adoration pulsate over me. The Aether is love. I am loved.

The knowledge is... heavenly.

I see those who I had inside me. Among the thousands I now possess are Claire, Chrissy, Sophia, Tegan and Lara, each one murdered by the Jade. Like on the field, their essences are tied to mine.

The Aether is among us. Inside us. Suffocating us with love. The feeling changes as purity melts, leaving only desperation.

My cynicism is quick to reinstate itself and snap my charges back into me, curling them into a ball too tight for even the Aether's claws to penetrate. Even Antoinette, who the Aether used to pull me in, has been released and now resides safely with the others, nested among their histories. Something else enters me. Not the Aether and not one of my dead. It brings with it such a strength of love, but oh! How long it has waited. Finally it is where it was meant to be. Nestling itself within my thick folds of quilted facets, it sleeps its well-deserved rest.

A tug, pulling me from behind. I turn, but there is nothing there. I look down. Only the Aether, except the colours are draining as the fractals collapse into chaotic whorls that consume the weak in a fight for dominance. This is the Aether I know. Not the facade it wears to fool the newly arrived and those who suffer near-death experiences and tell the world of a paradise that waits beyond life.

Another pull, the connection that ties me to Sun, an anchor to life. She reaches for me, but at the same time I'm pulling her in. I grasp for it, fighting my way out of the Aether and behind the curtain that separates life from death.

Sun should not be this strong. In a test of strength between her and the Aether, the latter should be the easy victor. I climb our connection, but not fast enough for my escape to go unnoticed. The Aether goes for those within me, but is unable to claim them. Its attention switches, grasping at my essence, a mass of memories and feelings, in the hope that it will find something too precious for me to lose.

It does.

So many memories, laden with feelings of such intensity they outshine all others. The Aether has them, its grip constricting and pulling me back. Ahead is the connection to Sun, solid and sure and reeling me home. I am failed regicide Robert-François

Damiens, tied to horses and awaiting dismemberment. But unlike Damiens, I can sever the parts of myself around which the ropes are tied. One, my connection to Sun and with it the chance to live. Cut that and I, and everyone inside me, will belong to the Aether. The other, every memory I have of Martina De Luca. Every feeling she inspired that I never spoke of; each day, remembered so vividly, that we spent in Antoinette's church doing little to nothing. Her smell, her warmth, the soft downy hair on her cheeks, the look in her eyes every time she saw me anew; a surprise so wonderful and perfect because there I was, waiting for her on the scarred wooden floor of a draughty church, unknowable until she stepped through the door.

Martina's life was the greatest gift I have ever known. Even though she was with me for such a short time, and the guilt of her death sits heavily on my shoulders and will ride with me until I die, I cannot imagine my life had I never known her. Martina, the only person I will ever love.

I scream into the Aether, begging it to release my memories of her, cursing what I am, an entity whose only purpose is to taunt with every life it takes. And here I am, begging for clemency. Offering anything else. Memories of my family, of Antoinette, of Sun-young and Laure. Every essence I have inside me. Anything but Martina.

But it knows. Because it has been watching me. Because it has been waiting for me. It knows, like I know, that Martina's life defines my own. Have that and you have me.

The pull from Sun grows stronger as the Aether's grip around my memories intensifies. I think of Sun, a growing friendship perhaps, and Laure, a younger sister who does not despise me. What I could have with them will never equal what I had with Martina. No connection with another person will ever come close. Yet I let them pull me as my memories of the few short years I spent with Martina dislodge and rise from my essence. I discard them not because I no longer love Martina, or because I have chosen Sun and Laure over her, but because something is telling me that I need to live. I sense it with such urgency, a plea whispered into my ear, begging me to let her go. The voice is one I could never refuse. How I've longed to hear it again.

My Martina.

Something is ripped from me. Long facets stretch and snap. They belong to the Aether now. I search inside me, desperate to see who it has taken and, among the thousands, find Antoinette and the murdered girls. Whoever it was, they were of little importance. There are too many inside me now to know their histories and I can only assume the Aether's reason for taking them was justified.

It comes at me now. Unsatisfied with one, it wants us all, but the pull from Sun is too strong and I am whipped away and thrown into myself with horrifying swiftness.

I am on my feet surprisingly fast for a body that was technically deceased only moments before. I look around to see the dead no longer encircle the Jade. They flee, the link between them severed. The Jade is surely dead herself.

The Aether renews its consumption, efficiently devouring the glut of existence on offer. The way before me clears as another scream rings out. There's shouting. Crying. I see the chair, and on it, the Jade. No sign of Sun or Laure. The final essences complete their life's purpose to feed the Aether, floating into the air and crumbling. As their forms collapse, they shatter into golden flakes and illuminate the exposed room, only moments before the Sun's morning light shines through the glassless windows and sections of missing wall.

Laure lies on the floor, sees me and pulls herself up. There is blood over her mouth and nose.

'She hit me.'

I run to her and kneel. Help her sit. I'm not sure if I'm supposed to hug her or keep a respectable distance when Laure decides for me by hugging me. I return the gesture, shocked by my ease of intimacy and desire to reassure.

I raise a hand, ready to finish the Jade.

'Not her,' Laure says as tears cut streaks through the blood. 'Sun.'

'Sun did this?'

I stand. Sun is not here.

I am unsettled. There are still too many inside me, their tumult so distracting it affects my ability to think. I fall, catching myself on the chair.

The dead burst from me in an explosive pulse as I'm forced to expel thousands in the hope that I can provide a home for a few.

The gentle morning is filled with cries as those who'd thought themselves safe are flung from Eden. Wave after wave they leave me, until enough have been expelled to allow space for those I wish to keep.

The Jade manages a strangled call for help. The way she looks at me... not like the Jade, even when stripped of her skin. I look through the Aether and see the essence hastily thrown into a body. See the thread that extends from the Jade and straight into me.

'Sun.'

I take her hands in mine, feel the cold death of her skin. She nods. Her lip quivers.

'Help me.'

This body is dying, forced to endure the release of so many and assaulted by the separation from its essence.

The Jade will have taken Sun's body, along with Monique's car, and will already be far from here.

There is nothing more I can do for Sun-young Kang. The body she is in will not survive the day. I failed her. Just like I failed Antoinette. Just like I will fail anyone else who gets close to me. Sun was right, all I do is bring misery to people. I am poison.

I touch my forehead to hers and extend my facets to prepare for the acceptance of one more essence. I take Sun in my arms, feel the lightness of her body, smell the stench of death eager to claim her. I tell her not to be scared and feel her nod in response.

'Release the life you hold so tight; welcome me and leave the light.'

34

I never visited the beach as a kid. It was only ever a promised attraction, there to make sure our rooms were clean or we didn't get in trouble at school. I was twelve when I realised we'd never go.

I could claim that's why I settled here, but it was really because someone had created a coast with a white sand beach and I didn't feel comfortable living so near everyone else. My first impressions of this place weren't great as thousands of us had just arrived with no idea where we were. Most took to shouting and a good many of those decided fighting would clear things up. Then the current residents got involved and the chaos that followed destroyed most of what they'd already created.

I did the only sensible thing I could think of and ran into the weird expanding whiteness. Things settled down at some point and, after that, it turned out this place wasn't so bad. I visit the town occasionally, spend time with the locals. I finally had lunch with Lara; I have lunch with her most days, actually. Not that we need to eat, or that days exist in this afterlife. But we pretend to eat things that look like food and that's good enough.

'Tea tastes better here,' I say.

'No, it does not,' Antoinette responds. She sits across from me on the wooden porch at the back of my cottage. It overlooks a small beach where I spend my time burying my legs or creating masterpieces from the sand with only a thought. Beyond that the sea extends forever, but only when you look at it from the right angle. Come at it from the side and it's just a thin line of blue. That was one of my tricks – things don't have to exist to be seen.

'Maybe you just don't have the imagination to improve the flavour,' I say.

'Sun, you cannot improve the flavour of tea. People have tried only to cheapen it. Tea is tea and this,' she says as she swirls the cup, 'is not tea.'

'Is there anything you like about this place?'

'The use of two hands,' Antoinette says as she flexes her fingers.

'I agree with Sun,' a voice behind me says. 'The tea is better here.'

Antoinette snorts. 'Being a god doesn't preclude you from being a philistine.'

I prepare the Archivist a cup, which he takes as he settles into the wicker chair to my left. It creaks as he sits. If I didn't know I was dead, I'd believe this was real. The strange thing is, it's not the flying or creating things with our minds or living with people born in 1604 that reminds me all this is fake; it's time. It's funny here. It passes differently to the outside world, but it also passes differently in here. Some who arrived when the Jade died are convinced they've lived years inside the Archivist, while others think it's only been a day. For me, it feels like six weeks, but as soon as the Archivist has his first sip of tea he says it's been four weeks.

He told me he died too when he faced the Jade, and it was our link that brought him back to his body. Only it wasn't just the link, it was the Jade too, pulling him in. He's the last archivist, she can't just let the Aether take him. Just like she couldn't let me die either, which is why she shoved me in that horrifying body of hers. In some ways I'm glad I won't grow old.

'Have you...'

'Sorry,' he says. 'If anyone can hide themselves, it's her. But I'll keep looking.'

'I expect she will find you before you find her,' Antoinette says. 'Pulling you back from the Aether was her final act as an archivist. Now she is nothing. No archivism. No money. But she will still have her mind and she will still have her cruelty. Do not fool yourself into thinking she has forgotten you.'

'Then I will wait,' he says.

'I hate to think of her out there, wearing my body, combing my hair, wiping my arse.'

'Be thankful you have a body,' Antoinette says. 'Mine's been turned to ash, as has everyone else's in here. Either that or they're horrifically decomposed or being molested by medical students. You may think of yourself as dead, but you're not. Not like the rest of us.'

'I suppose. But what if she commits a crime in my body? Or kills someone? Or what if she does find you,' I say to the Archivist, 'but she gets to Laure first?'

'I have explained to Laure that you are with me.'

'So? She doesn't believe you. Laure is stubborn and unless you give her proof, she'll keep believing that I attacked her and ran away.'

'She will come around.'

'Can I...'

'That's why I came. She wants to watch a movie tonight. I thought you might like to watch it with her.'

I spend more time projected onto the Archivist than any of his clients. It didn't work at first because I kept telling Laure how sorry I was and how much I loved her, forgetting that she can't see me. Everything I said came from his mouth in his voice and it made things awkward for a few days. Now I don't try to be me, not until I know she can believe it. So we just sit most evenings and I pretend to be him, but a better, more caring him, and that way I get to see Laure and know she's safe and has someone who listens. She tells me things she would only ever have told the old me, when I was in my body. I don't know if it's because she trusts the Archivist enough to open up, or because deep down she knows I'm in here. I don't dare ask.

'Four of the expedition teams are still out,' Antoinette says.

'The two that returned, did they find an edge?' he asks.

'One group disagreed over the direction they were supposed to be going in and before they'd realised their mistake, were back in the town.'

'The other group?'

I look at Antoinette and wait for her nod before I speak.

'They found something.'

'This could wait for another visit,' he says as the three of us trek through the whiteness. My cottage, the stretch of sand, even the sea disappears, leaving us alone with nothing visible to suggest we're going the right way.

We call it *the knowing*, partly because it's the best way to describe it, but also because it sounds like a shitty horror movie. When one person knows something about where we live, like what a building looks like or where something is, we all do. The knowledge isn't shared consciously, it just happens. And because it happens all the time as people push out into the expanse or create new rooms in their houses, the knowledge just grows without you realising, like armpit hair.

'It would be wrong to keep this from you,' Antoinette says.

'Is it a problem?' he asks.

'No, this doesn't affect anyone else.'

He looks worried. He knows less about this place than we do and I expect he's concerned that some of his own emotions or memories have leaked in, fearing the embarrassment.

It's not that at all. I kinda wish it was, because at least that would be funny. This is something else entirely. I don't know what it means except that for me, and my place in the Archivist's life, it's not good news.

'Everyone's naked when they arrive,' I say. 'Did you know that?'

'Yes.'

'It makes sense when you think about it. I guess the only reason ghosts in films wear clothes is because being chased by a naked man with his old man balls bouncing around his knees isn't all that scary. Well, it is, but a different kind of scary.'

He gives me a look and I keep talking.

'I have more control over this place than anyone else. Probably because of the link. So when I got here and saw I was naked, that was all it took for clothes to appear. Black jeans and my pink puffer jacket. It wasn't the same for everyone else. They were all naked and they stayed naked. Then they started fighting, but they were also trying to cover themselves up, so you had these guys fighting each other with a hand covering their dick the whole time. The women were just as bad, only they had more to cover. The people who were already here ran over with clothes that were plucked from nothingness, but that made it worse because now everybody could fight with both hands.'

'Sun, this is very interesting, but also deeply concerning.'

I take his hand. He's not comfortable with it and does not hold mine back. I don't let go. I know what's coming.

Arriving and leaving are the same here. One moment you're somewhere, then you're in the whiteness. Same the other way around; one second it's whiteness, then...

We're there.

'The team who found her came straight back,' I say. 'They spoke to her, but she never replied. Tried to take her home, but she couldn't be moved.'

He stares. Mouth open. Looks at me then at Antoinette. Confused, like he has no idea what's going on. I guess that's fair; we haven't a clue either. But I can't help feeling a little disappointed. I expected something more. He doesn't even squeeze my hand like I thought he would, just leaves it to slide out and slap against his thigh.

'You were wrong,' Antoinette says. 'She never grew tired of you. Never could grow tired of you. It was you who grew frustrated in your lack of abilities. Martina loved you with a devotion even I couldn't match. You were the only one who couldn't see it.'

'We thought it might be a memory,' I say. 'But I made that dress; she was naked, just like the rest of us. You never saw her naked, did you?'

He turns to me, his expression blank, and shakes his head.

I take his hand again and lead him forward. 'She's really here,' I say as I make him touch her cheek and run his fingers through her long Mediterranean hair. She looks fourteen. Antoinette said that's how old she was when she hanged herself in the church. I had misunderstood, thinking it was Antoinette who was responsible for her death. I know now that it was the Archivist.

'I don't understand,' he finally says.

'Neither do we,' Antoinette says. 'The Aether took her four years ago. She shouldn't be here.'

'No,' he says, and he slides his hands into his pockets, 'I don't understand why you brought me here.'

'To see her!' I nearly shout. 'To see Martina. She's here, inside you, just like the rest of us.'

Then I get it. I know exactly what he's going to say before he even opens his mouth. The blank stare, the confusion.

He has no idea who she is.

AFTERWORD

The Archivist was inspired by two deaths in 2010: my friend, Fay, whom this book is dedicated to, and my granddad, Peter. Fay's death was by far the hardest for me to process because she was 24 and, unlike my granddad, who was 84, I wasn't expecting her to die. To quote Antoinette, "there are few moments that truly define a person. Moments that change someone so profoundly that that change can never be reversed". I have had three of these moments in my 36 years of life, the death of Fay and the birth of my two children, Violet and Felix.

I don't believe in God or an afterlife. I wish I did, I think my life would be enriched knowing that everyone I've lost is waiting for me in paradise. But sadly, that isn't how my mind works. The Aether, facets and essences were my response to Fay's death, a creation that would allow parts of her, and everyone else who has died, a way to continue in those yet to be born. Not reincarnation, as such, but a subtle weaving of personality traits and memories across thousands of lives. I liked the idea and so chose it to be an integral part of *The Archivist*.

The second inspiration for this story was my granddad, Peter. His death was much like the first chapter of this book, with family members standing awkwardly around a room as he struggled to speak. I remember thinking how utterly shit death was. My granddad was desperate to talk to us, yet the nurse who leant over his bed couldn't make out the words. It wasn't a fitting end for an intelligent man who clearly had something left to say. That's where the idea of archivists came from, someone who could speak those final words for you, granting your death the dignity it deserves. From that idea, along with the Aether, facets and essences inspired by Fay's death, this story was born.

My thanks in helping me get *The Archivist* to this point goes to my other half; my parents, Simon and Jan; Esther Snell; Liz Duncan and Caroline Hattersley. I would also like to thank the Faber Academy for their excellent editorial critique, Neil Broadfoot for his highly informative line edit and everyone at Matador for the copy edit, proof read and all the other hard work that goes into publishing a book. Thanks again to Tiberius Lee for another fantastic, if not slightly creepy, cover. An extra special thanks goes to Emily Stammers who, many years ago, read a short story of mine called *The Boy with the Face of Death* that would become *The Archivist*. If it was not for Emily's praise of that short story, I never would have taken the time to turn it into a novel.

Finally, to you, reader, thank you for choosing *The Archivist*. I hope it got you thinking. Personally, I'm undecided if archivists are a good thing, so I'd love to know what you think. Feel free to get in touch.

V S Nelson - January 2022